The Larach

Alexandra Raife

CORONET BOOKS

Hodder & Stoughton

First published in Great Britain in 1997 by Penguin Books Ltd
This edition published in 1999 by Hodder & Stoughton
A division of Hodder Headline
A Coronet Paperback

A CIP catalogue record for this title is available
from the British Library

ISBN 0 340 73895 2

Printed and bound in Great Britain by
Caledonian International Book Manufacturing Ltd,
Glasgow

Hodder and Stoughton
A division of Hodder Headline
338 Euston Road
London NW1 3BH

The Larach

Alexandra Raife has lived abroad in many countries and worked at a variety of jobs, including a six-year commission in the RAF, and spent many years co-running a Highland hotel. She lives in Perthshire. Although she has written stories for years, *Drumveyn* was her first published novel, followed by *The Larach* and *Grianan*. *Belonging,* published by Hodder & Stoughton in 1999, vividly depicts the West Coast of Scotland and returns to the sea-lochs and hills of *The Larach*. Alexandra Raife's fifth published novel, *Sun on Snow* confirms her reputation as a page-turning contemporary storyteller whose warm and distinctive characters readily engage our affections.

Praise for Alexandra Raife:

'A real find … the genuine storyteller's flair' Mary Stewart

'A welcome new storyteller' Rosamunde Pilcher

'[A] warm, friendly, involving story with a page-turning quality that emerges less from the plot than from the characters who are perceptively drawn, real and (oh bliss!) likeable. A lovely book' Reay Tannahill

'*Drumveyn* had me hooked from the first page. A delightful book which I enjoyed enormously' Barbara Erskine

Also by Alexandra Raife

Drumveyn
Grianan
Belonging
Sun on Snow

For Sue

CHAPTER ONE

The morning she woke and could not remember the name or face of the man who had left her bed a couple of hours earlier Clare knew with absolute certainty that she must make a drastic and irreversible change in her life.

She could remember only the slack curve of thin back, the knobs of his spine as he sat on the edge of the bed rasping his fingers through his hair, presumably in an effort to rub some consciousness into his hungover brain. She had hissed at him not to wake Magda, who shared the top-floor flat above the hotel with her, but beyond that they had not spoken. Another guest whose eye would not meet hers as he paid his bill. His hands had been as small as a woman's, with thin greedy fingers. She shuddered as she remembered them on her body.

Self-disgust filled her, strong enough to make the moment a crucial turning point. She had known for some time that she was being pushed along a road she did not wish to take, and becoming in the process a person she did not wish to be, but it had been easier to submerge herself in the hectic world of Carlini's than face the memories and questions of the past. And she had nowhere else to go.

She would find somewhere, stop dodging, strip away everything she was using to blot out pain and guilt. Throughout the busy day – they were going all out on an ambitious Christmas programme this year – her mind fleetingly checked this resolve and each time found it still firm.

But how was she going to tell Magda that she was leaving? Magda regarded Clare as her property, just as much as the tall Georgian house by the river which she had converted into this highly successful restaurant and hotel. She also considered, rightly, that she had rescued Clare, lifting her out of the destructive inertia she had sunk into after Martin's death and obliging her brain to function again. Magda would definitely think Clare owed her long-term loyalty, but Clare had put in more than two dedicated years here, working all day and every day as Magda did herself. It had been rewarding in its way, but she knew it was a lifestyle that was ultimately wrong for her, and she had hit a downward spiral of alcohol and promiscuous sex which was frighteningly addictive.

Magda's mind would also leap at once to the question of the money Clare had put into the business. If it was crucial for Magda then it could be left there for the time being; it was not a consideration that would make Clare stay now. She could sell some of the shares which she had found so startlingly depleted after Martin's death . . . Don't think of that, keep to the present.

Two days later she flew up to Glasgow and by afternoon was crossing the Rannoch Moor in a hired Escort, too engrossed in herself to take much notice of the inhospitable landscape.

Magda had been exasperated when Clare had told her she was taking a couple of days off. As far as she was concerned they were in the run-up to Christmas and nothing else mattered.

'Oh, Clare, no! Can't it wait till after New Year, whatever it is?'

'I'm only talking about two days.'

'But why now? Are you having an abortion or something?'

'No, Magda, I am not having an abortion.' Justifiable question, though, Clare reminded herself, considering the way she'd been leaping in and out of bed lately.

'Well, I don't see what can possibly be important enough—' Magda had been ready for a fight, but had been buzzed by the kitchen — a crisis about the pheasant not having been hung — and she had shot off to deal with it. Impossible ever to have personal conversations in the hotel world, as Clare knew, and it had been no moment to try and make Magda understand her need to free herself from its incessant demands, to make some kind of objective evaluation of her life. She had tried twice to talk to her the following day but Magda had been dismissive, almost hostile.

'You're exhausted, that's all. Of course you need a break, who doesn't? Take a couple of weeks off in January, get some skiing. This is the worst possible time—'

'Magda, I just have to—'

While Clare groped for words that would not be too banal Magda had swept on angrily, 'I don't see how you can think of going anywhere at present. You know we've got all these staff to interview—'

'On Friday. I'll be back by then.'

How Clare had needed a drink, grinding through those two days. She felt actually ill as a result of this abrupt deprivation, everything around her unnervingly out of focus. But already a current of excitement and speculation was running, bracing her, and she knew the first step had been taken.

Not that abstinence had brought any rewards so far. As she had been channelled with the other passengers down the funnel which would shoot them into the Glasgow plane, she had found that not having a hangover to contend with was like walking round inside a different person, and an oddly vulnerable one. She felt as though she had lost a protective skin; everything was too close and clear and loud.

North of Onich the road writhed up the lochside in endlessly repeated twists. Signs warned of hazards like falling rocks, which Clare thought crossly one could do little about in the event. On the left the grey waters of Loch Linnhe or Leven – she couldn't remember which and didn't much care – looked sullen and cold, blurred hills beyond disappearing into yellow-grey mirk.

The solicitors, who she had discovered acted as house agents in Scotland, were easy to find in Fort William's basically one-street town, and how tacky and depressing that one street looked. Half the shops seemed to be in the process of changing hands, the rest were plastered with 'Sale' stickers. Clare couldn't let herself make any judgements, though, any more than she had let herself see the bleakness of the landscape she had just driven through, the featureless waterlogged moor, the dark, streaming rock and crowding ridges of Glencoe. If she looked she would never go through with this; and if she did not do this, then what?

'Clare Somerville. I phoned.' Her brusqueness was met with a cosy welcoming friendliness which shamed her into looking

3

properly at the grey-haired, cardiganed receptionist beaming over her high old-fashioned counter.

'Mrs Somerville, so you found us all right, then. And what kind of a journey up did you have? It's not a very good day for you today, is it, but perhaps tomorrow will be better. I'm afraid Mr Watts is seeing someone just now, but he'll not be very long, so meanwhile if you would be seated . . .'

Clare was seated, lodging her bottom in the brown rexine hollow of an upright chair. The gloomy hall was adorned with an umbrella stand with a leaking zinc tray and a cheese plant with one leaf; no pandering to the clients here. Amused, she relaxed for the first time that day. The momentum of the journey faded; all she had to do now was wait till summoned.

Mr Watts was benevolent, but obviously not able to take her seriously as a potential buyer of a remote and isolated cottage. She had the general contours of a knitting needle and weighed less than eight stone, and her fairness added to the impression of flimsiness. However, he did admit to having one or two properties available and Clare escaped as soon as she could with the schedules, acutely conscious of the shivery ache which was her body's demand for its normal dose of alcohol.

The evening in the Fort William hotel always remained a blur in her mind. Decorated in every shade of mud, it had varnished plywood corridors lit by opaque frisbees and furnished solely with ashtrays on hoover-scarred pedestals. Clare hoped she would never have to decode in extremity its clutter of emergency and fire notices.

She spent a long time lying on the unresilient bed, battling against the overwhelming need to go down to the bar and a rare longing to cry. But long ago she had learned that crying to deaf walls helped nothing.

She read the blurbs about the properties avidly, suppressing ordinary common sense let alone cynicism. That got her through the night, but didn't do much for her when confronted with reality the next day.

She was given into the charge of a large red-haired young man called Sandy Maitland. He was wearing an amazing suit of ginger tweed that looked as though it might have been made for his father – or grandfather – and which clashed teeth-wincingly with his curly hair and scarlet face. He seemed pretty malleable, though, and Clare soon had him *en route* to the most remote of the offered properties in spite of his obvious duty to save time and petrol by showing her the others first.

'Set in a Highland glen of great scenic beauty and having ample garden ground.' This translated into a weathered, cedar-shingled structure with metal-framed windows and a rotting verandah, with a solid mass of Sitka spruce looking as though it was about to march over it from the rear. Through momentary gaps in the cloud there were glimpses of the scenic beauty and glorious it was, but even Sandy was ready to agree that perhaps the house was not 'just the thing' for Clare.

He seemed briefly hopeful of the snugger amenities of a bungaloid growth separated only by its 'hard standing for two cars' from the busy A82 and a motel. Clare refused to go in.

Nor did she go into the next offering, though it was an appealing traditional cottage of just the type she had envisaged, with a view down the length of Loch Leven. But it was on the outskirts of one of the most depressing villages she had ever seen, crammed in below dark peaks at the head of the narrow loch. Clare was not particularly sensitive to atmosphere in that sense, but she couldn't wait to get away from the claustrophobic little place. As they drove back along the loch Sandy did tell her as a point of general interest that the sun never reached it for several weeks in the winter, and blushed when she fixed him with a cold stare.

Two tentative possibilities on the unbecoming fringes of Fort William itself were rejected out of hand, and they were through, and once more Clare found herself confronting alarming blankness. With the beginnings of panic she reviewed the houses they had seen. Surely one would do. Why not buy the Kinlochleven one, move in and look for something better? But the memory of the spooky village rushed shudderingly back and she knew she could never live there.

'There has to be something,' she said angrily to Sandy, staring away from him out of the car window so that he should not see how frightened and helpless she was beginning to feel. 'There must be hundreds of empty cottages around here. Don't tell me that's all you can produce.'

'Oh, there are plenty cottages,' Sandy agreed at once, in

his gentle non-estate-agent's manner, 'but most of them are on estates where the owners would never think of selling. Problems with access, water, future use of ground and so on. And there's been a lot of folk coming up from the south lately, snapping up anything they can get hold of—'

'Yes, and don't tell me what marvellous bargains they've found. I don't want to know,' Clare interrupted savagely. 'Come on, there has to be something, for God's sake. Something remote, basic, tiny – something your average punter wouldn't even contemplate. You've been wasting my time so far.'

'Well, there is one,' Sandy admitted, more out of self-defence than anything else. 'But Mr Watts won't be best pleased if I take you all the way out there for nothing.'

'What's wrong with it?'

'There's nothing wrong with it, *as such*. But there's no road in to it, and no power. It's quite out of the question . . .'

'I should think in that case your boss would be only too happy to get it off his books.'

After a hurried and greasy lunch they were on their way, shaking off the ugly northern straggle of the town and heading west, climbing over a moor as drably beige as last night's bedroom except where it was bog-black. Clare didn't look; she couldn't afford to. Having decided that she must break away from everything her present life contained she had scraped around among memories and associations and come up with a period that in retrospect seemed happy – the cottage in Rosthwaite, climbing, the marvellous summers. The fact that it was where she had met Martin (which had also incidentally meant the last of Rosthwaite for her) she had hurriedly suppressed.

But the Lake District was horribly overrun these days, too near, too familiar, and surely to go back in these untried circumstances would be a mistake. Somewhere like that, though. North Wales? Again memory had slammed shut a door. Scotland, then, with Fort William, as the best-known centre of the climbing area, the name that sprang to mind as the obvious place to start looking.

So here she was, holding herself in from too much awareness like someone who dreads the jolting of a broken limb, doing her best to cope with the clamouring need for a drink, being conveyed at Sandy's sober pace across this rain-veiled wilderness. The only sounds above the engine were the rhythmic clunk of the wipers and the thin swish of tyres on wet road and the only certainty in her mind was that she could not go back.

CHAPTER TWO

They came down off the moor in a series of steep unfenced loops which focused all Clare's attention and were in the village, and indeed through it, almost before she noticed.

'Inverbuie,' announced Sandy, who had not attempted to chat on the way, either intimidated by Clare's hunched silence or bothered about letting himself in for showing her another non-starter. 'Nearest shop, Post Office and so on.'

An impression of puddled empty carpark, open water beyond it, an uneven row of wet slate roofs, a scatter of cottages, then a high-arched bridge with a frothing stream pitching itself down a ravine on the right and winding away across a soggy field to the loch on the left. The road began to climb between hills lopped off by cloud and a dark block of plantation. Clare felt frustration – this long shot could not possibly come off – grow inside her like an aching bubble of despair.

The wall of trees on the left ended abruptly, they drove past a couple of empty fields and then Sandy was turning into a track of rough metalling and rain-filled potholes between wire fences. Whatever happened to stone walls? Clare wondered grumpily. A spread of buildings appeared ahead.

'What's this place?'

'It's part of Rhumore now, the farm out at the end of the headland. The house is empty but the steading buildings are in use. It belonged to Glen Righ estate at one time – the cottage we're going to still does. An old shepherd of theirs lived in it and they wouldn't sell till he died.'

'When was that?'

'A couple of years ago, it must be now. It's not everyone's cup of tea, as I told you.'

'We're going to look at it, so let up on the doom and gloom for a bit, yes?'

'Well, don't forget that Macrae, who owns Rhumore, has a right of pre-emption to buy. It has to be offered to him first . . .'

Clare didn't listen. Sandy had explained it twice already. It was too tedious, too clogged with potential problems.

Sandy parked in the muddy farmyard. Huge cylinders of hay were piled in an open stone barn, the windows of the farmhouse were boarded up. An icy wind knifed up Clare's skirt. Sandy was pulling on an enormous pair of green wellingtons and a heavy jacket with bulging pockets. Clare saw him glance doubtfully at her boots, which suddenly appeared absurdly elegant even to her.

'It's a bit of a walk,' he said unhappily, not for the first time.

'For God's sake relax.'

In fact she was disconcerted by the distance as they struggled over the ridge, pushed back by a vigorous damp wind. Sandy's face had gone a nasty raw-meat colour; Clare was glad he'd covered up the ginger suit. Impossible, surely, she thought, to lug supplies over here? But someone had; the place had been lived in; there had to be an answer.

She couldn't pretend there was one of those blinding moments of recognition and certainty when she saw the Larach for the first time. No 'this is it' as she stood on the rock slabs on the spine of the headland and picked out the grey shape of the cottage against the hillside. Yet there was some subtle appeal in its undisturbed look as it squatted there, a simple rectangle, unfenced, well back from a curve of pale shingle beach, facing south-west across the loch. If there was no certainty in that moment for Clare, at least there was a whiff of hope, a tiny upsurge of excitement, a 'this might just do'.

Sandy was getting more and more anxious and defensive as they squelched down the slope. 'It would cost a fortune to put a road in . . . there's not even a telephone, you know . . . the place would be completely cut off in bad weather . . .'

'I thought you were supposed to sell houses.'

'Well, but,' he protested, torn between the requirements of his job and his clearly winning better nature.

'No one could complain about your bringing me out here if you got rid of the place, could they?'

'But this is no place for someone like you,' he burst out, goaded. 'Not for living in all the time, anyway. It might just do as a holiday home.'

'I don't want a holiday home,' Clare said shortly.

Closer to, the cottage looked secretive in the drab afternoon light, its slated roof damson-coloured under the threatening sky. Could I possibly shut myself away inside that primitive stone shell, Clare found herself wondering apprehensively, with all my inadequacies and hopes and needs, and expect it to become the safe focal point of home? Bizarre thought, yet still there was that little tug of 'maybe, just maybe' . . .

It was difficult to remember later her first glimpse of the interior as the door opened under the impact of Sandy's shoulder straight into the main room. It was dominated by two dark blocks which were the triple-ovened grate with hob and open fire, and a high dresser which looked ready to topple forward and crush the first intruder. Brown and dirt prevailed. Doors, cupboards, furniture, the tongue-and-groove panelling halfway up the walls, the smoke-darkened ceiling and chimney breast, whatever the floor covering had once been, were all unrelievedly brown.

A door on the left opened into a bedroom with a wardrobe that was first cousin to the looming dresser, a chest of drawers dribbled with candle grease and an iron bedstead with a stained black-and-white striped mattress that made Clare shudder. A fall of soot spewed from the mouth of a tiny cast-iron fireplace across bare floorboards.

'Everything in the house is included in the sale,' said Sandy, consulting his notes.

'Great. No means of taking it away, I suppose.' How did the stuff get here in the first place? 'I hope that doesn't include . . .' Gingerly, then violently, she pulled at a sticking drawer. The pensioned-off estate worker had probably died in this room. Had they just carted him away and left everything as it was? Only yellowed newspaper ridged with damp, hairs, a shirt button.

Opposite the front door in the living-room two steps led through the thickness of the original outer wall into a narrow strip of kitchen and bathroom. No hygienic nonsense about the one not opening from the other. Here Clare was met squarely by the smell of damp – wet cement, rotting wood, earth, fungus.

It was nearly dark in the bathroom, its frosted glass window obscured by dirt and moss and frilled with layers of paint. Sandy's torch revealed a cracked plastic loo seat and a bath repellent with blue-green stains below a yellow tidemark. The floor was uncovered cement.

The kitchen was equipped with an alarming gas cooker, its cylinder beside it, a walk-in larder with tattered oilcloth on the shelves and, surprisingly, a stainless-steel sink in a cheap modern unit. The window looked on to a narrow space between house and hill, a dumping ground for netting, wire, broken slates, defunct buckets.

Ignoring the bleating Sandy, who had by now abandoned all pretence of wanting to make a sale, Clare went back to the sitting-room. A solid table stood at mid-floor, a couple of kitchen chairs tucked under it, the sort of table where you could plant your elbows, spread things out, get down to business. Two high-backed armchairs stood on either side of the fire, one handsomely carved, its grimy cushions still in the mould of its last occupant. Clare braved another look at the dresser. How marvellous its shelves would be filled with books. How less than marvellous was the smell which wafted out when she opened the cupboard doors below.

The fireplace she ignored, like someone at a party one knows one should speak to but hopes to be able to avoid.

'You'd have to heat your water with that,' observed Sandy, uncomfortably on cue, twiddling a knob which released a shower of twigs and tufts of sheep's wool. 'And the jackdaws are in it, by the look of it.'

'Well, it must have worked once,' Clare said curtly. Did she know even then that she was going to buy this impossible little place?

Sandy went outside and paced around with a condemning air and she followed. He said the chimneys would need repointing but grudgingly pronounced the rones to be fine; the guttering he apparently meant. He found a few slates missing, ground his thumb into window sills and humphed a bit, then went back inside and checked the loft, but the house seemed to have stood up well to its empty years. A knock-kneed shed, obviously sturdier than it looked since it was still there, was stuffed with more of the same rubbish that had been tossed behind the house.

As a last resort Sandy dragged Clare up the hill to locate the water tank, which was found to be brimming.

'Of course we've had a lot of rain lately,' he temporized, gazing glumly into the black depths fed by a swift-running little burn.

'Of course.'

'The rose will block with all the rubbish that comes off the hill.'

She didn't know what he was talking about.

'It's probably blocked now,' he pointed out huffily, and Clare laughed outright.

'Do you get commission?' she mocked him.

'You can't seriously be thinking of—'

'Somebody lived here. For a century or so, at a guess.'

'Yes, but, that's all very well,' he muttered, getting rid of his feelings by dragging the cover back on to the tank.

The mist was lower, the light fading fast. In silence they locked the door and slogged away, taking a somewhat uncertain line over the featureless headland.

'Do you know what Larach means?' Sandy demanded at last, sounding so aggressive that Clare knew his kindly soul was racked.

'No, what?'

'Old ruin.'

She laughed and laughed, and so after a moment did he, both of them reeling about on the oozy peaty ground like idiots. Clare knew her boots would never be the same again.

'You can't seriously tell me,' she said when they had recovered, 'that someone built a house and then named it "Ruin".'

'Well, actually it's "the site of a ruin",' Sandy admitted. 'There'll have been an older building here, probably going way back. It's a sheltered wee bay right enough.'

On the road back to Fort William, amicable now, they discussed the pros and cons more openly, except that Clare sidestepped the inevitable question as to why she wanted to come here at all. The house was habitable, the water supply adequate, the plumbing had presumably once worked.

'But how on earth did they get supplies in?' she asked. 'Coal and so on?'

She caught the surprised turn of Sandy's head. 'By boat, of course. Did you not see the jetty?'

Had she? She half recalled a stone pile at the end of the beach, so softened in outline by wind and water that it had looked a natural rather than a man-made structure. She certainly hadn't registered its obvious relation to the cottage.

'It's no way down the loch to Inverbuie,' Sandy was saying, then, alarmed, 'But you surely wouldn't be thinking of buying a boat?'

He didn't have to worry about that one. Launching herself on to the menacing waters of the loch was not included in this challenge.

When Sandy dropped her off at the hotel, with most earnest pleas to think it over sensibly, Clare asked for her bill and went straight up to pack. She was told, with a defensiveness which indicated they thought they were ripping her off, that she would have to pay for the room for two nights. What babes in arms they were, she thought with a large tolerance.

In half an hour she was heading back to Inverbuie. There was a hotel overlooking the harbour, she had taken note as they passed. What she had not noted was that it was shut from October to Easter. The lights she had seen belonged to the public bar which was open all the year round.

'Well, we are closed right enough,' said Ina Morrison judiciously, in Clare's first deathless memory of her, 'but that's not to say that we don't have a room.'

It was frightful, much, much worse than the Fort William one. Where did they find light bulbs so dim, wash basins so tiny, candlewick so lurid? Clare wondered in renewed exasperation, feeling the penetrating musty cold of off-season beginning to eat into her bones.

'You could put this on later, maybe,' said Ina, indicating a single-bar electric fire, its reflector furred with dust, her voice heavy with the hope that Clare would do no such thing. 'You'll have had your tea.' They had this way of doling out statements rather than asking questions.

'It doesn't matter,' Clare said. She would rather have starved than driven back across that moor. If she had demanded a meal she might not have got one since, as she later discovered, glen hackles were always ready to rise at someone with her voice and appearance, but her desire not to be a nuisance, as it was interpreted, at once aroused all Ina's bossy kindness.

'If you'd not mind eating with the family there's plenty to go round. It would be in the kitchen, though – and of course I'd have to charge,' she hastened to add repressively, in case there should be any silly mistake about it. 'It's ready just now.'

How Clare yearned for a hot bath, almost as much as for a gin, but she only had time for an irritated debate about whether it would be colder to keep on wet boots or expose her shins to the icy air. She kept her boots on, though walking into the kitchen a couple of minutes later she was nearly knocked backwards by the blast of heat, sound, light and fatty smells.

A huge television, its colour unnaturally orange and emerald, was delivering news that sounded somehow unfamiliar till Clare realized it was some parochial Scottish version. The room seemed full of people, two overalled young men at the table, Ina and two girls milling between microwave, grill and fryer.

The boys each gave Clare a jerk of the head and stared down at the table, where their forearms framed the spot on which the plate would land. The girls said hello and gave her inquisitive sidelong glances without raising their heads, taking in every detail of her appearance by a kind of visual suction.

Ina poured an avalanche of chips into her basket, gave it a spattering shake and lowered it with a violent sizzle into definitely pensionable fat, issuing at the same time a volley of commands over her shoulder.

'Just sit yourself down, Mrs Somerville. Morag, fetch up that chair – shift your feet, Lachy, what's got into you? Here, Karen, reach me that dish, will you, and watch the grill. One of you tell your dad his tea's on the table. And who's away with my holey spoon . . . ?'

The whole room was piled and crammed with a squalor Clare tried not to reduce to its component parts of nastiness. From the top of a mammoth refrigerator a cat regarded her sardonically from between a spike jammed with curling invoices and a carton of brown sauce sachets, as though it knew how bitterly she was regretting having accepted Ina's invitation.

Paying customer though Clare was, the sons of the house were served first, laden plates rimmed with dark fat planked in front of each by a flouncing but conforming sister. They dived in at once, heads lowered. A similar offering was put in front of Clare, less emphatically. Hamburger, tomatoes still in their skins, pallid clusters of chips, bullet-hard peas. She declined tomato sauce from a dribbled bottle, Branston pickle from a half-gallon jar. She thought of Magda and beat down giggles as she tried to decide where to start on this fearful penance. Offending the locals at this stage would not be useful.

Will Morrison came from the bar to take the head of his cluttered table with dignified calm. From time to time he addressed Clare. 'You will be here on holiday. You will be from London.'

She didn't contest these findings.

Every so often a distant bell pinged, presumably indicating that a customer, his own meal over, had arrived in the bar. Will took no notice, and soon a voice would call through the propped-open door, 'Is that you at your tea, Will? I'll just help myself then.'

'Aye, you do that,' Will would respond comfortably, holding out his cup for one of his females to fill.

The television was now offering a cookery programme in an unknown tongue. Trying to listen through the family bickering around her, Clare came to the surprised conclusion that it was Gaelic, which to judge by the amount of attention they were giving it the Morrisons knew as much of as she did.

When the boys had vanished, each with a nod in Clare's direction, and Will had paced majestically back to his bar, the problem was clearly what should be done with the unscheduled guest. It summed up Ina's opinion of her pretty accurately, Clare thought with irony, that the answer was to relegate her with a cup of milky coffee to the grim lounge, to sit solitary in a forest of hard chairs and too-low tables ringed with beer mats.

It was so appalling it was funny, and suddenly she was bursting to tell Magda about the day. They had shared everything for a long time. She had located the public telephone at the end of a dimly lit verandah alive with draughts, and had actually started to tap in the number, when she realized that she couldn't phone now. For one thing Magda would be in the thick of cooking dinner and calls at this hour from anyone who should know better very reasonably enraged her. But more pertinently, how could Clare expect Magda to applaud her cleverness in finding four stone walls enclosing dirt and dereliction for which she proposed to abandon the sophisticated comforts of Carlini's and the enterprise to which Magda was so passionately dedicated?

Seized by a paralysing loneliness, Clare hesitated in the freezing semi-darkness. The glass panes bulged under the pressure of a rising wind. The air was dank and stale with old cigarette smoke. The cold of the floor ate through the soles of her boots.

Picturing Magda in the charged pre-dinner activity of the kitchen at Carlini's brought back other images – of discreet comfort, pervading warmth, thick carpets, subtle lighting, elaborate flowers. It was a time of day which Clare herself had always enjoyed, that moment of coming downstairs to find the house moving smoothly into its evening mode, curtains closed, hall fire high, staff in crisp clean shirts moving quietly about the empty dining-room with its gleaming glass and silver, the bar still sparsely populated, tables polished, ice buckets and bowls of nuts newly filled, barman peacefully rubbing up glasses. She herself would be fresh from her bath, groomed, made up, ready for the long evening, forgetting already that she had been on her feet for most of a busy day, making the familiar circuit of the rooms, checking, drawing the curtain in the ladies' loo that was always forgotten, pinching a leaf off a plant, tidying the magazines, enjoying the way the place looked, these small, habitual attentions almost a caress.

But then her mind moved forward over the evening, the pace becoming more hectic as dinner wound on its strenuous course, the tended rooms crowded, the noise level increasing steadily, the full ashtrays, the endless dirty glasses, the meaningless exchanges with strangers and the increasing need to blur it, skate over the surface of it, which made her fill her glass again and again. And more powerfully there came back the memory of her sense of entrapment, her resentment of the cloying atmosphere of indulgence and extravagance, and disgust to remember that every night she would be there till the end, clinging to noise and company, to anything which would put off the moment of going to bed alone. So usually she didn't go to bed alone . . .

Well, it was over, she had broken clear. Tomorrow she would go back and have another look at the cottage. If she could manage to live in such a place there would be nothing between her and a long hard look at herself and at what had brought her to this crisis point.

She ought to find out all she could about the Larach, though. The bar was the obvious place. Could she cope with that? She wanted a drink with a gnawing physical need, but the memory of the enigmatic little house gave her courage. She opened the outer door of the verandah and headed resolutely for the public bar, buffeted by the salt-flavoured wind off the loch.

CHAPTER THREE

The wind was stronger than she had expected and Clare snarled as it lifted her hair and sliced through her too-thin clothes. She reminded herself caustically that she was planning to live in this place.

Later she was able to see her entry into the public bar on that blowy night from the glen perspective – cross, breathless female with 'townie' written all over her erupting into the masculine calm of slow-paced week-night drinking, darts and dominoes. After the first startled moment the turned faces became uniformly expressionless, though no one pretended not to watch her as she crossed to the bar. She made her judgements too. To her unaccustomed eyes a black-bearded giant in vast knickerbocker suit and tweed fore-and-aft cap with the flaps tied up on top of his head might as well have been in fancy dress.

Will Morrison, gentleman that he was, moved his bulk round the bar with surprising speed and pulled out a stool where he could keep an eye on her. Clare accepted it and watched half irritated, half amused as he tried to wrest free a bottle of orange juice frozen to the cooler shelf. She tried not to wonder how long it had been there. Behind her animation gradually returned.

Of course they chatted to her eventually. What could a female like this be doing in Inverbuie on a December night? And asking questions about the Larach, which was little better than a bothy. It was an excellent joke, spiced with the promise of some fancy snob from England making a fool of herself. They drank whisky when it was Clare's round. The fumes made her stomach knot as a nausea of longing rose in her throat.

They told her what they thought she wanted to hear, politely veiling their unanimous opinion that she was mad, but nevertheless she gleaned some useful facts. The water supply had never been known to dry up (they didn't mention the fact that it frequently froze up instead); the chimney was a 'good-going' chimney; and the wood of the roof had been renewed 'not all that far back'. After lengthy discussion, which became quite heated, this turned out to be twenty-five years ago.

Clare also learned that Angus from the shop would deliver anything she needed by boat, but would wait till he had enough other orders to make it worth his while and tended to be pricey into the bargain. Donald Macrae from Rhumore, however, was up and down the loch a couple of times a week and would never see her stuck.

Huddled under the meagre supply of blankets off both beds, pulling them over her nose to shut out the powerful smell of burning dust from the electric fire (would Ina burst wrathfully in at any moment and make her turn it off?), Clare mulled over what she had learned, trying to trick sleep with positive thinking. Useless. Curled up into a tense ball of misery, she moved from muddled fantasies to distorted dreams – of going down to raid the bar, of beating on doors till she could locate Ina and plead illness and be given huge solacing brandies, of being back at Carlini's and getting riotously drunk, one of a wild group all of whom seemed to be strangers.

Going back to the Larach alone was different. Her senses seemed keener, colours more sharply defined, wet stone dark against fawn winter grass, plantations dense green under a faint promise of sun as the mist thinned and shredded. She could hear the brisk voices of hidden streams cutting through the peaty ground. She could hear too – surely she could not have missed this yesterday – the endless suck and surge of the loch itself on the shingle of the beach.

The cottage faced diagonally across and down the loch. Above a narrow fringe of fields and scattered farms on the opposite shore, bracken-covered slopes climbed steeply and were lost in cloud. To the left of the cottage a rocky promontory cut off the village at the head of the loch; to the right Clare could see where the headland and the southern shore almost touched pincers.

She had no key today. She rubbed at the salt-encrusted

windows and cupped her hands round her face to peer into the dark rooms.

'You must be out of your mind,' she said aloud, but complacently, sure now of what she was going to do.

She was to say it often in the weeks that followed, and with a good deal more panic.

The battle to stop drinking took over her brain and being. Alcohol had been an integral part of her life for so long, needed stimulant, accepted partner of good food, a social pleasure which she had always enjoyed before it became a dangerous addiction. No one from Magda down helped her, apparently thinking that for her to refuse a drink was weird, ridiculous, even in some obscure way giving offence.

Magda persisted in treating the whole thing as a temporary and maddening aberration. Clare supposed it was the only way she could deal with it. It was a miracle that some level of workable amity survived between them, but they had come pretty close in the shared commitment of the past two years and it helped them now.

When Magda had 'found' Clare, she herself had needed support and help. Not as crucially as Clare, who had not even recognized for some time that there had been a two-way dependence, but Magda had not been blind to her own luck in running into Clare that day.

It had been in a pub near Grafham Water. Clare had been drinking glühwein after one of her solitary walks along the bleak water's edge, Magda sussing out a menu someone had raved about and, though she had never admitted it, hoping to do a little poaching of staff.

Youngest of a vast family of famous Italian restaurateurs but brought up for most of her childhood in England by her English mother, Magda had decided to make her mark here rather than tag along in the shadow of her father and brothers. She had done her training in Geneva, then for several years had run a successful wine bar off the Edgware Road before launching with heavy family backing into hotel-keeping proper.

When she met Clare she had owned the elegant late-eighteenth-century house in Godmanchester for over a year, and had worked her way with rip-roaring fights and dramatic sackings and walk-outs through various combinations of staff. She had come to the conclusion that she should run the kitchen (her real love) herself, and find someone else to handle front-of-house management.

Magda never lost much time in extracting facts, and perched on a bar stool beside Clare had discovered in a matter of minutes that Clare's background had been secretarial with translating and interpreting, and that her languages were French and Italian. Exactly what Magda needed, to deal with both the majority of her staff and a market she specifically targeted, and in spite of the way Clare had let herself go Magda made a swift assessment that she would suit her purpose. Also it was clear that Clare was available and that her resistance was conveniently low.

Magda had swept aside Clare's protests that she knew nothing about hotels. 'Common sense,' she'd said flatly. 'Standards. Adaptability.' Of course what she had chiefly wanted was someone she could mould.

They had been a good team and they had had a lot of fun. Magda was a volatile and ruthless person but she was also irresistibly lively and enthusiastic, and Clare had developed a deep respect for her knowledge, energy and creative flair. In the early days they had turned their hands to most jobs. They had had to. Magda's technique with employees was not conciliatory and whereas her Italian restaurant and kitchen staff screamed uninhibitedly back at her, but mostly turned up sullen and smouldering for the next shift because they needed the job, local girls simply flounced out with firm faith in the social security system. One pot-man departed leaving untouched the entire dinner wash-up because he had blocked both his sinks with grease and couldn't face dealing with them. It was Magda and Clare who had come down at six the following morning, baled out the disgusting stinking water, dug the build-up of peas and onion rings and diced carrot out of the plughole, poured down boiling water, cleared the U-bends, then attacked the towering pile of encrusted pans so that another member of the kitchen staff could have a clear start for breakfast.

There had been an occasion very early on when Magda had been away at some family celebration and Clare had found herself alone in the bar on an evening which had promised to be quiet and had become suddenly busy. She had floundered about unsure of measures, prices, or even which glass to use, watched with contempt and growing irritation by well-heeled customers accustomed to better service, and justified in expecting it at Carlini prices. That had not been a good experience.

There had been the morning poundings on the door of the flat with the smug voice of a waiter announcing that no one had come on duty to cook breakfast and she and Magda had dragged themselves groaning and swearing out of bed to fill the gap. There had been changing beer barrels by guesswork and peering ignorantly and hopefully into hissing loo cisterns; there had been the guest who came down to breakfast with a three-foot-long thread-like worm in his toothmug and loudly threatened reprisals, and the guest who died of a heart attack and was dispatched discreetly through the back door into the ambulance at five-thirty in the morning. There had been making every bed in the house and cleaning every room, hoovering the nail clippings and pared skin of some delightful guest from a red bedroom carpet, with Magda joining Pavarotti at full volume pounding out Neapolitan love songs.

The demanding pace and steep learning curve (one of Martin's expressions) had been just what Clare had needed. She had not wanted time off or holidays. She had had her fill of empty days, of facing the bald truth that there was nothing in the world she wanted to do and nowhere she wanted to be. Home, the family home of childhood, no longer existed. Her mother had died, the house had been sold and by some subconscious defence process Clare now thought of her father as dead too. It was less painful than the truth.

It had felt like shedding a hated burden to sell her own house in its turn and get rid of the possessions that reminded her of Martin and her marriage – the heavily buttoned green leather sofa and chairs, the Sanderson curtains with the pencil-pleat tops, the repro dining table, the matching everything, all objects that Martin's boss could not possibly take exception to when writing his annual confidential report.

She had kept the few remnants of furniture that had come from her London flat, pre-Martin, and they had fitted happily into the top floor of the hotel which she and Magda had converted into a comfortable retreat which they rarely had time to enjoy. These old friends would not come with her now. Her need to break with every detail of her present life was probably irrational, but it was the only way she could handle it.

The pressures of Christmas made abstinence harder than ever, but at least there was no time for introspection. She had had the sense to seek professional help in the end, and, though she was worried about transferring dependence to yet another addiction, sleeping pills did at least ensure an adequate amount of recharging oblivion.

There was one unexpected bonus – she wasn't missing sex. She had feared it was a drug as compelling as drink, but it seemed to have been largely related to it. Without the blurring of self-respect that alcohol brought, she was not remotely tempted to turn to that other source of reassurance. She had expected her body to have its own say on this score, but it was quiescent, inert in fact.

Belatedly she had had herself checked for AIDS. Waiting for the results of the test concentrated her mind frighteningly. She couldn't believe she had shrugged off this danger so glibly. She knew she didn't deserve the answer she got, and knew she couldn't regard it as total absolution either, but nevertheless she found herself weak with relief as she took it in.

The memory of the cottage kept her going and was the best help of all in keeping her from the unrelenting temptation to have just one drink. She couldn't picture it clearly by now, couldn't have said what she imagined she would do there, but it was an essential stepping stone and it was going to be hers. There had been no obstacle to the sale. The farmer, Macrae, had not taken up his option to buy, Sandy Maitland was soothing about rights to water and access, and she had enough cash to buy the place ten times over.

'But why buy it?' Magda demanded, for once giving two minutes of her life to Clare's concerns. 'Why not rent it, use it for a couple of months, get yourself together or whatever it is you feel you have to do?'

'Magda, I'm not coming back.' Clare had discovered with consternation that Magda was making no plans to replace her.

'But what's the *point*? If you can stop drinking and sleeping around while you're here with temptation right under your nose then why on earth do you need to dump yourself somewhere in the back of beyond? And remember, it was this place that sorted your life out in the first place.'

Magda had always assumed that it had been Martin's death a couple of months before they met that had reduced Clare to the state of shock and apathy in which she had found her. Clare had never told her the whole truth, or what she suspected to have been the truth.

'You'll hate it,' Magda persisted. 'What in heaven's name will you do with yourself? All you need is a holiday. We've both been working far too hard, of course we have, but the worst is over. The place will tick along now that we're established.'

The exhilarating hand-to-mouth emergencies of the early days might be behind them, but no place run by Magda could ever be described as ticking along. Present plans included the conversion of the stables into staff accommodation, extending the terrace and tacking a conservatory on to the dining-room.

Knowing of these plans, Clare had offered, reluctantly because she would have preferred to be truly free of it if possible, to leave her share of the capital in the business. Once Magda had established that this didn't mean that Clare wanted to keep her own position open, she had brusquely refused. Clare was thankful, wanting no lingering ties.

Through it all – the de luxe Christmas package, the New Year parties, the grim anticlimax after them when Magda had to take Clare's departure seriously at last and there were some ugly scenes – threaded the lifeline of a link with a different world. Discussing progress from time to time with Sandy Maitland Clare was amused to find that, though the sound of his voice produced immediate associations of damp, cold, mist and dirt, talking to him never failed to give her a reassuring buzz. And he dealt with the problems that nagged at her in the sleepless, anxious small hours with cheerful calm.

'Coal? That's Eck Geddes. Jean'll know his number.' Eck? Background shouts, obviously preferred to the technology of the extension. 'It's 702242. He'll deliver. Give him a bit of warning, though, so that he can fit it in with other orders going out that way.'

'But he won't know who I am.'

A laugh. 'He'll know the Larach, won't he?'

'Well, if it's all so simple, how about a mattress? Would someone deliver that?'

'No problem,' he assured her.

And there wasn't. Just calm Highland voices saying, 'The Larach. Oh, but that will be fine, though. And when was it wanted for? That's grand, we'll have that out to you, no bother at all.'

'Will you need a cheque in advance?' Clare had asked the motherly-sounding female at the coal merchant's.

'That will not be necessary.' The voice was cooler and Clare saw that she had been out of order. 'Angus will leave the line.'

What on earth did that mean?

A pro forma invoice was agreed on for the mattress. Clare kept her copy for a long time with its laconic message, 'Somerville, the Larach, Inverbuie – to go by Angus's boat.'

As Clare packed and jettisoned she reminded herself of the things she would have to do without, trying to acclimatize her mind. Would her brain work without a computer? Would having no telephone mean a mental isolation she would find unendurable? Would having no car make her feel a prisoner?

Selling the car did, in fact, have the greatest impact. Clare had decided that if she did the obvious thing and used it to take the final load north, she would not be able to trust herself to get rid of it once there. And with a car on hand how could she trust herself to stay?

It was the oddest sensation to walk away from the garage. She felt physically light, as though she had off-loaded a heavy pack at the end of a long day's walk. There was an unexpected feeling of Friday afternoons, of long-ago end of terms. But she felt alarmingly insecure. Who was this shell-less creature scuttling across busy roads, feeling strangely invisible to the encased individuals sweeping arrogantly by?

Magda thought the gesture so crazy that Clare even began to wonder if she would take her to the station. She did, of course, and it was awful. They stood shivering on the platform in an easterly wind, its unclean cindery smell niggling their pink nostrils. They were incongruous together already, Magda in her tomato-coloured suede coat over black sweater and skirt, Clare looking like the female half of a *Field* ad in check shirt, dark green cashmere sweater, moleskins, Barbour, all painfully new.

There had been nothing to say. After all the shorthand of jokes and sharing, their minds searched futilely for some offering. They had never gone in for contact. Clare was in the train before they touched and then it was with an awkward, urgent gesture, jerky, almost missing, Magda's hand like a little claw clutching at Clare's as the train began to move away.

'Promise me you'll come up, promise!'

One flashing, brilliant smile from Magda. 'I promise.'

Clare sat rigidly, eyes pricking, taking deep, steadying breaths. She could not let this long journey begin in tears.

CHAPTER FOUR

There was an inescapable sense of being marooned as Clare stood and watched the boat curve out from the jetty and saw the two men in it each raise an arm in salute as it vanished behind the promontory.

'It's not an island,' she said aloud. Her voice sounded revealingly bracing. She turned to look at the waiting cottage, unable to feel it had anything to do with her. Approaching it for the first time from the water it had looked smaller than ever against the great backdrop of the hills, and lonelier. Extraordinary that she was about to go inside it and eat there and sleep there and pass hours and days there. She felt herself shrivelling with cowardice. It wasn't a good moment.

In fact there hadn't been any good moments so far. Well, one maybe – the sight of Sandy Maitland grinning at her, his ears a horrid mauve against his red hair under the platform lights as the train pulled into Fort William over an hour late.

He had taken her to the hotel where she had stayed before and shared the sandwiches, appetizing as wound dressings, which was all they could be persuaded to produce. Then he had dealt the first blow.

Clare had had some basic work done on the cottage and succinct communications had arrived from time to time on yellowed quarto paper headed 'Thos McCosh, Plumber, Fort William, Est. 1904, Tel. 79' (which was no longer true by several removes). From these she had gathered that the cold water tank had been replaced, some lead piping exchanged for copper, that the new bath and lavatory seat had been ordered and the rones cleaned. (They did go on about these rones.) She had also been informed that the water supply was 'grand' and the septic tank 'best not looked at'.

When she'd rather anxiously queried this enigmatic comment Sandy had laughed and assured her nothing dire was implied.

Now he broke the news that the new bath had not been installed. 'McCosh says there's nothing wrong with the old one.'

'*What?* Nothing wrong with it? It's absolutely ghastly! It looks as though it's never been cleaned since it was put in. I couldn't bear to get into it.'

'It's cast iron,' Sandy put in pacifically.

'It's frightful. In any case, it doesn't matter what it's like or what it's made of, I arranged for it to come out and a new one to be put in. I'm the customer, I'm paying, I decide.'

'They're quite valuable, these old baths.'

'Sandy, that has nothing whatever to do with it. Where does this bloody McCosh man do business, if you can call it that, and what time does he surface in the morning?'

Thos McCosh, who was actually Thos's grandson Alec, was impervious to her protests and hectoring.

'No, no, no,' he said, gently chiding, his pale blue eyes ranging over the chaotic jumble of his yard (doubtless to hide his amusement at her stalking into it to do battle at two minutes past eight on an icy March morning, Clare thought sardonically). 'There's no sense in taking out a good bath like that and putting in some of your cheap modern plastic rubbish. I was thinking it was cracked, maybe, when you were wanting rid of it, but Kenny tells me it's just fine.'

'Are you refusing to do the job?' But a warning bell rang in Clare's brain. If she stormed out of here, where was the next plumber going to be?

'Oh, well now, I wouldn't put it just like that,' Alec demurred, permitting himself the glimmer of a smile. 'I've some stuff put by for you – what's this it's called? Well, I canna' mind just now, but when Kenny's next out that way he'll look in and give the bath a wee clean and it'll make all the difference in the world, you'll see . . .'

Clare got nowhere with him and still couldn't believe it as she found herself heading out of town on the 'Tuesday bus', on which, the sole alternative to the school bus at four, the planning of this entire journey had hinged. She was too angry about the bath to take in anything except that a woman in the seat behind her had a hacking cough and that it seemed to take five times longer to get to Inverbuie by this means than it had by car.

Once there she went eagerly to the shop, to be told by Angus that the household stuff she had sent on was not waiting at the Larach but was stacked 'in the back' at the hotel where Ina had kindly found room for it. There was worse. Prowling bad-temperedly round Fort William, filling in time before the bus left, she had muttered about the evil wind that plucked and buffeted, whirling rubbish about, chivvying the gulls whose summer-holiday cries sounded all wrong on the wintry air. But she had not related it to herself and her affairs. Even when she saw the white crests driving up Loch Buie as the bus wound its way down from the moor she didn't wake up to reality. She had made arrangements; her arrangements worked.

'But that stuff was meant to be there, in the house already,' she protested angrily to Angus, barely acknowledging the waiting customer who, sniffing the prospect of some rewarding drama, had obligingly allowed Clare to jump in ahead of her. 'It'll take ages to load and unload it.'

'Aye, well, it's no' just been flitting weather,' Angus told her with a grin she saw as both sly and patronizing, carrying on calmly weighing out potatoes.

'But when will you be able to go?'

Clare meant what time.

'Onions too, was it, Sheila? Four do you? They're no' all that big today. Well now,' he answered Clare, bending his knees slightly so that he could see a strip of loch between the notices stuck on his window, 'there's no knowing when this wind will drop. It could be a day or two days, but I've seen it blow like this for a week at this time of year.'

'What?' Clare felt her jaw drop. 'A *week*? But what on earth do you expect me to do for a week? This was all arranged ages ago, it's outrageous –' Exhaustion and frustration (and growing doubt) rose in her like a rocket and she faced up to solid, imperturbable Angus in fury. But just in time she recognized the classic scene – yet another ignorant Sassenach all set to teach lackadaisical Highlanders more efficient ways.

She made a huge, huge effort. 'Well, if you could let me know the moment it's possible to go,' she said stiffly.

'Oh, aye, aye, I'll surely do that,' Angus assured her solemnly but not unkindly, though his delighted customer broke out indignantly, 'Did you ever hear the like of yon?' as they watched Clare walk away, down on to the spray-soaked pier, and face into the tearing wind.

'She's a lot to learn,' Angus agreed, but he sounded more tolerant than offended.

They could not guess that Clare was doing her best not only to beat down rage but to deal with a frightening awareness of being alien and helpless. She thought she had done quite well, going to the hotel and calmly booking a room, which Ina of course had had ready for her all along. But Ina took one look at her face and substituted, 'I'll bring you some lunch through to the bar,' for the teasing, 'So you'll not have budged Angus?' that had been on the tip of her tongue.

Clare could never remember afterwards how she had filled the waiting time. She was in and out of the shop, ostensibly adding to the supplies Angus had ready in boxes for her but really not trusting him to organize her all-important trip down the loch the moment he could. Though the shop triumphed in such recondite offerings as Flymo blades and kit for smoking out moles, the food was far more dismal than she could ever have imagined.

She went for unambitious, unseeing walks along the three roads leading out of the village in turn, fuming at the persistent wind and rain. She ate with the Morrison family as the hotel was closed – and could have sworn that the same mound of ironing was still waiting while the cat still watched her through slitted eyes from its favourite spot on the humming fridge.

Yet the atmosphere was subtly different. Lunatic as the whole idea of her living at the Larach patently was, Clare now had the status of neighbour, and one guaranteed to provide rich entertainment at that.

Ina and the girls were mainly concerned with such questions as, 'But will you no' be scared, away out there on your own?', while Lachy and Ewan, once the serious business of eating was over, tilted back their chairs, picked their teeth and revealed that certain assumptions had been made.

'That'll be some price, getting the power in.'

'And the phone,' put in Morag.

'That'll be just the standard charge,' Lachy put her down automatically.

'But there's not even a road in, and it's miles from anywhere,' Morag argued.

'It doesna' matter where it is, you daft lump, you don't know what you're talking about.'

'You'd easy enough make a road though,' Ewan asserted confidently. 'Dougie Stewart was saying you'd only need a digger in for a couple of days, or a week at the outside.'

'I shan't be putting in a road, or a telephone, or electricity,' Clare announced crisply.

They gaped at her almost with hostility, so beyond their comprehension did this seem, and Ina rushed in with a little domestic organizing.

'The place'll surely need a good clean out from top to bottom. Why don't you stay here till the end of the week and Morag and Karen can go down at the weekend – oh, yes, you can, you've no call to go to Luig every Saturday, the dear knows what you find to do there anyway – and get everything scrubbed out for you. There'll be plenty of stuff there only fit for a bonfire, if I know anything about old Murdo.'

Clare only knew that she must get there as soon as she could, and alone, no matter how filthy, cold or uncomfortable the house might be. She had to complete this journey.

There was no feeling of sanctuary, however, as she went up from the jetty, following the path which still faintly indented the spongy turf, and into the waiting shell of the cottage. She knew she was lucky not to be spending another night at the Inverbuie Hotel, having seen the trouble the men had had getting the boxes on to the jetty. She was paying for Angus and his boat, but Donald Macrae had seemed to regard helping as a neighbourly duty. She had expected them to leave once they had dumped everything in the house but they had gone on tramping calmly about without reference to her.

They had swept up the soot on the bedroom floor while she was still groping past the fact that there was no hoover, had stripped the polythene cover from the gaudy new mattress (which Angus explained he'd seen no point in delivering any sooner just to get damp) and had chucked the noisome old one behind the house. They had taken the canopy off the sitting-room fire and had a look up the chimney.

'Kenny had the sense to do that much anyway,' remarked Angus. Each hid a grin.

Kenny? Oh yes, the henchman of the independent-minded McCosh.

'Best get it going.'

'I would think so.'

With Clare dodging about behind them trying to see what they were doing they laid the fire with the paper and sticks Angus had added to her boxes of provisions, and fetched coal from the shed. That at least had been delivered without anyone thinking of a better plan.

'I haven't even paid for it,' Clare remarked.

'The line's here.'

The mysterious line, a tiny, crumpled, damp, coal-grimed invoice.

Angus and Donald turned on the water, showing her where the toby was situated outside and where they were putting the key away afterwards.

'I thought I'd organized the plumber to do that,' Clare said.

'It's no good leaving the water on at this time of year without a fire lit,' they explained patiently, checking the taps and flushing the loo. (The new seat was in place, which Clare conceded had to be something.)

'That's a grand bath,' Angus remarked blandly.

How on earth did he know about that?

'Wretched man,' Clare protested, indignant all over again. 'I could have skinned him.'

'I was hearing he had an early morning visitor,' Angus commented without inflexion.

'Huh. But why does everyone go on about it being such a good bath?' she demanded, peering into its stained depths. 'It looks bloody awful to me.'

'Oh, but you'll never get enamel like that these days,' Angus told her.

Did she want to?

'And just look at the length of it. Though maybe that'll not matter too much to you,' Donald conceded, looking down on her from his six foot something.

They connected the gas cylinder to the cooker, then Donald, after a glance at Clare's face, disconnected it again and made her do it herself. They split kindling 'for morning' which would last her a fortnight, and Donald broke up a pile of gash wood over a boulder with his foot 'just to keep her going'.

Clare was torn between surprised gratitude for what they were doing and a base longing to get rid of them. She did at least remember to offer them tea, which they accepted politely. She guessed it should have been whisky but had none to give them, none within reach. And that was a strange feeling, in spite of the fact that she hadn't had a drink for nearly three months.

Why did it seem so dark, in later memories of that first dreadful evening? Donald had lit the oil lamp before he left and the fire was burning well. She supposed it was the contrast with what she was used to, the dirt, the penetrating cold. And fright. All her energies had been concentrated on fighting clear of a destructive lifestyle. Now she felt she had done it all too thoroughly, and was alarmingly conscious that she had only her own resources to fall back on here.

The blank black eyes of the windows watched her as she went back and forth assembling what she needed for a meal and for the night. There was nowhere clean to put anything down, no hot water to do any cleaning with, except what she could heat on the gas cooker which took an unbelievable time. She felt anger begin its familiar spiral within her, the anger even Magda had been wary of recently.

She found herself listening jumpily to the silence, or rather the absence of human sounds, for the wind was eerily vocal and behind it she could distinguish the sound of waves beating against the jetty. She found her cassette player and put on a tape, then realized that she was straining to hear over it. To hear what? It was too unnerving and she switched it off.

If she'd had a bottle of gin to hand she knew she would have drunk the lot there and then, giving up without a second thought the long resistance. She had imagined it would make self-denial easier with nothing to drink in the house, but instead it made her feel furiously defiant.

It was defiance with nowhere to go. What could she do about it? Outside the windows lay the dark miles of the loch, behind the house rose the open hill without paths or tracks. She could get over there somehow – and then what? There would be no passing cars on the road at this time of night. She could walk. Where to? To the sleeping silent village, the windswept tarmac spaces, the locked hotel. And then what? Bang on doors, shout for help, for contact, for the sound of human voices?

She pushed away the panicky images. The only comfort available to her was the prosaic one of going to bed and getting warm, if that could be achieved. A couple of hot-water bottles, a warm drink, the spare duvet she had brought against Magda's visit added to her own. She weighed the bottle of sleeping pills in her hand. She had been cutting back but this was one night when she needed the certainty of sleep.

CHAPTER FIVE

The pills had no chance against the cold. Clare dreamed she was swimming and couldn't lift her head out of the water. She woke to find her face aching with cold, her nose icy and her whole body temperature well below the point of comfort. Her feet were frozen lumps and even her kneecaps were icy, a phenomenon she didn't recall experiencing before. The second duvet had vanished. Reaching for her torch and sitting up to retrieve it she shivered and swore. She could dig out a sheet or something to anchor it but the thought of leaving even the semi-warmth of bed was exceedingly unattractive. She huddled the duvets around her, doing some rapid wriggling to stimulate warmth as she used to do in her sleeping bag on long-ago expeditions, and tried to persuade herself that the hot-water bottles were warmer than she was.

Then a new horror struck. There was a loud scrabbling somewhere across the room, the sound of something like a stone dislodged, rattling, falling. Jesus! In spite of the cold she sat up in panic. What was in the room with her? A rat? Scampering sounds behind the wardrobe. More than one? God, God, she couldn't take this. But she'd have to know. With shaking hand she reached for the torch again. Making herself search systematically she moved its beam round the room. Nothing. She leaned over and checked under the high bed. She'd have to check under the wardrobe too. And if she found something? If gleaming little beads of eyes stared back? But one way or another she was going to have to get out of bed since she was now colder than ever after sitting up in her skimpy nightdress, and even more urgently the cold was having an emphatic effect on her bladder.

With jaw resolutely set she swung her legs out of bed and

reached with her feet for her slippers. No way was she going to step on to the dirty bare floorboards of this totally unheated room. The slippers were little quilted slip-ons with thin soles, her dressing-gown a light wrap. Why on earth hadn't she thought of buying something more practical? Because she'd imagined March was spring, that's why, she told herself grimly. She steeled herself to go down on one knee and make a sweep with her torch under the wardrobe, holding her hair back with one frozen hand. She had to be sure. Nothing. In the wavering light of the torch the room looked bare but not threatening, no ominous dark holes in the skirting boards. Those sounds must have been in the walls. Nothing could get in here. She had to believe that.

She went shuddering into the mildew-smelling kitchen and filled the kettle. Did the water always run this slowly? Her fingers were almost too cold to fumble a match out of the box to light the gas. The match wouldn't light. Shaking, she stared at the box in the beam of the torch. Damp already? They couldn't be. And if the matches were damp, then how could she ever get any heat going? Then she remembered that there was another box of matches by the fire.

'Fool, fool, fool,' she muttered at herself as she fetched them thankfully and the gas popped into life. Should she try to light the lamp? But her fingers were too stiff and cold and she was afraid of breaking the glass or turning the wick the wrong way in the torchlight. The lamp could wait. And if she used up the entire torch battery then a replacement would be one thing Angus would be sure to stock.

The icy impact of the loo seat was something else she hadn't bargained for.

The kettle she had brought with her was too expensive, too heavy. The feeble flame took for ever to penetrate its base let alone heat the water. With a little sob that was more angry frustration than real tears she reached for the saucepan she had used to heat the milk. As she was filling it she remembered that the water in the hot-water bottles would at least give her a start. She was glad no one was there to see her fumbling her way through these elementary steps in survival. And there were three rings on the cooker. She found another pan in one of the boxes. But would this use up her gas too fast?

'God, don't be such an *idiot*! It's the amount of water you heat that counts, not the number of burners you put on.' A little ordinary logic was very steadying. What was she doing anyway, standing here with teeth chattering and arms wrapped round her waiting for the water to boil, with her ankles numb and the cold of the cement floor eating through her silly slippers?

She hurried to the bedroom, pulled on a big sweater, thick socks. Now the slippers wouldn't go on.

'Well, boots will.' Giggling by this time she padded back to where she had left them by the door and hauled them on. Her Barbour hung above them. Well, it was as cold in here as out of doors, colder probably. She put it on too. Now what would a good survivor do? What would Joe do? In this moment of extremis she didn't flinch away from the association, remembering only Joe the practical, Joe the competent leader. Get the blood moving, Joe would undoubtedly say.

With the torch on its back lighting up the smoke-grimed ceiling Clare began to dance round the table, stamping her booted feet, whirling and singing, coughing as the dust rose. What if some fisherman out on the loch should look across and see this demented torchlit scene? Would he send a boatload of police to take her away in the morning? What an excellent idea. For as the kettle first thinly then piercingly added its voice to hers, everything suddenly became perfectly simple.

There was no need to stay one day longer in this freezing, filthy, barbarous hole. It had served its purpose. The essential break had been made. There was nothing to keep her here. She could go to Inverness, Edinburgh, rent a flat, take stock, plan something sensible. Even if no other fool was prepared to buy the cottage from her she could write it off, forget it.

Damn, she hadn't heated any fresh water for a drink, she realized as she refilled her bottles. It didn't matter. Nothing mattered. Milk would do to clean the dust out of her throat. It was so cold her teeth jumped with pain; who needed a fridge here? But it was over, it was over, the dark and the dirt and the rats and the isolation she had naively thought she wanted. Anyway, she could probably be more anonymous in a city than she could here.

Warm, almost cheerful, shedding only boots and jacket, she

scurried into bed. Where would she be this time tomorrow? She didn't care.

The cold woke her again, but now it was daylight. The awful night was over; all she had to do was pack everything up again ready to be fetched away, take what she could carry and leave. Going through to the sitting-room to see if it would be warmer to dress in there than in the bedroom (it wasn't) she was repelled by its squalor in the grey light of a bitter morning. Even the memory of her wild dancing barely raised a smile. Nor did the discovery of hottish water coming out of the tap much cheer her. She had forgotten the existence of the back boiler and hadn't even checked the water last night, just gone on boiling the kettle like a zombie. She was not prepared for the fact that her tooth-paste was frozen (hardish anyway), that her nose had a permanent tendency to drip or that the butter refused to part with the knife.

No sound from the other inhabitants of the cottage. Well, they were welcome to territory they clearly viewed as their own. If all I want to do, Clare reflected mockingly, is sort out the lumber of buried memories festering in my mind and map out a new future, then surely I can do it somewhere warm and clean.

The problem was that even the time it would take to pack up and go would be unendurable without some form of heating, and there was only one source available. She stared doubtfully at the dead fire. All the makings were there.

Wearing rubber gloves and wincing at what was happening to the knees of her fawn moleskins, she set to work. Pulling out the ashpan too vigorously she discovered that it was about as functional as lace and she exclaimed crossly as the ash rose round her in a cloud. A bucket? There had to be something usable in that crazy shed.

She stepped out into a bright beauty that caught her breath away. While she had been muddling about as oblivious as a mole the sun had come up, pouring a steely brilliance over a scene she had been looking at from Inverbuie for two days and never seeing. The loch glittered, its waves beaten down to coursing silver, the mountains beyond were capped with snow and the air she had just gasped into her lungs filled her with elation.

What was I thinking about, she asked herself in disbelief, moaning and fussing and ready to be defeated before I'd begun? All I had to do was step through the door, my own door, and this dazzling splendour was waiting for me.

She turned back and, peeling off her blackened gloves, pitched them at the fire. Grabbing her Barbour she went down to the shore. Pure personal freedom, full of a great new simplicity and excitement.

The fire, however, was waiting for her when she got back. She couldn't get it to go. The hearth was covered with wisps of half-burned paper and the charred ends of twigs, with too-large lumps of coal and even an angry tear or two. She had adjusted every knob and lever she could see and could no longer remember how they had been when she started.

If I can't light the bloody fire I can't live here anyway, she thought despairingly. Simple as that.

She flicked back the hair that swung infuriatingly round her eyes and wondered why she had never noticed how it got in the way before.

She jumped shatteringly as a conversational voice behind her remarked, 'That's a grand morning, though.'

Her mind had so totally accepted her isolation that the shock was enormous, and she let out an 'Aaagh!' of a volume that visibly unsettled her visitor.

'Oh, here now,' he protested, drawing back his head exaggeratedly. 'I'm no' as bad as all that, surely?'

He had on a red cagoule over a high-necked black-and-white flecked sweater and what Clare now saw to be a postman's cap on the back of his head.

'My God,' she said unsteadily, 'I just about went up the chimney.'

'It's these boots,' he offered. 'They're inclined to come up on folk.'

Boots! She had supposed herself to be beyond the reach of human kind.

'You'll be having a wee bit of trouble,' he observed, his eyes going from her face (she discovered the state it was in after he left) to the messy hearth.

'I've done everything I can think of,' Clare said crossly.

'Aye, well, I can see that,' he commented, taking off his cap to reveal a high dome of skull laced with a few wild grey strands of hair.

Tutting and clucking, he stripped away her latest edifice and put together a new one. 'Air, do you see, air's the thing. Now what have you done here? You've the chimney shut off altogether. Here's this plate, and this wee handle opens and shuts it. Wait while I show you.' And taking out a dingy handkerchief he rubbed away at the knob in question, which turned out to be brass and to say 'Off' and 'On'.

'That's for your hot water, and this one is for your cooking oven. You'll have done your flues?' he enquired with sudden sternness and Clare was obliged to admit that she had not.

He embarked on a demonstration, winding up with the apparently irrelevant threat, 'And if I see that lad Kenny I'll have something to say to him.'

'But isn't Kenny the plumber?'

'And isn't seeing that you have hot water the plumber's job? Watch this soot now, I'll just away outside with it – and you'll be putting on the kettle maybe?'

Clare found herself smiling as she lit the gas and found some biscuits.

'Is Murdo's kettle not somewhere about?' the postman's voice asked from the sitting-room steps, and going past her he looked into the as-yet-unexplored larder. 'Aye, I thought it wouldn't have gone far,' he exclaimed with satisfaction, emerging with a sooty monster which he planked down on the draining board. 'That'll go on your fire, save your gas for you.'

He seemed to be in no hurry, discoursing affably about the weather and the general condition of the house. Clare fully expected him to enquire after her rones.

'But I didn't think a postman would call here,' she said, cutting across his peaceful monologue.

'Oh, no, I canna' call here,' he protested, horrified. 'They wouldna' hear of it.'

'Ah.' Even at that stage she realized that to ask, 'Then what are you doing here?' would be unacceptably blunt.

'But I could fetch your letters the length of the farm. It would save you going to the road end. I was having a word with Angus, and as you've no car I could lift your milk with me. Not every day, mind – three times in the week would be ideal.'

Clare watched him go up the ridge at an impressive speed, jacket ballooning in the wind, spry as a goat. She'd had in the end to ask him his name, which he hadn't seemed to approve of. Not surprising, she thought with a grin. Who'd like admitting to Nicol McNicol?

Her next caller knocked. Clare had her head in the cupboard under the sink, beginning to doubt if scrubbing would ever remove its indefinable smell, and she gave it a painful bang and crawled out trembling, wondering if her heart would stand this quiet life.

Kenny the plumber, dropped off by Angus who was delivering goods down the loch, was already in the sitting-room. Square and muscular, with shaggy dark hair and a cheeky grin, he seemed entirely at home.

He admired Nicol's efforts on the flues with bland innocence. 'Aye, he did a good job there, right enough. You'll no' be needing to look at those for a while.' He then lifted an assortment of ornaments off the big armchair by the now-blazing fire and sat down with a rhetorical, 'These cushions'll no' hurt, no?' He stirred himself only to lean forward and adjust the draught of the fire, subduing its gulping roar with the comment, 'You'll no' be wanting to waste your fuel,' then settled his stocky form comfortably.

It seemed churlish to raise the question of work. Clare went to put the kettle on.

When Kenny finally roused himself to apply Alec McCosh's miracle cure to the bath she rinsed out the old black kettle, filled it and set it on the hob. It seemed she was going to stay for the time being anyway.

'You'll be doing the place up,' Kenny stated when she went to see how he was getting on. She realized in time that his interest was professional and smoothed her hackles.

'No, I don't think so.'

'Oh aye?' said Kenny.

'Really.'

'Ach, the English always go mad for improvements.'

'Not me.'

'You'll be sending for me soon enough,' he said cheerfully, giving the bath a final wipe. 'How's that, now?' The bottom of the bath was paler blue, the disgusting yellow tidemark almost entirely gone. 'You'll no' be giving me the bother of bringing a new bath all the way out here now, will you?'

'So that was it. Quality of the enamel, my foot!'

'Ah, dinna' be like that, now,' Kenny protested, grinning slyly.

He ate his piece, the first time Clare had heard the expression, while waiting for Angus, and she had a very dull cheese sandwich. Where was she going to be able to get decent bread – and surely Angus must have heard of some other kind of cheese than Scottish Cheddar? The big old kettle was already whiffing out a straight jet of steam and she made the coffee from it. Kenny made no move towards the flask jutting from the corner of his grubby canvas lunch bag.

After a brief discourse on the history of the Larach plumbing and giving notice that he intended to improve the lagging before winter, he took himself off to the shed and began to sort out wood for burning.

'You'll need a chainsaw,' he stated, 'and a bushman.'

About to remark that she didn't feel she could be seriously attracted to a bushman, Clare realized this would strike a false note.

'A bushman?' she asked meekly.

'Do you no' ken what a bushman is? A saw.'

Suddenly there was comfort in knowing nothing, in having everything to learn. Responsibilities fell away.

'There's plenty wood on the cliff,' Kenny was saying. 'Easy enough dragged down.'

'But whose is it?'

He looked at her in surprise. 'Donald'll no' be wanting it.'

Angus, arriving shortly and accepting the tea Clare was getting tired of making, asked with a sidelong glance, 'So you're not wanting me to take you away then?' and she was ashamed to think how close she had come to giving up.

They scoffed at the idea of rats. 'Mice, it'll be,' they said.

'They must be wearing boots then,' Clare retorted huffily.

'They're not downstairs, though. They'll be in the walls and up in the loft.' And without further discussion they got up and went to have a look.

'At least you've no electric cable to worry about,' was Kenny's comment.

Lucky me, thought Clare.

She got rid of them at last. Hurrying up from the jetty she felt exasperation take over again. The idea had been to free herself of interruptions and demands and here she was with half the day gone and the huge, daunting task of imposing cleanliness and order on the cottage scarcely begun.

'I say, hello!'

Startled, Clare stared blankly round her.

'We're up here!'

In open-mouthed disbelief Clare watched as a white-haired, tweed-clad couple picked their way down the cliff, beating away two black labradors who were slavishly attempting to stay to heel.

'I do not believe this,' Clare said aloud. 'This *cannot* be happening.'

They met at the corner of the house, Clare hoping they had the dogs well under control.

'Now, we don't mean to keep you back –'

'We know you must be fearfully busy settling in –'

'Just thought we'd look in –'

'I'm Lilias Markie. How do you do?'

'Gerald Markie. Heel, Poppy, don't be such a bloody nuisance.'

'I know it's absolutely unforgivable of us to drop in like this but of course you don't have a telephone yet –'

Bruising handshakes, accompanied by a piercing scrutiny from two pairs of faded blue eyes.

'As we're your nearest neighbours –'

'Except for the Stewarts, of course –'

'Nonsense, we're much closer than the Stewarts.'

'What a preposterous statement –'

They broke off for the brief scrap, as dogs do, then returned to the joint attack.

'Now, we know it's maddening to have callers when you're trying to get organized –'

'But if there's anything at all that you need –'

'Please don't hesitate –'

They hadn't heard any of Clare's polite noises in reply.

'We just brought a little welcoming offering.' Two jars were thrust into Clare's hands.

She couldn't let them push off as she longed to do. After a bout of shouting at the dogs to sit and stay, though Clare was relieved to see that neither had shown the slightest hope of being allowed through the door, they were in, protesting about being a frightful nuisance but insisting all the same on sitting at the table ('Gerald's back, you know, such a bore,'), so that Clare had to shift the stuff Kenny had moved from the chair. She offered them tea or coffee.

'Oh, tea would be lovely. China if you have it.'

She didn't. She heard another brisk spat in progress as she recycled the mugs, but they were full of encouragement for her when she returned.

'I must say you've got your fire going beautifully.'

Had word spread already?

'Do a marvellous job, these old grates.'

'Oh, thank you so much,' said Mrs Markie, accepting her tea. 'We don't mind mugs a bit. It's so hard to find everything when you've just arrived, isn't it?'

'So glad you're keeping the dresser,' her husband remarked approvingly.

How did he think she would get rid of it?

'And Murdo's splendid chair. Awfully sad when these lovely old things are done away with.'

They seemed incapable of relaxing, insisting even as they drank their tea that they must be off and let her get on or bobbing up to hurl some discipline at the motionless dogs outside. They clearly longed to get Clare properly organized and to this benevolent end issued large-scale orders.

'You'll have to make a garden. Absolutely hopeless up here without a garden.'.

'You mustn't think of buying vegetables from Angus, perfectly dismal quality and fearfully expensive.'

'Plant potatoes. Clear the ground.'

'You've checked your water supply?'

'Is that loft of yours floored? Any woodworm?'

Clare resisted an inspection.

When they finally took themselves off, barking commands at the dogs and at each other till their voices faded away over the hill, she looked at the jars they had brought. Blackcurrant jam and rowan jelly. Yes, Lilias Markie was the kind of woman who would make rowan jelly.

Anger boiled up in Clare. The waiting work seemed suddenly so grim and disagreeable it felt for a moment quite beyond her to tackle it again. And what difference would mere cleaning make to this drab little place anyway? But more maddeningly, would people never leave her alone to get on with it? Then she was abruptly distracted by a mysterious rumble followed by supporting gurgles and knockings. Christ, the hot tank! She leapt for the kitchen tap to run off some water, swore at her own idiocy and rushed instead for the bathroom.

Oh, Thos McCosh, Alec McCosh, Kenny *et al*, you are forgiven and thrice forgiven. Never mind the wincing chill as she tore her clothes off, the dank concrete of the floor, the cloud of steam she had to flap away to find the tap to turn it off. Heavenly deep, perfectly angled, smoothly welcoming bath, she would cherish the memory of their first encounter for ever.

Soothed by the glorious warmth her ill temper faded, and she was at last able to acknowledge it for what it was. Though she had pretended to find it infuriating to have this procession of people coming to her door when she had imagined she had achieved complete isolation, she knew that really she was just run ragged with doubts and fears. Not fears connected with the immediate problems and discomforts facing her, but the much deeper fears about what would become of her, what she would be able to make of this new start. Did she have enough courage to carry through this drastic elimination of everything she was accustomed to? Had she gone too far? But warmth, the through-and-through warmth bestowed by the hot bath (though the moment of getting out was seriously unpleasant) and maintained after it by moving briskly about doing the unpacking she had had no chance to get at all day, made this evening very different from last night. And because there had been people in it, and because she had slept in it, more or less, the cottage itself felt

45

less alien. She undressed by the fire (she must do something about curtains since the loch seemed to have more traffic on it than she had bargained for), went to bed in full survival kit and slept quite soon. She was woken once or twice by the mice going loudly about their business and shouted furiously at them to get lost, which startled them into brief silence, but she could at least be sure that they weren't in the room with her.

Tomorrow she would attack the deep cleaning. Everyone had had a look at her now. With their curiosity satisfied and finding her unresponsive, surely they would not persist in harrying her. Her driven feeling would vanish and she would be able to unwind at last.

CHAPTER SIX

Clare had come to a standstill. If she unpacked the books on to the dresser shelves, now rich with polish, they would be covered in dust the moment she tackled the rectangle of beaten grime which called itself a carpet. She couldn't get at the carpet till she had unpacked the books, since she couldn't shift the boxes when they were full. Solo living. She felt the fierce exasperation which had become such a habit lately rise swiftly. For two pins she could have cried. There was so much waiting to be done. She looked at her watch from pure habit, used to racing through her days against the clock.

Then she caught herself up. There were no punters to please here, no rigid timetable of meals to parcel out the day. This check over the books was unimportant, a minor practical difficulty. And since there was no one to solve it but herself, getting worked up about it was ridiculous. She could unpack the books and stack them in the bedroom, or if that was too tedious put them on the shelves and cover them with a sheet or something. And more importantly she could do it whenever she felt like it. Her shoulders were aching after cleaning every inch of the bathroom and kitchen, though the larder still lurked in wait with its smell of rot and damp and its miscellany of uncouth abandoned objects.

She took off her watch, went to fetch the alarm clock from the bedroom and put them both into one of the dresser drawers. Then she looked across the room at the unworn hill boots beside her still-shiny green wellies under the row of old-fashioned cast-iron hat and coat pegs, but her resolution wavered. They were so very much the real thing and she, these days, so definitely was not. And they weren't broken in.

'So break them in.'

Was she going to talk to herself on a regular basis here?

Italian, soft as slippers, the boots didn't need breaking in. Watching their toes swinging up the narrow sheep track through the heather, Clare was transported – sights, scents and her own responses – back to Rosthwaite. It was one of the links that had brought her here, so it was natural enough that the associations should surface, but their vividness took her by surprise.

It had started at university, when she had followed her arrogant first love up every rock face on which he would tolerate her in North Wales and the Lakes. (Odd that memories of both should be tainted by Martin, though that came later.)

The affair had not lasted, but it had had its long-term effect. After coming down she had been lucky enough to be taken on by Marchant's, the internationally respected agency for secretaries, translators and interpreters. They had sent her to Paris and then to Milan for three busy and happy years. Once more London-based she had run into a girl who had a part share in a rented cottage in Borrowdale and was looking for someone to take it over.

Home with her father gone had become a chilly, stringently ordered place, relations with her mother more fraught with every reluctant visit, so for the next year or so the Rosthwaite cottage provided a refuge, a needed special place, a source of friendships.

Ironic that she had met Martin there. He had been in camp a couple of miles up the valley, running a training exercise for officer cadets. He and his fellow flight commanders had got together with the cottage group in a big mob at the pub and Martin had immediately singled Clare out with flattering determination.

It was a long time since she had thought of him as he had been in those days, in good physical shape, full of energy – and happy. She had had no way of knowing then that the tough outdoor image was largely role play, but later she could imagine how sardonically the other officers had watched the act.

She had been as happy as he was – and it was a long time since she had been honest enough to admit that. Later she had been able to look back and see that he had been totting up, just as Magda was later to do with equal self-interest, her qualifications and potential, in Martin's case assessing her suitability to be the wife of the senior officer he was sure he would soon become.

Only a few weeks later she had gone to Cranwell as accredited girlfriend for the squadron's passing-out and had seen the Air Force at its best – the civilized surroundings of the Royal Air Force College, immaculate parade, band, fly-past, even decent sherry. It had all looked quite bearable.

It had been not a big wedding but nevertheless a fairly pretentious one. Martin had insisted on the hackneyed arch of swords. Clare's mother had been less frosty than usual since she approved of Martin's ambition and was thankful to see her daughter 'settled'. Martin's parents, on the other hand, had been 'unable to make it'.

How could she have accepted that? Clare had asked herself so often and so guiltily since. Martin had taken her to see them once the engagement was announced and it had been ultra-tense. Martin's mother had been almost speechless with nerves, panicking about lunch, the way the house looked and about letting Martin down. His father had been protective towards his wife and largely silent, with the sort of silence that covers deep hurt. They had expected Martin and Clare to stay and had been disbelieving and disappointed when they insisted they had to get back after all, making their escape with too obvious relief, Clare recalled with shame. There had been the dreadful consciousness of loving preparations wasted, of polish and flowers and 'best' things brought out of hiding, of the larder stuffed with special food anxiously planned.

And why didn't I insist that they came to the wedding? she found herself wondering now. Did I really let myself believe it would be an ordeal for them, that they'd hate the whole scene? Didn't I know they would have been bursting with pride? Did I actually pretend not to know that Martin would have been embarrassed by them?

The wedding itself she remembered as a blur. That was probably fairly standard but for her, because the whole thing was so Air Force orientated, she had felt it was a show entirely staged by other people. And certainly Martin had seemed more aware of the various senior officers present than of her, and very twitched about her getting the service protocol right. No one else would have been worrying much about it, as she now knew.

The honeymoon – her mind skittered hastily away. Later knowledge had made that a memory not to be examined honestly. But she had recently come up too sharply against the dangers of evasion to let herself dodge it this time.

She had been so sure they would go back to Rosthwaite, or somewhere very like it. They could have had the cottage, their own special place where they had first made love. She winced, her face tightening. Martin had scoffed at the mere idea. Not his image. In fact, how could she not have realized it was no coincidence that during their engagement they had never even talked of returning? Weekends had been spent in her flat in London or Martin had booked her into some hotel near Cranwell. He didn't favour her staying in the mess as some of the other girlfriends did.

So the honeymoon had been spent in Amalfi and she had had a strange feeling throughout of being unable to get in touch with her surroundings. She had wanted to set out on foot, wander and explore and find the little bars and cafés the locals used. Martin had hired a car and when he wasn't stretched out on his lounger by the hotel pool, carefully working up his tan in the recommended stages, he wanted to go to Naples, Capri, the standard tourist haunts. One unexpected source of friction had been Clare's fluency in Italian. It was almost as though Martin had chosen Amalfi as a resort he knew would be up-market enough to talk about but had somehow not seen it as belonging in any particular country. He had seemed actually affronted by Clare's familiarity with the scene, as though she was not only cheating but making some kind of statement. It had been a difficult one to handle.

But the first two years after they were married weren't too bad, she told herself with practised facility.

'Oh, yes, they were, they damn well were!' she exclaimed aloud, halting dead in her angry determination to be completely honest for once. Then her attention was arrested by what lay around her.

She had been pounding on, head down, and had nearly reached the highest point of the headland. In a couple more seconds she was at the tumbled summit cairn and looking breathlessly around her at the huge view a few hundred feet of ascent had opened up. On her left the loch poured out through the narrows to the sound with its scatter of rocky islands. Across it rough moorland rose steeply above the fields and farms along the shore, blue folds of higher ridges stretching away and away beyond. To her right a narrow glen reached up into more dramatic hills than she had realized were so near at hand. Turning, she drew in a breath of pure excitement at the sight of the great range of mountains inland, snow still outlining their crests.

What a stupendous landscape to have arrived in more or less by accident. She must get a map, explore. Martin pushed summarily out of her mind, she went on eagerly, following the ridge which sloped down towards the tip of the headland till there appeared below her a spread of roofs, a solid stone house, farm buildings and barns. That must be Rhumore. What a place to live, she thought, facing out across that marvellous view. She didn't know much about westerly gales yet.

As she crossed the flat ground above the beach on her way back to the cottage, already conscious of warning aches in muscles used to high heels and thick carpets and very much looking forward to getting her boots off, she saw a boat heading in towards the jetty.

'Oh, no,' she groaned. These wretched people, were they never going to leave her alone? Who was it anyway? Even she could see that the boat was not Angus's wide-beamed workhorse, though the man at the tiller looked familiar. Donald Macrae, who would never see her stuck? Well, she had a list as long as her arm of things urgently needed and she had been wondering how she was to cart them back from the village. Also there was a great screed to Magda waiting to be posted. Perhaps, after all, this particular intruder could be useful.

She changed direction and headed down to meet the boat. Donald was already tying up, a black and white collie curving round his knees. Clare hesitated; dogs had never been her scene.

'So you've been having a look round?' Donald's eyes took in the boots and Barbour. He was wearing something just recognizably similar himself, a waxed jacket dark with age, its pockets sagging. It was creased and shaped to his broad contours, and approximately twice the size of Clare's.

'Was that all right?' It belatedly occurred to her that she must have been on his land.

'You're welcome to go anywhere you like,' he assured her. He didn't exactly smile; his face was less dour for a moment. 'That's a great view from the cairn.'

He'd spotted her? Clare realized she was going to have to get used to this.

'I'm just on my way to the village,' he went on. 'I expect you'll have found you're needing one or two things.'

'One or two,' Clare agreed, and this time he did smile.

'Well, you can give me a list, or you're welcome to come with me if you'd prefer.'

Those waiting jobs, but her list was pretty long and it hardly seemed fair to expect a total stranger to wade through it for her. 'I'll come with you, please,' she said. 'I'll get my bag and change my boots.'

'You're settling in all right then?' Donald enquired as the boat cleared the point and headed up the loch.

Something in the carefully bland tone made Clare give him a quick look. 'Now that I've learned how to light a fire, you mean?'

'It helps,' he commented, his face straight.

'Perhaps you'll also know that the bath is clean.'

'Is that so?' he enquired politely.

'And that Mr and Mrs Markie came to tea.'

'Colonel Markie.' A pause. 'So you'll be quite clear about what you have to do.'

Clare laughed. 'I'm to make a garden.'

'Are you now?'

She felt herself relaxing. This large self-contained man beside her, his big hand easy on the tiller, obviously had a sense of humour which his grim face belied. And what had she been in such a hurry to do? What could be better than being out on the loch on this crisp afternoon with the cloud shadows fleeing over the face of the hill and the colours of this new wide landscape changing by the minute as the sun came and went? She didn't even have to worry about the dog, which after one swift check had ignored her. It was up in the bows with its nose to the wind, its coat blowing back and its eyes closed to slits.

'Does Angus sell paint?'

'He does,' said Donald, 'and most other things besides. What else are you needing?'

'Mousetraps,' she said vengefully, and he actually grinned.

'Well, don't buy the shop out, I've one or two doing nothing at home.'

In Angus's shop Clare's list was considered a poor effort, omitting many items which it was clear to Angus, Donald and every passing customer she should have. A spare chimney for the oil lamp, a new flue-brush – and when she saw its bristly girth she realized what a ghost of a one she had – a saw, a carpet sweeper, mousetraps and a Tilley lamp, whose white brilliance was demonstrated to her there and then, had already been set aside by Angus.

The food on offer was grim, as she had already discovered, most of it panting to get out of sealed plastic, bacon that looked watery before it even reached the pan, pale discs of so-called ham, little cylinders of suspiciously pink paste. Bread was white and sliced. Fruit was Golden Delicious or black-speckled bananas. Vegetables consisted mainly of frozen peas, some very pallid and squashy tomatoes and large knobbly objects she would scarcely know what to do with – turnips, or were they swedes? Perhaps she would have to make that garden after all.

Donald suggested that she might like to look in on Ina while he dealt with some business at the garage. Clare thought grumpily that she had seen more than enough of the Inverbuie Hotel recently, but it was really the only place to wait. She was ashamed at her churlishness when she found herself given a warm welcome, along with stewed tea and a little mound of insulating foam coated in milk chocolate. She had not understood yet her own entertainment value.

Ina enquired avidly about the dirt, cold and loneliness of the Larach and seemed more amused than impressed that Clare was surviving. 'I've been expecting you back any minute. I was saying to Morag it was hardly worth changing your bed.'

Clare didn't tell her that if she had fled from the Larach she would not have regarded Ina's spartan establishment as much of an improvement.

'Though maybe you'll have seen quite enough of us for the time being,' Ina suggested slyly, getting rather too close for comfort. 'I often mind the rage you were in that day you arrived and couldna' get down the loch. Oh my, what a laugh that was! Fit to be tied, you were. If you could have seen your face . . .'

Ready to bristle defensively, Clare saw in time that there was no real unkindness here. Ina was just relishing something she had found highly diverting and wanted to share the joke. With salutary clearness Clare saw her own absurdity on that frustrating day and during the two days that followed. She had been unable to relax, had held angrily aloof from everyone and must have looked a complete fool. In fact, considering how uncommunicative and impatient she had been, she saw that everyone had been remarkably tolerant with her. Laughing shamefacedly, she relented and fed Ina some of the horrors she longed for – the mildew, the mice, the tuft of rushes growing in the wall in the corner of the bedroom.

Ina had wanted disasters; Donald wanted facts. And he didn't go in for the statement-questions of the other locals, which always seemed to Clare to have an overtone of poking fun.

'So is everything working all right in the house? You're managing to keep yourself properly warm?' he asked as the boat headed at an easy pace down the loch and the village fell away behind them once more.

'Not really,' Clare admitted. 'Too many years of central heating, I suppose. I wear a lot of strange things in bed. I did wonder about lighting a fire in the bedroom, but I think the chimney's blocked.'

'Jackdaws. I can sort that for you, but you'd be best with a gas radiator.'

'Off a cylinder? I hadn't thought of that. But would it use a lot of gas?'

'Don't worry about that. It'll be no problem to keep you supplied. Those heaters go for a song in the saleroom now that everyone is getting central heating put in.'

'Where's the saleroom?'

'Luig, on the next loch to the south. There's a sale on the second Monday of every month.'

Couldn't she order a new heater through Angus? Everyone seemed determined to save her money for her and she couldn't decide whether this was native Scottish frugality or kindness based on the assumption that because she was living somewhere like the Larach she must be hard up. It didn't occur to her that that could be a point in her favour.

'How are you finding life without electricity?'

'It takes a bit of getting used to. Not being able to switch on some form of instant heat is the worst, but without the appliances around it's actually not as frustrating as having a power cut. I suppose living in the cottage seems more like camping than anything, and I was expecting things to be pretty primitive up here anyway.'

Since Donald's expression didn't alter in the slightest degree Clare remained oblivious to the chill this tactless comment produced.

'And you don't miss television, being on your own?' he asked politely after a moment.

'I hardly ever watched it. I was running a hotel, and television doesn't figure much in that existence.' Incredible to think that she had been in that plush environment only a few days ago.

'Where was that?' He was the first person to take any kind of real interest in her as an individual with a life outside Inverbuie, and Clare found herself telling him quite a lot about Carlini's and Magda, prompted by quiet questions. But he didn't ask why she had come here, and for that she was grateful.

He wasn't forthcoming about himself.

'I saw your farm from the hill this afternoon,' Clare told him. 'What a marvellous position.'

'Some of the time.'

'Have you been there long?'

'Long enough.'

'Do your family like living in such an isolated place?'

'I've only one daughter and she's away now. Married and living in Perthshire.' He didn't seem inclined to enlarge on that either. He must be older than he looked, Clare realized. She had put him at fortyish, but people here seemed fitter than in the south, their faces less harried, their skins healthier, and their clothes provided an unfamiliar camouflage.

Donald not only helped her to lug her purchases up to the

house but stayed to set the two mousetraps she had bought and supervise her first attempt at lighting the Tilley.

'I think I'd have found that a bit alarming,' she confessed. 'But what a fantastic light.'

'A bit better for reading all those worthwhile books you're going to have time for at last.'

'How did you guess? *War and Peace*. I've never got round to it. It's hung over me for years.'

'It's *The Struggle for Europe* that's waiting for me.'

She had glibly classed this man with Angus and Kenny; had she made it obvious?

'Speaking of books –' Together they dragged the heavy boxes into the bedroom so that she would be able to get at the carpet.

'Are you going to clean it?' Donald asked.

'Kill it, I think.'

'You'll need a hand shifting it then. That table must be just about growing out of it by now.'

'But aren't you in a hurry?' Clare remembered to ask.

'Not till lambing starts.' Donald effortlessly lifted Murdo's heavy chair and carried it through to the bedroom.

Had she been missing his jokes? Clare asked herself as she held back the door for him to drag the unsightly smelly bundle of ancient carpet through.

'You could do with a new clothes pole,' Donald commented when the carpet had been disposed of behind the house, as he first rocked then wrenched out bodily the weathered, swaying post. 'That's been well used,' he added, pointing out the middle section which had been polished to perfect smoothness.

Clare put her hand out to caress the silky surface. 'What did that?'

'My stock,' he said dryly. 'Back scratching. I owe you a new one.'

On the whole she was pretty lucky in her neighbour, Clare decided as she came back to her bright room after seeing him off from the jetty. Now that he had disposed of the appalling carpet, did she have enough energy left to scrub this floor tonight? Checking the water she found it too hot to touch; plenty for the floor and for a bath afterwards. Get it done.

She had rolled into bed exhausted on more nights than not

in the hotel, but it was years since she had felt this satisfying muscular tiredness or the lovely drowsiness induced by a large dose of fresh air. She didn't decide not to take a sleeping pill; she didn't stay awake long enough to think of it.

CHAPTER SEVEN

Two days later came the rain. Nothing dramatic, just a fine relentless drizzle which blotted out the Rhumore headland and the hills across the loch and made Clare feel she was stranded on the shore of some limitless sea. The loch itself was grey, flat, pitted like hammered metal. And damp seeped and spread and took over her life.

Getting up late, since the room was so gloomy it was hard to believe it was really morning, she found the clothes she had left round the fire the night before clammy to the touch. Shuddering with distaste she dressed, confronted once more with the basic problem – she couldn't dry anything till the fire was lit and she couldn't light the fire till she had gone outside for wood and coal. In the sitting-room the damp air hung visible and the room smelled fusty again, the fresh polish of the dresser shelves finely filmed. The walls of the bathroom were sweating, its floor dark and dank. The kitchen walls where she had scoured away mildew stains with such satisfaction once more showed yellowish patches with faint grey marling.

Fire first. Without it there was a deadly drabness about the whole house on such a day. Like an idiot she had tidied away the newspapers to the shed and had improvidently burned the paper bags and wrappings from the shopping; another lesson. Then she remembered that Angus, blessed man, had put in a packet of fire-lighters. Never mind that he had remarked slyly as he did so, 'We wouldn't want you having any trouble with your fire, now would we?' Even with their help the fire was surly, the smoke reluctant to go up the chimney, and it was a long time before there was any noticeable change in the temperature of the room.

Faced with a day indoors, Clare took stock. What had she planned to do, picturing this before she came, being imprisoned by rain or gales, or even snow if she stayed long enough, which didn't seem likely at present? She had thought it would be luxury to be alone, peaceful, cosy, busy. Well, she wasn't short of things to do. There was this wood to strip for a start. The layers of smoke-darkened varnish would have to go before she could apply the white paint she longed to see everywhere. She had never used paint-stripper before. The instructions seemed straightforward.

Full of determination she launched into a long and frustrating struggle. The chief problem was lack of light. In spite of Donald Macrae's assurance of keeping her supplied with fuel she dreaded running out, not sure how much oil the lamps would consume or how often he would call, and all too conscious of the impossibility of getting heavy supplies in without help. But even in the areas where the light was best she couldn't see properly to clean the grooves of the old panelling. She tried opening the door, but even damper air poured in and she hastily shut it again. Then her happy image of the wood coming up free of stain with one application was far from the reality. She had to take a knife to the accumulated filth along the skirting boards. She rubbed and scoured and scraped, broke her nails and skinned her knuckles, got up to fetch a band to keep her hair out of her eyes and found the knees of her trousers filthy. How on earth was she going to get those cleaned, and why had she never foreseen that dry-cleaning would be a problem here? What had been going on in her brain during those weeks of so-called planning?

Keeping off the bottle, that's what. God, what wouldn't I give for a glass of chilled white wine right now, she thought yearningly. But this is what I came here for. To get down to basics, test my resources.

'What resources?' she jeered at herself aloud, flinging down her scraper and deciding that even if there was no wine on hand she could have lunch. The kettle was simmering on the hob. She had all day to do this – and probably several more days after that, she amended, peering out at the grey mizzle that domed the cottage like a dirty muslin lampshade.

She did her best. She worked away at the dark unsightly wood, thankful that since the dresser was immovable there was a huge section behind it she wouldn't have to tackle. She failed to get Radio Three but put on a tape, and at intervals she sat by the fire and drank black coffee, since the thought of going over the ridge to the farm for milk in this weather was not appealing, and she tried to read.

It was no use. After a couple of lines her mind was away, darting from one trivial worry to another. She couldn't believe it. She had always read. 'I am a reader,' she announced to the room, where only the hiss and flicker of the fire and the quiet song of the kettle answered her. But was it still true? Reading had vanished with so much else in the demanding immediacy of hotel life.

The feeling that she had thrown away the freedom to run her own life grew as the hours passed. It was the very opposite of all she had expected or intended. She felt trapped, restricted, restless and increasingly angry, with no one to direct the anger against but herself. The day seemed endless, yet she found herself as reluctant to go to bed as she had ever been at Carlini's, afraid of the thoughts that would come as the light went out. The idea of having a drink obsessed her. Sherry before dinner, fastest to hit the blood stream, most warming of drinks for a dismal day. Wine to improve the dullness of a steak pie which the gas oven seemed keen to burn round the edges, one of them anyway, before it properly heated up the middle. And the rest of the bottle to help her through the long evening.

The next morning she woke to an unchanged scene and was conscious of a sinking feeling of foreboding, not about what was going on around her but about what was happening in her head. The window was blurred with condensation. When she discovered it was on the outside she felt colder than ever. In the kitchen the doors of the sink unit glistened; sweeping her hand down one her palm came away wet. The silver in its basket was beaded with moisture. Drops of water oozed from the wooden salt mill. The stains on the walls had spread and darkened. The floor was puddled.

Out of doors the needle-fine rain drove down as though it would never stop; a wall of mist hung between the Larach and the outer world. Grimly Clare set to work to clean out the grate and lay the fire, dry paper and sticks ready on the hearth today.

Not a single job tempted her. She hated the cottage at that moment, profoundly regretting her blind obstinacy in coming here. The place felt as repellent as if she had never put in all those exhausting hours of washing and scrubbing and polishing. Everyone had been right, from Magda to Ina Morrison. If only there had been some word from Magda. If only they could talk. A week since she had left; a week was long enough for Magda to have written. Perhaps the letter was waiting at the farm, though Magda was not an ardent writer of letters, as Clare knew. But the need for some contact with what represented home grew into an ache of longing, and the absence of a telephone seemed to assume huge importance. If she decided to give up the struggle to decorate this room, for example, how could she find a painter, how could she arrange for him to come? And if she went on with it herself, how could she get the paint and materials she needed? She was running out of paint-stripper already. Did she have to wait for days till some neighbour turned up in his boat?

But what was really frightening about that day was the more fundamental question it forced her to face. If she abandoned the Larach, then where did she go? She could certainly improve on her surroundings; anywhere warm and dry and clean would do. But as well as being on her own again in yet another strange place, she would have to take with her this time the knowledge of failure. And worse still, she had distanced herself from Carlini's and knew, really, that there could be no going back. She had viewed that way of life objectively and was sure she had been right to leave. But this rushing to the other extreme, planting herself in such a miserable hovel, had shown up with disastrous speed her own lack of inner strength. Her restlessness, her ability to sleep even with the help of pills, to concentrate on a book or stick to a job, her irritation at the state of her hands and clothes and hair, were all born of fear, a fear of her own limitations. She had even put on her watch again, needing to be able to place herself in the dragging hours.

What would she do here for weeks, months, on end? What would she do anywhere? She had planned this, had meant there to be no protective buffers between her and ... what? Some sort of discovery of who she was? Well, she had made that discovery. She was an ordinary unadventurous female who couldn't function without the support of day-to-day human contacts and job demands and familiar habits and objects – and who desperately needed a drink. And she had cut herself off from the only place where, however uneasily or temporarily, she had belonged.

She gave up any pretence of working, huddled in the big armchair pulled close to the fire and went down, down, into a hopelessness and sense of futility more complete than she had experienced even after Martin's death. And she knew the only thing that would help her through it.

She sat it out till early afternoon then, in a sequence she knew well but had combated with fierce resolve for nearly four months, she began to make the moves to go. It was as though one isolated part of her, stronger than intelligence, conscience or even her own wishes, took over. Whatever protests her brain made had no effect on her actions. She had a bath and put on clean cords, clean shirt and sweater. She pushed a few basic necessities into her leather satchel, put the guard over the fire. She stamped her feet into gumboots, rammed shoes into her bag too, realized it would gape open in the rain and found a plastic carrier. All this she did without any of her earlier exasperation, going methodically from one thing to the next, emotions on hold. She did up her Barbour, drew the hood round her face. There was the beginning of a feeling of reckless freedom in abandoning everything in the house to its fate, not caring, not interested, driven by the single compelling need.

There was one slight check, a moment when the decision might have been reversed. Stepping out into the steady downpour she found the air mild and sweet, the rain against her face soft and not disagreeable. Perhaps instead of grouching indoors she should have come out and walked, at least gone as far as the farm. She had walked often enough in conditions a good deal worse than this. It was a moment of balance but the old addiction won. Head down, face set in an unattractive frown of resolution, Clare set off, not making for the farm but aiming at a line which would bring her out on the glen road above the village.

It was surprisingly hot walking done up in her Barbour, particularly as she met all kinds of setbacks and had to cast about for a feasible route so often that it would have been quicker in the end to have gone via the farm. First she had to negotiate the wet and treacherous little cliff behind the cottage, then an unscalable fence of squared netting with barbed wire along the top and no visible gate, which pushed her east as far as the plantation. Then the plantation itself, densely planted and surrounded by deer fencing, blocked her way. Attempting a direct line from there to the village she was checked this time by the burn, much swollen by the rain, which crossed the level fields at the head of the loch. Angry with herself, she paused to get her breath back, dragged off her hood and turned up her face to the cool rain. If her mind had not been focused so exclusively on the one vital objective she knew she could have foreseen and avoided most of these obstructions but she had just gone on and on in angry blindness.

Battling her way out at last on to the road, Clare ran into the first piece of luck, it seemed to her in her present self-pitying state, that she had had for days. A Hotpoint engineer who had been up Glen Righ fitting new hoses on a washing machine which he had failed to persuade its owner to replace was not going to drive past a nice little blonde, however bedraggled, who turned to gaze at him with such a look of appeal.

For Clare, seeing the familiar name on the side of the van, it was like emerging from the fogs of nightmare. Normality still existed.

She didn't let him drive her right into Fort William. The first hotel they came to on its outskirts would do. She supposed she must have thanked him. She didn't remember doing so, but headed up a slope of rain-dark tarmac towards a hideous one-storey sprawl of mock sandstone adorned by a row of sodden flags plastered limply round their poles. There was a moment of panic when she thought the bar might not be open, stilled by the prosaic, 'A large gin and tonic. And will that be with ice and lemon?' of the fat, untidy woman who appeared to serve her.

It was nectar, solace, essential drug, bringing order to her jangled nerves and calming the frightened fears darting about her mind like creatures in a trap. Peace flowed through her as she sat with closed eyes to let the cold, tangy, delicious liquid slide down her throat and start its work.

She didn't drink fast; she needed to savour this acute pleasure.

The bar was an arid rectangle of dark red dralon and 'dark oak' furniture with a row of small windows above head height. It suited Clare perfectly. It could have been any bar, anywhere. When a couple of customers came in she moved away to the bench seat along the rear wall, partly to avoid conversation and partly to pace her drinking. Leaning back and deliberately relaxing she drifted in and out of formless thoughts which did not reach beyond the immediate present.

A barman with a pink shirt and tartan bow tie came on duty presently, eyeing her with a professional assessment which made Clare grin. After-work drinkers came and went, menus for bar suppers appeared, two or three groups settled round the tables, the bar stools were nearly all occupied. The tape which began with 'Come O'er the Stream, Charlie', succeeded the tape of 'I will go, I will go, when the fighting is over', as it had done since Clare arrived. The barman came to take her order for food and she booked a room at the same time. People, nearly all locals at this time of year, glanced at her with curiosity, the few women with disapproval, the men more covertly and with interest. On her first trip to the dingy loo Clare had tidied herself and put on make-up in automatic response to her surroundings, changing into shoes and squashing her gumboots into the carrier bag in their place.

Sometime during the evening, as the bar grew noisier and cigarette smoke thickened and mingled with the smell of beer and fried food, Clare was joined by a well-fed young man in a tight suit with too much shirt cuff showing and a signet ring on the wrong finger. She had known it would happen; he had been eyeing her for some time. She had let it happen. She didn't want to be alone. He was clean, freshly shaved, his hair smooth; he had harmless brown eyes and he was not as confident as he would have liked her to think. His line of chat was comfortingly amateurish. In a strange mood of inevitability, laced with a remote, cold, completely ineffectual self contempt, Clare set out on the familiar path. He might not know what was going to happen, but she did. He was probably fantasizing about the out-come of chatting her up, but she could have told him there and then that this was going to be his lucky night. It was as though the vocabulary came back with the whole familiar sequence, and with it the disillusionment that took over before the process had even begun.

He was called Lennox. He sold photocopiers. He was based in Dundee. Good, thought Clare muzzily. The barman was by now serving her almost undiluted tonic water and doing nicely out of it, but over the hours she had drunk a great deal and eaten very little. Even so instinct told her that she wanted this place, this evening, to have no connections with anywhere. Limbo. Indulgence. And soon, she hoped, oh how she hoped, the gratification and oblivion of sex, that release and fulfilment which would surely bring the dreamless sleep she so needed.

Lennox talked about photocopiers for a while. Clare didn't care; she talked about them as well. Why not? She knew he needed to build up his confidence and that confidence would, after all, be crucial. And some time must pass anyway. Her thoughts floated with the heat and smoke. Where was her room? She'd find out in time. Somewhere beyond her reach the real Clare hovered, appalled, but for now she was letting her body take over with its well-remembered demands and needs.

Lennox was beginning to realize with mingled excitement and terror that he might have bitten off more than he could chew. He wasn't in the habit of chatting up strange women, though he thought about it often enough in the long miles of driving. This girl was a bit classy, and as soon as she'd opened her mouth he had been sure she was out of his league and that he'd wasted a pricey gin and tonic on her. But then she had definitely given him the signals and now she seemed to be giving him a few more he hadn't bargained for. Well, go for it, he told himself, having taken himself off for a pee and a think. What have you got to lose? He had a girlfriend in Wormit who'd skin him alive if she ever found out, but who was there to tell her?

Like the bar itself, Lennox had no connection with anything in Clare's life. He was so unlike the smooth operators who had chatted her up at Carlini's, and with his cheap suit and light shoes and pale indoor hands equally unlike the men she had encountered in Inverbuie. But his eyes were kind; he would be gentle at the very least. He had a wholesome-looking stocky body and she wanted it; wanted the simplicity of closeness without words, without worrying about motives or reactions or tomorrow morning.

It was nearly closing time, but a table in the corner was being wiped clean of beer rings and plates of sandwiches still covered in clingfilm were being put out. The background rumble of the bar suddenly rose an octave as a gaggle of women came in and milled round, taking off their coats, fussing about where to sit, settling like roosting hens, tucking their handbags carefully round their feet. Some female committee meeting or outing just concluded, Clare decided idly, Lennox's views on the folly of thinking fax copies were an adequate substitute for proper ones not quite holding her attention. Did they all go to the same hairdresser? she wondered, marvelling at the crinkly grey perms. Then abruptly the no-time, no-place capsule she felt so safe in cracked open. One of those yattering women falling greedily on the tuna sandwiches was someone she had seen. Where? In Angus's shop a couple of days ago, taking a friendly interest in Clare's shopping, saying, 'You'd best not be too heavy-handed with that bleach, it does no good to the septic tank, or so my man's always telling me . . .'

As the memory clicked into place the woman's eyes met Clare's, and Clare read the little sequence of recognition, ready friendliness, then doubt as she took in the full picture, followed by a sort of defensive withdrawal as though she wasn't sure what was going on and wanted nothing to do with it.

It said everything to Clare. It brought pouring back the memory of the kindness she had received – from Sandy and Jean and Mr Watts on that very first day, to Ina and Will, Angus and Donald and Kenny, the Markies, Nicol McNicol – everyone, in fact, she had met. They had accepted her in good faith, accepted, with whatever private reservations, what she was attempting. She was not in some impersonal strange place here; she was just outside Fort William, a few miles from the village, still in their territory. This woman across the bar knew who she was, would certainly say to someone that she had seen her.

Instead of being resentful of this as invading her privacy Clare saw it as a most lucky and timely reminder that she had already, in the most tenuous way it was true, formed some links with this place. She had drunk too much gin to reason it out clearly, but she had been brought up with a sharp jolt. With the memory of kindness and help and humour saner values returned. She remembered the last man who had shared her bed; remembered her own profound disgust.

'Lennox' – she swung back to him in urgent concern, cutting ruthlessly across what he was saying – 'I know one of those people.' It was the easiest and kindest way out. He would understand that; worrying about what someone would think would seem quite natural to him.

'You're going?' He had enough male pride to sound indignant, even to feel it for a moment, but what he primarily felt was relief. He wrapped it up quickly – she'd led him on, she thought she was too good for him and had been playing some game of her own. Anyway, when it came to it, he'd never have cheated on Pam.

'I'm sorry,' Clare said, putting her hand on his arm, making him look at her. 'Truly I am. I've behaved so badly, but I just – it was—' There was no possible way of explaining to him. She felt tears springing to her eyes. 'I'd better go.' She slung her bag on her shoulder, had a brief and queasy struggle stooping to line up the handles of the carrier bag and stood up, swaying as the gin hit her.

'You OK?' Lennox was on his feet, his warm hand under her elbow, his anger forgotten.

'Um. Must have drunk more than I realized.' She kept her eyes away from the group of women, imagining the censorious faces. 'I'll be fine.'

'Come on. Where's your room?'

'Don't know.' Her head was spinning, the noise in the room beating unpleasantly in her brain, the fuggy heat almost overpowering her.

'Come on,' Lennox said again. 'You'll be OK.'

Cool air hitting her, a bright overhead light, a wall swaying beside her. Another male voice. The barman's? A strong arm round her, a key turning.

'There you go, you'll be fine now. Sit here a minute, lean forward.'

Was that really such a good idea?

'I'd better get back. There's no one else in the bar.'

'That's all right, mate, on you go. I'll look after her.'

'She'll be fine after she's had a kip.'

'I'll get her shoes off. Is this all she's got with her, a pair of wellies?'

'That was all she had with her in the bar. I'd best be off.'

'Cheers, mate.'

Clare felt herself lifted and dumped on an unforgiving bed. A cover of some kind being pulled over her was like obliterating sleep itself.

Waking in the narrow bed in a slit of wooden-walled room with purple tweed curtains roughly pulled across the square window, the first thing Clare's fuddled brain recalled about these exchanges was their unthreatening quality. She had known she was being looked after. She had known the two men had meant well. It seemed part of being here, she thought gropingly, frowning. People helping; people accepting each other. Even fleeing to what she had thought of as an impersonal town, Inverbuie and the Larach had not let her go. Anonymity didn't exist here. It might just as easily have been Jean from the solicitors looking in surprise and sorrow across the bar at a Clare about to fall into bed with a man she'd picked up a couple of hours before.

Something else was surprisingly clear in those wincing waking moments. She was going back to the Larach. A tiny link had been established and she needed it; she had no wish to be completely rootless again.

She pulled herself up cautiously, gave her throbbing head a few moments to get used to that, then got out of bed and went to push back the ill-fitting curtain. The thin morning light reflected back from glistening tarmac and pewter loch was blinding. The mist was higher, more silver than grey. The rain had stopped. Shivering in spite of the generous heating Clare stripped off her clothes and made for the shower.

Stepping outside there was a hollow emptiness to the drenched monochrome scene. Only three cars were parked outside. Clare felt the shudderiness of hangover compounded by the early morning bleakness; her stomach was achingly hollow. Her boots made a tiny squelch in the silence. What if no one was up? She had to pay. She hated the thought of having to hang around. She wanted to start out at once along that gleaming deserted road, heading for what already, tentatively and more by default than anything, seemed like home.

Turning the corner of the main building she saw a lighted window and heard faint sounds of Radio Two. A woman in a red and white apron with a white hat clinging precariously to a fuzz of yellow hair glanced up in query, then waved Clare to the door.

'Off early?' she asked matter-of-factly. 'I can give you your breakfast if you're wanting it.'

Clare was not wanting it. 'I'd love some coffee.' She heard her humble tone and smiled inwardly. Did she think this woman would know or care that she had had a heavy night and most bitterly regretted it?

'You can have it in here if you like,' the woman said. 'Save me running aboot laying tables. Bit of toast? Fresh bap? I brought them along with me. Most days the van doesn't get this length till breakfast's over and done with. Daft, isn't it?'

She asked no questions, humming as she got out a frying pan and began peeling bacon from a huge pack. Clare sat and let the coffee diffuse through her system, as welcome as yesterday's gin had been. What was she doing here, in a motel kitchen, with somewhere along the row of rooms Lennox and his wrinkled suit? But how good he'd been. She had behaved so badly and he had looked after her without question.

'Would you be able to give me my bill?' she asked the friendly cook after consuming three mugs of coffee.

'Ah, that I canna' do. And the office won't be open till eight.'

'How much is it for a night?'

'Do you know this, I haven't a clue? I've never asked. It's less than an hour to wait, though.'

'Could I leave a cheque with you?'

'Well, that'd do, maybe. If you put your address on the back.'

I have left a signed blank cheque in the hands of a woman I never set eyes on till half an hour ago, Clare thought with a sort of rich satisfaction. It's part of being here, my response to the way they behave towards me. I bet Lennox and the barman never even opened my handbag last night. And if I'm stung then serve me right.

She left a note for Lennox, stuck under the wiper of the car with the boxes in the back, judging that he would probably prefer not to see her, and set off westward with a surprising exhilaration considering what she had drunk last night – or assumed she had drunk. A couple of workmen's vans met her; no one was going her way. She didn't care, light-headed, removed from practical reality, carried along by relief and gratitude that she had been saved by chance from destroying this new uncertain beginning.

She had forgotten that the school bus would have to go out to Glen Righ to collect its passengers. The driver had taken her to Inverbuie on the shoppers' bus a week ago and pulled up as soon as he saw her.

'You're out fine and early,' he commented, his mind turning over the possibilities.

'I am,' Clare agreed.

CHAPTER EIGHT

The mist hadn't lifted completely as she walked along the farm track – over the moor the bus had been driving through it for most of the way – but it seemed to be slowly, slowly filling with white light. She collected the milk and a Nightingale's catalogue forwarded from Carlini's. She was momentarily irritated to see it, then remembered that shopping by post would be useful if not vital here. Perhaps Magda had thought of that when she readdressed it.

'Don't be a fool, of course she didn't,' Clare told herself. The writing wasn't even Magda's. The girl who was now helping in the office had seen to the small chore. And Magda hadn't written. That was the true source of Clare's irritation, and she knew it.

How would the waiting cottage welcome her? she wondered as she went on. She knew that walking back into it would be a more significant test even than the strange disconnected moment of first taking possession after Angus and Donald had left her alone there.

Extraordinary what one evening among strangers, one night in a spartan motel room, could do. As she opened the door the cottage already had the faint feeling of home. The furniture pulled into the middle of the room, the newspapers on the floor with her brushes and scraper and rags, the splendour of the dresser with its rows of books to the ceiling, the guard she had put over the now-dead fire (the fire which she had managed to light even in the worst of the damp) – all these things were hers, familiar, claiming her. Here was refuge from the near-disaster of last night, from eyes that had witnessed the pathetic backsliding which today she could hardly believe she had succumbed to.

Would word of it spread round Inverbuie? She was certain it

would. And, surprisingly, she minded. Brief though the various encounters had been, she found she did not want to lose the respect of people like Ina and Lilias Markie and Donald Macrae. Well, some self-respect might be a good start. Fire first, sleep second, work after that. How commendable a programme. But though she mocked herself she looked at the dim, messy, unheated room with a new affection.

When Donald Macrae called early the following week to see if she needed anything from the village he was impressed by what she had achieved. Not enthusiastic exactly, but his slow nods as he looked around inside and out were approval enough from him. Nothing in his manner towards her had changed, Clare was relieved to see, finding herself unexpectedly self-conscious and tentative with him. He had heard nothing of the flight to Corpach, she decided with spirits soaring, though reminding herself mockingly that that dour face of his could hide anything.

Feeling chastened had certainly been wonderfully productive. Waking on the day she came back after a long sleep which had made the events of the previous twenty-four hours seem remote and unreal, she had found that although the sun had not broken fully through the cloud the day was brighter, the air mild. She had spent the remaining daylight hours attacking the mess behind the house, wrestling wire netting and bucket frames and shapeless lumps of rusty iron from the overgrown grass and encroaching earth, collecting up broken glass and crockery and slates, heaving away at half-buried bed-ends and rotted fence posts which always had hidden tangled wire stapled to them somewhere. It had been good therapy to which she returned in the fine spells of some changeable weather, in between scraping paint, polyfilling holes, pulling out sundry superfluous nails and tackling the larder. Where the unsightly heap of rubbish she was collecting would be disposed of she didn't know, but whereas in the depression of a few days ago this would have seemed an overwhelming problem, now she decided that someone would find an answer.

There had still been the all-pervading damp but that was another problem which seemed to recede when the door could stand open and the gloom had lifted. There had been bad moments, though – one when she had stripped away the stained and torn oilcloth covering the larder shelves and revealed horrid dark stains mottled with fresh-looking spots of some white and orange fungoid growth. Another, much worse, came when, sanding down a shelved recess in the corner of the sitting-room which she wanted to paint, she had put her foot through the floorboards.

That had given her a bad night, harried by waking and sleeping images of the whole floor giving way, of rot or woodworm riddling the entire place, of the roof collapsing, windows falling out. Only this time she didn't decide to flee when morning came, which had to be some kind of progress.

'I've a bit of flooring somewhere about that'll do nicely,' was all Donald said when she showed him this catastrophe.

'But what if it goes through somewhere else?'

'The rest of the floor's sound enough. If you clear away a foot or so of earth along the outside wall you'll find it helps. And if you go right along the back of the house you'll make a big difference to the kitchen too, though that cement floor will always be a bother in damp weather.'

If the solution was that simple Clare couldn't help wondering why Murdo hadn't resorted to it, but she was willing to try anything.

'The damp's got a hold,' Donald went on, wrenching up another section of floor Clare would have left in place for the time being. 'With the fire going and some air moving it'll soon dry out, particularly if we get a half decent summer.'

'I can't budge a single window,' Clare confessed, feeling useless.

'I'm not surprised. They'll not have been shifted for years. I'll see what I can do with them.'

'Would it be difficult to get some plain glass put in the bathroom window? Who could I get out here to do that? I hate that frosted stuff and I can't get the moss and dirt off the outside. And come and look at the way it's been painted.'

'Not what you'd call professional,' Donald conceded, surveying the cracking layers of green and brown and a lingering maroon. 'Ten-minute job to replace it. Want to learn how to do it?'

As they went down the loch to the village, Clare's list even longer than last time, she asked what he thought she could do about the rubbish she had gathered. The pile had grown alarmingly when she had started on the contents of the loft.

Donald dealt with the problem in the same easy way that he had promised to fix the floor. 'Don't worry, we can get that shifted for you easily enough. Not that Glen Righ shouldn't have seen to it long ago, but it won't be much use complaining to them.' He sounded grimly amused about it.

'But what will you do with it?' Clare asked.

'Take it away and bury it. JCB,' he added, seeing that she still looked worried.

It didn't help her much.

Donald had brought a new pole with him for the clothes-line, neatly finished with a cap to shed the rain and a small cross bar. He had also brought a length of new plastic-covered cord with eyelets.

'But I could have got that at Angus's. You must let me pay for all this,' Clare exclaimed.

'I had this by me. It won't be needed,' Donald said briefly. No washing flapped and slatted these days in the stiff winds of the Rhumore headland.

He had his chainsaw in the boat and together they went up on to the promontory and dragged down branches. Clare fed them to him as he buzzed through them over a buckling old saw-horse she had unearthed in the shed and which Donald called a cuddy.

'I'm thankful to get this lot cleared away,' he remarked between the howls of the saw.

Clare couldn't honestly see that the fallen wood had been doing much harm where it was but didn't argue.

But the swing back to optimism after Donald had made light of the disasters she'd been so worried about, the pleasure of doing jobs together, of learning basic skills, even of being ticked off for not having done enough preparation before starting to paint, had ended in a clash that made her writhe to think of for days.

She had meant well. 'Donald, it's so good of you to help me like this,' she had said, watching him as he got the kitchen window free at last, leaving the edges of the frame saw-toothed with old paint. 'I don't know what I'd have done without you. It was such a pain trying to get these local clowns to do anything.'

She said it lightly, without malice, as she would have to a friend. She felt so much at ease with him, and spoke without thought.

'They managed to get one or two things right for you, I believe,' Donald said after a fractional pause, making sure the window would shut and open again, and Clare had seen with horrified shame the tide of red deepening the tan on his neck.

'Oh, God, that sounded awful. I didn't mean—'

'I know what you meant,' he said shortly, brushing paint fragments from the sill into his palm and depositing them in the pedal bin. Then he straightened his long back and gave her a level look which brought a blush to her cheeks. She wouldn't have believed quiet, easy-going Donald could look so hostile.

'Donald, I—'

He didn't let her continue. 'You're here because you choose to be here, I take it,' he said, and he gathered up his tools and went down to the jetty, Trim the collie glued punctiliously to his heel as though sensing his anger, and Clare was left appalled and furious with herself, wondering if that was the last friendly visit and kindly help she would receive, from Donald or anyone.

Surely she hadn't used those words? Surely it hadn't been as bad as it sounded? But she knew it had.

'I've often thought of you in that wee cottage all by yourself. Are you sure you're managing?'

Clare, in Fort William to do some shopping, had called in at the solicitors to see if Sandy could meet her for coffee and had been surprised to find herself welcomed like some cherished protégée. There was Jean the receptionist beaming at her over her dock, Sandy appearing scarlet with pleasure and even Mr Watts pausing for a paternal comment as he said goodbye to a client. They must lead uneventful lives, Clare thought, but was pleased in spite of herself.

'How did you come in?' Sandy asked.

'Don't ask.'

'The school bus?'

'What a nightmare.'

It had not been like rolling in the other direction over the misty moor in subdued silence two weeks ago. In fact it had been a considerable cultural shock as the bus had gradually filled with turbulent passengers. The racket had been daunting and she had appeared to be the only person not smoking. But the route had been spectacular; she couldn't believe she had noticed none of its beauty till today.

Sandy grinned. 'So you'll want to make sure you get the early bus home.'

They arranged to meet and Clare plunged into shopping with misplaced optimism. Carpets and curtains headed her list, but violent colours and mad patterns clamoured on every side. Books and tapes seemed equally hopeless, though she did find a delicatessen which was a big improvement on Angus's shop.

When it came to clothes, however, she was finally in step. Directed by Sandy to a big sports shop she had a busy hour before he found her, by this time among the maps. They had coffee and she showed off her haul: huge sweaters, wool shirts, jeans, padded gilet, trainers – the clothes of someone she scarcely knew.

'No survival bag?' But Sandy was tolerant of it all.

'Won't it be marvellous? Warm at last.'

'How are you going to get it home? I could bring it out for you this evening if you like.'

'Oh, Sandy, that's kind of you, but Angus has a delivery to make down the loch this afternoon and I arranged to go back with him.' Were shopping trips with Donald over?

Sandy looked rejected and ate another cream cake. 'I didn't think you'd last this long,' he confided.

How nearly he had been right. How nearly the first threat of serious discomfort had defeated her. Well, he needn't be told that, nor need he know that she saw the Larach as a temporary refuge and would probably be gone by autumn. How shocked he would be if he knew all this reckless spending was just to see her through any remaining weeks of cold weather.

'But aren't you bored?' he persisted. 'What do you find to do with yourself out there?'

'Do? Putty, polyfill and paint. Dig, saw, burn.'

He laughed. 'I must say I never thought someone like you would go in for all that.'

There are times when I'm not too sure of it myse.
me. 'What am I like?' she asked.

'Well, you know, sophisticated, elegant. I mean, it's not ʊ
luxury living at the Larach, and there's no one to talk to.'

'No one to talk to! You sold me that house under false pre-
tences, telling me it was isolated. Having no road doesn't work.
I need a moat.' Brave words; was that still going to be true?

'Well, but, it's not exactly what you're used to.' Sandy clung
doggedly to his point, passing over the professional reference.

'No, it isn't,' Clare agreed, relenting, as her mind went back
to the world she had left, the competitive edge to everything,
the facile manners and calculating eyes, the price tags, her own
frightening sense of losing touch with who she really was. 'But
I find things I want there. I like the silence. I like waking with
the whole day waiting like an empty page. I like the feeling of
everything being down to me . . . well, I like it most of the time.
And I'm beginning to look about me – I don't mean exploring
so much as *seeing*.'

Sandy looked solemn, gratified to feel he was being taken into
her confidence, Clare guessed. 'I was afraid you were just wanting
to get away from something – or someone,' he hazarded daringly.

'Yes, me,' Clare said dryly, and after a surprised moment he
laughed out loud.

Sandy might laugh but it couldn't be done, Clare reflected
wryly as the Tuesday bus ground slowly on, stopping to drop
passengers or goods at cottages or farm tracks, at a caravan site
or a box nailed to a post with empty moor on every side. And
simply resisting hopping into bed with a Rank-Xerox rep hadn't
provided any magical solutions either. Except that she now knew
she would stick to her original intention and stay at the Larach
until she could plan some future that seemed right for her.

Sweeping the bare boards of the bedroom floor and pondering
the carpet prospects at Rory McMunn's sale next Monday,
Clare's mind turned regretfully, as it often had during the last
few days, to the disagreeable little clash with Donald. He must
have known she was joking – but she hadn't been joking. If not
deliberately unkind, she had certainly been unforgivably patronizing. But she had heard Donald making dry comments about

.enny and Alec McCosh himself. Yes, but he belonged here. That was the crux. She had spoken like a disparaging outsider and moreover had expected him to mock with her. It had showed how relaxed she felt with him but there was no way of offering that as an excuse. Anyway, it was no excuse; what she had said was awful.

She swept the dirt into the dustpan, leaned her broom against the wall and reached to open the door. The handle came away in her hand. She felt for a horrible moment as panicky as a child with its head stuck between the banisters, convinced it will be there for life. The window in here had not received Donald's attentions before he had packed up and gone striding off. It was immovable, warped with damp and solidly painted up. She had been happy to have it like that to keep out the draughts and so, no doubt, had Murdo.

It might be days before anyone appeared. Now that she had insulted them, no one might ever come. Well, wasn't that what you wanted? she asked herself angrily, fighting down hysteria. It was a couple of very unpleasant moments before she remembered that she could break the window, and she understood people dying in blazing rooms because this didn't occur to them.

It seemed rather excessive but she couldn't stay where she was indefinitely. She had a shoe poised to strike when she saw a boat come round the western arm of the bay. Donald? Could it really be Donald? She had never been so pleased to see anyone.

'How long had you been in there?' he asked as she spilled out, too relieved to worry about looking a fool. Most unexpectedly, as he had always seemed the least demonstrative of men, and even more surprisingly in view of the way they had parted, he put an arm round her shoulders and gave her a little bracing squeeze, laughing at her but examining her face with a swift appraising glance, satisfying himself that she was all right.

Clare was taken completely unawares by the gesture, but even more by her own startlingly strong impulse to turn into that arm. She was close enough to see the smooth healthy texture of Donald's skin, the grey in his thick brown hair, close enough to breathe in the heady male mix of ancient jacket, salt air, dog, farm. She wanted to bury her nose against his shoulder and inhale it. Thoroughly disconcerted, she moved hastily away.

'About two minutes,' she exclaimed, gathering her wits. 'And I'm never going to shut that door again!'

'Oh, I think we'll be able to fix the door,' he said, with his hint of a grin. What would he think if he knew the longing that just swept her? 'Were you planning to stay there long?' he enquired.

'I was about to break the window when I saw the boat.'

'Oh, you'd thought of that.'

The quiet wind-up she had begun to get used to and enjoy, voice and manner exactly as they had always been, no hint that she had ever offended him. Had she exaggerated it, like the panic about the dry rot and wet rot and whatever? But no, it had happened, and it was a lesson she mustn't forget.

Shaken by thankfulness and gratitude, and surprise at the strength of her own physical reaction a moment ago, Clare said breathlessly, 'I think I need an intake of coffee after that,' and dived across the room to push the kettle on to the heart of the fire before escaping to the kitchen. Donald rootled peacefully in the dresser drawer for a screwdriver.

Spooning coffee into mugs Clare tried to calm down, dismayed by what the small drama had revealed to her. In all the sexual encounters and brief affairs since Martin's death she had felt real attraction only once and had fled from it, unable to deal with it. And to think of Martin himself in connection with sex was now utterly repugnant to her. With an involuntary shudder she picked up the tray and went down the steps.

'I'd better get the rest of the windows to open,' Donald remarked. 'There's some fine weather on the way by the look of it. And I've brought the brushes to do the bedroom chimney, though maybe that's not as urgent as it was.'

Clare put down the tray and faced him determinedly. 'Donald, I was totally out of order the other day and I'm sorry.' It was surprisingly easy to say, in the face of his equable unaltered friendliness. 'I do feel so grateful to everyone—'

'Forget it,' Donald said, and though the words were curt he gave her a little nod of acceptance. 'I over-reacted anyway. Let's get to work.'

'Donald?'

'Mm? This needs drilling out. I'll take it home with me. And

I'd better have a look at the other door handles while I'm at it.'

'But why?' Clare asked abruptly. 'I mean, why do you help me with everything like this? Why does everyone? Moving me in, taking me shopping, Nicol bringing my milk to the farm, the Markies coming to call.' And Lennox who had forgiven her and been kind to her, and even the blowsy blonde cook who had given her breakfast.

'Just being neighbourly.'

'It's more than neighbourliness. Look at the things you've done — putting up the clothes-line, cutting that great pile of wood for me —'

'It would have taken you for ever with the bushman,' Donald pointed out reasonably.

'I've been pretty churlish, haven't I?'

He regarded her, weighing his words. 'Unhappy, it seemed to me,' he said after a moment.

Clare was astounded to feel the prickle of tears at this unexpected perception. Perhaps Donald realized, for he went on without any obvious pause, 'It takes guts, to do what you've done. Maybe we just feel you need a bit of a helping hand.'

'Guts? I thought you'd see it as running away, dropping out. Not much guts about that.'

'A lot of people find themselves in situations that aren't right for them. Not many of them do anything about it.' His face was suddenly dark.

'I needed to stop. Think. Decide what I wanted to do with my life.'

'Well, that takes courage. You chose a good time of year to arrive, at any rate, though it's been a bit colder than you'd normally expect.' She knew he was saying he would ask no more than she wished to tell.

She accepted the offered escape route. 'I'd actually planned to come in February but Magda had to go to Italy to talk to her brother about the hotel partnership.'

'He bought you out? Did you retain any interest in the business?'

'No, I'm not involved in it now.'

'But you keep in touch with your friend?'

'Oh, yes.' Still no word from Magda.

'You haven't kept the door open a crack in case you want to go back one day?'

'I'd only been marking time there, awful as it is to admit that about more than two years of one's life.'

'It is,' agreed Donald, though she had the impression that he was speaking more to himself than to her.

'I leapt into it when – well, at a bad time,' she said. 'Then I got caught up in it – hotel life hurtles you along – then I started drinking too much—' She checked. She could not tell Donald of the other refuge she had found. And had he heard by this time about her night in Corpach, now as unreal and confused in her mind as a hateful dream? Suddenly she needed it to be out in the open. It must have been talked about and she didn't want to go on wondering what everyone had thought. 'I'd given it up, in fact, but I fell by the wayside after I got here, I'm afraid.' What a phrase, but she felt more awkward than she could have believed possible putting it into words to Donald.

'I heard something about that,' he said. 'But you don't have any alcohol here, in the house?'

'I gave you tea at the flitting, didn't I?'

'You're learning the language.' When Donald smiled it was the most rewarding pleasure; his whole face lit with warmth and kindness. But he didn't let himself be sidetracked. 'And you didn't bring any alcohol back with you after that one night? You've had nothing to drink since?'

Clare shook her head; his understanding and insistence on the positive moved her so much that she couldn't speak.

'You're sticking to it. That's the hard part,' he said. 'Even harder after you've once gone back.'

'It's odd, but it feels as though it's something separate from this house,' Clare said frowning, looking away from him through the window and out across the loch. 'It doesn't occur to me to buy anything to drink here. That belongs to the world outside.'

'Just hang in there,' Donald said. Was he referring to living at the Larach as well as sticking to abstinence? Somehow Clare thought he was.

'I want to, I mean to. And Donald, I truly am grateful for the help I've been given here. I couldn't have coped on my own.

And then to have said what I did. You must have thought me so unappreciative.'

'Oh, we hadn't quite written you off. Now, how about these jobs?'

Donald preferred action to words, Clare deduced, and liked jobs properly done. For he reverted to his stony look when, discovering that the bedroom chimney was blocked solid with old nests, Clare said lightly, 'Oh, let's leave it. You keep telling me the weather's going to get better and who knows if I'll ever need a fire in here anyway?'

Still no letter from Magda. Carrying the milk back from the farm Clare reminded herself that it was only three weeks since she had left the hotel, hard though that was to believe. In any case, what was she so anxious to hear? Carlini's had dropped out of her mind and she knew she really only wanted some response to her babblings about the Larach and the glen, craving some endorsement of what she had achieved. More than anything she needed to know when Magda was coming, Magda who represented the only home link Clare had.

The thought reminded her of how her life had emptied, a process which, though she hadn't noticed it at the time, had begun as soon as she met Martin. Though they had lived in London during his tour at the MOD after they were married, she had allowed him to alienate her own friends there in spite of the fact that she had still been working for Marchant's. There had been plenty of socializing but somehow the group they mixed with had consisted entirely of those of Martin's connections who, as she plainly saw now, would be in a position to enhance his precious career. They had dropped away at the next posting.

It had been to RAF Marbury – and what a popular pair we must have been there, Clare thought, Martin throwing his weight about as second-in-command, I critical and detached. She had hated the place, hated being penned up behind the high security fencing, hated the dreary landscape beyond it of flat fields and laid hedges with cattle-trodden gateways, the sad remnants of old woods. And the absence of any kindred spirits – till she met Joe . . .

She was jolted out of her thoughts by hearing a tractor behind her. Dougie Stewart, the Rhumore tractorman, sent by Donald to put a fence round her vegetable plot. Mossy posts and sagging wire were all that remained of the old fence and she had patched it with netting of a similar vintage unearthed from the shed. No one had thought much of it.

'Baby rabbits can get through the tiniest holes, you know,' Lilias Markie had said when she came bringing a begonia and an ivy (which she had kindly pointed out would survive the coldest conditions).

'What's this then, knitting?' Nicol McNicol had demanded on a day when he had fancied a walk over the headland.

And, 'You'll no' keep out much with that,' Angus had informed her, dropping in after a trip down the loch.

Donald had simply rocked one of her newly hammered-in posts and shaken his head.

Now Dougie, without wasting time on social chit-chat, started to uproot the lot with the damning pronouncement, 'This'd no' stand so much as a puff of wind.'

'But it's mine,' Clare protested.

'Aye well, it'll be Rhumore stock that'll be knocking it down,' he retorted, unperturbed.

She thought she might as well learn how to make a proper fence since he was here, though she mentally ran through a few well-phrased exchanges with Donald as she tottered about carrying larch stobs and knee-buckling rolls of rabbit netting.

Dougie was not the greatest of communicators but before he left he surprised Clare by saying awkwardly, 'You could mebbe call in on the wife sometime. She canna get out much, what with the bairns. Just if you're passing, mind.' Scarlet with embarrassment, but protected by this disclaimer, he revved up his engine and drove off before Clare could answer.

Of course she wouldn't go, but surveying the neat rectangle of completed fence she felt the tentacles of kindness once more looping her round. It had been no part of the plan. She had come here expecting, intending, to be alien and solitary and she was being offered the sort of friendship she had not known since Joe had vanished.

From habit her thoughts winced sharply away, then she caught them back. Twice today she had arrived at this point. Hadn't she come here to deal with guilt? She picked up her jacket from the boulder where she had slung it when she grew too hot working, and set off along the eroded lip of turf above the rock and shingle of the beach.

CHAPTER NINE

It had been hard to adapt to married-quarter life. Magnolia walls and cow-pat brown carpets; metal-framed windows that grew black spots overnight; soulless G-plan furniture among which Clare's own pieces had looked ill at ease; idiotic rules which said you mustn't so much as mend a fuse and then expected you to wait five weeks for someone to come and do it for you. The thud of the door closing behind Martin, leaving her in the blank morning silence surrounded by objects from which dust must be removed. The suburban feeling that all along the row of identical houses other wives confronted identical mindless chores. The flat rectangular gardens enclosed by concrete posts and wire, though to be fair many had well-grown shrubs and trees too. The nagging instructions about compost heaps issued periodically by the Families Officer – though Clare discovered that in fact Martin himself generated most of them . . .

She had wanted them to buy a house but there had been some policy afoot just then about senior officers setting an example by living in quarters, and that had been enough for Martin. His increasingly neurotic desire to be seen to be doing all that was required of him extended now to Clare. In London she had been safe from Wives' Club activities, the flower roster in the Officers' Mess, coffee mornings and playgroup and the endless fund-raising. Not any more. Martin had impressed upon her that Marbury was an important posting for him, since as it was a small station he was second-in-command though still a squadron leader. He insisted that she play her part.

Reaching the tip of one of the rock ribs that made tiny bays along the shore, Clare paused to look about her. The evenings were lengthening and the loch glittered under a still-warm sun. Surely there were more birds about than when she first came and they weren't all gulls, were they? She must ask Donald.

Finding her mind ready to be beguiled away by this agreeable thought, she dragged it determinedly back to Marbury. It had been easy to pretend that everything had gone wrong between them because Martin was obsessed with his job, but their problems had been more profound and had begun on that tense and unsatisfactory honeymoon.

Love-making had been good – she had to cling to this belief – in the stolen afternoons in Rosthwaite, with the legs of the flimsy holiday-cottage divans tied together after one hilarious untimely parting of the ways. They had laughed – talked. And when they were engaged the weekends in London and Lincolnshire *had* been happy.

So what changed after they were married, during the time in London? Martin had been absent more and more, busy supposedly with arcane military matters beyond Clare's comprehension, and she had never questioned the endless evenings on duty. Also love-making had become a very different thing. She made herself admit it at last, with a sudden vivid memory of Martin lying on his back, head turned sideways, eyes screwed shut, face self-absorbed, and of her own chilled realization that he had forgotten her, was aware only of the service her body was performing for his. After a while he would make love only with her turned away from him. How bereft and separate I used to feel, she recalled; no words, no kisses, no eyes intent on mine, reading the messages of sensations shared; and above all, far worse for her than anything, never achieving orgasm.

She had tried to talk to Martin, assuming that he must be as unhappy about it as she was, but he would never let her get near the subject. In the first year or so they had glossed over the cracks; by the time they were at Marbury they were quarrelling. And it was at this stage that Martin began to drink more and more heavily, though with phenomenal control. By now he would only make love to Clare when he was tanked up after some function in the mess or some duty dinner party. He would never speak and Clare knew now he must have been deliberately blanking out the knowledge of who she was.

Oh, those functions in the mess, the Saturday Steak Nights, the parties for Valentine's Day and Hallowe'en, the Battle of Britain cocktail party, the Summer Ball, the Ladies' Nights that seemed to crop up every other month. Worst of all had been the Ladies' Nights. As a wife Clare had always felt an incongruous interloper in the traditional scene: the long candlelit tables, the gleaming heavy mess silver, the white-gloved stewards, the mess sergeant at his post behind the PMC's chair, his watchful eyes everywhere, the just-too-loud music from the uniformed ensemble (a word whose final syllable, whatever was done with the first two vowels, was universally pronounced 'bull'). The food had been variable – always elaborate but not always successful. The company had been consistently poor. No, be fair; occasionally there had been someone lively and intelligent beside her, but always there had been the wariness she now perfectly understood. No one had trusted Martin, therefore no one had trusted her. The wives frankly avoided her, replicating faithfully their husbands' attitude to Martin.

Once and once only on one of those evenings the barriers had briefly come down. A WRAF flight lieutenant had come across to talk to her during the muted drinks-before-dinner phase, a smiling dark girl with a figure trim enough to make the blue mess dress look actually elegant. She had introduced herself as Jackie Copeland and without a single maddening service abbreviation had explained that she worked in station headquarters as one of Martin's junior officers and looked after personnel matters. There had been that instant certainty of communication which at Marbury Clare had almost forgotten existed, and though this first conversation had been brief and Jackie had soon flitted off on a round of the ante-room where she appeared to know everyone present, she had come back after dinner to find Clare and they had talked some more.

'I'm glad you're here,' Jackie had confided after a while, grinning. 'Most of the wives get a bit tetchy about my being here on Ladies' Nights, especially the ones who were WRAF officers themselves. They think I see quite enough of their husbands at work, but there was a three-line whip because so many people were on leave so I didn't have much choice. Dining-in nights are a lot more fun though.'

'I can imagine it,' Clare remarked. 'Don't you hate us taking over like this?'

'Well, you're the first wife I've ever known who sees it in that light,' Jackie said, impressed. It had been the beginning of what could have been a good friendship. If Jackie, not an officer who liked to spend the day behind her desk, spotted Clare on her dashes about the station she always stopped to chat. They ran into each other in town once or twice and without discussion went off for coffee together, talking eagerly. Once when Jackie's car was being repaired by the MT corporal who ran the Motor Club, Clare had brought her back and they had gone up to Jackie's 'suite' in the mess. This consisted of two square rooms badly in need of redecorating, identical except that a wash basin was stuck in one of them. They were furnished with the familiar G-plan and gaudily patterned curtains and stretch chair covers that made Clare's head spin. Who on earth chose those, or invented them in the first place? But the careless clutter of Jackie's books, plants, guitar, tapes, videos and dressmaking cloaked its dismal bareness and Clare had felt at ease there. She had enjoyed hearing about Jackie's life, at last getting a glimpse of the Air Force that was new and refreshing. Jackie loved it, and loved her job, apparently finding the dramas and crises she dealt with every day fascinating. To Clare they sounded terrifying, and she was impressed by the level of responsibility and breadth of knowledge the job entailed.

Martin had destroyed the friendship before it had the chance to take root. Easy to see from this distance that the warnings had been there, but Clare had not yet grasped the level of obsessive anxiety Martin felt about his service image, and the reason for it was still an unguessed-at faraway dark shadow.

First there had been the row about the party at the Station Commander's house. Clare had been delighted to see Jackie there though, as Jackie had gravely explained, she really shouldn't have been.

'Makes the mixture uneven, you see. You've got to have the different branches represented, with the right intervals between invitations *and* the correct balance of rank. It's a worrying business. I think they should really have cancelled the whole thing rather than hauling me in at the last minute to make up the numbers.'

'Come on, Jackie,' Clare protested. 'It can't seriously be like that. And anyway, why shouldn't you be here?'

'I'm another Adminner. That's bad enough, but *I work for Martin*. Squadron Leader Somerville I mean, of course.'

She grinned and Clare laughed. Martin did not allow junior officers to use his Christian name even on social occasions. Not that you could describe this as one, Clare thought with impatient distaste, observing the wary waltzing and circling.

'Is it always like this?' she asked Jackie.

'Absolutely not. I wish you could get a tour on a flying station. Marbury's a backwater, being wound down anyway, as I'm sure you know.' Clare didn't; Martin would not tell her such a thing. 'Supply courses, fuels courses, odd little units that will soon be tucked in somewhere else. And the CO won't ever make group captain and he knows it.' Had she lowered her voice quite enough? Clare wondered, quelling giggles and resisting turning her head to check who was within hearing. 'He's an old has-been with a frightful wife. This is a quiet corner for him to die in. MBE probably as a sweetener, then the boot.'

But it was the buffet that did it. The catering had obviously been done by the mess. 'Garnished to the eyeballs,' Jackie sniffed as she and Clare, who had been chatting so engrossedly that some of the men had not waited and had actually helped themselves before them in spite of their annual confidential reports, surveyed the elaborate offerings. A mousse in the shape of a salmon, fearsomely decorated, every scale and fin in place, had been respectfully left intact by the docile shuffling queue.

'Soon sort that out,' said Jackie, lopping off its head with a single swipe. It was Clare's delighted laugh that alerted Martin. He really thought it mattered. The rest was strife and grief.

The end came when she asked Jackie to lunch one Sunday. They were luxuriating at the time in a spell of baking weather and it had occurred to Clare that the exposed and parched lawns around the mess were not ideal for the inmates to lounge and sunbathe at weekends.

'How did you guess?' Jackie asked gratefully. 'It is a pain. It's one thing I really miss about home in fine weather, hopping in and out of the garden wearing not very much. You're a gem to think of it.'

Clare told Martin that Jackie would be coming at breakfast on Friday and missed his outraged look. When he came home at lunchtime he announced, 'I've cancelled the arrangement for Sunday, by the way.'

'Cancelled it? But why?' Clare checked with the salad bowl halfway to the table.

'Jackie is one of my junior officers. It's not appropriate to have her coming here casually.'

'But you're always complaining that it's part of your duty to meet your junior officers socially!'

'Yes, when I invite them. In strict rotation. To a formal buffet or dinner. With other suitable guests.'

'You sound like the station commander. I just thought Jackie might like to get out of the mess and relax in a house – or garden – for a change.'

'Not in my garden. Let her go to some flight lieutenant's if she must. You simply don't understand how these things work. I don't want you to encourage her any more. It undermines my position – and it could make things very awkward for her.'

Clare had been incredulous and defiant; she had certainly not taken in his implied threat. But when she had phoned Jackie she had been forced to accept that Martin actually could and would make trouble for her over this issue if Clare persisted. They had seen little of each other after that and now for the first time it struck Clare with a chill of belated realization that soon afterwards Jackie had left Marbury. Fortuitously? In the normal sequence of posting? More than probably not. And how would her tour there have been assessed?

Why had she stayed with Martin? Clare asked herself with fresh shame. It had been as much from need of some familiar background as from lack of courage. Her mother had died shortly before the end of their tour at the MOD. Home no longer existed. Though the Vernham Dean house – and a rather surprising amount of money – was now hers, Clare knew she could never have lived in its chill perfection, particularly after what she had learned when she made herself face the task of sorting through her mother's desk. Her mind skated hurriedly on. It had not been a time for launching out alone. And in any case soon after Jackie had gone something had happened that had made it more bearable. Into the featureless days, the numbing boredom of 'wives' activities', rapid blind walks in a countryside that held no appeal for her, shopping in a town clogged and thronged with cars and people, its ancient beauty of hilly streets and black and white architecture vandalized by plate glass and supermarkets and multistorey carparks, had come Joe.

Clare had a short time before begun helping out in the station library, volunteering to do a couple of evenings a week as a relatively painless way of keeping Martin quiet. Joe had come in regularly for books on crafts and hobbies, a tall, lean corporal, one of the PEd instructors, with a reddish tan and fair hair of the yellow-gold variety. He had an easy friendly manner which was balm to Clare after the wariness she normally encountered at Marbury.

Joe had never chatted her up. They had just moved naturally into what had seemed to her the best kind of friendship. She had relied on it without question, which was why it had been so hard to accept his disappearance without a word, and his later rejection of her, his total refusal to listen.

Don't think of that part yet, she warned herself hurriedly.

On the shore the light was going, cut off by the Rhumore promontory, and she turned and went fast up the hill to try to reach the cairn before the sunset faded, working off the pain.

The early days, concentrate on those, remember the feeling of liberation as the Land Rover pulled up outside the quarter on a Friday evening, running down the concrete path, Joe coming towards her with his light stride to take her pack, giving her the smile she'd waited for all week. The trainees silent at first, not sure of her, exuberance tamped down. The obligatory stop in Llangollen for fish and chips, the noise rising, the reek of vinegar mingling with the nostalgic smell of boots and rucksacks, the weekend feeling taking over as Joe swung the Land Rover up the curves of the A5.

He had asked Clare to help him out because airwomen were not allowed to go on these expeditions unless a female officer or NCO was present. After a conversation in the library one evening, when she had been talking about the Rosthwaite cottage and the Lakeland hills, it had occurred to Joe that as OC Admin's wife Clare might be equally acceptable. As the decision fell into Martin's direct area of responsibility there had been, to Clare's amazement, no difficulty; indeed he had chosen to see the plan as an admirable contribution to his own image. Clare could only suppose that since a corporal was so lowly there was no threat of social bounds being overstepped. Only now did she see how thankful Martin must have been to have her out of the house.

Mostly they had used the Army camp at Capel Curig, available to all three services for expedition training. Leaning against the cairn above Rhumore, watching a changing pattern of ragged clouds darkening against a lemon and peppermint sky, Clare found herself smiling at the memory of her first evening there. She and the two girls in the party were put into a barrack hut with twenty beds and twenty lockers and nothing else at all – not even curtains. Within seconds every window had been plastered white with male faces. The girls, of course, had shrieked rewardingly and been answered with joyful yells and whistles. Clare had begun to see why she had been invited.

As they had been the only females in the camp that weekend, the women's ablution block had not been opened and the men's block was allocated to them for fifteen minutes. The moment they were inside the door was kicked open and a jostling crowd filled it. Clare had wished for once that she had some rank, as the two girls hyped up the drama by screeching and squawking. Suddenly Joe had appeared and barked one sharp order. The doorway had emptied by magic and the girls had been left looking sheepish.

Then there had been the party of sailors cleaning up their area of the big kitchens, sluicing buckets of water about with much frantic swabbing to the roars of a petty officer. It had been a relief to find that Joe operated in a more laid-back style, and she had luxuriated in the long-forgotten feeling of belonging as they drank cocoa at one of the long tables and the kids wolfed down bread and tinned marmalade. Martin had seemed a long way away and she had been conscious of a tight knot of tension unravelling inside her.

The air had a bite to it, but the sky was too dramatic to miss. Clare tucked herself down against the cairn and pulled up the hood of her jacket. In this setting perhaps she could at last get past the barriers of all that had gone so fatally wrong and think of the good days, the Snowdon Horseshoe on May Day, nursing the group along Crib Goch in blinding flurries of snow, then suddenly sunshine brilliant on white ridges and jewel-blue lake, and stopping to sunbathe before they came down. Dark Welsh rock in mist and rain; running over the sun-warmed slabs of Moel Siabod; the happy playground of the Milestone Buttress; evenings in the pub, welded into a cheerful unit by the demands of the day, stretched, amicable, content. And for her the special pleasure of relaxing because Joe was there to whip them in, take them home, see to everything.

It was a long time since she had thought honestly about what he had meant to her in those early days. They had never mentioned Martin, but Joe had seemed to know that the weekends represented a vital escape for Clare. He made her feel safe; he made her feel *liked*. He banished her sense of purposelessness. He was a natural leader, like a firm nannie whose affection is never in doubt. The boys role-modelled on him and the girls fell for him – and received no encouragement whatsoever.

He and Clare had talked when they could, often sitting on in the empty kitchens late at night, with great stainless steel monsters humming and hissing quietly round them. Clare learned that Joe was involved in all kinds of voluntary work, his special interest being remedial gymnastics for the disabled. He packed more into twenty-four hours than any person she had ever known and still gave the impression of having energy and resources to spare.

There had been no sexual spark between them, no indiscretion and no guilt. Clare had fantasized about him, of course, in the grey weeks when she had to live with her own self-contempt for clinging to a foundering marriage for reasons she acknowledged to be cowardly, but her imaginings were pure escape, romantic fiction, and she knew it. When she was with Joe she didn't even remember them. He was absolutely straight, innocent if that wasn't an absurd word to use. She had found in Donald Macrae something of the same quality.

She was stiff and chilled. The wind was getting up, the wisps of cloud gathering into dark threatening masses. Across the loch scattered lights shone, the pencil lines of occasional vehicle head-lights brushed the face of the hill. All at once she felt devastatingly alone, out of step with the rest of humanity, excluded from those warm lighted houses where families were eating, watching television, washing dishes, doing ordinary things.

She was glad that the farmhouse of Rhumore was out of sight from where she stood. She knew she was a fool to find it especially unbearable to picture Donald Macrae relaxed in just such a dom-estic scene, but she felt a bitter envy for the woman who could share with him the normality and security that had evaded her.

Depression crushed her. She had failed Martin, allowed Joe's career to be ruined, let Magda down for nothing more than a selfish whim. Coming here had been intended as a positive action, getting hold of her life again, no longer allowing herself to be moulded and directed by others. As she started down the shadowy slope, shivering in the strengthening wind, it seemed merely irrational and futile.

CHAPTER TEN

'Hello there! How did you fare in that little blow yesterday?'

Gerald Markie's red face peered at Clare in dreadful dishar-mony over a neatly trimmed beech hedge beginning to show hints of new green. She had been perfecting her route to the village and had come off the hill at the bridge beside Tigh Bhan, the Markies' square white house (which Clare had not yet realized was what Tigh Bhan meant).

Little blow! 'Fine, thanks,' she called, taking her time fastening the gate. Perhaps he'd be satisfied with that and bob down again.

No chance. 'Come in and say hello to Lilias, she'd be delighted to see you. Yes, yes, of course you will, come along . . .'

The neat stretch of tarmac drive between squared-off hedges, the manicured garden, the gleaming paintwork and shining brass door knocker and handle defying the salt air did not especially appeal to Clare, but the Tigh Bhan kitchen did. Its wide window looked straight down the loch and it was big, light and warm, smelling of baking and full of clutter. Binoculars, maps, reference books; *The Times Literary Supplement* open on the table with a spectacle case beside it worn to the metal; garden catalogues and seed packets and a plan of the garden scored and arrowed; hillocks of needlework, newspaper cuttings and letters pushed aside to make room for a rack holding two golden sponge cakes above which Lilias held a poised spatula ready to spread a creamy filling. Dog baskets and bowls and what looked like a dismembered hedge-trimmer occupied the floor. Plants rampaged on the long windowsill.

'My dear, what a pleasure! We've been so looking forward to seeing you again. And how clever of you to arrive just when this cake is ready and waiting to be eaten.'

Clearly no gossip had reached them about drunken and dissol-
ute behaviour. Might have saved her from being hauled in like
this if it had, Clare thought ungratefully, but deep down she
knew she was glad. The dogs, who had met her in the garden
and escorted her in, decided to check her out officially and
vocally and were beaten off with furious commands. Not that
she much minded; Donald's collie Trim had begun to convert
her.

They sat at the kitchen table and drank Earl Grey tea and ate
not only the feather-light sponge cake but scones and bramble
jelly.

'We thought of you in the gale,' said Lilias in her turn, 'but
I saw Donald this morning and he said you had survived.'

A telephone would have been sheer extravagance.

'I did learn one or two things,' Clare admitted. 'Not to open
the door with the kitchen window open at the same time
was one. Not to take the ash out was another – fairly obvious
really.'

They laughed with her, lined old faces bright and sympathetic.
'Is the shed still there?' Gerald asked.

'Oh, certainly. When I went out for coal the wind picked me
up bodily and plastered me against it. It was held up by the sheep
sheltering behind it, I should think, hundreds of them.' The
Markies made token noises of concern but on the whole seemed
rather proud of what their weather could do. 'I thought the
whole thing would take off with me in it. The racket inside was
indescribable. And then when I lit my fire the smoke billowed
all round the room and nearly choked me to death. However,
I got it to go up the chimney eventually . . .' The prospect of
shivering hours without heat or hot water had provided a considerable incentive.

It had been impossible to sleep much with the sound of the
wind howling outside, squally showers battering against the
window and the rattle of hooves as the sheep milled and shifted
in their refuge behind house and shed, though Clare had been
surprised by the stillness and sense of safety inside those thick
walls.

She didn't confess to Lilias and Gerald her renewed feeling of
imprisonment when day finally came, or how her heart had sunk

to look out once more on horizontal rain, driven loch and streeling clouds. But she had come further than she knew. She had got on with painting the larder shelves, a dull job she had been neglecting in favour of more alluring work outside, and she had actually found some satisfaction in doing it. There had been no impulse to run this time. Slowly, laboriously, the cottage was changing; it was becoming hers.

Common sense had told her nothing could move on the loch in such conditions, but somewhere at the back of her mind all day had been the feeling that Donald would appear, and towards evening he had come . . .

'You'll have to keep a supply of fuel indoors in the winter.' Lilias's voice cut bossily across her thoughts. By winter Clare intended to be tucked up somewhere a great deal cosier than the Larach, but she didn't think it necessary to say so.

'Where do you expect her to put it?' Gerald was demanding scathingly.

'There's plenty of room –'

'Of course there isn't –'

'Well, she won't be able to get the door open if there's a real storm –'

Clare decided that if you ignored these rattler attacks at each other, and could take a double dose of contradictory advice delivered in the form of direct commands, they weren't bad company. And they were undoubtedly useful.

'Oh, my dear child' – not disagreeable at thirty-three – 'you mustn't buy eggs from Angus, they sit there for ever. Barbara Bailey, who bangs round here from time to time under the misapprehension that she's cleaning the house, keeps chickens and bantams and ducks. You must get your eggs from her. In fact we'll go round and see her now. The dogs could do with a walk.'

Barbara Bailey was a large lady with a square jaw and a cast in one eye and a lower lip which seemed to be permanently and ominously folded over the upper. She explained to Clare about which tray to take eggs from if she was out, which trays not to touch *on any account* and where to look in the nesting boxes if the trays should be empty. Clare thought in that event she would probably do without eggs. 'And mind you bring your own box,'

Barbara shouted down the path after them like some nightmare undertaker as they left.

'How is your garden progressing?' Lilias enquired as they returned to Tigh Bhan after a call at Angus's where Clare had shopped as surreptitiously as she could. 'I gather the new fence is up.'

Clare had a sudden light-hearted sensation of giving in and swimming with the tide. 'I've dug most of it,' she said meekly, wondering if Lilias would wish to inspect her blisters as proof. The job had gone a good deal more rapidly after Donald had explained that she didn't need to lug away the lumps of field she had hacked out. It was quite permissible to turn them in as the grass would provide valuable nutrients. It had speeded up even more when he had put in a few rapid rows himself – rows which Clare had to admit could not be mistaken for her own handiwork.

Donald had also pointed out, exaggeratedly resigned at her surprise and delight, mint and chives coming up, the pink knobs of rhubarb struggling through clogging grass, and overgrown blackcurrant and gooseberry bushes in an unkempt straggle below the cliff.

'You must have seedlings from us,' Gerald ordained. 'Broccoli and curly kale. And you should get some seeds going in a warm window. You have bought your seeds?'

'Some,' Clare said guardedly. 'I went into Luig.'

The bus had been like something out of Enid Blyton and had stopped not only for anyone who waved at it but also for shopping bags hung on garden gates. The route along the loch and over the hill had been glorious every yard of the way. 'I found seeds but not much else. Where does one get decent food short of going into Fort William?'

'Hah! You didn't look far enough,' Gerald pounced, wagging a stubby garden-grimed forefinger at her.

'The meal shop in the old mill,' Lilias rushed to get in first. 'Only been open a year or so but *such* a boon. Run by an English couple. He pots. You'll find all kinds of goodies there, local cheeses and smoked fish and so on, as well as the usual beans and flour.'

Clare expected her to make out a shopping list for her there and then.

'You make your own bread, of course.'

Of course I don't.

'That coal oven of yours at the Larach would make marvellous bread,' chipped in Gerald. Much he'd know.

'It would hardly be worthwhile making it for one, would it?' Clare temporized.

She had barely looked inside the oven, let alone contemplated putting food into its rusty maw. Those unenterprising days were clearly over.

'Make small batches.'

'Try soda bread, no yeast.'

'Homemade bread keeps beautifully anyway.'

A tour of the garden was mandatory, and Clare stifled yawns at the vegetable strategy for the year and the mercilessly pruned stumps of bushes, each greeted tenderly by name, but liked the sheet of daffodils sloping down to where the river tumbled out of its wild little gorge. She barely had time to enjoy it, though. Having rashly said that she was going to try the Luig sale for carpets and curtains on Monday she was summarily whisked into the house and taken up to a large sewing room, where she was offered anything she liked from a ceiling-high cupboard stacked with curtains of every description.

'But can't you use them?' she asked dutifully, her eye drawn to a white ground decorated with gold and brown flower sprays. 'What about your family?'

'There's only Stephen. Half of these came from him and Lucy anyway. Army, you know, perpetually on the move. How about these?'

Clare gratefully accepted the sprigged curtains, and an enormously long pair of once-red velvet ones.

'Have them, have them, I'll never need them. Too big for your house, I know, but cover cushions, make a sausage for the door, do anything you like with them. We'll leave them at Angus's and he or Donald can take them down for you.'

'How are you getting in to Luig for Rory's sale, by the way?' Lilias asked as Clare was leaving with a loaf of gingerbread, a selection of bread recipes, some last year's seeds and the assurance of an endless supply of books and classical tapes.

She thought for a moment that Lilias was going to offer to

take her, and her mind boggled at the thought of what she might end up buying. 'Donald has arranged for Dougie Stewart and his wife to take me in.'

'Oh, yes, they need something for the children's bedroom.' Lilias gave Clare a searching look. 'Have you been to see Margaret yet?'

Wrong-footed, Clare floundered.

'You should, you know.'

Really, the cheek of the woman.

'She's on her own with those two appalling brats,' Lilias went on, 'and Dougie works long hours. And she is your nearest neighbour –'

Flinching at the prospect of a rerun of the who's-nearest-to-the-Larach argument, Clare made conciliatory noises and took herself off.

In fact she called on Dougie's wife the very next day. Nothing to do with Lilias's instructions, she assured herself. She had been walking up the glen road and had been given a lift by a Forestry Commission van (driven by the black-bearded giant of that first December night in the hotel bar which now seemed to belong to the life of a different person). On her way back she passed the Stewarts' house, a bare white bungalow in a patch of rough grass adorned by chewed sticks and fragments of toys and cars. 'The Birks' was burned into a slice of peeling varnished tree trunk nailed to the gatepost.

Good intentions were a serious mistake, Clare decided, finding herself in a sauna of a kitchen pulsating with sound – telly at full volume, dogs barking, cat hissing from the windowsill where it had failed to find an exit route, and Sheena and Lynn, aged three and two, eyes round and mouths square, bawling their horror at the sight of a visitor.

Margaret was speechless with embarrassment, but eased the moment of social constraint by applying her toe to the dogs and her hand to her daughters, then fleeing to the kettle for moral support.

Later Clare learned to check before sitting down and this time only just avoided a spat-out sweet and a kitten, but through all the squalor Margaret's good nature shone serenely. She had, Clare was to discover, a squandering, live-for-the-day generosity which had its own charm and she was the gentlest of girls, completely at the mercy of those two fiends, her daughters. And she was desperate for company. Her only contact with the outside world seemed to be hanging out the washing and she made no attempt to hide the fact that she thought Clare a complete freak for living at the Larach, though Clare had the impression she barely knew where it was.

There was lots of 'And are you no' frightened, away out there on your own?' and 'You'll surely be getting a car soon?' and 'You're never telling me you walked this length?'

When Clare explained that she had walked not from the Larach but almost from the head of the glen Margaret was frankly disbelieving. 'You'd think you were at the top of the glen, but you wouldna' have been,' she said kindly.

'There's a huge place like a castle stuck up on the hillside.'

'Aye, right enough, that's Glen Righ House,' Margaret agreed, awed. 'That's where the Finlays live. They used to own the whole glen but most of the land belongs to Rhumore nowadays. The old laird is daft in the head and there's only the one grand-daughter to come after him.'

'What happened to her parents?'

'They were never here, seemingly, always off in one of those wee private aeroplanes and it blew up on them, and the son, Catriona's brother that was, he was drowned in the river beside the big house and the laird went in after him and hit his head and went mad.'

She gabbled off this melodramatic tale with great complacency. Clare felt it could do with some expansion from a more reliable source.

The children scuffled and whined at a distance of two feet from Channel Four racing and Clare reluctantly accepted weak tea and a wrapped milk chocolate wafer. She was hotter than she'd been since leaving Italy, but somehow she didn't mind.

Margaret seemed to think she had Clare to thank for the prospect of going to the Luig sale. 'I've been at Dougie for long enough about a cupboard for the weans . . .' Margaret had been brought up in Glasgow. A cupboard for the wains? Clare turned the phrase over but it made no sense to her. '. . . but he was always saying he was too busy. But then Donald said you were needing a few things and we could take the farm van, so Dougie said he'd go. Donald wasn't sure he'd manage along himself, though. Well, he can never say, can he?' Seeing that this meant nothing to Clare she added, lowering her voice, 'With Ishbel, like.'

His wife? Didn't she let him out?

'With Ishbel the way she is.' Margaret's voice had taken on an enjoyably portentous note.

'Is she ill?' Clare asked. It occurred to her that she should have wrapped that up a bit. But Donald had never mentioned anything of the kind.

'I made sure you'd have heard.'

Was there some innuendo there? But it seemed not.

'A matter of months, so they say.' Margaret compressed her lips, folded her hands across the bulge of her stomach and nodded meaningly, but would not utter the dreaded word.

Clare walked home thoughtfully, wishing she had kept her mouth shut on a certain point when Donald had arrived after all on the day of the gale.

CHAPTER ELEVEN

Though the wind had lost some of its ferocity towards evening the loch was still too rough for a boat, but Clare had not been surprised when she heard the familiar double knock. Donald opened the door and Trim's nose appeared round it. Delighted, Clare rushed to pull away the rug she had jammed into the worn hollow of the step.

'Wait till you're invited,' Donald admonished Trim. But it was a formality; she always came in now.

'Of course she's invited. Quick, both of you, and get the door shut.'

'So you're still in one piece.' Donald surveyed the bright fire and warm room and the paint in her hair. 'And I see you found yourself something to do.'

'Come and look.'

'An improvement,' he allowed, his fingers finding one or two pockmarks in the shelves which Clare knew she should have filled.

'That's good enough for me,' she mocked him.

'I thought you'd have finished *War and Peace* by now.'

'No time for such indulgence.' How it transformed the house to have him there, with his quiet voice and quiet tread, stooping his tall head through the doorway, going to sit as of habit in Murdo's chair, filling it with his broad shoulders and long thighs.

'Did you get much sleep last night?' he asked.

'Not much. Particularly after the sheep arrived.'

A flicker of a smile. 'They always come down in a storm. We'll be lambing here soon so let's hope that's the last of the spring gales.' He moved his feet as she went to fill the teapot, watching her as he always did, as though still entertained to see her there. 'And you didn't mind being cooped up alone all day?'

She knew what he was asking. 'Nothing I couldn't handle,' she said, and knew from his assessing look and slow nod that he had understood. 'Have you walked over from the farm?'

'No, the headland's passable, but I had to leave the Land Rover the other side of the burn. Too much water to get across today. You'll have to tidy up that ford of yours,' he added slyly.

'You sound like Gerald Markie.'

'Oh, here now.'

'It was good of you to come.'

'I wanted to be sure you were all right.'

Trim oozed out from beside his chair to the middle of the hearthrug now that tea-making was over and Clare took a cushion and joined her, stroking the silky head, contentment filling her. She told herself not to be a fool. Donald had come because he regarded her as an incompetent who needed looking after. There was no more to it than that. And he was right. She had not fled this time, but she had had to make an effort to relax and accept the novelty of her enforced isolation.

'You'll be a real survivor by winter,' he remarked, 'digging in and not caring what the weather does.'

'I shan't be here by winter,' she answered out of her thoughts. 'This is only a temporary hideaway.'

'But you bought the place,' he began, sharply for him, then seemed to catch himself up. 'I suppose that's what made me think you'd be staying. There are plenty of places about to rent.'

'I needed somewhere of my own after the hotel.' She knew she sounded dismissive and wasn't surprised when he let it go.

'Whereabouts does your family live?' he asked, after a pause during which Clare concentrated on Trim.

'No family.' She had rapped out the words and apologized. 'Oh, Donald, I'm sorry. I don't mind you asking. It's just that it's all a bit bleak and I'm not used to talking about it.'

'You can talk to me.' If he knew the effect that quiet comprehensive statement had on her.

'Nothing much to it really.' Her voice sounded high, not quite under control, taking her by surprise. She had thought she was quite calm. 'My father vanished ages ago – couldn't stand my mother and who could blame him?' A brittle note there and she hurried on. 'And she told me a couple of years later that he was dead.'

She had made Clare feel that it was disloyal to her personally to be devastated by the news. She had explained that by leaving them Clare's father had forfeited all right to their grief. Eleven years old, Clare had had to cope with the loss and the memories alone.

'When my mother died too, after I was married, I found out . . .' To Clare's annoyance her voice betrayed her again, wavering dangerously. She had not known she would find such difficulty in putting this into words after a gap of so many years. As Clare had stopped stroking her, Trim gave a deep sigh and subsided into sleep against her hip. Donald waited, saying nothing.

'There were dozens of letters, horrible bitter letters, about money and divorce – and about me. My father had been alive all the time, was married again.'

'Did you go to see him?' Donald prompted as the silence drew out.

'I did. He didn't want to know. He just didn't want to know.'

'Come on, lass,' said Donald gently, as she had heard him say to Trim. He leaned forward and reached for her hands, folding them comfortingly in both his own, and Clare bowed her head over them, fighting down tears.

'He – and his wife – came to the door. They wouldn't even let me into the house.' The words choked her, but she couldn't have stopped now. Martin had dismissed it with an impatient, 'Well, what did you expect?' when she had reached home shaken and distressed. He had not wanted her to go in the first place, had refused to see any point in it.

'They said it would upset the children.' She could recall with the most painful clarity standing on that inhospitable doorstep and learning that she had half-brothers and sisters, and in the same instant having them taken from her again. 'They said things about my mother. They seemed to feel I'd been to blame too in some way for refusing to keep in touch after he had left—' It poured out in jerky anguish. 'My father believed I hated him as much as she had and he wouldn't listen, he absolutely refused to listen.' That had been the unbelievable, unendurable part.

'Poor lass,' said Donald's deep voice above her. 'Poor little lass.' His sympathy melted Clare and her eyes brimmed with tears she could no longer control. Donald gave her a handkerchief, neatly folded but smelling bracingly of tar, and that made her giggle and stemmed the incipient flood.

'That's better.' He stretched past her to edge the kettle on to the flames, pushing away a solicitous Trim. He gave the impression that he would have liked to settle in and talk for hours, but after a second round of tea he looked at his watch and said reluctantly that he would have to go. Clare stood at the corner of the house in the fine, wind-driven rain and watched the Land Rover thread a route up the sodden hillside. She was conscious of an ache of loss and need that had nothing to do with the past.

Waiting in the draughty tin-roofed shed for Rory McMunn's sale to begin an unpleasant thought struck Clare. She had told Donald she had no intention of staying at the Larach for longer than the summer, so why should he continue to concern himself about her comfort there? Only now, when it was obvious that he was not going to appear, did she realize how confidently she had expected to see him tonight.

At least Margaret was happy. It was clearly an occasion for her. She was wearing a frilly blouse under her anorak, tight trousers and teetery little shoes, and had applied at least an half an hour's worth of make-up. There had been traumatic scenes as the children were abandoned for an evening with their aunt and cousins, and every adult present had reasoned with them at the full pitch of their lungs, but once the van was heading safely along the loch shore Margaret had let the exhilaration of unaccustomed freedom take over.

Though saleroom etiquette seemed to call for down-turned mouths and disparaging mutters, she dived excitedly at the pile of carpets on Clare's behalf. The gaudy corners she turned back were like the horrors that had been available in Fort William and Clare's heart sank. Then she saw suspended on the wall behind them a huge spread of pinkish-brown, badly hacked round the edges, but muted, plain. She climbed over to it. Wool, soft and dense.

'That's always there,' Dougie said dismissively.

'Why? Isn't it for sale?'

'Oh, it's for sale right enough. It's just that no one's about to buy it.'

Before Clare could find out more the auctioneer, a lank-haired, unwashed individual, took up his position with an air of weariness and disgust.

'Is that Rory McMunn?'

'That's his son, Lachy. There's Rory over there.' Dougie jerked his head discreetly towards a fat man at the back of the room, tightly buttoned into a pale yellow sheepskin coat, a tiny tweed hat somehow adhering to his bald head. He visibly oozed satisfaction as he surveyed the malleable herd, faces turned meekly up to his son, pockets waiting to be emptied.

A lot of dismal rubbish changed hands in the first half hour and Margaret set her heart on a green fluted bowl with five stem dishes but said she was too shy to bid for them. Dougie was protesting that she didn't need them when Lachy made everyone jump by roaring, 'Less noise, the lot of youse! I canna' hear myself think. If there's any more of it I'll close the whole thing down and we can all go hame.' Clare could hardly imagine that he would want to be left with this dross on his hands, but a breathless silence fell.

Clare won the dishes for Margaret for two pounds which she hoped wouldn't cause too much marital strife.

They had reached the gas heaters she was interested in, and she was about to make sure of the first one that came up when a tall figure loomed at her side and a hand on her arm warned her to wait. Donald had come after all. Clare felt a surge of pleasure which was not connected in any way with the prospect of acquiring a heater.

The second one went to 'Rhumore' for twenty-five pounds.

'In better condition,' Donald explained.

'How do you know?'

'I had a look this afternoon. It had the full cylinder too,' he added blandly.

'You switched them?'

'No sense in carrying an empty one home, now is there?' he reproved her, his face innocent.

Clare laughed, feeling exuberantly happy. How it altered the evening to have him there, his big frame solid at her shoulder. The Stewarts too responded to his presence, Dougie competing fiercely for a warped cupboard of coated hardboard and Margaret, pink-cheeked, eyes sparkling through the thicket of mascara, having to be restrained from reckless saleroom fever.

Clare bought a little oak bookcase and a chest of drawers and Donald rather surprisingly lashed out three pounds for a washing basket full of oddments, though belatedly Clare thought the basket itself would have been an improvement on her plastic one.

Lachy came to the chairs, each temporarily vacated as it came under the hammer, except one which was sold with an old lady dozing in it whom nobody wished to disturb. There was a check at a dumpy bedroom chair with tattered chintz flounces.

'Ah, come on now, I'm no' here for my health,' Lachy exclaimed petulantly, his cold eyes raking his motionless audience. 'Someone will give me a pound, surely?'

Rather to her own surprise Clare found that she had. But then it was she who brought proceedings to a standstill, or rather Donald did so on her behalf, when she realized that the brown velvet sofa to be sold next would convert into a bed.

'I was going to get one for when Magda comes,' she hissed to Donald.

'Let's have a look at it, Lachy,' Donald called with authority and a space was cleared while he and the two assistants, and in the end Lachy himself, grappled with the mechanism. Even Rory McMunn moved closer to watch as it became obvious that the sofa had rarely, if ever, been called upon to perform its secondary function. 'A drop of oil is all it's needing,' pronounced Lachy.

'Mimie Ross's?' enquired Donald, examining a chalk squiggle. 'Front room. Hardly been sat on let alone slept in. I wouldn't normally buy a bed from the sale,' he added to Clare, without bothering to lower his voice, 'but you'll not go wrong with this one.'

An uncontested fifteen pounds.

The carpet section began with the beige-pink monster. When Lachy announced a starting price of fifty pounds and everybody laughed, Clare thought it was because it was so absurdly cheap. She was ready to plunge but Donald restrained her.

'Leave this to me,' he ordered.

There was a lengthy pause. People began to shuffle their feet and glance impatiently towards the brighter glories to come, now vacated by the punters who had been relaxing there eating pies and crisps and drinking from flasks and cans.

'He's just trying it on,' Margaret whispered disgustedly to Clare. 'Fifty pounds! That's plain daft. No one's ever going to give that.'

But Lachy had somehow sniffed Clare's interest and guessed he had a chance to get his wall cleared at last. Donald waited impassively and Clare did her best to appear equally indifferent, quite unaware that she was holding on tightly to his sleeve.

Taking part in the proceedings for the first time Rory McMunn gave one slow nod.

'Forty-five pounds then,' said Lachy, aggrieved, 'and what use there is opening the doors in the first place I'll never know.'

Donald didn't move a muscle and Clare gave an anguished tug at his sleeve. The silence stretched, then Lachy moved on. The carpet was lost to her; he'd called Donald's bluff.

'But—' Clare began. Donald gave one shake of his head and heroically she kept quiet.

With a ripple of disappointment at the fizzled-out drama the crowd turned its united gaze to a shaggy lime-green hearthrug being flapped before them as enticingly as a bull-fighter's cape. For a moment Clare thought Margaret would want it to go with her green dishes.

The last item was a white Indian rug which had been hidden at the bottom of the pile and which, after Donald had made them measure it and had decided it would fit the Larach bedroom, Clare acquired, then everyone who had bought surged forward to besiege the harassed clerk.

'Cash only,' said Donald, before Clare could start in about the carpet. 'That all right with you?'

'Well, if cash doesn't include cheques or Visa, no, it's not,' she said, taken aback.

He laughed. 'I can't see Rory turning down a cheque from you. But how about, "All goods to be uplifted at close of sale"?' pointing to a roughly scrawled notice above the clerk's head.

'But how can they expect that?' Clare demanded, rattled.

'I could get some of the small stuff into the van,' Dougie put in helpfully.

'And we could probably get the cupboard into the back of the Land Rover.'

Clare stared from one dubious face to the other.

Margaret relented. 'They're having you on. McMunn's lorry will bring it all out.'

'We'd best go and settle up,' Dougie suggested, grinning at the successful wind-up.

Clare found that her 'line' included a forty-pound item she had not expected. Some message had evidently passed between Donald and Lachy; face had been saved and the big carpet was hers. They exploded from the saleroom in triumph. Even Donald allowed himself to look pleased.

CHAPTER TWELVE

Donald took Clare home. She was thankful not to be squashed into the van choking on waves of Margaret's cheap scent and Dougie's cigarette smoke, and to be spared the probable dramas and certain hospitality of collecting Sheena and Lynn.

What rubbish, she mocked herself, you want to be with Donald. You want to be here in the Land Rover roaring over Luig Hill, watching a bright moon sailing in and out of white trails of cloud, looking across Loch Buie and knowing that one dark dot on the opposite shore is home.

She glanced at Donald's profile beside her, clear-cut, strong. Just being with him gave her a sense of peace, of childish all's well. A few weeks ago she would have despised everything about the evening they had spent, the objects for sale, the level of humour, the company.

'We'd best get those carpets of yours laid before lambing begins,' Donald said.

Still the generous, taken-for-granted 'we'. So good to hear.

'Couldn't I lay them myself?'

'How do you think you'd be able to move the dresser?'

'I could cut round it.'

'You'll do no such thing.'

Clare smiled at the sailing moon.

'Your wee house is going to look quite smart once that stuff is in.'

'And Lilias gave me curtains.'

'I hope you liked them?'

She laughed. 'Luckily yes. How will they deliver the furniture? By Angus's boat?'

'They'll put it into the barn at the farm and we'll bring it over on the bogey.'

Bogey? 'Did you arrange that?'

'I did.'

'Oh, Donald, how can I ever thank you for all you've done for me?' She felt helpless to convey what it had meant to her.

'We'll think of something.' She wished that was the sort of suggestive hint she would once have taken in her stride but from Donald she knew it couldn't be. How ironic the situation was. She had thought nothing of affairs with married men in the end, having decided that their moral problems were nothing to do with her, but she had no wish for Donald to behave as they had done. Also his respect mattered to her, and she wanted to respect herself in everything to do with him. He had given no sign of being physically attracted to her, but could she seriously believe any man would do what he had done for her if he wasn't? Or were the rules different here? One thing she vowed there and then, she would not spoil the happiness she found in being with him by hankering for something that could not exist.

Donald drove past the farm, put the Land Rover in four-wheel drive and started up over the headland.

'Donald, that's good of you but I'm quite happy to walk. I know you have to get back.'

'No hurry. Ishbel's sister is staying. One of her sisters,' he amended feelingly. But once on the ridge he pulled up and sat looking at the steel and ebony of land and loch and sky. Clare felt sharp disappointment that he had changed his mind and the evening was ending.

'It's a grand night, not too cold. You say you want to walk down?'

'Yes, of course. I'd enjoy it.' Clare hurriedly gathered up her bag, hoping she hadn't given herself away.

'Come on then.' He was getting out, going round to open the back, pulling out the basket of bits and pieces he'd bought.

'What are you doing?'

'Taking you home, of course,' he said, putting out a hand as though to take hers, but waving her forward instead.

Swung back to ebullience, Clare trotted beside him down the slope. It was magical to be out on the hill at this hour on a cool

April night, the cloud and moon patterns flowing before them over the rough ground. She had a sudden vision of the overheated, busy hotel.

Donald lit the lamp and raked the fire together. Clare made coffee and assembled a scratch supper, wishing for the first time that she had a drink to offer him. Then they had a look at what was in the basket.

Stone jars, butter pats, a set of rusted icing nozzles, blackened bread tins, a flit gun which Donald said was brass, what looked like the beginning of someone's beermat collection and a pair of flat irons.

'These are what I was after. You have to be the only person in the glen who'd have any use for them. Mind you, I could probably have found most of this stuff in the attic at Rhumore. It's crammed with all kinds of rubbish going back a hundred years.'

Clare wished she could have the run of it. 'Have you always lived there?'

'I was born there. So were my father and grandfather, come to that.'

'It must be marvellous to belong to a place like that from generation to generation.'

'Humph,' said Donald.

'No?'

'It has its disadvantages.'

'Such as?'

'Oh, obligations.' He sounded curt and Clare thought he had disliked her English effusiveness.

'Margaret told me that most of Rhumore had once belonged to Glen Righ estate. She also gave me the impression that all the Finlays are a bit odd.'

'They're in a sad way nowadays, true enough. There's only Fergus and his granddaughter Catriona left of the whole family.'

'How did they lose the land?'

'Oh, that's one of the good old stories. Let's see now. Fergus's grandfather it would be, he was one of twins and when he inherited he made over the promontory of Rhumore to his brother and built a house there for him, on the understanding that it would revert to the estate if there was no family to succeed to it.'

'And twin didn't stick to the bargain?'

'Just so. He'd got hold of some local yarn that he was the elder, or that no one had known which baby was which, I think it was. So in revenge he went off to Canada and tracked down the Macraes, who'd been evicted by his father from the township in Righ Bay – I'll show you the ruins sometime' – Clare tucked away the nugget of this promise – 'and he sold Rhumore to my great-grandfather for a guinea or some such paltry amount.'

'And what became of him?'

'Oh, he shot himself.'

'Of course. So then what about the rest of the estate?'

'Simple economics. The Macraes farmed with burning zeal, having so unexpectedly come into possession of a piece of what they regarded as their ancestral homeland, and the Finlays continued to live beyond their means.'

Clare liked his dry humour, liked hearing him talk, above all liked to see him relaxed and in no hurry at her fireside.

'That's continued into present times,' Donald went on. 'Catriona's father was always desperate to get out of the glen. He wasn't interested in shooting or fishing or the land or the tenants, he only wanted to have a good time on the proceeds. He ran up enormous debts while he was at Cambridge and Fergus sold the ground on the east side of the glen to the Forestry Commission to meet them. Then Alastair married a girl who loathed the Highlands even more than he did and between them they simply emptied Fergus's coffers. Most of the time they dumped the children here, Catriona and her brother Iain, and poor old Fergus looked after them as best he could.'

'And the boy was drowned?'

'Yes, went over the terrace wall into the gorge beside the house. Fergus went in after him, an incredible leap for a man of his age, and was dragged out unconscious much lower down. They reckoned he'd had a crack on the head; anyway, he never fully recovered. He'd always been a bit vague and had become very unsociable after his wife died, and more and more distressed by Alastair's lifestyle and general extravagance. Losing Iain, who was to be all his father had failed to be and take the estate in hand when he grew up – you know the sort of thing – tipped the balance.'

'And what about Catriona?'

'Poor girl, she's hardly been out of the glen since. They tried sending her away to school but the old man got into a terrible state. I think in the end she refused to go and there was one useless governess after another. Now Catriona just drifts about getting more and more like Fergus every day.'

'But that's awful. How old is she?'

'Let's see, a couple of years younger than my daughter Fiona, so about nineteen or twenty.'

'But what does she *do*?'

Clare saw his mouth twitch and realized how conventional she must have sounded.

'Very little, I should think.'

'So you're turning into the laird?'

'I'll never be that.' His face darkened. Oh, God, have I been flippant about some sacrosanct hierarchy? Clare wondered in dismay.

It broke the mood, whatever she had said, for Donald was on his feet saying courteously, 'What am I thinking of, blethering away like this, keeping you up . . . ?' and Trim was awake on the instant and slipping like a shadow to the door.

'I'll let you know when McMunn's bring that stuff over,' Donald said, hitching his shoulders to settle his big jacket.

'Thank you for the basket.'

'Just junk,' he said, lost to her.

Restless and dissatisfied, Clare went down to stand for a while on the end of the jetty after he had gone, a dark shape moving rapidly up the moonlit face of the headland, but the vast scene was suddenly empty and intimidating, the air off the water penetratingly chill. She was glad to turn and go in to the refuge of bed.

The carpet-laying turned into the flitting she had never properly had. Donald had warned her that Lilias and Gerald intended to come and she began to realize that it would be regarded as something of a party. She thought, not too enthusiastically, that perhaps she'd better have some food on hand, and certainly something to drink. She had learned that much by now.

'It ought to be whisky, oughtn't it?' she asked Donald on the way up the loch to shop.

'You stick to whatever suits you,' he said firmly. 'I mean about having no alcohol in the house. No one will question it.'

'That's one of the nice things about living here,' she said. 'People accept you as you are.'

'More or less,' he said, with the suggestion of a grin.

'I think I could have alcohol in the house now,' Clare said slowly and caught his quick glance.

'That's good,' he said, and she knew he was genuinely pleased. 'In that case,' he went on, 'Dougie would like a dram, I probably wouldn't say no to one and Gerald Markie will down as many as he's given. The ladies will take tea.'

'Really.'

She wondered, as she had once or twice lately, what comments were being made about Donald taking her so openly under his wing. Or did she only assume there would be gossip because he attracted her so much? If Donald had nothing on his conscience the consideration probably wouldn't enter his head.

It gave her a definite buzz of private satisfaction to buy wine, gin and tonic, a malt of Donald's choice. Handling the bottles she felt that the urgent, frightening need was gone, though what it would be like actually having them in the dresser cupboard in the Larach she wasn't sure. And if she allowed herself a drink to be sociable when the others were there, would she be able to stop?

What she was going to give them to eat was another worry. 'God, that place is *hopeless*,' she complained to Donald as she swung herself down into the boat and stacked under the thwart the bulging much-used carrier bags he handed to her. 'Why on earth can't there be some decent food on offer occasionally?'

Donald cast off without responding, yanked at the outboard, raised a hand to an acquaintance on the jetty and roared away in a sharp curve out on to the loch.

Clare knelt on the bottom-boards to rescue a toppling bag, pushed a couple of items back into its gaping mouth and settled it more securely against its neighbour. 'Honestly,' she went on over her shoulder as she pulled herself back to sit in the stern beside Donald, the engine now cut back to its normal throaty purr, 'you'd think there might be something more imaginative than that damned yellow Cheddar occasionally, wouldn't you? And it doesn't really have to be butter or margarine or nothing these days, does it?' The butter at the Larach now lived permanently on the sitting-room mantelpiece, along with the salt.

'You can't expect Angus to have everything,' Donald said. 'He supplies what his customers want.'

He spoke with restraint and Clare didn't even realize he was angry. She had no feeling of making a personal attack on Angus; she was merely venting her frustration at not being able to get what she had wanted, just as she and Magda would have done about their local shops on the rare occasions when they were forced to use them.

'Well, don't tell me all his customers want sliced bread or that ghastly bacon that spits white-speckled water when you put it in the pan, or Mr Kipling cakes a week out of date.'

Donald said nothing, his eyes on the point of the Larach promontory.

'Anyway,' Clare pursued, still thinking they were having a general conversation, 'how can he know what people want unless he gives them a choice?'

Now Donald turned to her and his face was grimly angry, taking her totally by surprise. 'A choice? You want Angus to put – what was it I heard you asking for? – Cambozola on the shelf and then wait for you to come in, but maybe you don't appear that week or you don't want it when you do, and nobody else likes it or can afford it so in the end he has to throw it out. And how many people do you suppose he gets asking for black olives or French wine vinegar?'

'Lilias Markie would buy them,' Clare retorted, flurried into defensiveness by this unexpected attack.

'Lilias has the good sense to order any fancy things she wants from elsewhere or get them when she goes into Fort William. And you seem to forget that Angus has been able to provide every mortal thing you've needed so far for that cottage of yours, from curtain hooks to wood glue, and from sewing thread to a new ashpan.'

'Yes, I know that,' Clare snapped, getting angry in her turn. She resented finding that a few routine grumbles about inadequate supplies should have landed her in a confrontation on such a personal level. 'I just think a little imagination would do no harm.'

Donald didn't reply and she was even more annoyed with herself for persisting in an argument which she didn't really care about. A boat is not a good place for a fight, she decided, taking a look at Donald's stony profile out of the tail of her eye. Worse even than a car; no dramatic exits possible. Damn, how had they reached this point?

The mile down the loch gave her time to see the unpleasant spat from Donald's point of view. To him she was a patronizing newcomer from the south having one more contemptuous dig at the locals. As he closed the throttle to nose gently in to the Larach jetty she said awkwardly, 'I wasn't making a personal attack on Angus, you know.'

Donald didn't seem to hear. He tied up and began to sort out Clare's shopping from his own and lift it out. He told Trim to stay where she was.

'Donald –'

'I heard you,' he said, taking the box of bottles under one arm and a fistful of carrier bags in his free hand. 'Can you manage the rest?'

Clare followed him up the path, frowning and uncertain. Was he simply going to dump the stuff and go back to the boat and leave without any further reference to their argument? Well, she wouldn't let him. As they swung their burdens on to the big table she turned to him determinedly. 'I truly wasn't being unkind about Angus. That wasn't what it was about.'

Donald looked down at her for a moment, his face unreadable, and she felt the colour come into her own.

'That shop's not part of a chain, you know,' he said at last. 'The shop is Angus. You can't have a go about it and not mean him. You're intelligent enough to see what space he has available and what he manages to provide – and to realize that what he mainly provides is a service. He understands the needs of a place like this and he remembers all kinds of individual preferences and he takes endless trouble. Do you remember the time,' he went on, raising his voice very slightly as Clare opened her mouth to interrupt, 'that Angus enquired after your plans for doing up this room? He said to me he could see there'd be a serious run on white paint coming up and he made sure he had it in before you even asked for it.' I'm being lectured, Clare thought, astonished and actually quelled by the steamroller quality of his criticism. 'He does all he can in the same way for everyone in this community. Do you seriously think it's worth his while to go on making deliveries to those isolated cottages down the loch? He does it because there's old folk and pensioners living there, often without cars or neighbours who can help them. You—'

'Donald, don't, I can't bear any more! I only complained because Angus stocks such boring food.' Clare threw up her hands in surrender. 'I am grateful for what he's done for me, of course I am. Please, please don't make me feel guilty about the old age pensioners as well.' In spite of her real regret that she had spoken so unthinkingly – or that she'd annoyed Donald – she began to laugh.

'Yes, but you don't think,' Donald told her, not angrily now but still seriously. 'You just react from habit, without considering different circumstances, different needs.'

'And you don't intend to let me get away with it?'

At last he smiled. 'That's right, I don't.'

How lucky that the Larach was so far from the village, Clare reflected as she saw him off. It would not have felt good to leave this unresolved between them. And how lucky that Donald was prepared to tell her what he thought of her. On her first visit here last December she had decided, purely from self-interest, that it would be unwise to antagonize the locals. Now she found, slightly to her surprise, that as well as their goodwill their good opinion mattered to her.

★

Not only the Markies and Donald turned up for the carpet-laying, but Angus just happened to be passing and swung into the bay to help (which hammered Donald's point home pretty forcefully), and Margaret broke all precedent by letting Dougie tuck her and the children on to the trailer among the furniture and carry them off into the unknown wilderness beyond the road.

Murdo's hideous chest of drawers was carried out to be added to the bonfire of the old carpet, flat and stiff as lino, and other accumulated rubbish. Donald's estimate had been accurate and the Indian rug fitted the bedroom to within a few inches and turned it instantly into a different room. Clare had shortened and hung Lilias's flowered curtains and now caught her eyeing the ragged cover of the dumpy chair with pursed lips and a calculating expression.

The men had a hot and dusty struggle with the big carpet, but they made a most professional job of cutting and laying it. Clare couldn't believe the effect in the now white-walled room and wandered about rapturously getting in the way while her helpers shook their heads and got on with the job of lugging the furniture back in. Donald as usual went one step further and not only fitted the bathroom with one off-cut but laid another down the narrow kitchen.

'Keep your feet a bit warmer,' he observed. Clare could only smile at him, wordless, but caught his satisfied look as he gathered up the scraps to take them out to the bonfire.

The Stewart children refused all food and drink on offer and howled every time Poppy or Topsy blundered near them. Gerald barked at the dogs and Lilias barked at Gerald. Trim behaved perfectly, tucked against a boulder looking superior, though occasionally lifting her lip when the non-workers came too close. A capricious wind made the smoke impossible to dodge and Clare was awarded two out of ten for her first attempt at bread-making, but the sun shone, the cottage looked more comfortable than she had ever dreamed it could and she recognized one of those moments of unreserved happiness which remain a bright picture in the memory for ever.

It was not till they had left that she found her second glass of wine half full on the windowsill where she had put it down and forgotten it. She had been right in what she had said to

Donald. The Larach seemed a place somehow separate from that dangerous compulsion; she felt no fear of ever being in its grip again.

CHAPTER THIRTEEN

It was still almost dark when Clare was woken by the sound of the cottage door opening. Quiet steps, flicker of torchlight through the open bedroom door, the tiny squeak as the glass chimney of the lamp was lifted off, the scrape of a match.

She jerked up guiltily. 'Donald? I'm sorry, the alarm can't have gone off. I won't be a minute.'

'Go and get her up then,' she heard him say and the next moment Trim's wet paws were up on the bed, her cold nose nudging into the warm hollow of Clare's neck.

'Trim, that's horrible!' But she gave the dog a hug and received a couple of quick sideways licks before Trim slipped back to Donald.

'Whatever time is it?' Clare called. She could only just pick out the grey square of the window.

'I'm early,' Donald told her. She heard the pop and roar of the gas fire igniting, then the sound of it being trundled across the room. 'Here, dress by this. I'll put the kettle on.'

He shoved the heater inside the bedroom door and went away. Disgusted with him but resigned, Clare huddled for one last luxurious second in her nest of duvet then reached to light the candle. No other man in the world would behave so scrupulously.

'I was going to have the room warm and the kettle boiled by the time you got here,' she apologized, going into the kitchen where Donald was making toast.

'Don't worry. It's not half past four yet.' He sounded grim and the lamplight carved deep lines in his face.

'What's wrong?'

'A cow went down last night and the vet was out on a call. I haven't been to bed.'

'Poor you. Is the cow all right?'

'Couldn't save her.'

He must be very tired, Clare thought. He was usually philosophical about the hazards and disasters of farming. 'I'm sorry, Donald.' She understood more now of the sort of loss this represented.

He pulled out the grill pan and propped the toast against the marmalade jar. 'That enough?'

'Plenty, thanks.' She liked the way he had become so much at home at the Larach.

'That damned daughter of mine – and her useless man.'

Fiona had come, protesting, to look after her mother while Donald was busy with the lambing since all Ishbel's sisters were married to farmers and fully occupied themselves. Clare knew from Donald that Fiona hated the remoteness and wild weather and hard work of Rhumore and had escaped them by marrying a man called Norrie Marr she'd met on a package holiday in Majorca. He had some indeterminate job in the financial world, small-time, and Donald referred to him as 'that damned moneylender'. Every time he had come up to Rhumore to see Fiona during the last couple of weeks he had done his best to persuade her to go back with him.

'Bloody idle pair refused to get out of bed,' Donald growled. It was unusual to hear him swear and Clare knew his anger was not for his lost sleep or even his lost cow. 'Come on, then, let's see after these ewes,' he added, pushing himself upright from where he'd been leaning against the sink and turning to rinse out his mug.

The thrill of being out in the dawn making the round of the lambing ewes with Donald never failed. The first morning he had been on his way home when he had looked in at the Larach and Clare had been just up. He had gratefully accepted the offer of breakfast and had taken his time over it.

'I was tempted to buy this for a lambing bothy when I had the chance of it,' he'd remarked, glancing round the comfortable room with his glint of a smile. 'It's not worked out too badly after all.'

'Did you really think of buying it?' Clare asked with a flurry of panic even now to think her ownership could have been threatened.

'It seemed a wee bit of a luxury. Sheep farmers don't have that much spare cash these days.'

'I'm glad,' she told him cheerfully.

'Well, I'm not complaining just at the minute,' he had conceded.

He had watched her closely when he suggested, only half seriously she thought, that she might like to go out with him some time and see what it was all about. The first morning she went had been a revelation, with sunrise still half an hour away, the air fresh and sweet with a tingling keenness to it. A pallid disc of moon had hung in a downy sky and as the light grew the landscape really did look new-washed, like a beach scoured clean by the tide.

It had been a delight to watch Donald, absorbed, expert, unhurried. He and Trim seemed to work in one coordinated flow of anticipation and action. Clare hardly knew which sheep Donald had his eye on before Trim was there, singling it out for him. At first she had been afraid of being in the way, doing the wrong thing, but Donald had been very relaxed, talking easily, explaining what he was doing.

'That old madam for example, just look at her. You'd think she'd never seen me in her life before. Whisht now, you daft ould thing.'

The ewe was stamping a narrow black foreleg and rolling a yellow eye at Trim, who was flattened to the ground a couple of yards away and looking very businesslike. 'She was born just about here herself,' Donald went on, 'and she's at this spot every lambing. Very territorial, these Blackfaces. Given the choice they'd spend their whole lives on the same few yards of hill.'

'Don't they have to be inside to have the lambs?'

'Some breeds. These are hill sheep, very hardy. And they're not used to being herded close. They're used to spreading out on ground where the feeding's sparse.'

Clare loved watching his big hands bringing a lamb, checking that the airway was clear, swinging the limp body to make sure breathing had started, returning it to the anxious nuzzling mother.

'They can't give birth on their own, like animals in the wild?'

'Very often they can and pretty well always if there's only the one lamb, but we're trying all the time for higher lambing percentages, more twins and triplets, and that's when you can get complications and they need some help. Then again a ewe will rarely be able to feed three lambs so you've to take off the third one and put it to another ewe who's lost her own lamb.'

Clare had expected these trawls of the hill, sometimes in the Land Rover putting out the high-protein feed that increased the ewes' milk yield, sometimes on foot, to be strictly business, and she was careful to keep her thrilled excitement at the beauty around them to herself. So it was always an agreeable surprise when Donald would choose a comfortable rock for them to sit on to watch the sun come up, or take time to point out the various landmarks to her, name hills and farms and houses, trace out the old and new marches of Rhumore.

She learned, too, a few of the hard facts about sheep-farming. 'Hundreds of small farmers who can't diversify are selling up these days. Subsidies are way down and we're being told all the time to cut production. Prices aren't the disaster they were four or five years back when top price for a ewe was about sixty pounds, the average was more like thirty and lambs were going at twenty pounds for a pen of four, but even with a pen of thirty realizing a hundred and sixty a head last back end at Stirling nobody's going to make his fortune . . .'

Why don't I find this utterly boring? Clare asked herself. The truth was she enjoyed it. There was a satisfaction in knowing that the end result of this work directly fed basic human needs – wool, meat. And there was the unexpected and novel thrill of seeing new life come into being, watching staggering little creatures just out of their mothers' wombs at once struggling to their feet, beginning to feed. The space and starkness of the scene, her own freedom to come and go as she wished within it, added up to something intoxicating and precious in a way she had vaguely hoped for when she made her decision to come here but would scarcely have been capable of defining then.

It was about this time that Clare found her way to the Old Mill in Luig. A former woollen mill, it was a large rectangular building of dark stone with three floors and many narrow windows, hard on the bank of a turbulent little river. A Range Rover was parked outside with a yellow labrador at the wheel.

A section of the ground floor had been partitioned off and formed a crammed and aromatic meal shop, where a tall girl with a lot of long brown hair, wearing a faded tan fisherman's smock, presided over a chaotic medley of every kind of pulse and bean and flour. Dried flowers and herbs and strings of onions and garlic hung from the ceiling; solid-looking brown loaves were piled in washing baskets like the one Donald had bought at Rory McMunn's sale. Clare's eye was caught by the flowing firm shapeliness of the writing on the labels of a long line of spice and herb jars.

The girl was dealing with a gargantuan list scrawled on the back of an A4 envelope but gave Clare a wide smile, and her customer also acknowledged her with a friendly nod. Happy to wait, Clare sniffed and looked, opening her senses to mostly delicious gratification.

'You're Clare,' the girl said when the customer had left.

Clare goggled, then laughed.

'Trudy Thompson. Lilias said you'd be in. How are you getting on in your cottage?'

Falling into chat with Trudy was like slipping into a warm bath. She was one of those direct people with no axe to grind and no patience with pretension.

'What made you come up here?' Clare asked, when Trudy had fetched coffee for them both, with the warning that she probably wouldn't get the chance to drink hers.

'Ben and I were both teaching in Watford and came home one January night exhausted, frustrated and each individually ready to hurl ourselves into the nearest river. Luckily we said so, and decided there and then to do something about it. We sat down and worked out what we really wanted to do and where we really wanted to be, drew a circle round a big chunk of the west coast of Scotland and as soon as we could drove up and looked around.'

'And found this. Do you live here too, in the mill?'

'Come on, I'll show you . . . cancel that' – as a customer came in – 'but hang around a bit if you can.'

As she hadn't been served yet Clare thought she might. They didn't in fact have the opportunity to talk much that day but Clare walked back into the centre of town with a warm certainty of laughter and friendship there for the taking.

'Trudy's one of the best,' Donald affirmed, when she told him about it. 'She's done a great job with that shop and she handles the back-up for the pottery too, accounts and ordering and so on.'

'What about Ben?'

'Didn't you meet him?'

'He'd gone to see some other potter down near Drishaig, Trudy said.'

Donald nodded.

'So what's he like?' Clare persisted, chiefly interested in more background to Trudy.

'Well, let's see. Very little is allowed to come between him and his art.'

'Ah.'

They were as close to the fire as they could get their chairs, gently steaming, numb hands coming painfully back to life clamped round mugs, stockinged feet companionably pressed against the oven door.

Lashing rain mixed with sleet driven on a fierce wind had convinced Donald that Clare wouldn't dream of leaving her bed and he hadn't called for her. She had seen the Land Rover lights picking a slow way across the hill and had been incensed to be left behind. She had caught up with Donald to find him kneeling in the lights from the Land Rover beside a weary ewe, her draggled fleece and the ground around her muddy with her struggles.

'You must be mad,' Donald had said briefly, finding Clare at his shoulder, but he hadn't sounded as though he minded.

'You should have called for me,' she said indignantly.

'Aye, well, let's save that for later, shall we? I could do with a hand now you're here.'

'What do you need?' She expected him to ask her to dig something out of a pocket or fetch something from the Land Rover.

'Can you help with this ewe? She's having a terrible time and I'm hurting her more than I'm helping her.'

Clare didn't stop to think about it. The pelting rain, the semi-darkness, the mud, the foundering sheep, all created an immediacy that left no room for squeamishness. She knelt beside Donald and followed his instructions carefully, inserting her hand, feeling for the tiny hooves.

'See if you can bring them round.'

Too caught up in what she was doing to feel any revulsion she carefully manoeuvred the small slippery knobs in the right direction, got a grip above them.

'A steady pull,' Donald said quietly.

'I can't shift it,' she gasped in dismay.

'Keep a firm hold. I'll help you.'

The sight of that slimy little bundle emerging on to the churned-up ground was one of the great moments of Clare's life. She couldn't remember afterwards exactly what she'd said but she did remember the amusement in Donald's voice as he reminded her, 'She'll maybe need a hand with the next.'

The second lamb was no trouble, and astoundingly the ewe was up and searching for her offspring even as Donald rubbed it down and steadied it on its spindly, swaying legs.

'Feels pretty good, huh?' he said, looking into Clare's face with his warm smile.

'Oh, Donald!'

'We'd have been in a bit of bother without you.'

'Yes, well, who left me behind?' she demanded, remembering.

He laughed. 'Come on, you've earned your breakfast today.' He put an arm round her shoulders as they turned to the Land Rover, and that rough wet embrace, with the rain dripping off her hood and cuffs and her filthy jeans clammy round her knees, meant more to Clare in that moment than any romantic gesture ever made.

CHAPTER FOURTEEN

Going into the old dairy at the farm Clare was delighted to see a letter from Magda on the slate slab beside the milk. A long letter, too. She hastily skimmed a couple of densely word-processed pages about Carlini affairs in search of what she wanted.

Magda was too busy to come, the deal with her brother had not been finalized yet, at the last minute his wife had refused to live in England, Paolo was commuting between hotel and family in Italy and Magda would not be able to get away till the matter was settled. She made no comment whatsoever on Clare's life.

Clare told herself robustly that all she'd wanted anyway was a bit of ego massage, an acknowledgement from 'home' that she had done something positive rather than desperate in coming here, but she couldn't pretend that she didn't feel horribly let down. Replying, she took care to sympathize with Magda's anxiety over the partnership (it sounded more like fury actually), but begged her to find time to come north before the busy summer engulfed her. Then she buried her disappointment in work.

She finally made herself attack a job she had been putting off because she was always lured outside by something more tempting – cleaning the loft. Grey-green cobwebs as disgusting as old J-cloths obscured the two small cast-iron skylights and hung from the rough beams. Smelly rolls of rugs chewed by mice, a rusty fender, a gas ring with perished rubber pipe, a cracked and speckled mirror, a cardboard box of jam jars which fell apart at a touch were huddled on woodwormy planks and old cupboard doors across the joists. Down it all came and was piled with the last of the rubbish from the shed and everything else they hadn't been able to burn for Donald to take away and dispose of once lambing was over. Much more enjoyably she went on bit by bit with the job of clearing away the build-up of earth and grass, nettles and dandelions against the cottage walls, and in the process discovered big stone slabs buried under the turf at the door. She also began to attack the nettles springing up where Donald had run the clothes-line for her, and spent happy hours rebuilding the old ford across the burn, hours which had to be classed as mere footling since the ford no longer had any function.

She allowed herself plenty of time for stopping and looking, hardly able to take her eyes off the loveliness on every side produced by the spell of warm weather which had suddenly arrived. The first seeds were in the garden, the seed potatoes Donald had given her were sprouting in their boxes, the herbs contributed by Lilias were flourishing and the freezing dark days when she had arrived seemed far away.

She often walked to the village now that Donald was so busy. Like the farm it seemed oddly nearer. Having thoroughly lost track of time, not helped by getting up at dawn and going to bed whenever she felt like it, she had provided some entertainment for her friends, as she felt so many of the people in the glen and village had become, by going shopping on a day which turned out to be Sunday. She had been found standing blankly outside the closed shop by the Markie family in full force on their way back from church. Stephen and Lucy and their two self-sufficient children, Oliver and Libby, were up at Tigh Bhan for Easter. Clare had been swept off to have lunch with them. Lilias was basting the roast before the others were out of the cars, still wearing her little tweed hat which matched her heathery suit and round which her white hair curled jauntily.

Clare was ordered to the drawing-room which was bathed in sunlight and calm, full of the scent of pheasant-eye narcissus, with faded Persian rugs on the pale floor, fat downy cushions on welcoming chintz-covered sofas and books everywhere. Gerald, wearing kilt, tweed jacket with leather elbow patches and very prickly-looking stockings, crashed about in brogues which Clare was sure were nailed, fetching as each thought struck him ice, lemon, tonic, Shanghai nuts and a bowl of pumpkin seeds devoid of taste or colour.

The children, as aware as the dogs that this was no time to be underfoot, withdrew to a gigantic jigsaw laid out on a table in a big curve of window. Stephen attempted to take on some of the trips to the kitchen for his father but was ordered to sit.

'No reason for everyone to be on their feet. You look after Clare. Drat, now where's the knife? Damned woman, never puts anything back. I don't think I can stand much more of her.' Crash, crash, crash.

'Barbara Bailey, I think,' Stephen said gravely.

Clare laughed. 'Should I offer to help?'

'Wiser not, probably. Lucy will hover about a little and she and Ma will get on each other's nerves, very politely of course. But the food will eventually arrive.'

Lucy interested Clare. She seemed so separate, not aloof exactly, certainly not hostile, but somehow not part of the scene. She was a totally different physical type from her beefy husband and stocky children, slender and droopy, her movements fluid and indecisive. She had a mass of soft unbrushed dark hair and floaty clothes. She was courteous and smiling, gentle with the children, and the dogs pantingly and embarrassingly adored her, but she seemed to elude all contact.

Lunch was very, very good. The words 'home-grown' and 'organic' hung in the air. Gerald carved fussily but competently and Lilias, pink-cheeked from the oven and the large gins Clare had seen going to the kitchen, sparkled at the foot of her table. Thankfully they were both too busy answering Stephen's questions to Clare about the Larach to have much time to spare to be at each other's throats.

'Which reminds me, Clare,' Lilias said, interrupting her own account of how well her ex-curtains looked in their new habitat, 'that little chair you bought for your bedroom. I've looked out some material which will do perfectly for it. Will you be able to make a new cover yourself?'

'Well . . .'

'Then bring over the old one and I'll show you what to do.'

'Do it for you,' Clare caught a murmur from Stephen as he offered her a pudding of cream and summer fruit ('must get the freezer emptied before summer') whose brown-sugar topping was crisp and golden from the grill. 'Just say yes.'

There was some bracing teasing for Oliver, due to go to Gordonstoun in the autumn, which he took quite well though

Clare thought it a bit brutal, but it was Gerald who held the floor when they reached the cheese (Stilton or nothing) on the subject of a regimental history he was writing. Stephen, a lieutenant-colonel in the same regiment, commented with marked restraint, banking on the hope, Clare suspected, that it would never see the light.

She was not surprised when, after a noisy group attack on clearing the table and arguing about what to stuff into the dishwasher and what to leave for Barbara Bailey the next morning, Lucy folded herself down on the floor behind the piano with *Queen Victoria's Highland Journal*, Volume I, and seemed not to hear when a route march was organized to escort their guest home.

What Clare loved most at this time was going out with Donald each evening to pair the ewes and lambs for the night. The lambs had reached the gang stage, butting each other from rocky outcrops, showing off in back-breaking bucks, making mad concerted rushes along the hillside and staying out till all hours. They had numbers sprayed on their sides – many of which Clare had put there herself – but as few of their mothers could count to two and made no objection to having one offspring adrift, it could take some time to reunite them.

Golden evenings, the tide of new green higher up the hill each day, birds busy along the shoreline (Clare could tell an oystercatcher from a seagull now), long shadows stretching, dazzling gilded light spreading across the loch, and Donald with his crook, a bawling lamb under one arm, muttering about useless females.

As the lambs grew bigger 'giving an eye' to the flock became a matter of making sure all was well and Donald seemed quite happy to sit and chat, often till the last of the light had faded, so much later than Clare was used to in the south.

'Make the most of it before the midges start,' he would warn her sardonically if she became too euphoric. He seemed in general not prepared to let her off with any woolly preconceived ideas about her new environment. These idyllic evening hours were not entirely passed in harmony.

Donald had been telling her about a run-in his shepherd,

Calum Macdonald, who looked after the ewes lambing on the low ground around Righ Bay on the north side of the Rhumore headland, had had with a group of walkers with two dogs. Calum had been out till dark, with his wife to help him, reuniting ewes and lambs after the flock had scattered in panic.

'I don't think walkers really know it will be a problem,' Clare remarked, thinking back to her days in the Welsh mountains. She had passed sheep then with as little awareness as if they had been animated versions of the rocks among which they grazed.

'Then they damn well should,' Donald said roundly.

'But the hills can't really belong to anyone, can they? I don't mean enclosed land like this, but there are miles and miles of mountains that can't produce anything. Surely people should be able to walk on them.'

'And what about the shooting and stalking?'

'But they're barbaric anyway,' cried Clare, sure she was on safe ground here since Donald was a farmer. 'And how can it be more acceptable for people to go on the hills for recreation to kill creatures than to walk and look and enjoy them?'

'Do you seriously believe that airy-fairy notion that no one owns the hills? Good God, Clare, I credited you with more sense. Someone's capital is tied up in every inch of ground and that someone needs a return on it. Shooting is one resource, stalking is another, and it's also essential if deer numbers are to be kept under control and feeding preserved for the sheep. And what about employment? Apart from jobs for the keepers and ghillies, what about the spin-off, bringing customers into the area for the hotels and shops? And that makes business for the suppliers and tradesmen as well.'

'Well, I still think walkers have a right to go on the hills,' Clare argued, though rather taken aback by Donald's forcefulness.

'Maybe, if they stick to routes where they can't do any harm and take shooting seasons and lambing time into account. And if they keep their dogs under control and don't leave plastic bags or cans about or climb over high-tensile fences and leave gates open, or even worse shut gates that were open so that stock could get to water – and a few other things I could think of.'

'Walkers aren't all totally ignorant.' But she was beginning to laugh and knew that Donald was partly teasing her now.

'And to go back to this barbaric matter of shooting,' he said, shifting his point of attack, 'I take it you'd eat grouse and venison without too much protest?'

'I certainly would,' she agreed cheerfully.

'Then you'd best come out on the hill and do some beating for me and see what goes on, then we'll have another discussion about it.'

'But do you have shooting? I thought Rhumore was a farm.'

'Some of the land we've acquired from Glen Righ over the years is grouse moor and deer forest and the income from it enables me to keep on farming.' He was master of a dry but not unfriendly sarcasm, and by the gleam in his eye Clare knew he relished using it. 'And since we've got that settled we'd best be making our way back,' he added with a glance at the sky. 'My mother's ideas on supper are fairly lavish and she'll be looking for me soon.'

His daughter Fiona had not lasted out the lambing and in the end Donald's mother, who lived in Fort William, had come to help out.

'Does she enjoy being back at Rhumore?' Clare asked as they went along the shore.

'Not entirely,' said Donald with restraint.

Clare looked at him.

'Two women in one house,' he enlarged, with a resigned chuck of his head and lift of his eyebrows.

'Did she like living there before – when your father was alive, I mean?'

'She loved it. Now—' But he changed whatever he had been about to say. 'Well, she's getting on a bit for hand-rearing lambs and that kind of caper.'

Clare felt a sharp stab of jealousy to think of Ishbel doing it in the past, sharing the life of the farm with Donald, expert, at home in her familiar world. Then she was ashamed of herself; the woman was ill, for God's sake, probably dying.

It was during those quiet evening hours of looking, talking and not talking, that Donald first spoke of Ishbel's illness, though briefly and with a sort of suppressed anger which Clare supposed was the only way he could face its implications.

'You'll have heard about Ishbel?'

'Yes.'

He gave her a small nod which acknowledged the directness of her answer. 'That she has cancer?'

'Yes.'

'So someone's actually uttered the word, have they?'

'Lilias.'

'Ah yes, Lilias.' He was silent, his face sombre, and Clare waited uncertainly.

'Ishbel won't say it,' he said harshly after some uncomfortable moments. 'Won't let the word past her lips. To hear her talk you'd think she had indigestion or something.'

What on earth do you say to a man who is watching his wife die? Clare thought with anxious compassion.

'We have to keep up this damned pretence.'

'That must be very hard for you.' Perhaps it explained his reluctance to go home, his readiness to spend time with her, someone outside his real life.

Her words had been trite enough but her sympathy was real and Donald must have heard it. He turned to her quickly. 'You lost your husband, didn't you?'

'Yes, three years ago.'

'Do you mind my speaking of it?'

'No, not at all – truly.'

'What was it?' Clare knew he was seeking help, even if it was only the solace of shared experience.

'An accident.' I shall never know, an inner voice cried. The unanswered questions could still torture her. Would she never be free of them? 'Icy road. His car hit a lorry.' Had Martin walked out on that December morning desperate and determined? Had he known what he would do? Clare had watched him with revulsion and pity as he went to the car, pathetically summoning the military walk, the brisk staff-officer persona which it had become harder and harder for him to assume.

She had not realized she was trembling till Donald's big warm hand came down over hers.

'I'm sorry, lass, I don't know what I was thinking of. I should never have asked you that. I was too taken up with my own affairs. The last thing I wanted to do was to upset you.'

'No, no, you didn't, it's all right,' Clare cried, feeling that comfort had come close and was in danger of being lost again. 'I don't mind, honestly. Because it wasn't – it wasn't as it seemed.' The hidden pain, the doubts and deception and shame, seemed to swell like a festering abscess which had never been lanced.

Donald gave her a sudden alert look. 'Have you ever talked about it?'

'No.' She could hardly hear that whisper herself. 'No. There was never anyone I could tell.'

'Would it help to talk?'

To you, oh God, yes, it would.

'I'd wondered if maybe you'd come up here to get over losing your husband,' Donald continued in that comfortable way of his that steadied her.

'Not exactly. Well, I suppose it was part of it. I'd never really faced up to it. I'd let the hotel take over, fill the days . . .'

'I know what you mean.' He looked away across the loch. Clare thought his mind had returned to Ishbel but he said, 'You talk if you want to, if you think it would help. There's no one else to hear. And I sometimes think talking is the only healing there is.'

What could she tell him of the uncertainties that had surrounded Martin's death, the suspicions that sometimes seemed so nebulous and absurd, at other times so utterly convincing? How could she put into words her own profound sense of failure, her guilt that she had never attempted to help Martin, except by agreeing to preserve the pretence of their marriage? And why had she agreed to that? Why had she stayed? At this distance the decision seemed inexplicable, cowardly. How to begin to talk about such things to straightforward Donald, in his sane clean world? But it would be a relief to tell him some of it. She heard her own voice, high and priggish, the voice people use when they think they're not being self-conscious about words like 'penis' and 'vagina', saying, 'He was a homosexual.'

'Go on,' Donald said, and Clare felt his absence of shock, yet his understanding of the giant step she had taken in saying this at last.

'There were . . . I should have realized sooner—' But she could not tell Donald or anyone else of the sickening shock it had been to walk into the sitting-room of their house that afternoon,

136

turning back unexpectedly from a walk because the heel had come off her shoe, to find the room full of the blare of *Grandstand* and Martin sprawled back in his chair, his shirt pulled out, his trousers open, his hands busy, with a look of ecstasy on his face which she had never seen there before, oblivious, absorbed, not knowing she had come or gone. She had never put into words her intense feeling of rejection, of fundamental inadequacy as a female. She turned hastily to another memory. 'Once, in the mess, well, I didn't exactly see anything –'

She wasn't sure afterwards how much she had managed to convey to Donald of that brief vignette, though it was starkly clear to her in every minute detail still. She had walked along the dim wide corridor, needing a respite of coolness and quiet away from the party, and she had seen through the half-open pantry door the narrow boyish shoulders and thin neck in the white steward's jacket, the fair hair and golden downy cheek, and the hand reaching out to touch that glowing skin with the most perfect tenderness – Martin's hand . . .

'He must have lived in torture. He was in a sensitive job, staff officer to someone very senior. Image was everything, you know the sort of thing. He'd begun to drink more, getting deeper and deeper into a terrible private struggle to maintain appearances. It was a nightmare to watch. I tried to talk to him but it was hopeless. We were two completely separate people sharing a house and keeping up a façade.'

'Why did you stay?' Donald's voice was so gentle it sounded like her own thoughts.

'I hardly know now,' she confessed. 'I suppose I believed it would have ruined his career if I'd gone, because he couldn't have stayed in that post. That's what he always said anyway. For him it would have been one more crack in the make-believe self he was trying so hard to hang on to. It was like watching someone being dragged down by some dreadful unstoppable suction.'

'It must have been pure hell for you, living like that.'

Clare was surprised at this view; she had seen it for so long as Martin's nightmare.

'You were glad when he died.' Simple, direct, the words were out, offering her the chance to face them at last.

She turned to look at Donald's watchful, compassionate face and knew he would make no judgements.

'I was so thankful,' she said, relief flooding through her.

Donald put his arm round her and she allowed herself the luxury of burying her face in his shoulder. For a long slow count of moments she drank in peace, comfort, and a lightening of conscience long delayed.

CHAPTER FIFTEEN

Magda was more than two hours late. Clare waited for her at the hotel, anxiously reviewing the directions she had given her and eyeing a threatening sky. She had an uneasy feeling that she had pushed too hard for this visit which Magda had so suddenly found time for. Ina was frantically busy with high teas and the whole place smelled of frying.

Then Magda was there, and waiting and impatience were forgotten in unequivocal pleasure to see her bounce up the steps with her familiar energy, vivid, confident, ready for the next thing. Clare hugged her closely in her delight, remembered they didn't do that and tossed the thought aside.

'My God, I haven't seen a house or a living soul for the last fifty miles!'

'I thought you'd got lost.'

'Lost! There's only one road!'

'It's *so* good to see you.'

'What on earth have you done to your hair?'

'Not much.' The sun had bleached it almost white round the temples and privately Clare had thought it looked not too bad against her tan, but she had been doing some hacking to keep it out of her eyes and her hand went up to it with a gesture she knew to be defensive.

'I can see that.' Magda paused long enough for one scarifying look which made Clare conscious of her battered jeans and mud-stained trainers before diving back into her own concerns. 'I had to check out the most marvellous place on the way up –'

What?

'– buried in the Cheviots, miles off the beaten track, and you wouldn't believe the menu. Look, I pinched one.'

'Show me later. I've left a casserole in the oven.'

'Can't we have a drink first? Or me anyway.'

'You can have one at home.'

'Oh, come on, Clare. I've been driving for hours.'

Two minutes later they were in the bar. 'You're quite right, it's ghastly,' Magda pronounced, gazing round with a shudder. 'You certainly weren't exaggerating.'

Clare's cheeks flamed. Will Morrison was behind the bar and Magda's voice was always emphatically confident. He must have heard. And how remote now seemed the person she had been on her first invasion of this room.

'So how about Carlini's? Are you madly busy?' she enquired hastily.

Magda was still refighting her battles over the conservatory roof, dry rot in the staff block and the kitchen porter's dermatitis as they swept over the hump-backed bridge, past Tigh Bhan and up the glen. 'You can't be serious,' she said when Clare told her to turn left. She loved her Porsche, most blatant and conventional of status symbols, inherited from a brother and past its first youth as it was. Clare had more than once wondered if it was some kind of penis substitute in Magda's arrogantly manless life. 'But where on earth are we going? Ouch, poor car! Is that the cottage?'

'That's the farm. We leave the car here.'

'Leave it here? But we can put it under cover somewhere, can't we?'

'It'll be fine.'

'But where's the cottage?' Magda demanded, staring round her at the steading buildings.

'By the loch.'

'So where's the loch?'

'Magda, you know it's a mile away.'

'You have to be joking.'

'Which suitcase will you need tonight?' But Clare knew the answer even as she asked.

'Oh, God, I don't know. I left in such a tearing hurry, had to fling everything in. You know what it's like.'

A vision of the attic flat they had shared rose before Clare's eyes; she knew what it was like. She made Magda put on what she called boots, high-heeled suede affairs that barely reached past her ankles, and a silky-textured pale trenchcoat. Clare felt the first touch of rain on her cheek as they set off with a cream leather suitcase apiece, a clinking plastic carrier bag and Magda's Gucci satchel which would have done as an overnight bag on its own.

Clare was thankful that the rain didn't get beyond a light mizzle though the distinction clearly meant little to Magda as she picked her way with disbelieving curses over the damp ground. By the time they reached the Larach she was much too enraged about the state of her hair and her feet to appreciate how welcoming the cottage looked, with everything lovingly polished, a big jar of lupins from Rhumore in the alcove by the fire and the fire itself high and red, both to cook the lamb and to make quite sure there were no mistakes about the bath water.

Another gin and a flurry of present giving, the warmth which Clare had grown unused to in summer and found stifling, and a squawking horrified tour of the premises restored some of Magda's equanimity.

'How absolutely revolting!' she cried at the sight of the bath, recoiling from its blue depths. 'Why on earth didn't you put in a new one?'

'I must have told you the saga of Thos McCosh. Anyway, you should have seen the state it was in before.'

'I'm glad I didn't. You don't expect me to get into it, do you? Don't you have a shower?'

'Water pressure's not good enough.'

'Can't you put a pump in?'

'Running on?'

'You don't mean to tell me you're still not connected? Even up here they can't be that useless. What's the hold-up?'

Clare stared at her, dumbfounded. Magda must surely have understood—

'God, what a museum piece! Aren't you terrified of blowing yourself up?' That was the gas cooker, but she was even more appalled when Clare took the casserole from the black depths of the coal oven.

'I thought you'd approve of good old country cooking,' Clare said, sounding more acid than she had intended.

'You dreamer.'

But it was undeniably fun to be with her again, back in the furious flow of argument and laughter.

'That's not some supermarket plonk I've brought you, you know. You can't open it for at least three days.'

'Relax, you're not flogging it to a customer. Shut up and open a bottle. Stick it on the hearth.'

'Sacrilege . . .'

'I knew the lamb personally, by the way.'

'That is unnecessarily primitive.'

'My own herbs –'

'Oh, spare me.'

The room had grown smaller, wildly strewn with Magda's belongings, but Clare knew it was good to have her solitary lifestyle shaken up.

'That dresser's a beauty. What would it fetch, do you think?'

'Forget it. It won't go through the door.'

'That chair's not bad either.'

'Hands off.'

Later Magda asked, 'You're drinking again?'

'Not much. Socially.'

'You really kicked it?'

'It's not been a problem here.' The single episode when she had succumbed seemed never to have had anything to do with the Larach and was in any case so blurred in her memory that it was as easy to dismiss as a bad dream. 'The whole way of life is so different.' But as she searched for words to attempt to describe the vastness of the difference Magda said, 'You dropped me in it, though, didn't you, taking off like that?'

Clare gaped at her. 'Magda, you can't still be—'

Magda paid no attention but rushed into a long tirade about the family strife she appeared to think Clare had caused. Paolo had bought the shares but was not prepared to involve himself in the actual running of the hotel. Not only the entire Carlini family but Paolo's wife's family as well had become embroiled in the argument. It was so intricate and of such passionate interest to Magda that it occupied most of her attention till it was time to go to bed.

There was no discussion as to who would sleep where. 'What

a fiendish contraption,' Magda said damningly as Clare began to impose her will on the sofa. 'I hope you've got a decent mattress on that hideous bed next door.'

It took Clare a long time to get to sleep. Not that the sofa-bed was uncomfortable, once she had deferred to its demands, but she was stirred up by the talk and wine and acutely conscious of another presence in the house. The room was unpleasantly warm, littered and unfamiliar, hung with the smells of food and Magda's scent. She had made such an issue about the door being locked that Clare felt it would be unfair to get up and open it to the cool, clean night air.

She felt even more restless while waiting for Magda to surface the next morning and was dismayed by her inability to settle to anything. Was her new independence so flimsy?

Magda staggered out from the bedroom eventually in a mood Clare knew well – refuelled energy erupting through sleep-blurred grumpiness. Without the carapace of make-up she looked ten years older, her olive skin greenish, her face sagging in sour morning lines. Clare was pleased when she crossed at once to the door – the morning was bright, her new world looking glorious – but Magda only wanted to shut it, complaining petulantly, 'It's absolutely freezing in here.'

'It's probably warmer outside,' Clare suggested. 'I usually—'

'Isn't that uncouth object a heater?'

Huddled by the gas fire, her small hands claws round a mug of black coffee, she asked fractiously, 'Are you sure we can't get the car any nearer? There must be a road somewhere.'

'We won't need the car.'

'Of course we will. I'm going to take you somewhere decent for lunch.'

'I thought we could just potter about today, have lunch here. I can show you—'

What could she show her? Had she seriously imagined that Magda would want to wander idly along the shore or sit up at the cairn and feast her eyes on the expanse of loch and hills, islands and sound dreaming in the blue July haze? Suddenly Clare saw it through Magda's eyes – spartan little hovel furnished with saleroom junk, grass and sheep outside the door, nothing whatever to do.

With most apposite timing, Magda asked aggrievedly, 'What on earth do you find to do with yourself anyway?'

Where had the contented weeks gone? Out of all the hours spent on house and garden Clare was unable to pinpoint a single job worth showing her. And what else had she done? Sat in Margaret's kitchen and laughed over such trivia as Mrs McGillivray from Glen Righ backing the school minibus into the burn to the delight of the children. Established a light-hearted friendship with Trudy Thompson in gaps between customers, with endless coffee and frivolous chatter, and finally met Trudy's vague and disorganized husband Ben. Sat on the terrace at Tigh Bhan eating marvellous al fresco meals, spent hot scratchy hours helping Gerald to brash their small plantation, browsed through their hundreds of books. She had grown fond of Lilias with her shrewd humour, her undiminished thirst for information on every imaginable subject, her brisk competence.

Sandy Maitland had come over several times to fish; they had feasted on sea trout and she had longed for a freezer. Dougie Stewart had taught her to drive a tractor and she had wuffled hay. She had tried her hand at clipping sheep and had helped Calum Macdonald's wife, Peggy, with lunches and teas for the men. She had gradually put names to faces; she had settled in.

And always there had been Donald. On seeing him, talking to him, clashing often as their different views and backgrounds met in head-on collision but always able to arrive at an acceptable truce, working alongside him at unfamiliar jobs, learning from him, enjoying his quiet humour and sound sense, she knew her contentment had been founded. And as she hesitated, knowing she could never make Magda understand how satisfying this had been, she heard Donald's step outside.

She knew Magda was just up and detested being caught with naked face, but not then or later did Clare think there was any excuse for the way she behaved.

Donald had come to ask if they would like to go with him to a farm on the far side of Loch Luig where he wanted to look at a baler, and he had brought with him an old-fashioned milk-pail full of thick yellow cream.

'A boat trip?' Magda shuddered. 'Nothing I'd hate more, thanks. I intend to keep as far away as possible from all that water. You'll have to look elsewhere for a fare, I'm afraid.'

Horrified, Clare leapt in. 'Magda, Donald's come miles out of his way to give us the chance to go with him. It would be perfect out on the sound today.'

'He had to deliver the milk, didn't he?'

'It's cream, and it's a present, you idiot. Donald, thank you so much for thinking of it, and for offering to take us with you. I'd have loved it. You'll stay and have coffee, won't you? Come and sit down.'

Trim, having greeted Clare, padded across to inspect the stranger. Magda shrieked, jerking up her arm and splashing coffee over her chair. 'Ugh, get away, don't come near me! Clare, do something, you know I can't stand dogs.'

At a flick of Donald's fingers Trim was beside him and he was opening the door and ordering her out.

'Quick, Clare, get a cloth. It's gone over my skirt.' Magda was angrily on her feet, turning her solid hip towards the light. Donald stood wooden-faced just inside the door. Clare gave him one pleading look as she went for a cloth, afraid he would be gone when she came back. He must have caught it for he paced across to the table, pulled out a chair and sat down.

How Clare wished she had let him go as Magda released some of her annoyance by patronizing him outrageously, while Clare herself felt she could hardly apologize openly for the behaviour of her guest. Not surprisingly, Donald did not find much to say in response to such remarks as, 'We did our best to stop her rushing off to the back of beyond but she was absolutely determined – though I suppose it's not so bad for someone who lives here all the time.'

He wasted little time over his coffee.

'Thank you so much for bringing the cream. It was really good of you,' Clare said again as he got up to go, wanting to send him some placatory signal.

'Oh, yes, the cream. Do you have change?' asked Magda, and before Clare could stop her she had reached for her bag and handed him a ten-pound note.

Donald gave her one considering look and turned to the door.

'Magda, don't be idiotic! Donald's giving us the cream. I told you. Donald—'

'It's all right,' he said, checking her firmly, and went out with a nod to Magda.

Clare rushed after him. 'Donald, I'm so sorry. Magda didn't realize—'

'You go back to your friend.' She had never seen his face so unrelenting.

'I'll come and see you off.' She always went down to the boat with him.

'Not today.' She could feel his anger, solid as a wall.

'Magda didn't understand.'

But Donald merely shook his head and set off with his long stride down to the jetty. Nothing had ever looked so uncompromising to Clare as that rigid back. Is that what Donald saw in me too? she wondered appalled, turning back reluctantly to the house. No wonder he was so ready to jump down my throat when I was tactless and critical. But was I ever quite that blatant about it? She was terribly afraid that she had been, and more clearly than ever she saw how much Donald had taught her. It was largely because he had saved her from so many obvious pitfalls that she had been accepted here with such general goodwill.

CHAPTER SIXTEEN

'How *could* you?'

'What are you talking about?'

Clare was nearly speechless with anger and distress. 'You know Donald's a friend. You know how good he's been to me.'

'I thought it was the local boatman touting for custom.'

'You thought no such thing. I told you who he was.'

'Well, the name didn't mean anything to me.'

'But in my letters—'

'Oh God, Clare, I never had time to read them. They were all exactly the same anyway.'

Clare blinked at her, shaken at the scale of this rebuff, not sure whether tears or rage would overtake her first. Magda knew that she had gone too far. Clare saw it in her eyes as she swiftly changed tack. 'Oh, come on, this is silly. I'm sorry if I wasn't nice enough to your pal, but he did seem a total . . . all right, all right, I won't say it. Look, why don't we head off right away, find somewhere to have lunch, give you a change of scene?' Clare suspected that the word 'treat' had been on the tip of her tongue and was glad she had amended it. 'I'll have a quick bath –'

'You can't, there's no hot water.'

'Are you serious?'

'You used it all last night.' Magda's horror at the bath had disappeared when it suited her.

'Well, don't you have an—?'

'An immersion heater? No, I don't.' Clare's carefully level tone got through.

Magda gave an elaborate shrug and went off muttering, 'Really! I don't see how anyone could possibly bear . . .'

Clare took a few deep breaths, cleared away the coffee things and washed up.

Magda reappeared in her slip (she had put on weight, Clare observed) and carrying her blouse. 'Can I iron this?'

Clare stared at her.

'Oh, for God's sake,' Magda groaned. 'Well, what do you do?'

'Flat irons.' Donald's flat irons – I should have gone after him. 'When the fire's going.'

'I don't believe this. So what do you suggest?'

'Wear it as it is. Wear another one.'

'They're all in the same state.'

'Borrow one of mine.' Not tactful, but it wasn't meant to be.

'What about your peasant chorus? Can't we borrow an iron from one of them?'

'Magda!'

'Go and iron there, then. Whatever.'

Clare knew that Lilias was in Fort William, probably shopping for the dinner party she was giving two days hence for Magda, and that Ina was run off her feet, but she must have been out of her mind, as she told herself more than once afterwards, to take Magda to Margaret's.

The children had just been given a crème egg each and were masked in the revolting contents. The young collie was banging a saucepan against the skirting board in an engrossed effort to remove the last morsels of food from its dents. The remains of a very sloppy breakfast were still on the table. Margaret was scarlet with mortification as she struggled with an ironing-board with a scorched cover and produced an equally blackened iron, the kinks of its flex pulling with it from the cupboard as it came a horrid collection of stained and stiffened rags.

'How could you take me to such a—?'

'How could you be so rude and ungrateful?'

They were hissing venomously at each other before the door was shut behind them. Clare asked Magda to stop in the village, as much to have a couple of minutes to cool down as to ask Angus to send some baps with Nicol the next morning. Magda followed her into the shop, however, and entertained herself by poking though the tins of cook-in sauces and the Bonnie Scotland tea-towels. Angus was looking very boot-faced by the time Clare hustled her out.

Magda was vociferously appalled at the resources of Fort William. Clare's own first reaction had been the same, she reminded herself, trying to be fair, but Magda's assumption that Clare would laugh with her at the natives made her feel hotly protective and defensive now. They ended up in Inverness, snarling up the crowded A82 past caravans and laden holiday cars, and Magda at once went off to bully or bribe a hairdresser into giving her a shampoo on the grounds that she couldn't face the Larach bathroom.

Clare sat for a few minutes on a low sun-baked wall, watching the slow drift of tourists and getting her anger under control. A child buffeted by arguing adults dropped his ice cream and was swept on yelling unheeded protests. Clare looked at the white splat on the pavement: albatross dropping. The omens were bad.

I've put this behind me, she thought rebelliously, the crowds, the traffic noise, the tainted air, the hideous encrustation of advertising on once-dignified buildings. What on earth am I doing here on this perfect day when I could have been in Donald's boat, or swimming in the loch, or lying in the sun on my own beach?

Donald. The memory of his closed face had been with her all day. Would he feel she had condoned Magda's behaviour? She was oppressed to realize that briefly and fatally she had seen her life at the Larach through Magda's eyes.

'Shall we stop off for a drink?' The Porsche was already sweeping round to park outside the Inverbuie Hotel.

'I thought you despised the place.'

'Must have something to fortify me for that hike to the cottage.'

'I ought to get the fire going so we'll have hot water later.'

'Do you mean to say you didn't leave it lit?'

'We were only supposed to be going out for lunch,' Clare pointed out. Every conversation seemed to be a confrontation.

'All the more reason to have a gin, then,' Magda said, banging the car door in a way she swore at other people for doing.

She disappeared after the first drink. Clare made stilted

conversation with Will, who would not meet her eyes, and wondered what Magda would have to say about the ladies', and if she'd say it at the top of her voice as she came back. She was away for ages. With a sudden dread that she might be taking a professional interest in Ina's activities, Clare went in search of her. She found her coming down the stairs, flushed and triumphant. Had she been having a quick screw with a member of the bus party? Clare found that being with Magda again made her thoughts and language revert to a level she had abandoned here without even being aware of it.

'Ready to go?' Magda called gaily, as though it were she who had been waiting.

'What on earth have you been doing?'

'Having a bath.'

'Without asking?' Clare really hated her in that moment.

'Of course I asked. I wanted a decent-sized towel for one thing – some hope – and a piece of soap bigger than an After Eight.'

'You pestered poor Ina?'

'You look like a very cross goldfish. Whatever's happened to you these days?'

'You went barging into the kitchen when Ina's up to her eyes putting out about a hundred high teas? I can imagine how pleased you'd be if someone—'

'Oh, Clare, lighten up. I gave her a fiver, can't be bad. Anyway, I did you a favour, now you don't have to worry about that fire of yours.'

I might like a bath myself, Clare refrained from saying.

They did get round to talking in the end, not without wounds.

'I'll say this much for your inarticulate chum, this is gorgeous cream,' Magda said, spooning it liberally over the chicken tarragon.

'He's not inarticulate.'

'Well, he didn't have much to say for himself this morning. You don't fancy him, do you? You can't be that hard up.'

Clare slammed down the handful of silver she had been about to take through to the sitting-room. 'What is it with you? Why do you want to attack him? Or do you just want to attack me?'

'OK, OK, don't fly off the handle.'

They smoothed down their feathers and got on with dinner (Magda even approved of the fresh tarragon) but it didn't take much to make Clare release some of her simmering indignation. She had got up to push the kettle on to the fire ready for coffee and Magda had commented, exasperation unmistakable through the attempt at teasing, 'All this Boy Scout rigmarole. You've got a cooker next door, remember, such as it is.'

Clare turned on her, goaded. 'Why are you being so bloody-minded about everything? Why don't you at least try to understand why I came here, what I was searching for?'

'I know why you came here. You were stressed out and you needed some space. But you can't expect me to believe that you really enjoy this. It's awful! And you must be going out of your mind with boredom.'

'I haven't been bored for a single moment since I came.'

'Oh, come on, you know that can't be true. You've got a first-class brain, qualifications, ability—'

'You aren't listening to me. You never listen. You haven't the slightest interest in anything outside your own affairs.'

'You were glad enough to be included in them when your own life had fallen apart.'

Clare held on to control. 'Yes, I was, and you know I was grateful. But you never asked why my life had fallen apart, did you?'

'You'd lost your husband,' Magda said, genuinely surprised.

'He killed himself.' Clare must have been shaken to the depths, she realized with a flash of objectivity, to face this at last, to say it. For of course that was how it had been.

'I didn't know that,' Magda said, forced into a tone of grudging apology. 'But it's more than three years ago, Clare. You have to get on with life.'

Clare was thunderstruck, then amusement took over. 'Of course you're right,' she agreed humbly. 'Silly me.'

Magda gave her a sharp glance then looked shamefaced. 'Oh, well, I'm sorry, but this' – with an irritable wave around the cluttered room – 'can't have anything to do with that, surely?'

'Look, Magda, we both know the state I was in when we met and I'll never forget what I owe you for giving me a job, getting me motivated again.'

'But?' Wary, hostile.

'You must have realized there were things connected with Martin's death that I never talked about, had never made myself face up to. When I started working in the hotel all I did was bury the memories deeper. In the end I felt I was living a lie, losing control of my own life, being carried along in a direction I hadn't chosen for myself, a direction that was wrong for me.'

'Being pushed by me, you mean?' Magda's face showed her impatience and distaste. She loathed introspection and what she always dismissed as 'deep' conversations. The air was suddenly electric with challenge.

'Yes.' It was said. 'You are a stronger person than I am. You were consuming me.'

'How melodramatic!' Magda exclaimed. 'How ridiculous!'

'By coming here I was trying to make myself free of extraneous influences and pressures, decide what sort of person I really am. Nothing too profound,' Clare added, trying to keep things light.

Magda would have none of it. 'It's called dropping out, isn't it?' she said viciously. 'And coming to a place like this! It's bizarre, self-indulgent, pointless. You're completely out of touch, you haven't a clue what's going on in the world, you don't meet anyone, you don't even have television. You can't get to theatres or concerts' – since when had Magda had the time or the inclination for either? – 'and this absurd business of looking like some teenage scruff, dirty jeans, no make-up, living in squalor—'

'I've found things here that I value,' Clare said, refusing to be rattled.

'What, for example?'

'Peace.'

'Peace! Is that what you call it?'

'I don't mean the lack of noise.'

'Well, that's all very well for a while,' Magda said, suspecting irony and passing irritably on. 'But you'll have to come back to the real world sooner or later.'

The real world. How simplistic. But Clare knew nothing would be achieved by saying what she thought of Magda's values. And equally Magda would froth with impatience if she tried to describe the pleasure she had found here in simple ordinary things, the discoveries she had made about a world she had never taken time to look at properly before. Nor could she risk attempting to explain to Magda her pride in having survived cold and loneliness and the need for alcohol, her gratitude for the kindness she had received, her sense for the first time she could remember of putting down roots.

'You can come back to Carlini's any time you like, you know.'

Clare jerked out of her thoughts. 'Come back?'

'I know the first couple of years were hard but we can take things more easily now. If you didn't want to live in again you could buy a house, come in whenever it suited you, just run the office. You wouldn't have to chat to customers or empty ashtrays or check in wine deliveries on winter afternoons. We'd get a receptionist for the nitty-gritty. I want to concentrate on the food. The demand is definitely there and we've had one or two terrific write-ups recently. I brought a couple to show you, hang on . . .'

Clare stared at Magda's back incredulously as she stooped over the sofa to fish in her bag. This was why she was here. She would never have considered coming if it hadn't suited her own purposes. Everything had been mapped out. Paolo may have agreed to come in but Magda still needed someone to take the tedious admin off her hands. And I, thought Clare with ominous calm, would be conveniently softened up by now by isolation and discomfort and mental stagnation.

'So that's why you came.'

'Look, this food writer came. She drooled over the place. She's been back since, in fact, strictly privately, turned up with di Senzo of all people.'

'I thought we were friends. I thought you had come to see me.'

'What?' Magda glanced at Clare's stiff face and turned down her mouth dismissively. 'Well, of course, but you could hardly imagine this would be my scene, could you?'

'You only came to persuade me to go back?'

'It's a good offer, Clare. You can make your own terms.'

She was quite unaware of any other issue. The friendship Clare had clung to had not existed. Theirs had been a working relationship, functional, enjoyable even, but entirely dependent on the shared enterprise of Carlini's.

'I'll make the coffee,' Clare said.

'This lot drove us nearly demented for two days,' Magda went on, studying a photograph with satisfaction. 'Worth it, though.'

In the kitchen Clare stood clutching the edge of the sink, staring down at the stacked-up pans filled with scummy water, a clutch of spoons sticking out of them. She was filled with a dull anger at her own naivety.

CHAPTER SEVENTEEN

'I still don't see why you don't get wheels,' Magda panted, breaking a silence bursting with suppressed antagonism. 'You could get over here in a jeep or something, couldn't you?'

'I could, most of the time.'

Magda paused to scowl at Clare, resting her suitcase on a rock intricately patterned with whorls of grey-green lichen. 'That's what's so idiotic. You're deliberately making everything more primitive than it needs to be. If you must live here you could perfectly well afford to put in electricity, a phone, heat the place properly. You could build on, have a decent bathroom and kitchen. You could drive over, get a boat even. What's it *about*?'

Too late, too aggressive. But that wasn't why Clare didn't answer. Having seen it through Magda's cynical eyes she wasn't sure any more that she could adequately explain or justify what she was doing here.

No time was wasted over farewells. 'The offer's there,' Magda said. 'Let me know if you change your mind.' She was convinced that Clare would see sense eventually.

It was like the end of an affair when there is nothing left to say but you cannot bear to accept that it's over. Aching with a profound sense of loss which she knew Magda did not share, Clare watched the Porsche weave carefully along the track, then surge away down the glen road to vanish in seconds behind the plantation. What rival establishments would Magda plunder for ideas on her way south? she wondered.

Two nights and one day, after waiting so long for this visit. Hollow, tired, disliking the almost forgotten sensations of having drunk too much red wine last night and with a strange feeling of disconnection from everything around her, Clare started for home. Then she remembered the milk and turned back to the old dairy. Nicol had brought the extra baps she had asked for.

Halfway to the Larach she remembered Lilias's dinner-party, but felt unable to face her yet with explanations and apologies. Instead she went blindly on, to shut herself up in the untidy house and sink into the sort of depression she hadn't experienced since Martin died. She found herself arguing endlessly in her head with Magda, raw at her callousness, feeling betrayed by her easy dismissal of their friendship. But she didn't resort to drinking this time, though the means and the temptation were to hand.

She tried not to think of Donald, hurting again at the memory of his shut, unforgiving face. She knew from her own experience how angry he could be when faced with the sort of arrogance Magda had displayed and wished desperately she had not let him go without insisting on putting matters right.

It was the knowledge that Donald would expect better of her than this self-pitying inertia which made her rouse herself in the end. Though as she sorted out the mess which seemed to have spread into every corner of the house, wondering as the sofa sprang like a trap into its daytime mode whether it would ever be slept on again, she told herself that after the way Magda had treated him she would be surprised if she ever saw him here again.

Then she walked to Tigh Bhan. It was a bad time to choose. Lilias was talking on the telephone in the hall, Gerald panicking to find himself suddenly in charge of dinner.

'Damned inconsiderate of Stephen. He should know better than to phone at dinner time,' he fumed, snatching at a saucepan lid and leaping back with a cry of pain, flipping his fingers to cool them. The dogs milled about his feet in the reasonable hope that something would shortly come their way.

Damned inconsiderate of her too, Clare knew. She suggested coming back at a better time, perhaps after dinner, but Gerald wouldn't hear of it and launched at once into the turmoil of getting her a drink. So, annoyed with herself for her thoughtlessness, she pushed a couple of pans to a cooler spot, made sure no crises were imminent, and waited uncomfortably for Lilias. She came in at last, her mouth a moue of displeasure and reserve, her face strained and tired. She didn't meet Clare's eyes as she greeted her, which was not like her in the least.

'I hope you told him he was ruining my dinner,' Gerald grumbled with splendid selfishness.

'He was going out,' said Lilias crisply, taking a pan to the sink to strain it. 'You'll stay, of course, Clare? There's plenty of everything.'

Clare knew she hadn't given her much choice about the invitation. 'No, honestly, thanks, Lilias. I'm sorry to come at such a bad time. I just wanted—'

'Gerald's given you a drink?'

'Yes, thank you. I came to tell you that Magda's had to go back. I'm so sorry about tomorrow.'

'I heard this morning that she had left.' Lilias flapped steam away from her face and gave Clare a very buttons-off look.

These damned people, thought Clare with irritation. Was everything public news? But her annoyance was sheer bad conscience and her cheeks burned. 'I really am sorry. I should have let you know at once. I do hope you haven't gone to a lot of trouble.'

'I have, as it happens,' Lilias said. 'Not that it matters. Everything can be used or frozen.'

This was not the moment, Clare saw, to try and tell her how she herself felt about Magda's departure. She had been looking for comfort, sure Lilias would be on her side. It was a disagreeable shock to find that Lilias, like everyone Magda had upset or patronized, seemed to hold her, Clare, responsible. There was nothing to do but apologize again and go before she disrupted their evening any further.

Clare did some serious thinking during the next couple of days, during which she saw no one, turning over possible future plans and even making herself consider the option of returning to Carlini's. Her findings were definite. She wanted to stay where she was until she had some compelling reason to leave. Everything she had found in this place was important to her. She would make her peace where possible, and as far as Donald was concerned she would not clutch at another relationship based on her own need. There was nothing in the past to cling to; she accepted that at last. She had this house and whatever future she could establish for herself, and that was all.

There remained one loose end connected with the past, however, and she had put off dealing with it for far too long. She must write to Joe and put the record straight. He was unlikely to be at RAF Eland still, but she had an idea there was some central clearing house for Air Force mail and was fairly sure that anything sent to him there would be forwarded.

It wasn't easy to decide on the tone of the letter. She planned and replanned it during a long walk beyond Righ Bay, the scene that afternoon in the Officers' Mess when she had learned the truth about what Martin had done returning with all its outraged disbelief sharp and fresh.

They had left Marbury by this time and Martin was in the staff officer post he had so much coveted. He was utterly committed to pleasing his 'master' and more than ever insistent on Clare's support. He was up early and away to the office or frequently to the residence, or off on those high-powered visits which could not be left to the ADC. He was often on duty for evening functions and occasionally away overnight, which Clare soon came to regard as one of the bonuses of the post. He became fanatical about his appearance and Clare could find herself ironing a dozen service shirts a week and never seemed to be out of the dry-cleaners. He also agonized over the increasing paunchiness his drinking and too many lengthy official lunches and dinners were producing. There was a lot of meticulously planned entertaining and endless storms about what Clare thought adequate and he did not. Worst of all there were far too many uneasy gatherings of the staffs of the various air officers who, since they all did the same job, were arbitrarily considered a social unit. What Clare chiefly loathed about these occasions was the way Martin and the senior staff officer relentlessly pulled rank, even at so-called relaxed gatherings like barbecues or pub suppers. The wives of the ADCs eyed her without favour; she could hardly blame them.

Once more she was obliged to involve herself in Wives' Club activities and it was on one of those afternoons when she had grudgingly given up a couple of hours to the tedious pursuit of doing table arrangements for a dining-in night that she heard the shattering news. She was standing at a pantry draining board stuffing unnatural-looking florist's flowers into riddled oasis and morosely wondering whether it was more endurable to be here doing this than passing the time alone in the house they had bought in the village. (The new boss thought every forward-looking officer should be in the property market.) She had been paying no attention to the indiscreet conversation going on behind her till a name alerted her.

'Not the lovely Joe Parfitt? I don't believe it!'

'It's true. Terry told me.'

'Posted for chatting up an officer's wife?'

'That's what he said. And a bit more than chatting up by the sound of it.'

'You have to be joking. Joe was such an old stick in spite of the way he looked. Anyway, we never got very far, did we?'

'All that agonizing keep-fit at Whitmore! Totally wasted.'

Giggles. 'So come on, what went on?'

'Apparently she used to take part in those weekends Joe ran in Wales, camps or something.'

'How did she manage that? We were never invited.'

'She must have had something. Anyway, she obviously didn't like where it got her and complained to her husband that Joe had leapt on her or something.'

'*Joe?*'

'I know, incredible, isn't it? Anyway the husband happened to be OC Admin, so it was easy to have Joe quietly buried. Had him sent to RAF Eland of all places.'

'Never heard of it. So there wasn't a court-martial or anything heavy?'

'No, it was kept very low-key evidently. There must have been something in it, though. Terry says Joe will never make sergeant now.'

'But didn't I hear he'd been recommended for a commission at some stage?'

'Yes, that's right. I'd forgotten that. Poor old Joe. What a bitch . . .'

Clare had walked back to the village in a blur of rage and shock, remembering the inexplicable chill she had encountered at Marbury after Joe had so suddenly disappeared, and the absolute clamp-down on news of him afterwards. She had waited tensely for Martin to come home, and could remember her choking helplessness at his bland stone-walling. First he had pretended not to know who she was talking about, then had vaguely recalled the corporal who had run the Welsh weekends from Marbury. Then he had simply fallen back on the tried and true protective screen of service confidentiality. But once or twice that evening Clare had caught him looking at her with what seemed a furtive, even excited, triumph.

Having decided to try to speak to Joe, Clare had been amazed at the ease with which the switchboard operator had run him to earth. His familiar voice was answering before she had time to calm her thumping heart.

'Joe?' Her voice wavered, prepared words fled.

'Yes?' Alert, placing.

'Joe, it's Clare.'

A fractional pause then, very brisk, 'Yes, ma'am, what can I do for you?'

'Joe, I must talk to you. I've just found out—'

'Sorry, ma'am, if this is a personal call I'm not allowed to take it while on duty.'

She had thought at first he was simply being discreet. 'Then when could I phone? Can you give me another number?'

'I can't give you any information about that, I'm afraid, ma'am.'

Was someone else there? 'For God's sake stop calling me that! But listen, Joe, I've just found out what happened.'

'As this isn't a service call I'm afraid I shall have to clear the line.' Obdurate, controlled.

'Please, Joe, it's important—'

He had cut her off. She had been shaking so violently she could barely replace the receiver.

Then she had done nothing. How could she make public the fact that her husband had had an NCO posted for what she presumed were motives of personal jealousy? And how could she risk any investigation that would involve Martin, already suspecting what she did about him?

And after Martin's death the issue of Joe had become second-ary, almost unimportant, compared to her fear that what she had suspected about Martin would finally be uncovered. She had stayed in the house alone, shutting the door to the effects officer appointed to look after his affairs, the Benevolent Fund representative, the padre, to his 'master' as she had detested Martin calling him, and to the well-intentioned wives.

Uncertainty and anxiety had tormented her. There had been the discovery of unexplained payments out of the account, regular but lately steeply increasing, which she had known nothing about. As an administrative officer, Martin had been accounts trained and looking after their financial affairs had always been his province. Clare had rather enjoyed the luxury of being able to leave it to him. All she knew was that there was always enough for her needs, household or personal, and she trusted in his expertise.

Her mother's house had been sold during the period when the housing market was doing astonishing things. Even the purchase of a house Martin had considered appropriate for his present rank and future prospects (and if he succeeded in pleasing in this post they would be very good indeed) had left a most adequate slice of capital which he had carefully invested – and, she had found, drawn on heavily in the last year. Horribly, inescapably, Clare had seen how these withdrawals tied in with his slow disintegration under pressures she could still only guess at, pressures which had grown so insupportable that he had almost certainly taken his own life. The service was remorseless on the subject of homosexuality and swift to act if the merest suspicion of it arose. In Martin's position the ramifications would have been far-reaching in terms of damage and drama. He would not have fallen from a great height alone. She was harried by the fear that if someone had been blackmailing Martin he could threaten even now to expose him.

Sometimes, almost incapable of rational thought after another sleepless night, she would wonder if she had a duty to inform someone of her suspicions before a monumental service scandal broke. Then she would see that this was more a desperate need to share the burden with someone, perhaps receive some reassurance that she had imagined the whole thing, than any responsible or useful action. Perhaps Martin's death had been pure accident after all. Then a dozen images, momentary glimpses which had meant nothing at the time, would come crowding disturbingly back, explicable at last.

She had withdrawn into herself completely, hardly moving outside the house, doing literally nothing for hours on end, for days at a stretch. Until she had met Magda.

She breathed in with deep thankfulness the scent of bog-myrtle and salt air and sea-wrack, allowing the details of her present surroundings to reclaim her. Recently clipped ewes, white and leggy, grazed the rich summer herbage beside their rounder grubbier lambs; patches of vivid colour glowed in the sun where bell heather was already out; the rocks below her were golden with lichen above the tideline, black below; wading birds were busy on the wet sand, gulls drifted up the thermals and two fishing boats phutted peacefully up the sound. Clare was aware of a fierce impulse of possessiveness, of determination to hold on to this no matter what.

Surely all she needed to say to Joe was that she had known nothing of the reasons behind his abrupt removal from Marbury. It was not necessary to refer to Martin. Even so, it took her most of the evening to write the letter.

She walked over to the farm to catch Nicol with it the next morning, but missed him. Her milk was there and a communication about a building society merger. Written neatly in intermittent biro on the back was the succinct message: 'Donald said to tell you he'll not be. Nicol McNicol.'

'He'll not be.' The elliptical phrase rang with an empty and final sound.

It was a prompt test of her new resolution to stay. The decision had been based on many things and had not been solely dependent on her feelings for Donald or his continuing friendship, but she knew life here would be very different if that had truly been withdrawn. She had not believed it possible till she read those bald words. He had often been impatient, as she was well aware, with what he saw as her unthinking and superficial criticisms of the way of life she found here. Had he thought she had condoned Magda's behaviour? Had he seen them as on the same side, as it were? Surely she had made it clear that she was furious with Magda? If only she could talk to Donald about it, get the whole thing out into the open. If she never had the chance to do that, if he vanished, she was going to mind very much. But as she set off to the village to post her letter she felt resolve harden. Even if Magda had gone too far with Donald for fences to be mended there were other people who deserved apologies for her behaviour, and Clare intended to waste no further time in offering them.

CHAPTER EIGHTEEN

Margaret was the person most heavily on Clare's conscience and the one among Magda's victims she would have thought the least likely to forgive or forget offence, so she was prepared for embarrassed reserve at best when she knocked on the dog-scratched door of The Birks. To her astonishment Margaret gave a squeak of pleasure at the sight of her and made an awkward little clutch at her arm, which Clare thought might have been an embryo hug.

'Come away in,' Margaret said without hesitation, adding with a darting questioning look over her shoulder as they went into the house, 'Dougie told me your friend was away again.'

'Yes, she's gone. It was a total disaster, as you probably gathered,' Clare told her, getting to the point at once. 'I came to say—'

'Well, I'm glad she's gone, that's all I can say,' Margaret burst out wrathfully, stopping dead and swinging round to face her. 'She had no right making a fool of you that way. I didn't know where to put myself. It was as good as saying your house wasn't fit. I could have seen her far enough, I can tell you, shaming you like that . . .'

This view was entirely unexpected. 'But I came to apologize for being such a nuisance,' Clare protested.

'Oh, she didna' put me up nor down,' Margaret declared, airily and untruthfully. 'She's nothing to me. When Dougie told me she was away I said to myself, well, that's the best thing I've heard for a long time. Who needs the like of yon?'

It was borne in on Clare that Margaret had no idea that her

household arrangements had not come up to scratch. What Clare had interpreted as mortification at their deficiencies had been indignation on her own behalf.

'I know she's your friend and that,' Margaret was shouting over the reassuring roar of water jetting into the kettle, 'but to my way of thinking you're a lot better off without that sort.'

Clare realized that pure partisanship had given Margaret the courage for this unusual outspokenness and she was warmed by relief and gratitude.

'Oh yes, Margaret was like a bantam hen ready to fly at all comers in your defence,' Lilias told her. 'And Ina was just as loyal and indignant. In her view by demanding a bath at the hotel Magda was announcing to the world that you couldn't look after your own guest properly.'

'It never crossed my mind they'd react like that,' Clare admitted, amused but also rather humbled.

'I think everyone felt sorry for you.'

Except Donald, Clare thought with a stab of pain.

Lilias had surprised her too. 'Oh, my dear, I'm so glad you've come,' she had called from the depths of the herbaceous border when Clare had gone in search of her. 'I was so horrid to you the other evening, it's been on my conscience ever since. I went over to the Larach the next day to apologize but you weren't there. I was intending to go over again this afternoon to try to find you.'

'But, Lilias, you had every right—'

'I was upset about something else,' Lilias interrupted firmly, emerging backside first from among the delphiniums and beating earth from her filthy gloves. 'The truth is, I'd had some rather disturbing news. It was fortunate for Gerald that you were there or it would have been his head that was bitten off.' She gave Clare a little smile of deprecation.

'I should have let you know at once that Magda had gone. It was awful of me to leave it till evening.'

'Well, yes, it was rather,' Lilias agreed matter-of-factly. 'But I'd put everything on hold as soon as I heard she'd gone through the village on her own. And no one else was involved in the party. If I hadn't been so worried about Stephen's news I should have insisted that you came on your own anyway.'

'Bad news?' Clare asked tentatively, recalling Lilias's strained look which Clare had attributed to anger with her.

'Oh, worrying, I suppose. Oliver is due to go to Gordonstoun in September, as you know, and Lucy has decided that she doesn't want him to.'

'But it must have been decided long ago, surely?'

'Years ago, of course. There was a tremendous amount of debate about it originally, but Lucy did finally agree. And Oliver takes it for granted that he's going.'

'Does he want to?'

'Dead keen. It will suit him ideally, too.'

'So what's Lucy's objection?' Clare offered the question diffidently, not sure how much Lilias would wish to tell her about a family row.

They had walked back towards the house and Lilias stopped at the bottom of the terrace steps as though she could not tackle them. She looked suddenly crumpled and old, and Clare was moved when she accepted the offer of an arm which normally she would have disdained. 'They are so different,' she said tiredly, as though to herself. 'Lucy versus the barbarians.'

There seemed nothing to say.

'Come along,' Lilias exclaimed, summoning up her characteristic vigour again. 'I picked pounds of currants this morning. You can help me to pick them over while we have tea and then you must take some home with you. Yes, I insist, you know perfectly well that we can't use a quarter of the fruit we grow. I offered some to Ina, but she told me kindly that it's easier to use pie filling. Her tone implied it was a good invention I would never have heard of.'

Clare knew she was meant to laugh, but she felt too concerned to be very convincing. Lilias was so lively and domineering it was easy to forget that she must be well into her eighties. It was sad to see her worried and showing her weariness. How glad Clare was that she had misread her sharpness when she had come to tell her Magda had gone. To lose Lilias's good opinion would matter to her now.

Angus was cool for a while, and Clare had to listen to several home truths about the English from Ina, but the general reaction to Magda seemed to have been resentment on Clare's behalf which surprised and touched her.

Even Trudy had heard about it. 'Glad you didn't bring her here,' she said, busy packing new supplies of mackerel from the local smoke-house into the depths of the freezer.

Clare passed her the next pack. 'She might have met her match.'

'True – oh lord, is that the bell? I've been trying to get this lot away for about an hour.'

'I'll go on with it. Is it all the same?'

'Salmon goes on the left. Then this stuff has to go back starting from this end. You're a star. Shan't be a sec.'

The storeroom on the ground floor of the mill, with the river shouldering past just outside the barred windows, was shiveringly cold on the warmest day and Clare got on with the job as rapidly as possible. Ben, no doubt, was peacefully potting, warm, leisurely, undisturbed, satisfying his creative urges.

'Oh, Clare, you are a dear. I go nearly mad racing up and down. I know it's marvellous to be so busy, and people often spend more in the shop than they do in the pottery, but it gets a bit frantic when I don't have the time to check deliveries in properly, or if I know food's sitting down here thawing out.'

Not too much chance of that, Clare thought, folding her numb hands under her arms.

The bell rang above.

'I'll finish this, if you like.' Had she really said that? 'You stay in the shop.'

'Would you? That's great, thanks.' Trudy vanished, her big turned-out feet in sandals slapping on the stone steps. 'Oh, do you mind bringing up that sack of adukis when you come?' she called from the top. 'Sorry, forgot.'

'Does it go on like this all the time?' Clare asked, having braved the hurricane-whirled kitchen end of their vast open living area and made coffee which she had brought into the shop.

'More or less.'

'Well, you know how long I have to wait for the bus. Could I help?'

'You're on.' Trudy wasn't the hesitating type.

She seemed to tap some new reserve of energy as she served briskly and at the same time kept an eye on Clare, directing her to shelf or bin like a traffic policeman, adding up Clare's orders simultaneously with her own and making scurrilous comments on the customers as they dived into some sack together. All three of them wolfed down bread and cheese in a brief lull, Ben and Trudy drinking lager out of cans, ripping open mail and pitching it at a buried desk from which most of it slid disregarded to the floor.

'How would you like a hand for a few hours a week?'

'You don't mean it?' Trudy stared at Clare in incredulous hope, a wholemeal doorstep in one hand, a piece of khaki-coloured goat's cheese impaled on her knife in the other.

'That's good of you, Clare, but—' Ben began.

'I don't want to be paid.'

Trudy's feet and Ben's can came down with a synchronized crash. Lager splashed over the table.

'We couldn't let you do that,' Ben said.

'We'd pay you in dried apricots.'

'Trudy, you know we can't.'

'On principle?'

'Yes, of course on principle.'

'Then speak for yourself. My principles are well under control, thank you.'

'Three or four hours between buses?' Clare suggested. 'Two, three days a week? Would that be any use?'

'Whe-e-e-ey!' screeched Trudy, leaping up to squeeze the breath out of her. 'Would you really?'

'If I survive this,' Clare gasped, struggling out of her muscular embrace.

'Well, it would give Trudy a break,' said Ben nicely, reaching a sketchily washed hand to ruffle his wife's hair (quite superfluously) and going off to his pottery leaving his plate and lager can on the table.

The few hours a week which Clare spent at the Old Mill,

undemanding and voluntary as they were, nevertheless made her feel that she was no longer playing at living at the Larach. She enjoyed Trudy's forthright company, meeting people, the shop itself, but mainly she was glad that it gave her something to do which kept her mind off Donald. Only now that he was absent did she realize how her days had revolved round the time spent with him. Over and over again she found herself listening for the sound of the boat coming into the bay. Once or twice she even imagined a shadowy movement at the door and thought Trim had come to warn her he was on the way. She missed his teasing, the dumbfounded way he would shake his head when she showed off some amateur job she'd been quite proud of. She missed his interest in everything she did, his patient teaching, even his touchiness at what he saw as an innate English feeling of superiority and his refusal to let her get away with glib preconceptions or lazy thinking. She missed the long conversations when she lured him to talk about the farm and glen. Above all she missed his physical presence, the pleasure of watching him, the comfort she drew from his bulk and strength and calm. She supposed she had seen what she wanted to see in him. The Donald who had meant so much to her would hardly have sent that curt message via Nicol, or been so readily offended by Magda.

She was determined not to repeat her mistake over Magda. She would draw on her own resources to make something of this new life. To start with she would improve the cottage, just as Kenny had prosphesied, putting into action a plan she had often toyed with when the westerly gales raged up the loch and straight under her door.

With a strong feeling she couldn't quite suppress that Donald should have been consulted, and very much missing his advice, she put out feelers and learned without surprise that Kenny's brother Pete worked for a builder and did 'homers', and that he would certainly be 'skint' when he came back from his holiday on the Costa Brava. Angus brought him down the loch, plus Kenny, one August evening. They clearly wanted the job but were not noticeably enthusiastic about Clare's plan.

'But you'll not want just the one door?'

'There's only one door now.'

'Right enough, but that's the front door. You canna' have folk coming in through the kitchen, can you now?'

'My wife wouldna' stand for that,' Pete asserted officiously.

'Lots of people use their kitchen doors,' Clare pointed out.

'Aye, but they've another door besides.'

'And when you come to sell,' Pete added as a clinching point, 'there's not many people would fancy that idea, is there?'

'We could make the new door before we close off the existing one,' Kenny offered. 'Then you could see.'

Clare thought they might have to do that in any case.

'Do you think it would spoil the house from the outside though?' she asked, for this was a consideration that had been bothering her. 'Turning the door into a long window?'

'Oh, is it a patio door you're wanting?' they asked, cheering up at once.

'No, a double-glazed sealed window with a sill to sit on,' Clare said firmly, dragging them outside to see what they thought.

But on the aesthetic aspect they were not prepared to commit themselves. 'You'll know best yourself,' they said. And, tolerantly, 'The house is nothing much anyway, is it?'

Kenny extracted full mileage out of the English never being satisfied and having money to burn, they sat for an hour drinking tea and Clare had to suppose that some deal had been struck.

The prediction that they would be short of cash had been accurate. They were back the following evening in a borrowed boat, now joined by Ina's son Ewan. They set about knocking through the end wall of the larder without bothering about refinements like clearing the shelves first. As daylight appeared Clare wished more than ever that she had been able to discuss this with Donald.

'You're staying then?' Kenny asked, tipping rubble yards from the spot she had designated.

'So it would seem,' Clare agreed.

'I never thought you would.'

Suddenly Clare felt extraordinarily pleased with herself, for no particular reason that she could account for.

CHAPTER NINETEEN

Clare was restocking shelves in the shop and trying to decide whether some rather bashed packets of herbal tea were fit to sell when she became aware of a waiting presence beside her. As Trudy was free she ignored it, particularly as the edifice she had created had taken on a threatening wobble and the light, slippery packets were beginning to teeter in every direction.

The presence remained, silent, small, patient. Putting her arms round the imminent collapse on the shelf, Clare glanced over her shoulder. She had seen this girl before, in Angus's shop weighed down with the most dilapidated Barbour Clare had ever seen, and on a couple of occasions almost invisible behind the wheel of an equally dilapidated but stately Bentley cruising up the glen road.

'I know you're busy.'

'This lot's about to come down on both our heads, that's all.'

Tall Trudy came to the rescue, reaching over Clare. 'They're battered enough already, can't afford to let them hit the ground again. This looks like one for you to take home, Clare.'

'Bergamot. Must I?'

'Do you know Catriona? Catriona Finlay.'

'We've seen each other, I think,' Clare said, released, nodding to the small figure today shrouded in an olive-green wool shirt roughly twice her size hanging over dusty black cords.

'I think Catriona wanted to ask you something,' Trudy prompted, nannyishly but kindly.

'Yes, of course,' Clare said. What could she tell her that Trudy couldn't? she wondered, her mind still on the shop.

But Catriona gazed at her nervously through a thick uneven fringe of dark hair and remained mute. Trudy uttered a sharp expletive as the step-ladder nipped her finger, and took charge. 'Are you going back up the glen, Catriona? Clare came on the bus.'

'Oh, of course you must come back with me. Not until you're ready, that is.' But Clare saw the tiny suppressed movement to raise a wrist hidden in buttonless cuff, and remembered Donald saying that Catriona could never be away from her grandfather for long.

She also remembered him saying that he doubted if Catriona had ever taken a driving test, as they swayed over Luig Hill in the Bentley with a large golden retriever anchoring himself with a heavy chin over Catriona's shoulder or Clare's impartially, while a white terrier rolled about on the back seat like a football.

Catriona's hands on the wheel were tiny and brown, or dirty. Her wrists were like a child's and as the shirt sleeves flopped back Clare saw that the watch she had refrained from looking at was gold, minute, and set with what looked like diamonds. Its delicate bracelet had been mended with fuse wire.

Catriona took Clare to the farm, lurching along the track at the same steady pace at which she had taken the road over the moor – and the village, come to that.

'You were going to ask me something,' Clare finally reminded her. Catriona had hardly uttered a word since they had left the Old Mill, receiving Clare's attempts at conversation with a shy smile. Now as much of her as was visible through sticking-up shirt collar and rough hair blushed.

'I didn't know you already had a job.'

Intriguing. 'Only helping Trudy out for a few hours a week.'

'It doesn't matter really.'

'Tell me anyway.'

'Only Lilias said that you knew Italian.'

I might have known Lilias would be at the bottom of it, Clare thought. 'Well, come on, you can't leave it there.'

She was glad she had persisted when she heard what Catriona, not very coherently, had to say. She wanted Clare to help her grandfather with a family history he was compiling, specifically to translate the letters and diaries of his Italian great-aunt.

'I know you've lots to do and it's probably awful of me even to mention it, but if you could perhaps look through them for him, give him some idea of what's in them. We'd pay the proper rates, of course, though I'm afraid I don't know what they are, and I could come and fetch you and bring you back, if you decided to do it, I mean. Only I think the papers are probably in rather a mess so it may be a hopeless idea . . .'

Clare couldn't wait to get her hands on them and said so, filled with pure mental greed at the prospect. Reassured, Catriona relaxed at last and her small face lit up in a transfiguring smile.

'I've seen you once or twice on the glen road,' she confessed abruptly as Clare got out, 'only I never quite dared to stop and speak.'

She was spared the embarrassment of any answer Clare might have made by the shrieks of the terrier, who took violent exception to Clare speaking to his mistress through the window of the car in which she had recently been a passenger.

'You set that up,' Clare accused Lilias.

'Of course.' She was leaning comfortably against a boulder, head back and eyes closed against the uncertain sunshine. The rug on which she was sitting was pulled round her like a shawl, patterned with bits of grass and sheep droppings. Her brown scaly legs stuck out before her, ending in squelching gym shoes.

The family were at Tigh Bhan once more – the Twelfth was upon them – and an argument which had taken place when Clare was over there one day, about the sewage outlet in Inverbuie which Gerald seemed much exercised about, had ended in an invitation for them to come and swim in Larach Bay and have lunch at the cottage. Clare had not thought that Lilias and Gerald, or even Stephen and Lucy, would necessarily swim. Lucy did show her good sense by wandering off along the shore with a book but the rest plunged valiantly off the jetty, and Clare hoped no one would die before lunch, over which she had taken some trouble.

Cooking it had not been entirely straightforward. Pete and Ewan had arrived, without warning and very pleased with themselves, bringing the new door.

'Ah,' Clare said, hands suspended over her mixing bowl as the plastic sheeting was summarily ripped away from the end of the kitchen, 'I think perhaps we are going to be in each other's way.'

'You'll not be in ours anyway,' Pete responded cheerfully, and he was right. In five minutes he and Ewan had the cooker and cylinder set up in the shed and had obligingly filled the kettle for Clare to make their first cup of tea.

In the end the hanging of the new door turned into something of a celebration. Markie family conflicts were put aside. Pete and Ewan downed most of the beer Stephen had brought and pretended to like herb quiche, the last of Magda's wine was polished off and Clare's bread-making was pronounced to have improved slightly. There was generous approval for the new-style kitchen. Clare had been so intent on making the sitting-room draught-proof that the changes to the kitchen had been second-ary, a mere means to an end. Now she saw that from a gloomy strip of galley it had become light and airy. Its new glazed door would let in the morning sun and was only a couple of steps away from the shed, which was going to be a great boon in bad weather.

'Nice sheltered corner, this,' Gerald commented. 'You'll have to close off this gap, lay a few paving stones, and you'll have a splendid little sun-trap.'

'So you've decided to stay with us,' said Lilias, as Kenny had done, and though she spoke teasingly Clare heard a satisfaction in her voice that pleased her very much. She nodded, smiling, and Lilias gave her a brusque hug, her bony body moulding surprisingly aptly to Clare's.

'That's *good*,' she said.

'Grandfather's potty, of course. I expect you've heard that,' Catriona said, leading Clare into the library at Glen Righ House.

Clare had come up the glen with Mrs MacGillivray the game-keeper's wife, who was on her way back from delivering grouse to the game dealer in Fort William. Feathers blew about the jeep and stuck to the blood on the floor. Mrs MacGillivray whiled away the drive by battering Clare with questions about her age, her marital status and her income and sniffed audibly at her guarded replies.

'Just go round to the front,' she had instructed Clare, pulling up in a sunless stone courtyard with a jerk on the handbrake that made the jeep put its nose down like a refusing pony. 'Give a shout in the hall if Catriona's nowhere to be seen.'

The house dozed in afternoon quiet as Clare crossed a terrace of huge slabs of stone, the aubretia and stonecrop once planted in the cracks being throttled by grass and speedwell, the only sound fast-running water somewhere out of sight reminding her of the tragic story of Catriona's brother's death. A slumberous air of decay hung over everything, redeemed by the beauty of weathered granite, the splendid proportions of the house and the immense vista of the glen stretching clear to Righ Bay.

The hall clearly did duty as a garden shed. Stags' heads, crowned with dust so that they all looked as though they had been shot in old age, gazed down on trugs, gloves and hanks of twine, Flymo, barrow and a huddle of tools. Clare was not surprised to see a saddle over one side of the banisters and a Barbour she recognized acquiring a new bulge on the other.

'Hello?' she called. Too tentative and feeble by far for the empty cubic feet which reached away past panelling and armorial shields, dark paintings and elaborate chandelier to a green-streaked cupola above.

'Hello! Catriona!' she bawled, and listened to the solid silence return.

Then there was a dull thud far away, a nearer slam and the sound of claws skittering on stone. The dogs shot into the hall, breaking respectively into one mellow woof and a barrage of hysterical yaps, and Catriona appeared behind them wearing a man's check shirt, its collar worn through to the interlining and most of its buttons missing, below which appeared two inches of denim skirt.

Fergus Finlay rose to greet Clare from the piled chaos of his library, tall and bony, with transparent skin and a look of silvery cleanness in spite of his darned and faded tweeds. He clearly had no recollection that she had been invited, but welcomed her with great charm.

The papers on which he had been working looked not unlike Trudy's business correspondence. The diaries, fourteen of them, were eventually collected up, while Catriona made worried apologizing faces at Clare and the dogs disinterred a bone from the depths of a hide-covered sofa and quarrelled over which of them had put it there.

Densely written in fading sepia ink, the leatherbound volumes roused in Clare a passionate craving she had almost forgotten. She put her hands behind her back while Fergus embarked on a rambling explanation of how Great-Aunt Sofia had fitted into the family tree. The letters, hundreds of them, yellowed and curling, were crammed into Gordon's gin boxes and the sort of plastic trays that looked as though they should have been returned to the baker. Clare suggested taking some of them home with her to look through, but there was instant alarm. Fergus hugged a diary to his soup-spotted tie and Catriona put a reassuring hand on his arm. Clare said hastily that of course she could come up whenever they liked and they deflated with relief.

Clare would quite happily have started work there and then and foregone tea – particularly when she saw it. There were fragile pink and gold cups, all chipped. There was a tea strainer in spite of the fact that the strings and labels of teabags sprouted from the lid of the tarnished teapot. There was sugar on which the spoon lay as on marble. There was toast with Gentleman's Relish for Fergus and for Clare and Catriona some yellow cake from Angus's shop with its wrapper trailing from it and a sell-by date that made Clare blink.

Braan the retriever sat with puckered forehead and long trails of saliva swinging from his jowls. The terrier, Chippy, fixed Clare with bulging toffee-brown eyes while quivers of greed ran over his white coat like catspaws on water. Trim never begged, Clare thought.

'Would you really help Grandfather?' Catriona asked doubtfully when Fergus had risen, leaving his cup full and toast on his plate, and headed back to his library unconscious of their presence.

'I'd love to.'

'It might be a bit frustrating. He won't always remember that you've been here before.'

'I shan't mind that.'

'And you may never get anywhere. I mean, I'm sure you can do the translating and everything perfectly, of course, but I'm not sure it will ever be finished, the history itself . . .' Her voice trailed away unhappily and Clare guessed that she didn't want to be disloyal to her grandfather. It also occurred to her that perhaps it would be convenient if this harmless and absorbing occupation for Fergus should never come to an end.

'I do understand,' she said. 'I'd love to get into all that fascinating material. The end product isn't important. I'd be delighted to come as long as you think it's useful.'

'That's so kind.' Catriona had a lovely little face when she smiled. 'We haven't talked about what you should be paid, though,' she added, the anxious look returning. 'Of course anything would be quite all right.'

Clare didn't think there would be much ready cash to squander on translator's fees, which would certainly be a shock to Catriona, and quoted a figure somewhere above the going domestic rate which she accepted serenely as quite normal.

'Grandfather loses track and gets into a terrible state sometimes,' she confided as she drove Clare down the glen. 'The whole thing gets beyond him and there's nothing I can do. This will be such a help to him and I can't tell you how grateful I am.'

Clare didn't think anything she could do would much affect Fergus, and was more interested in Catriona herself. She seemed contented enough, apart from her concern about her grandfather, but during the days that followed Clare found her thoughts returning frequently to her odd and lonely situation.

CHAPTER TWENTY

From the hill above Tigh Bhan where she often walked now to
keep clear of the busy moors higher up the glen, Clare watched
Donald's boat head down from the village towards the promontory which hid the Larach.

'*Yes!*' she exclaimed, jubilant, then remembered how far away
she was and that from this point she wouldn't be able to see
whether Donald turned into the bay or not. She plunged down
a slope of heather and bilberry and scattered rocks and raced up
the next ridge, but the headland dropped away too steeply and
her view was blocked. By the time she could see into the bay it
was empty. She sank down breathless and angry with herself.

'Idiot, you're thirty-three, remember, not thirteen. Chasing
round like some besotted teenager.' Something she had learned
by chance yesterday had sparked that momentary hope. Lilias,
giving her a lift into Luig, had remarked gravely, 'Somewhat
ominous, I fear, Ishbel Macrae being sent home.'

'Sent home? From where?' Clare had asked, puzzled.

Lilias had shot her a surprised glance. 'From hospital. You
know she's been in for tests for the last two weeks? They've
decided not to operate again and they're even giving up on the
chemotherapy it seems. It looks very much as though nothing
more can be done, I'm afraid. Poor Donald has been driving in
every day, often twice a day. With all he has to do at this time
of year the poor man must be worn out. I can't imagine how
you missed hearing about it.'

It was grave news and Clare felt a pang of anxious sympathy
for Donald. It sounded as though the end might not be far away
and she tried to imagine how he must be feeling. Could that
have been the explanation for his absence? she wondered as she

walked home, with a surge of selfish eagerness she could not quite suppress.

And now, thirty-three years old notwithstanding, her heart was not beating very evenly as she approached the cottage. Would there be some sign that Donald had called? The little house gave nothing away. Mattock, barrow and flat stones waited as she had left them by the new door. Exasperated with herself at the sharpness of her disappointment, she made up her mind, not for the first time, to do something positive about contacting Donald. But she could hardly write or phone. Besides, what did she want to say? Apologize for Magda? But had sane, equable Donald really taken serious offence over that incident? And how could she say to a man who had never treated her with anything more than ordinary friendliness, a man whose wife's present condition must be occupying all his thoughts, that she missed him?

She was thankful she was so busy these days, and especially glad to see so much of Trudy who, with mortgage, interest rates and the cost of overheads climbing round her, with Ben leaving everything from buying the loo paper to placating the bank manager in her hands, was still bouncingly cheerful, still capable of glorious bouts of giggling about sliding down the storeroom steps on a tide of chick peas from a split sack, or about a tourist asking if the ewes' milk for the cheeses came from the wild sheep on the hills.

Trudy was delighted that Clare was helping Catriona, which was how she saw the work for Fergus – as indeed Clare herself did – and she could never hear enough about life at Glen Righ House, based as it was on a splendid indifference to any form of comfort.

'You are lucky, I'd love to see it. Never mind about boring old Aunt Sofia. Tell about lunch.'

Catriona invited Clare with great cordiality to the most terrible meals. Clare had rather expected her to go in for all the gardening and harvesting and freezing and cooking favoured by Lilias and her pals, but Catriona seemed to wander about in some Edwardian daughter-of-the-big-house time warp, giving the impression that the few chores she did, though dealt with quite uncomplainingly, were ultimately nothing to do with her.

Apart from feeding herself and her grandfather, barely, and the dogs rather well, she rode most days, brushed Braan more often than she brushed her own hair, kept the top section of the huge sloping lawn roughly mown, occasionally hacking back the encroaching jungle around it, and read omnivorously. There was a handyman, Watty Duff, whose main passion (non-cosmetic) was the Bentley and who maintained with less interest the other estate vehicles. He also burst in from time to time with logs, performed acts of heroism with the wiring, and delivered bulletins about lead flashings, down-pipes and the boiler to Catriona, who took no notice of any of them.

She was equally oblivious to the shooting which appeared to be run by MacGillivray without reference to anyone. These days the glen road was alive morning and evening with expensive off-road vehicles packed with hearty men in tweeds, with long melancholy dog faces peering out of misted-up rear windows. Some, Clare knew, were headed for Rhumore, where Donald ran the shooting himself. She remembered that once he had suggested she should do some beating for him and see for herself what went on. How she longed now to have the chance to be up there on the moor, involved, part of it. Barbaric, had she said? The grouse would have to take their chance. She remembered, too, that Donald had told her how busy he. was when harvest coincided with the shooting. Another probable reason, she was able to persuade herself, why she never saw him these days.

Dougie Stewart, like everyone else on Rhumore, was working during every daylight hour and as often as she could Clare called on Margaret who, like Trudy, loved to hear about Glen Righ House.

'And you're no' frightened of the laird?' she would enquire, eyes round, longing for drama.

'Margaret, he's the gentlest person in the world, unless it's Catriona.'

'But I mean, he's no' right in the head, is he?'

'Just forgetful.' Clare would often arrive to find the front door propped open as it had been all night by the dogs' drinking bowl, a hand-painted Victorian chamber-pot, and neither Fergus nor Catriona visible. She would start work in the mist-hung library and when Fergus discovered her there with courteous surprise she would tell him who she was once more and they would settle down contentedly together.

'Catriona can never leave him, not even for ten minutes,' Margaret pursued.

'She goes into Luig every week.'

'Aye, but he rages about the place like a mad bull, calling on his wife and tearing down the furniture. All the electric fires have to be locked away from him.'

Clare recalled Donald telling her how distressed Fergus had been when Catriona was sent away to school. Legend in the making. Mrs MacGillivray's making, by the sound of it.

'And do you know this? He has eighteen pairs of new shoes in his dressing-room. Eighteen pairs, still in their boxes . . .'

Here Lynn pulled the aerial out of the back of the television and stuck her finger in the hole. As Margaret believed this to be live, it was a useful diversion.

'You're exactly what Catriona needed,' was Lilias's verdict.

Unusually, Clare had found her alone. Stephen was shooting and Gerald and Lucy had taken the children to the Sealife Centre near Oban, not, it seemed, without some dissension. Lilias's exasperated comment that she hoped Lucy would refrain from loosing too many creatures to the wild provided a clue as to why Grannie had not joined the expedition.

'We've done our best,' she said, still on the subject of Catriona, 'but she won't go anywhere without Fergus and of course wouldn't think of inviting anyone to Glen Righ House – mercifully, perhaps. It will be good for her to have you there. Maybe you'll be able to persuade her to tidy herself up a little.' Tart as she pretended to be, Clare had observed that Lilias spoke of Catriona with the same protective affection she seemed to arouse in everyone.

'Cook a little, would be more to the point.'

Lilias gave a bark of laughter. 'And drive?'

'Poor Catriona, she's not that bad. It's just that she treats the Luig road like her own drive, expecting everyone who comes round the corner to be a friend.'

'Have you thought about getting a car yourself, now that you're out and about so much more? There are plenty of small four-wheel-drive vehicles to be had these days. Stephen could help you to find one if you liked. Of course, even with four-wheel drive you wouldn't get over the hill in winter, or even along the farm track if we had much snow, though Donald could get Dougie to clear it for you, and really we hardly ever do get snow down here.'

'I have thought about it. I'm beginning to feel rather guilty about accepting lifts. But I don't want the Larach to lose its feeling of remoteness. I love that stepping out of the door on to the open hillside, setting off everywhere on foot, out in the air and the scents and sounds – and the gales and rain, I know, I know.'

'My dear, I do understand. You go on enjoying it as long as you can. And there is absolutely no need to worry about lifts. People like meeting the glen oddity.'

Clare laughed, but was conscious of the mental equivalent of crossing her fingers. She knew it was only by a hair's breadth that she had avoided making herself highly unpopular here. Her decision to live at the Larach had been sufficiently bizarre to make people feel she needed looking after and she had been particularly lucky in gaining Ina's support. And Donald with great firmness had saved her from many a pitfall of criticism and ignorance. What comments had been made about her wild fling in the Corpach motel she would never know, but she suspected it was owing to the unshaken friendship of these two that it had been forgiven her. Her link with Tigh Bhan and later with Glen Righ House would not carry the same weight.

She hadn't given Lilias her real reason for putting off buying some kind of vehicle. The truth was that she hoped Donald would call for her again when his trips to the village resumed. Though she also knew that if Donald really wanted to call the fact that she had a car would make no difference.

She was picking spinach one evening, wondering how Gerald had managed to dragoon her into growing it and why she felt obliged to eat it now that she had, when she saw a man with a large back-pack heading down towards the bay. Where was he making for? Walkers mostly preferred the high ridges to the east of the glen. Donald wasn't too keen about campers down here, either. When she next looked the man was quite near, in silhouette against the setting sun which outlined his head dramatically in gold. Gold; tall; a walk that seemed strangely familiar. She wasn't sure afterwards of the exact moment when she had known . . .

'Hello, Clare.'

'*Joe!*' A wave of shock washed over her, leaving her knees trembling and her stomach churning.

'Thought I'd look you up when you told me where you were.'

So easy, so normal, after all the anxiety and guilt. Clare clasped the washing-up bowl of spinach to her chest and gazed at him speechlessly. He had come up to the fence and was grinning at her, very relaxed.

'So how are you keeping?'

She couldn't find words.

He laughed at her. 'You look completely gobsmacked. But you did write, remember.'

'I wanted to explain—'

'Oh, that business. Forget it, water under the bridge. Here, give me that.' He took the bowl from her and held out a hand as she stepped over the fence. 'Some place, this,' he commented, gazing round him appreciatively. 'Aren't you going to ask me in?'

Clare had a wild feeling that they were reading from different scripts. 'But I thought you— Yes, of course, you must come in. Have coffee or something.' What time of day was it? 'A drink?'

'Come on, Clare, get your act together. You know I don't drink.'

He sounded casual, teasing, as though they had seen each other last week, instead of – how long? – four years ago. Of course Joe didn't drink, how could she have forgotten that? And with this factual detail reality returned. Here, smiling at her, in person, was Joe, the Joe she had last seen walking down the path of the married quarter at Marbury, turning to wave as he went round the back of the Land Rover where the trainees waited to be taken to hand in kit. Everything in between vanished.

'Oh, Joe!' she exclaimed, grabbing his arm in her greenish hands. 'Goodness, I'm glad to see you.'

'That's better,' he mocked. 'I was beginning to wonder. You've not half fallen on your feet here, though. Does the cottage belong to you?' He swung off his pack, propped it by the door and followed her in, and suddenly she was eager to show everything off to him, exuberant, sure of his approval. It took her half an hour to produce a mug of tea, half an hour of exchanging fragmented superficial news, ignoring looming questions.

Joe bore it all patiently, making himself at home at once in the remembered way, foraging in cupboards, collecting what Clare had forgotten, not concealing his satisfaction at his reception.

'Made your day, have I?' he enquired complacently, putting down the tray and settling on the sofa beside her.

'You can't imagine how pleased I am that you've come. But what are you doing up here? Are you on leave?'

'Terminal leave. Coming out.'

'Leaving the Air Force? But, Joe, why?' Then she felt hot embarrassment to realize that if he thought her responsible for his abrupt posting and non-promotion then he might consider her partly the cause.

If that was so he gave no sign. 'It's changed a lot these days. Gone security mad. Cutbacks every other week it seems like. Then I was offered this job, just the sort of thing I've always wanted, so it seemed a good move.'

'What is the job?' Her conscience could wait.

'There's this activities centre outside Glasgow, run by the Council. They're adapting part of it for disabled kids and they wanted an instructor. I'll be in on the ground floor, involved in setting it up, course design, the lot.'

'Joe, that's marvellous. There must have been tremendous competition for a job like that.'

He launched happily into details of qualifications and selection and poured out his plans for future courses as the sunset light died and dusk filled the room.

'This place is brilliant,' he said, as at last Clare made a move and went to light the lamp. The room seemed bigger now that the coats and boots were in the porch formed by the ex-larder, but she wished Pete and Ewan would come back to put in the new window.

For the first time it occurred to her to wonder where Joe planned to sleep. A swift sequence of thoughts fled through her brain. The sofa — would he think an invitation to sleep there implied more than she intended? But surely Joe of all people could be relied on not to do that, particularly if he believed that she had reported him to Martin ... and so back to what lay unresolved between them.

'Let's have supper,' she suggested, shelving both issues for the time being.

'I can kick in with some compo — that should take you back a bit.'

'No need, thanks, you've hit the jackpot. Someone left a brace of grouse hanging on the shed door yesterday.' Stephen Markie, she had supposed, finding a succinct note written on a page torn from the back of a diary. 'Shot Friday' it had said in a firm military-looking hand.

Then it crossed her mind that Joe might disapprove of shooting and not be prepared to eat grouse, but he only remarked, 'Living off the land, I see,' with what sounded like approval and added teasingly, 'How about plucking them?'

'Did it this afternoon.'

'I'm impressed. And then there's that pile of spinach to eat up.'

It was nice to be teased. 'And my own potatoes.'

'What can I say? Better get the tent up first though, while there's some light left.'

That was what it had always been like with Joe, problems dealt with. Why had she ever worried?

'I'll help you,' she offered, suddenly sure that when the moment came they would be able to put right all past misunderstandings with the same simplicity.

CHAPTER TWENTY-ONE

'Joe, why wouldn't you talk to me when I phoned you at Eland?'

Clare knew this had to be cleared up. Joe was cockahoop with the success of the surprise he had given her and his welcome, and he had behaved all evening as though nothing but time had intervened between their last weekend in Wales and his arrival at the Larach. But Clare found herself excited and stirred up by seeing him again, and not prepared to have any renewed friendship jeopardized by lingering misconceptions.

Joe was obviously unprepared for the direct question and equally obviously wished she hadn't asked it. 'Oh, well,' he hedged, 'it was a bit awkward, wasn't it? Service line and all that.'

'Come on, Joe, you know it wasn't that.'

'No need to go raking things up at this stage, is there?' he muttered, getting up to nudge a log on to the fire. His tone was cajoling, but he could not quite hide an underlying wariness.

'We can't just ignore it!' Clare exclaimed.

'It's over and done with, isn't it?'

She frowned at him, puzzled at something in his manner. He had spoken airily, almost patronizingly, but he was careful not to meet her eye and she thought his high colour had nothing to do with the heat of the fire.

'But didn't you believe you were posted from Marbury because I had reported you?'

'What? Reported me? Don't be daft, of course not. What are you talking about?' He was looking at her now, genuinely startled. 'Reported me for what?'

They stared at each other, thoughts as confused as slides coming in the wrong order.

'But I heard some of the wives talking one day in the mess, saying Martin had had you posted because I'd told him you tried to chat me up—'

Clare jumped as Joe kicked the log in with sudden violence. 'That bastard!' he exclaimed in a tight voice, laying his forehead down on his clenched hands on the high mantelpiece. 'Jesus, that total bastard! Oh, I know he was your husband and I know he's dead – oh Christ, I'm sorry, Clare – but how could he say that, when he—? Jesus almighty!'

Clare stared at him in shock as he took a couple of jerky steps across the room, his face taut with rage, turned back to put his fists on the mantelpiece again and stare down into the fire between his braced arms. She could see the muscles of his jaw jumping.

'Joe, what on earth is it?' she asked in consternation, getting up to go to him, laying her hand on his arm uncertainly. It felt like an iron bar.

He gave a shake of his bent head.

'Joe, listen, I don't give a damn what you say about Martin, but I need to know what really happened.'

He hesitated; Clare could feel the current of his tight-held anger transmitted to her hand. 'Tell me, Joe,' she urged softly. 'What did he do?'

'He told me something different, that's all,' he got out after a moment. 'Nothing to do with you. I never thought for a second that you had anything to do with it.'

'Well then, why wouldn't you talk to me?' There were things here Clare couldn't fathom and didn't like.

'I told you, we weren't on an outside line. You know how they listen in half the time. I couldn't risk talking about anything, and I wanted to be clear of it all. I mean, he was your husband, wasn't he, and I didn't know what he'd told you. And the job he was in by then, he could have fixed anything he liked. He'd dropped me in the sh— he'd dropped me in it anyway, my career was up the spout and I didn't want any more trouble. Surely you can see that?'

'But if he didn't tell you I'd reported you, what did he say? How could he have you posted because he was jealous? Why didn't you fight it? No one can abuse the system like that, can they, and get away with it?'

'That's all you know. Bloody officers, they can do anything they like.'

Clare didn't think they could, but Martin appeared to have got away with this. 'Is it the reason you're leaving the service?'

'Partly. I just felt I'd had enough. In fact I wonder now how I stuck it for so long.'

The service to which he had been so committed, which had been his whole life. Clare felt again the baffled conviction that there was more to this than she was ever going to discover.

But Joe dismissed it with sudden impatient anger. 'What are we doing wasting our time talking about this crap anyway? It's finished, over. I'm out, all but, and we're here in this fantastic place. Why don't we have a coffee, get our heads down, then tomorrow you can show me this glen of yours?'

Clare recognized that Joe had come back into her life at a moment when she was ripe for some emotional relationship. For months she had been trying to deal with a serious attraction for a man who didn't feel the same way about her, who was not free and not even fair game. Now Joe was here, and the guilt of four years had suddenly been wiped out. His liking for her had never changed, and he could be associated once more in her mind with images of peace, escape and uncomplicated happiness. He was the ideal person to share with her everything she enjoyed in this new place. Also the sexual revulsion which had driven her to change course had been short lived, had not even been strong enough to deter her from hopping into bed with poor Lennox, alcohol had done that, and she had been battening down some very strong feelings for Donald. She found herself responding with pleasure to Joe's ready smile, his energy and fitness, his lean muscular build.

She tried to push Donald out of her mind, though uncomfortably reminded of him whenever she saw Joe's tent. So blatant a signal, visible for miles, and on what was virtually Donald's own ground. I have a man staying with me. But to see it in those terms was to imply that Donald felt about her as she did about him.

It was fortunate that her summer's activities had left Clare in good shape, for with Joe's car available he could trot her over a far wider landscape than she had explored on her own, heading for areas where they would not disturb anyone's shooting. Now it was down to the village call-box first thing in the morning for met reports; it was meticulous route planning, brisk calculations in Ks, emergency rations, first-aid pack and proper kit. Clare's muted rural look was not considered acceptable and she was hauled off to buy bright cagoule and overtrousers. She felt a good deal more self-conscious in them here than she ever had in North Wales.

This apart, being with Joe was balm after the warfare of Magda's visit. Clare reduced her working hours as much as she reasonably could and Joe obligingly went with her to the Old Mill when she did her stints there. He delivered orders for Trudy – tuning up the van rather pointedly after his first run in it – did the stocking up and even created some order in the dusty muddle of the storeroom. He got on well with Ben and spent a lot of time watching him at work.

Trudy was preoccupied these days and finally admitted to having the end-of-year audit on her mind. 'I was going to ask you if you'd mind having a look at the books for me,' she admitted, 'but it appears you're going to be too busy. Not that I grudge it to you for a minute,' she added hastily with her old grin. 'Time you had a bloke around.'

'A bloke who'll be down in Glasgow,' Clare reminded her. 'Of course I don't mind having a go at the books if you're worried about them.'

'Would you? I'm afraid I seem to have got a bit behind though.'

Clare could imagine it.

When Clare went up to Glen Righ House the plan had been that Joe should go off and walk, but before Clare could warn him he had accepted Catriona's invitation to lunch. Luckily it was nothing actually life-endangering that day – tongue from a tin Clare saw opened, cream crackers soft but not fusty, delicious Victoria plums, bruises, wasp holes, bit of leaf, sap and all, and gaspingly strong coffee, sent up from Drysdale's in unvarying quantities for the past thirty years.

Joe was marvellous with Fergus. Clare realized that she might have foreseen as much, but even so she was touched by his patience and the way he drew Fergus out to talk, and she felt proud of him in a possessive way that amused her when she became aware of it. She found herself jarred by his comments, however, as he drove down the glen.

'That girl needs help, hadn't you realized? She shouldn't be left up there on her own with that old bloke, he's a total fruit-cake. She should have a break sometimes, as a full-time carer. Has she tried the local health service? Her GP could get her some info.' Nor had he been impressed with Glen Righ House. 'Place needs a good clean-up, it's not hygienic. That coffee pot was supposed to be silver, wasn't it? Same colour outside as in, I didn't fancy it at all. And that plate she gave me was cracked, only I didn't like to say anything.'

'Just as well you didn't, since they're all the same,' Clare said, slightly too breezily.

'And it was a bit parky, wasn't it? Don't they have any heating?'

'The radiators are sometimes faintly warm.'

'You should refuse to work, you know, if the temperature's below the legal limit. What do they pay you anyway?'

But this Clare refused to discuss.

What she had wanted for so long and then tried to put out of her mind now happened. She saw Donald. She and Joe had been walking on the eastern side of the glen and had come down the boring forestry track which curved away from the road shutting off the views of the loch and outer sound.

They had left the car in a lay-by just inside the curve, and while Joe was taking his boots off Clare went down to open the gate in the deer fence. As they had turned in that morning she had felt a pang of loss to see the Rhumore track leading away opposite. Now Donald's Land Rover was coming out of it, and she was aware of a swift unmixed delight to see it that wiped out the empty weeks without him, wiped out Magda, Joe and everything else.

Donald pulled across into the wide sweep in front of the forestry gate when he saw her. She knew a big silly grin was spreading over her face as she went to speak to him but could do nothing about it. It was so good to see him again, his bulk, his brown hand on the wheel, his clear tanned skin, his direct gaze under the brim of his flat cap.

'Donald! How lovely to see you!' she exclaimed with a spontaneous pleasure which was overtaken by uncertainty as he nodded to her, saying nothing, his eyes watchful. 'How are you?' she added more formally.

'I'm fine.'

'It's ages since I saw you.'

He made no comment.

Conscious that Joe would appear at any second, Clare plunged on. 'I've been wanting to say – I wasn't sure if I should write or not – I'm really sorry about that day when Magda was staying. I shouldn't have let her—' Clare broke off, suddenly seeing the thicket of tactless inferences into which she was heading.

'Oh, that. It didn't matter,' Donald said dismissively and convincingly. But he was still watching her, as though waiting for something.

Clare wrenched her brain with an effort from what had seemed to her the one vital point. 'Donald, I was so sorry to hear that Ishbel had been in hospital.'

'Yes. She's been home for a few days now.' Another avenue closed.

'How's the shooting going?' It sounded ridiculously social, the question everyone asked, but absurd from her who knew nothing about it.

'Not too badly,' Donald replied politely, but looking for a second faintly amused.

Clare felt herself blushing. 'Oh, good.' She had not imagined that meeting him again would be like this. Angry as he had been when she last saw him there had been many weeks of solid friendship before that. With a horrid blankness she realized that they had carried no weight. Yet he had stopped to speak to her, an inner voice pleaded.

'You've been making some improvements at the Larach, then?' Of course he would have heard. 'Have you changed your mind about staying after all?'

Clare's thoughts tumbled like the fragments in a turned kaleidoscope. She had so honestly believed that her decision to stay here had nothing to do with Donald; yet now she was near him again that seemed impossibly naive. But her chief concern in this flurried moment was that he must never suspect that such a consideration had entered her mind. Then she reminded herself that it would never have occurred to him, and thought how surprised he would be at this emotional mish-mash. Just give some practical answer, she told herself angrily.

'Oh, it all adds to the value of the property when you come to sell, doesn't it?' she said brightly.

Donald's face, after another searching look, became perfectly blank. He turned to stare ahead of him, down the road. 'Yes, you're right. Nothing much to stay for in a place like this. I probably shan't be here much longer myself.'

About to say that wasn't what she had meant, Clare's attention was arrested by this much more startling news. 'You're leaving?' Her voice sounded creaky with shock.

'There'll be no point in staying.' He wasn't looking at her, his face set in grim lines. 'Sheep-farming has had its day. I've certainly had enough of it, anyway. I'm thinking of going to Canada. My sister lives there, haven't seen her for years. Have a look around . . .'

When Ishbel is dead. The harsh unspoken words hung between them.

'Yes, of course.' What was there to say?

Donald's head turned away from her. Past him Clare saw Joe's car coming down to the open gate, heard the scrunch of loose stones as he pulled up.

'You'll be enjoying doing a bit of exploring,' Donald said courteously, looking at her again with eyes like bits of grey glass; the walker, the tourist. 'I'll be on my way, let you get home.'

'Donald!' But what could she say to him? She wanted to reach out to touch his hand, his sleeve. Her hand felt as though it had moved of its own accord, so imperative was this need. But it hadn't. She unhooked her aching fingers from the slot where the window ran and stepped back.

Donald had raised his hand to Joe, an acknowledgement that he knew he was in the way and was about to get out of it. For one second as the Land Rover moved forward his eyes met Clare's, probing, cold. With the most formal of nods he accelerated away.

It had happened in seconds, emotions whirling up then left suspended. Clare went automatically to shut the gate, thankful to have a few moments in which to try and assimilate the one devastating fact.

'Chum of yours?' Joe asked, rolling down to the road and punctiliously checking for traffic before pulling out.

'Just one of the local farmers,' Clare answered, impressed by her own ordinary tone.

CHAPTER TWENTY-TWO

After Lilias's ticking-off over the dinner party for Magda one thing Clare did not omit was to call and thank Stephen for leaving the brace of grouse. To her surprise she found that he and Lucy and the children had already left.

'Did he take some birds over?' Lilias asked, surprised. 'I can't think when he found the time. Of course I'll thank him for you when I next write.'

'I'm sorry I didn't see them to say goodbye. I thought they were going at the end of the week. I must have got it wrong.'

'You were quite right,' said Lilias. 'They left early.'

Clare looked at her quickly. Lilias's manner was very controlled, but there was a tenseness there which hinted that the control was fragile. Gerald too was unusually subdued, the whole atmosphere fraught with things needing to be said. It was impossible to talk with Joe there, champing at the bit to get away for an ambitious day in Glencoe, but Clare felt torn as they left, suspecting that it would have taken very little to break down the barriers and wishing she could have stayed.

'Snooty old pair,' Joe commented. 'All that plum in the mouth stuff's a bit over the top, isn't it?'

'They are perfect lambs,' Clare said unguardedly.

'Perfect lambs?' he mimicked, seizing on the phrase. '*Perfect lambs?* Come off it, Clare, their sort went out with rationing.'

'They've been very good to me.'

'Can't say they're my type. Now, what do you say we push on a bit, then perhaps we can get down in time to have a look at the Nevisport sale on the way back?'

Clare enjoyed the day. She had decided to let everything else go as long as Joe was on leave, temporarily abandoning Fergus, giving up the pursuit of Pete and Ewan, leaving the stone-paved corner half-laid, neglecting house and garden. There was certainly no time for thinking about the Markies or Donald or anyone else on the wicked ridge of the Aonach Eagach, which was challenging enough to absorb all her attention. Joe was at his best, watchful, encouraging, professional, and not stinting of praise after an exhilarating run down. They were in time for the sale where Joe made a killing, equipping himself for the new job, the new life, as recklessly and excitedly as a small boy. They went home well pleased with themselves, swinging over the headland in the chilly dusk feeling they could go for miles, coming in to find the cottage warm, the water rumbling promisingly in the hot tank, the oven ready for the chicken Kievs Joe had picked up.

It was good not to be alone, Clare thought, good to unwind, potter about together getting dinner ready, good to stretch out in front of the fire afterwards, muscles relaxed, skin glowing, eyelids drooping.

The only problem was that Joe wasn't making the right moves. Clare felt drowsy, sensuous, ready to be amorous. She wanted his arms round her, his hands caressing her. She longed with sudden acuteness for the remembered silky feel of skin on skin, the slow awakening of the senses, the delicious fulfilment and oblivion. She wanted Joe's long limbs against hers, wanted to sleep in the curve of his body. She had found that she was increasingly conscious of him now, aware of every small contact as they huddled in the lee of a rock together to eat their sandwiches on the hill, as he reached a hand to her crossing a burn or threw a casual arm round her shoulders in a gesture of mutual congratulation as they made the last few yards to the car, coming down after another strenuous and successful day. But it wasn't enough. Joe was affectionate, demonstrative even, but nothing ever developed, and he seemed quite unaware of the response he was arousing in Clare. Each night he departed to his tent apparently perfectly satisfied with the arrangement, leaving her restless, too conscious of his nearness, anxiously going over the evening's signals, wondering where she was going wrong and if he wanted some lead from her.

So often the message would have seemed to her unequivocal,

the mood perfect, and she would be drifting on a slow uncomplicated tide of desire when Joe would bounce up to make tea or
change a tape or build up the fire which never satisfied him
unless it was blazing like an advertisement for British Coal. Clare
would remind herself that the way she had been living during
those last months at Carlini's was not the norm. But she was
burning for involvement, for some kind of commitment. She
found herself scraping round for excuses for him. Once he was
out of the Air Force, free of its associations, settled in his new
job, things would develop naturally.

It seemed that she was right when, after final clearing from
his station, Joe arrived driving an Isuzu jeep to the door. Clare
could not control a moment of pure outrage at the sight of it
there, but fortunately Joe was so intent on his new toy that he
didn't register it. She resolutely thrust down the feeling of
invasion, understanding this was a big moment for Joe.

The cottage was swamped in seconds with kit, presents, mem-
entoes. 'There you are, how's that?' Joe asked proudly, propping
a crudely made station plaque on the mantelpiece. 'Where can
this go?' Out came the inevitable tankard, fulsomely inscribed.
'On the dresser? What do you think?'

I think you could have kissed me.

'Won't you want that in your new flat?' she suggested. 'What's
it like, by the way?'

He had dropped off most of his kit there, though not nearly
enough by the look of it, on his way up.

'No, this can live here. The flat's OK. Anyway it'll only be
for four nights a week, won't it?'

He moved a bowl of Tigh Bhan apples and put the tankard
in the centre of the dresser, surveying it with satisfaction. As in
the matter of the jeep, this was no time to dash his elation. As
he seemed to be making statements Clare wondered in passing
whether the tent would be put up tonight and felt a small shiver
of sexual anticipation.

'Won this in the draw,' Joe was saying, rummaging in a holdall
and pulling out an object wrapped in a sweatshirt. Under Clare's
appalled eyes he uncovered a china shepherdess with aspirations
to the ballet since one toe was higher than her head. 'Listen to
this.' Joe twisted the figure rapidly on her grassy base and set her

on the table where she slowly untwirled to the tune of 'The Lass of Richmond Hill'.

'Joe, how—'

'Ghastly' Clare had been about to say in joyful horror, when Joe gave the shepherdess another turn and said proudly, 'Just the thing for here, isn't she? Cottagey. Bit of luck getting that. You should've heard the lads, but I don't give a monkey's for any of that now.' He made passes with the mutedly tinkling figure, trying her on bookcase and windowsill. 'Or shall I take some of the books off the dresser and make room for her there? Those rows need breaking up a bit.'

'Let's decide later, shall we?' Clare said, and then was ashamed of the sham heartiness in her voice.

Joe seemed content, however, delving once more into his grip. 'Got these for you, you don't treat yourself very often.' A huge box of milk chocolates; Clare's throat closed at the thought of having to eat a single one of its nauseating contents. 'And I thought we could have a look through this lot after tea.' He lifted out a set of albums, gold-lettered, gold-tasselled, each covered in a different coloured plastic over sponge, and an HMSO folder bulging with loose photographs. 'I'll have to get a couple more albums, then we can stick this lot in some day in the winter when the weather's too rough to go out.' By 'go out' Joe meant into the hills. He had to put the stacks of *Fitness* and *Climber and Hill Walker* and all his maps on the floor for the time being, but his country and western tapes had their own rack. Why hadn't I expected this? Clare thought wildly, escaping to start dinner. But wasn't it exactly what I wanted? she reminded herself.

Joe slept on the sofa-bed and Clare lay alone in her chilly bedroom, every nerve jumping with need, imprisoned by his presence outside the door, baffled and angry – mainly with herself. She couldn't read, couldn't relax, and certainly couldn't sleep. She longed to rush out and have a tremendous row along the lines of, 'How dare you clutter up my house with this hideous junk and then not—?' Not what? Not try to get your leg over? She tried to stifle her hysterical giggles, then realized that Joe, like any other man who ever lived, would have fallen obliviously asleep long ago.

She hated waking the next morning and seeing the jeep parked outside. Joe was delighted with it.

'Can't think why you never got yourself something like this ages ago,' he said more than once. 'Even in bad weather I should be able to get over here most of the time. You'll have no problems getting your shopping now, will you?'

She knew she could never make him understand. Casting round for something positive to say she offered, 'We could take the empty gas cylinder to be changed.'

'There you are, you see! What would you have done about that if I hadn't bought the jeep?'

Clare couldn't bring herself to reply.

But when Joe went to the shed to collect the cylinder he called after a moment, 'Where is it, Clare? I can only see a couple of full ones here.'

'There should only be one full.' But when she went to look she saw that both cylinders had their paper discs still in place. 'How odd. It must have been changed before Magda came.' She frowned, unable to work out the timing.

'You're going as bananas as all the rest of them up here,' Joe teased her, pleased to have caught her out.

It was a good weekend on the whole, though. Joe was in tremendous spirits to be free of the watching eye of the Service, so much a part of his life for years that he had almost forgotten it was there but giving an extraordinary sense of personal liberty once it was withdrawn. He was excited and confident about the new job and it was no moment, Clare felt, for her to make any distracting claims of her own.

She saw him off on Sunday afternoon at the hump-backed bridge before the village, looking forward to walking home over the hill. As she went through the gate she saw ahead of her a toiling figure in a Burberry and her mind at once registered something odd about it. No dogs.

'Lilias!' Clare ran to catch up. 'Hi! Lilias! Are you on your way to call on me?'

Lilias slowed, wavered, and as though with a great effort turned her head. Coming up to her Clare was startled to see her face set like a mask, cheeks wet with tears.

'Lilias, darling, whatever has happened?' Clare put an arm

round her and it felt as though she could have crushed the frail collection of bones without effort. Lilias leaned against her with a gesture of relinquishing control that was absolutely alien.

'Lilias, please, tell me what's wrong. Is it Gerald?'

'No, not Gerald.' She seemed to have difficulty in finding the breath to get the words out.

'Stephen? The family? Oh, Lilias, what is it? Whatever has happened?' Clare carefully flattened the anxiety in her voice.

'They're all fine.'

'Is it Topsy or Poppy?'

Lilias shook her head helplessly.

'Come on,' Clare said gently, loving concern swamping her at that defeated gesture, 'let's go back to Tigh Bhan. It's bitterly cold out here. Then you can tell me what's wrong.' And Gerald might be there and able to explain if Lilias couldn't.

'Lucy.'

'What about Lucy?' Clare felt a chill of fear as she turned an unresisting Lilias in the direction of the house.

'She's gone.'

CHAPTER TWENTY-THREE

Lilias, though mute and shocked at first, was gradually able to tell Clare what had driven Lucy away. She had been fighting all summer against sending Oliver to Gordonstoun. On the day Stephen returned from seeing him off to school, he found her gone. She had left a note saying that Libby, whose term didn't start for another week, was at a friend's house.

Stephen was due to spend most of the week at Ministry of Defence meetings in Whitehall, and Gerald and Lilias had decided to take charge. Clare never discovered whether Stephen wanted them to, since the only conversation she had with them centred round the firm proviso that wherever they went and whatever else happened they were not going to drive to London. Clare put them on the train at Fort William and drove back to Tigh Bhan in their Metro, hoping she had assimilated a complex time-table, menu and health programme for the dogs, and trying to forget the picture of the two anxious old faces smiling bravely as they waved goodbye.

Barbara Bailey was to look after Poppy and Topsy during the day and Clare had agreed to sleep at Tigh Bhan. After a lot of misinformation from Strathclyde Regional Council, she got through to Joe to tell him what was happening then turned to her own affairs.

There were Trudy's books to prepare for audit, and Fergus was badly on her conscience. She drove up to Glen Righ House on a morning of pelting rain, knowing that she should be grateful to have the car which Lilias had insisted she used while they were away, but slightly oppressed by a feeling of ordinariness. Braan and Chippy came baying and grinning out of the courtyard door to meet her and Catriona rushed out after them.

'Oh, Clare, something so awful!' she cried. 'I don't know how to tell you.' Have I heard this somewhere before? Clare wondered. It had the ring of drama rather than of tragedy, however, and it didn't sound as though anything had happened to Fergus.

'Come and look,' Catriona wailed with theatrical despair. The dogs jostled them along the icy passage as though they knew exciting things were afoot. Catriona led the way into a murky boot-hole and with a wave of her arm revealed to Clare the fate of Great-Aunt Sofia's diaries, or Clare's version of them at least. 'Grandfather had a bad day – he does sometimes. He thought someone had been using the library and he was annoyed and he did this before I realized.'

'Hamster litter,' Clare said cheerfully. No point in getting excited about a job as thorough as that. Even as she thought this it crossed her mind that a few months ago such a disaster would have thrown her into quivering rage.

'I thought you'd be furious,' Catriona gasped. 'I've hardly slept.'

Clare looked at her more carefully. Her eyes had huge bruised shadows under them and her mouth was trembling as she gazed worriedly at Clare.

'Don't look so desperate,' Clare said, half laughing at her tragic expression but harrowed to imagine Fergus's distress and Catriona having to cope with this sort of thing alone. 'I can do it again, if you still think Fergus wants it done.'

'Oh, he does, he does. It was only that one day when he was confused. He's been searching and searching for the translations everywhere since he did this. He used to read them over and over again. He was getting so frantic that I even thought of coming to fetch you, to ask you to write a bit of it out again to calm him down, but Mrs MacGillivray said your friend was still staying with you. I think Grandfather has a vague idea that he's done something with them himself, but he can't work it out and it's upsetting him dreadfully.'

'Don't worry, I'll get something on paper for him today. I don't mind redoing it. I can always improve on it. But what we need is a word processor, then we can't lose the lot ever again.'

'I'm not quite sure I know exactly what a word processor is,'

Catriona said humbly, 'but wouldn't it be terribly expensive?'

'Not necessarily.' There was no way of knowing if the way they lived was habit, indifference or actual poverty. The only things always in lavish supply were Fergus's gin and dog food. I must ask Donald what he thinks, Clare decided. No, I must work something out for myself, she instantly amended.

Feeling that Catriona needed therapy as much as her grandfather, Clare decided at lunch-time (having also seen what was on offer) that she would teach Catriona to make omelettes.

'I thought you had to whisk them.'

'That explains those slabs of bath sponge you produce. And I suppose the brown bits underneath would have been rust,' Clare added, examining the pan Catriona had given her.

It was a relief to hear her giggle.

'Butter in the pan – about an eighth of that, thank you, Catriona – draw it towards the middle, let the rest run to the sides. Here, you do it.'

Catriona hooked her hair behind her ears and concentrated.

'Tap the handle to slide it out, flip it over with the edge of— Oh, well, close.'

But Catriona was entirely satisfied, diving in there and then with the bent old fork she had used to beat the eggs. 'We can always make more. Um, this is *good*.'

Clare seized her chance. 'Catriona, have you ever thought of getting help with Fergus? Just so that you could get out a bit more?'

Catriona's face closed immediately, threatened, stubborn.

'Come on, you can talk to me. It's such a lonely life for someone your age.'

'I like it. And Grandfather hates having anyone else in the house. If I'm not here he gets into a frightful state.'

Received version. 'Does he get into a frightful state every time you go into Luig or out riding?'

Catriona said nothing.

'Isn't there someone on the estate who could stay with him – be in the house while you're out?'

'He can't bear Mrs MacGillivray,' Catriona objected.

'Not the most soothing person,' Clare agreed. 'But there must be other people.' Though in fact, as she knew by now, most of the Glen Righ estate cottages stood empty or were already derelict.

Catriona had stopped eating her omelette and was standing with head bent, hair swinging forward once more in a protective veil.

'Or is it that you don't want to change things?' Clare pursued very gently. 'I don't want to butt in, so tell me to shut up if you want to, but I can see how easy it must be to go on from day to day in the same way. Yet you seem to like being with me, and you enjoyed meeting Joe the other day. Aren't there any friends you'd like to get in touch with again?'

There was a highly charged pause. Clare knew if Catriona rejected this opening there would be no excuse for interfering again.

'It's not only being out of touch with people,' Catriona burst out abruptly in a voice full of desperation. 'I feel as though I don't know anything about – anything. Literally. I feel as though everything outside this glen is modern and sophisticated and utterly beyond me, as though I wouldn't know how to use a telephone or buy a ticket or drive on a motorway. I feel as though I don't know what people are wearing, or eating, or saying or reading. I don't know about word processors!' she wound up with a sniff and a gulp, laughing at herself tremulously.

'I could help,' Clare offered, almost holding her breath.

'But you do. You have. I haven't enjoyed being with anyone so much, just laughing and talking, doing ordinary things, since Iain died.'

Six, seven years? 'We'll work something out,' Clare promised, her voice husky, hugging her.

'Do you know one thing I'd really like to do?'

'What?' Clare couldn't imagine what it could be.

'See the Larach. Everyone talks about how nice you've made it – nobody ever believed you'd really stay, you know – and it's always good when estate houses are lived in again.'

Had she remembered Clare had bought it? But if that was all she wanted in the world, to see a cottage on her own doorstep . . . 'It certainly seems an ambition not entirely beyond realization,' she assured Catriona, and was glad to hear her laugh again.

Clare made plans as she drove back to Tigh Bhan.

Living there was strange. For one thing she had never looked after dogs before, but once Topsy and Poppy had organized her to their satisfaction, which they did without delay, she was no further trouble to them. She enjoyed the comfortable, well-furnished rooms, the paintings, the collection of beautiful and fascinating objects from the years of travelling, the music and books, and knew she should also enjoy the luxuries of even heat throughout the house, endless hot water with no fire to worry about, warm bathroom, battery of machines. But somehow it was too bright, too perfect, too stifling.

It was useful to have a telephone though, and Joe, full of the new things that were happening in his life, was delighted to be able to chat at every opportunity. Lilias's daily calls concentrated on the safe subject of the dogs, who Clare swore were missing her though certain they were incapable of any emotion beyond greed and self-interest. A great silence had fallen about Lucy.

On Wednesday evening Joe phoned to say that the duty roster had been changed and he was off till midday on Saturday. He was going to drive up first thing in the morning and wanted Clare to meet him at the Ballachulish Hotel so that they could do Bheinn à Bheithir.

'Joe, I can't tomorrow, I'm sorry. I promised I'd help Trudy with her book-keeping.'

'She'll understand when you tell her my days off have been changed.'

'I can't let her down, Joe. Why don't you have a day on Bheinn à Bheithir on your own?'

He did his best to persuade her, but Clare was firm and in the end he said he'd come to the Mill and wait until she was free. She didn't feel it was an ideal plan and hoped he wasn't going to spend the whole day chivvying her. The question of where he would sleep on this visit had been glossed over. Lilias had said that of course he must stay at Tigh Bhan, but Clare didn't feel happy about it. It might be disastrous, like an eagerly antici-pated sexy weekend which dies at dinner on the first evening and leaves two bored, frustrated people stuck with each other in strange surroundings. Nor could she gauge what Joe would want or expect. Then there would be Barbara Bailey appearing in the morning, though it was a bit late, Clare reminded herself, to worry about anything Barbara Bailey might relay to the village and glen when Joe's tent had been regularly pitched outside the Larach for all the world to see, its presence doubtless a well-enjoyed joke.

In any case, Clare couldn't fool herself that it was glen opinion in general that she was worrying about. It seemed so long since she had seen Donald and she knew his whole attention must be concentrated on Ishbel, in whose condition no change was reported since she had come back from hospital, yet somewhere always at the back of her mind was a restless need to explain to him about Joe, to justify Joe's presence, even have a fight about Joe. And she still hated the idea that Donald might have seen her in the same light as Magda, equating them in their patronizing intolerance. She cringed to remember how thoughtlessly critical she had been in her first weeks here, doing her best to adapt but tense and anxious, deeply unsure of herself. It seemed now, the thought growing more and more exaggerated as she worried about it, that she had complained to Donald about everything – the squalor Murdo had been content to live in, Ina's cooking, the resources of Fort William, the school bus. No wonder he had given her up as a bad job.

'Why on earth didn't you ask me to sort this lot out long ago?'

Clare was kneeling on the floor of the living area of the Old Mill, wrinkled ethnic rugs and dusty wood invisible under piles of invoices and statements.

'I hadn't realized it was quite this bad,' Trudy confessed, pushing back her long brown hair with a hand holding a fan of petty cash chits. 'Do you think you can do anything with it?'

'The shop side probably. There only seem to be a few blank cheque stubs for the pottery.'

'Ben regards bills as a compromise of his liberty as an individual.'

Clare knew nothing useful would be achieved by saying what she thought of Ben, who had strategically removed himself to an exhibition in Birmingham. Perhaps it was easier anyway to get the broad picture clear without him.

Soon after an abstracted lunch when neither of them could pull their minds away from the job in hand, Joe arrived, elated, bursting to talk, impatient for Clare to come away with him and salvage what was left of the day.

'I'd really like to get further with this,' Clare said. 'I did promise Trudy I'd be here all day. You wouldn't like to keep an eye on the shop for her while we carry on?'

'Oh, give me a break,' he protested.

'I thought you might not mind. You were quite happy to help out before while I was working,' Clare reminded him.

'But I'd turned up out of the blue then, hadn't I? This is my weekend off, our weekend.' It didn't seem worth reminding him that it was Thursday and that it was he who'd changed the plot.

He prowled around restlessly till Clare sent him to do some shopping, but she knew she would have to abandon the accounts when he came back. At least she now had a rough idea of how they stood. There would then be the last weeks of the accounting period to go through, stock-taking . . . and exasperating as the prospect was, she would have to interrogate Ben, and probably make him turn out his pockets, before she could do much more. She would have liked to suggest taking Trudy out for a pub supper, but she knew Joe felt he deserved some attention by now and reluctantly gave up the idea.

Once back at Tigh Bhan he gloated openly over the house – where Clare for the time being ducked showing him to a room.

'You've done pretty well for yourself here. Bet you're enjoying a bit of luxury for a change, eh?' On went the kettle, off came his sweater. He'd brought his washing. 'Bit of forward planning there, see,' he said, tipping his bag out on to the kitchen floor and filling the washing machine there and then. 'Anything of yours to go in?'

Lilias would expect them to make themselves at home, would be positively annoyed if they didn't, Clare tried to persuade herself.

'You should bring your sheets and stuff over while you've got the chance,' Joe said, stuffing in the jeans Clare had handed him. He was perfectly serious.

After dinner he pulled her down beside him on to one of the big downy sofas. 'This is the life,' he remarked with gratification, arm round Clare, legs stretched out, remote control within reach.

'I miss the telly at the cottage. You'll have to get power over there soon.'

Clare felt rebellious and edgy, uncomfortably conscious of dodging the issue of where Joe would sleep, resenting his casual arm and his absorption in some noisy drama, and even more indignant when he took time off during the commercial break to kiss her. Then she was turned on by the kiss and, which was worse, must have shown it.

She felt the instant stilling of Joe's body, his mouth withdrawing, his arms slackening. 'Better behave ourselves, hadn't we? Whatever would your friend have to say?'

Clare knew then that he wouldn't stay, had never thought of staying. She bit back the protest that Lilias wouldn't mind. Joe's morality was the product of an early background where everyone worried about what the neighbours would think, reinforced by dated service codes, and he would be ill at ease and disapproving if she tried to override it. And how much fun would there be in that?

The dogs were not impressed to have their usual last-thing couple of minutes in the garden turned into a round of the windy fields between road and loch, while Clare attempted to walk off some of her frustration after Joe had driven away. They hurried into their baskets with reproachful looks the moment they got home.

CHAPTER TWENTY-FOUR

By the time Joe's next visit was over Clare was beginning to feel more than a little driven, not only because once more he had slept at the Larach and she at Tigh Bhan and she was getting tired of cosy affectionate evenings and lonely nights, but because when he was there for his days off everything else had to be shelved.

Gerald and Lilias, looking weary and oddly smaller, had come home and had begged Clare to stay on with them for a night or two. She saw that they felt in need of cosseting, which she was only too happy to provide, but she also guessed that each wanted to talk to someone outside the family. Reticently at first, with conscientious riders about there being two sides to everything and how wrong it was to make judgements, their grief and pain found words. Each added to the picture when alone with Clare, and each returned continually to the question of Gordonstoun, refusing to see that it was only a battle and not the war.

'It was all agreed. Lucy had accepted it. You can't suddenly start playing fast and loose with a boy's whole future.'

'Where did she imagine he could have gone instead, at no notice?'

'Stephen was quite right to insist.'

'It's so hard on poor Oliver.'

What hurt and bewildered them most was that Lucy had left no trace behind her, and no one knew if she ever intended to see the children again. Stephen would not search for her, nor would he pack up her belongings or discuss the future.

'We feel so fortunate to have you here,' Lilias told Clare as they put most of dinner uneaten into the fridge. 'We could hardly have borne to have come back to an empty house.'

'Good of you to stay,' said Gerald in his turn, patting her arm as she took him his coffee by the drawing-room fire. 'I don't think I always say quite the right things.'

What an admission, Clare thought with affection. But she could see for herself that it helped them to be able to focus on her, to ask how the dogs had behaved, whether Barbara Bailey had looked after her properly, if the car had started on cold mornings. They were eager to be entertained by crises at the Old Mill and dramas at Glen Righ House, horrified by what Fergus had done with Great-Aunt Sofia and emphatic about how good it was for Catriona to have Clare there.

Catriona – another matter neglected, Clare was guiltily reminded as she settled into the Larach again. There had been no chance to invite her down yet, which after all had been such a simple thing to ask. She must do something about it soon, before the impulse to break out of the cage died again.

It was the end of September already. Pete and Ewan seemed to have vanished and several other jobs were pressing. Joe wanted to be out as much as possible whenever he was there, Glasgow having been a considerable shock to the system and the transition from service to civilian life a good deal harder than he had expected. His usual energy had a slightly frenetic edge to it these days and Clare didn't find him restful company.

He was now generally accepted as her boyfriend. Lilias had invited them both to dinner the following week, Trudy and Ben had talked about the four of them going out somewhere one evening, and even Catriona had insisted that Clare mustn't think of coming to help Fergus when Joe was at the Larach. And they had come face to face with Donald one morning in Angus's shop.

More shaken than she had imagined she could be by such a chance encounter, Clare had done her best to make the introduction casual and had only succeeded in sounding offhand, her voice infuriatingly too high, too English. Beside Donald's breadth in his work-worn waxed jacket Joe looked lightweight, his bright blue sweatshirt holiday garb, his fair hair boyish. The two men shook hands, locked eyes for one second, then exchanged brief nods and a few careful remarks about probable conditions on the hill. Clare didn't know if the tension was in them or in her, but decided that the rest of her shopping could wait till she got to Fort William.

During a grey day on Bheinn à Bheithir, a plan which hadn't gone away, with an approach through well-grown plantations and a second peak so like the first it seemed superfluous to go up it, she did her best to order and subdue the feelings that brief glimpse of Donald had stirred up. She had not even asked about Ishbel, too cowardly to put the question and ashamed to realize that her chief concern had been not for Ishbel's condition but for Donald's plans.

She tried to wrench her mind away, but found it turned instead to other worries, more mundane it was true, but urgent just the same. There were so many things she should be doing at home. There was a stack of wood waiting to be sawn, which she had hoped Joe would help with in view of the huge fires he favoured. The new door to the kitchen should be primed and painted before winter weather made the job impossible. Lilias's curtains had to be altered to fit the new window, should Pete and Ewan ever reappear to put it in, and there was the cushioned seat to be made for its sill. The paved corner for sitting out would have to wait till the spring, and the steps to the jetty, which she'd been looking forward to working on, weren't a priority now, she thought with a pang. But one thing that couldn't wait was cleaning out the water tank. The heavy rain of the previous week had carried down a mass of accumulated summer debris and Gerald had warned her that if she didn't attend to it right away she would be in trouble.

Joe had said he would help her, but after living so long in barracks he had a tendency to think such jobs looked after themselves. Clare had imagined that as the outdoor survivor type he would enjoy them, but he showed no inclination to get involved and as he usually had a full programme worked out when he arrived they invariably ended up yet again in the expedition training mode.

Clare finally gave up hope of his helping and decided to tackle the job on her own, encouraged by an afternoon of mellow sunshine, Luig Hill a coppery mass above pale harvested fields, the loch dancing and sparkling under a gentle wind. It was rather agreeable to be on her own, she thought with slight guilt, then wondered if she might not regret it as the heavy lid of the tank threatened to defeat her before she began. She managed to work it gradually aside, however, successfully diverted the inflow, and indulged in some nice wet work dredging the burn and the overflow while waiting for the tank to empty. She was flat on her face struggling to free the rose, which was only just within her reach and seemed to be welded on to the pipe, when with a heart-stopping shock she received a vigorous nudge under her armpit which all but broke the tenuous hold of her splayed feet on the sloping ground.

As she yelped, paddling air with her hands, a voice ordered, 'Come out of that, Trim,' and a strong hand took a grip of Clare's ankle and heaved her back the couple of inches necessary to restore her balance.

'God!' she exploded, rolling away from the lip of the tank while a hideously smiling Trim licked her effusively in welcome or apology. 'You nearly had me in, dog!' She pushed the collie away and looked up. Donald, a colossus against the duck-egg blue sky, was smiling down at her. Thank goodness I've got every excuse to be out of breath, she thought.

'All right?' Donald enquired, reaching a hand to pull her to her feet.

'I think my heart's going again, thanks.' In quite painful jerks, she could have added.

'Having trouble?' he asked, nodding at the tank. 'I saw you from the loch.'

'Cleaning it out. Gerald's orders.'

'Ah well, he's right enough for once,' he said, with that glimmer of a smile of his. 'It's a good long time since this tank was last looked at.'

Today there was none of the reserve in his manner which Clare had so much minded at their last two brief meetings. He was already taking off his jacket, tossing it across a clump of heather and lying down to reach for the rose which came off sweetly at his touch. 'That was badly needing cleared.'

'I'm surprised anything was coming down the tap,' Clare agreed, wrinkling her nose at the little pile of black muddy fragments he was tapping off it.

'Are you getting down in the tank or am I?' Donald asked, rinsing the filter in the burn.

'I take it that's a rhetorical question?'

He steadied her as she lowered herself into the last couple of inches of water and brownish-green slime. 'God, do I drink this stuff?'

'Not what's below the pipe,' Donald explained with exaggerated patience.

Clare found it hard to keep her feet and it was oddly spooky down there. She baled away, glad he was there; glad, glad, glad.

With Clare out of the tank again and the rose back on, Donald seemed in no hurry to go, improving on the clearing of the overflow channel Clare had begun. They worked away contentedly, recapturing without effort the mood of early summer, catching up on news, sharing their concern about Gerald and Lilias, and Donald, like Lilias, expressed his approval for the help Clare was giving Catriona. He told her that one of Ishbel's sisters was staying at Rhumore at present with her three children for half-term, but didn't sound as though he would welcome questions. For Clare the peace his presence brought was as warm and perfect as the day.

Then from far and high above them a thin gabbling music penetrated their talk, and they abandoned work to squint up under their hands into the cloudless arc of blue.

'Geese! There they are.' The fluid wavering echelon, the calling voices, awe at the instinct that impels these beautiful creatures to the long journey; and being there, on this sunny hillside with the gleaming loch stretching away below them, seeing this sight with Donald, caught Clare by the throat.

Donald glanced down at her, smiled and said softly, 'I know. I've seen them every year since I can remember and it gets to me every time.'

Clare turned hastily back to work to hide whatever else her face might reveal.

Donald unblocked the inflow, watched the clean water running in for a moment, slid the cover back over the tank with no apparent effort and stooped to pick up his coat. He was going; Clare felt an instant clutch of loss.

'You'll come in for coffee?'

She heard the too-urgent note in her voice. If Donald heard it too he gave no sign. He began to gather up the strange assortment of tools she had thought suitable for tank-cleaning and set off down the slope with his measured stride. But he hadn't replied.

He mustn't go; she couldn't bear it. 'Donald, I wonder if you'd mind looking at something for me. Giving me your advice –'

'Shall we turn the taps off first?'

Clare had forgotten that detail. The teasing note in his voice steadied her. 'It's about the alterations to the cottage. I'd be glad if you'd tell me what you think.'

She outlined the plan, told him about Pete and Ewan's reservations and her own fear of spoiling the exterior by closing off the door. Donald paced solemnly about, stood well back from the house and considered, went inside and had a look from across the room, turned down his mouth and shook his head judiciously. Clare wished Joe hadn't left so many of his belongings lying about.

'No good?' she asked, disheartened by Donald's dubious expression. 'Silly idea?'

'It will be the making of the place,' he pronounced.

'Donald, you so-and-so! What a wind-up.'

'So why isn't the window in yet? Can't you get hold of Pete?'

'I paid them for what they'd done so far,' she admitted.

'That's no use.'

'I didn't think I should go to McCosh's yard to send a message via Kenny.'

'No, that wouldn't be exactly ideal,' he conceded, almost smiling.

'All right, I don't want to know all the ins and outs of their activities, but the question is, will they get the job done before the winter?'

'I'll see to it that they do.' How good that sounded to Clare. 'Let's have a look at what they've done so far.' He nodded approval of the kitchen and larder, though he ran his thumb along the edge of a couple of new shelves and did some disgusted muttering about bevelling.

'And here, outside, I wanted to close off this gap between the house and the shed, only I wasn't sure, would the whole thing blow away, including the shed, if there was a bad storm, do you think?' Clare knew that she was babbling and didn't care. She was fizzing with a reckless happiness just to have him there, just to be able to snatch this brief time with him.

'Oh, I think it will last a year or two yet,' Donald replied temperately. 'Which reminds me, did you find the grouse I hung on the door, or did the fox get them?'

'The grouse? You? Oh, God, Donald, I thought Stephen Markie had left them. I hadn't realized you'd even been here.'

'So who do you think changed your gas cylinder, the Loch Buie monster?'

Clare gaped at him. 'I thought I must have got muddled and had a full one all along. I never thought of you – I mean, after I got your message.'

Donald was suddenly alert, rather dauntingly so. 'What message?'

'The one you sent by Nicol.'

'What did he say?'

'I didn't actually see him. He left a note with my mail at the farm saying you wouldn't be calling at the Larach any more.'

'The message was,' Donald said very carefully, and Clare found herself hoping that she would never make him seriously angry, 'that I couldn't take you to the village for your shopping as long as I was busy with the grouse.'

Clare remembered him explaining that although stalking started in July and grouse shooting went on through November, on high ground like Rhumore, and with no gamekeeper but himself, each took its turn.

They stared at each other, fitting the pieces together.

'I've been by more than once,' Donald said, 'but you've always been out. Then – well, latterly you've not needed anything, have you?'

Clare couldn't cope with that one just now. 'But you must have wondered why I said nothing, about the gas cylinder or the grouse, that day I met you up by the forestry gate.'

'I did. Not that it was important, but it wasn't like you.'

'Oh, Donald, I'm sorry. But that day I thought you were still angry about Magda.'

He looked at her, frowning, then said briskly, 'Where's this coffee you were talking about?'

Clare was disappointed; she hadn't thought he would simply shelve a sore point. 'Donald, can't we clear it up? Everyone else has forgiven me.'

'Can't we have our coffee while we talk?'

What he said was entirely unexpected. Sitting beside her on their favourite boulder, the sun warm on their faces, he was silent for a moment, then launched into the narrative style he jokingly used to employ for telling her what he called tales of the glen.

'Once upon a time, in the far distant past, a young man called Donald Macrae set off to the university in the grand city of Aberdeen – since, contrary to what you may suppose, one or two folk hereabouts know how to read and write.' He shot her a sardonic glance and Clare realized that though she hadn't moved a muscle he had read her surprise. 'Just to read agriculture, you understand,' he added with irony. 'Nothing too fancy.'

'Donald, tell me properly.'

'Oh, it's not a new story. I met a girl there and fell in love.' There was self-mockery in the three syllables, but also, even now, there was tenderness, nostalgia, and a tolerance for the young man he had been, and Clare felt a wave of hot jealousy, such as she had never felt over Ishbel, rise up and nearly choke her.

'We were very happy, moved into a little flat together and thought it was all going to be for ever. Then I went to stay with her folk and she came to Rhumore.' Clare glanced at what she could see of his dour face and held her tongue. 'Her father was a solicitor in Chester. They lived in an old mellow-brick house with a paddock and a tennis court. Her mother was so polite to me it set my teeth on edge but her father had several farmers among his clients so he was able to talk to me man to man.' Donald gave a little grunt of laughter; Clare could feel the long-ago helpless discomfiture. 'Then Annabel came to stay here. My mother did her best, but my father showed her exactly what he thought of her, the thrawn old bugger.' It was rare to hear him swear, or indeed speak so forcefully. 'I nearly went then,' he said, as though the memory could still surprise him. 'I'd always wanted to travel, have a go at something besides sheep-farming, be free of the old man for a while, though it had always been understood that I would take on the farm eventually. Anyway, Annabel pretended to accept that. I think she thought that if once she got me away she could see to it that we never came back. Only she made one big mistake. She couldn't wait to let me see what she thought of us, my parents, the house, our whole way of life.'

He paused for so long that Clare thought she should make some comment, but frankly didn't have the courage.

'Well, that's it,' Donald ended brusquely, shrugging. Then as Clare opened her mouth to protest that it wasn't, and demand what all this had to do with Magda, he went on in a hard voice, 'From the day Annabel left to the day I met your friend I had never again encountered quite that brand of arrogant contempt. That was exactly how Annabel spoke to my mother.'

With a shaky feeling of dismay Clare saw the rest. 'And you felt I was the same, that I looked upon everything here in the same way?'

Donald hesitated and Clare felt her heart beginning to beat in slow, heavy thumps. I don't want to hear this, she thought in anguish. But he seemed to reject whatever he had been about to say. 'You had your moments,' he said, with his ghost of a grin. 'But you had a lot to adapt to. Good God, even anyone accustomed to this environment would have had trouble getting used to living without power or a road in or a phone. And the things that threw you were always practical difficulties. You were used to being in control and being able to get more or less what you wanted, and suddenly you were at the mercy of the weather, of isolation, of a different pace and different standards. You always got on well with the people, even someone as shy as Margaret Stewart – or Catriona, come to that – though you made a few digs about the peasants in general—'

'I never said peasants!'

'– you never had a hard word to say about any individual, and that's what mattered. No, I never for a moment classed you with that so-called friend of yours, and once I'd cooled down I meant to come and see you. But then, what with one thing and another . . .'

One thing and another. His dying wife. Overcome with shame

at not having enquired before Clare said, 'Donald, I'm sorry, I should have asked. How is Ishbel?'

He looked away from her for a moment, out across the loch. 'She doesn't come down now. She's so filled up with pain-killers I don't think she knows where she is half the time.'

'I'm sorry.'

He nodded. 'I'd best be getting back.'

She went with him down to the jetty as she always used to. She had the feeling that something important had come close and drawn away again. They had put right one misunderstanding but nothing else had changed. Except that Clare knew she was going to have trouble dislodging from her brain the memory of his voice speaking another woman's name in a tone of such tenderness.

I forgot to thank him for helping me, she thought emptily, as she stood watching the dark wedge of the boat curve away from her through the bright water.

CHAPTER TWENTY-FIVE

Joe's days off were changed once more at no notice and Clare was obliged to rescramble her plans. A recent breakthrough had been persuading Margaret to go to WRI meetings, which Clare had learned was the Scottish version of WI, but since Dougie never knew when he would get home during stalking the arrangement hinged on Clare's baby-sitting. Certain that Joe would not react favourably to an evening with Lynn and Sheena, or be impressed by the state of Margaret's kitchen, she had reluctantly called to tell Margaret that she wouldn't be able to come this week.

'I'm not that bothered anyway,' Margaret said instantly, which was exactly the reaction Clare had feared. 'I can stop going altogether if you're not going to be able.'

'It's only this once. Normally Joe will be in Glasgow during the week.'

As Clare went on to Tigh Bhan from The Birks she made up her mind that whether Joe was at the Larach or not she wouldn't let Margaret miss another meeting.

Lilias took her apologies about the dinner party surprisingly well. 'Your friends do create problems for you, don't they?' was her only comment.

'I'm really sorry, Lilias. Do you want to give us up as a bad job?'

'Certainly not. The Urquharts are fairly quiet in the hotel by this stage in the season, so I'm sure they won't mind, and we can easily find another evening when John Irvine isn't on call.'

There was one small clash as Joe and Clare were getting ready for the rearranged dinner party a few days later. Clare came out of the bathroom to find him in her bedroom, long legs braced to look into the too-low mirror, combing his hair into shape and wearing a suit. It hadn't occurred to Clare that he would think of bringing one to the Larach, but of course he had been in the Air Force for a long time.

'Oh, Joe, I should have said. I'm afraid it will be rather casual.'

'Why, what are you wearing?'

'What I usually wear, only cleaner. I have to walk everywhere as a rule.'

'Yes, well, you don't have to walk everywhere now, do you?' he said snappishly, and Clare realized that he was nervous. 'I'm not going out in jeans and that's flat,' he added, taking another look at himself in the mirror and evidently liking what he saw.

Clare was aware of his indignant surprise as Gerald led them into the kitchen at Tigh Bhan where the big table was laid for one of Lilias's robust meals with a great basket of delicious-smelling rolls, pats of Jersey butter whose providers Clare passed on the Luig road a couple of times a week, low bowls of bronze chrysanthemums and a promising array of glasses.

In the overhead lights still on for cooking Joe's suit looked more blue than grey, its lines undeniably sharp. John Irvine, a GP in practice in Luig, was in sagging cords, Gerald in a cherished mustard-coloured cardigan dragged down by pockets stuffed with screws and string and knife and cigar cutter – and quite probably marbles and conkers as well, Clare thought lovingly.

Jeanette Irvine, a chatty friendly creature Clare had seen once or twice when shopping, cornered her at once about keep-fit, badgered her briefly to join a ski group, then said she'd let her off if she contributed instead to the children's Highland dancing which Jeanette ran. Noisy protests to protect Clare from her methods of extortion arose on every side.

Clare had met both Urquharts at the Old Mill. 'Ardlonach Hotel,' she said. 'Large amounts of muesli.'

'A nice wholesome way to be identified,' said slight, gentle Una, giving her a friendly smile.

And where Stephen went grouse shooting, Clare could have added but guessed, rightly, that references to him would be avoided this evening.

Tony Urquhart had been in the Navy, but had resigned his

commission on inheriting a biggish house with land on the Luig peninsula, which he had decided to turn into a hotel. Looking round the group Clare saw how carefully Lilias had planned it with Joe in mind; the medical and service links, the young-middle-aged average. Everyone was very relaxed, giving Lilias a hand or leaning on the Aga getting in her way, sitting on chairs pulled out from the table or sprawling on the dingy corduroy sofa where the dogs welcomed human migrants. Clare had warned Gerald that Joe wouldn't drink, but could do nothing to stem the hospitable attempts to urge him to some non-alcoholic alternative.

Argument was raging about the Scotland–Fiji game. Joe, drawn in kindly by Una, said he preferred football. Discussion moved hastily on to the demise of a local fish farm and the rival advantages of the skiing at Glencoe and Aonach Mhor.

Clare saw Joe jib at the sherry in the consommé and hoped that his doubts about the dice of savoury custard enriching it would not be as plain to Lilias as they were to her. Lilias certainly didn't miss Joe's lack of ease as the confident voices rose around him and she soon made an opportunity to ask him about his new job, firmly drawing in John Irvine who may or may not have been primed but who was certainly there to field that particular ball. Jeannette, an ex-PE teacher herself, joined in with some trenchant views, which luckily coincided with Joe's, and he was off, talking right through the hare pâté (which he hardly touched) and the salmon (name, rank and number supplied by Tony).

Clare saw Una, obviously a dedicated cook, heroically forego a discussion with Lilias about the sauce (had Joe detected the wine in it?) and give him her complete attention, as everyone else gradually did. He'll never understand if I try to head him off, Clare thought helplessly.

In spite of being convinced that the success of the evening had rested on his shoulders he hadn't enjoyed himself. 'It was an insult, having us sat in the kitchen like that. And not even putting the dogs out.'

'I love the kitchen. And anyway, who was being insulted? The Irvines? Tony and Una?'

'It was because they knew you wouldn't dress up, living out

here. And because I'm a corporal, I bet you anything.' He said it defiantly, not seriously believing it but needing to pick a fight.

'Joe, I never heard such complete rubbish! You know that's not true.'

'A colonel and a commander, give me a break,' he muttered, but he had the grace to look slightly ashamed of himself.

'I can't believe you could even think such a thing.'

'The food wasn't much though, was it? I mean, that thin soup with those slimy bits in it. I couldn't have kept them down if you'd paid me. The pâté was whiffy too, I was surprised no one noticed it. And you were going it a bit, weren't you? I thought you'd stopped drinking.'

As soon as they reached the cottage he made tea. Clare thought of Gerald's pale sherry, the perfectly chilled Chablis, the port and brandy after dinner. How idiotic of her ever to have imagined that Joe would enjoy such an evening.

'Poor Joe, I'm sorry you hated it. We'll have a lovely day on our own tomorrow. Any idea on a route?'

He cheered up at once, on safe ground, and out came the map. 'Might be a good idea to fit in this lot over in the Mamore Forest. The hour goes back soon . . .'

Perhaps it was an omen that the day began with leaving the jeep in creepy Kinlochleven, with the mist lying level as a tablecloth a couple of hundred feet above the black waters of the loch. They trudged away towards Am Bodach in a landscape drained of colour, russet and copper muted to beige and dun. Joe seemed very charged up, navigating fussily, keeping up a driving pace, determined to take in a couple more tops of little merit which Clare had never even heard of, and she felt guilty and rebellious in turn.

Looking back on it later, she was sure that Joe had decided during the day what he was going to do. Perhaps he even felt it was already accomplished since he startled her by saying as they settled down with their coffee after dinner, apropos her acquiring some 'decent' clothes so he could take her out, that it would be easier for her to shop once she was down in Glasgow.

'Am I going to Glasgow?' Clare asked in the jocular tone of someone trying to temper startled hostile reaction.

'Well, midweek. Or whenever I'm working, if they can get their act together about the roster. What they need is a few good corporals to sort them out.'

'They've got one,' Clare pointed out, cravenly trying to deflect him.

Since he took this as read he ignored it. 'No, I mean when you're down in the flat. You should see the shops in Glasgow, they're out of this world.'

'But Joe, I live here.'

'Well, let's face it, this place is OK for weekends at present, but who'd want to be stuck here for the winter with no heating and no electricity?'

Oh, Joe, not you too; not you of all people.

Before Clare could think of some non-controversial way of quashing this plan before it could take shape, Joe had seized her. Instead of the low-key cuddling which he had gone in for up till now, the hand playing with her hair, the arm round her shoulders, the kisses on cheek or neck, he was suddenly into full-scale onslaught. Clare could feel the ridged muscles in his arm as he scooped her towards him. He was pressing her head hard against the back of the sofa and she had a panicky sensation of entrapment, a moment's deep blind fear that he was a stranger and would not release her, no matter what she said or did. But it was Joe, and this was what she had wanted, longed for. She did her best to respond.

Joe was kissing her in quite a new way, his mouth voracious, his tongue probing. His free hand had come up to her breast and had first grabbed it like something he was about to throw up in the air and hit with a racquet but was now pressing on it like a plate. Then he began to rotate the hand so that her nipple became not only hard but hot and sore. Submerging again in that frightening feeling of being trapped, Clare opened her eyes and found his eyes watching her, a strange glitter in them that reminded her of something which she could not immediately track down but which rang a definite warning bell. Joe's face was blurred and formless, his body a dead weight on hers. There was no current of feeling between them, no moulding or accepting of their limbs.

With a shudder she could not control Clare broke free. She

couldn't imagine what her face showed in that second of revulsion but she couldn't help it. Joe leapt up instantly and even at such a moment seized on the subterfuge of rattling their coffee mugs together and taking them through to the kitchen. Clare pulled herself upright and slowly wiped her mouth, feeling a need to huddle herself together protectively, trembling with shock because her brain had clicked up the buried association of that slack-muscled, glittery-eyed expression of Joe's. The long-ago Saturday afternoon when she had walked back into the house and found Martin . . .

Well, Joe can't stay in the kitchen all night, she told herself shakily, taking refuge in the practical from the implications of this association. And poor man, what must he be feeling? She hauled herself up from the sofa, feeling oddly exhausted, and went across to the kitchen steps.

Joe was standing leaning against the frame of the old larder door, defeat and misery in every line. Clare stayed where she was, thinking that touch or even her nearness would not be acceptable to him.

'Joe,' she said, 'it's all right, truly.'

He lifted his head and stared at her, defenceless, and she saw that his cheeks were wet with tears. 'I thought – with you – it would be OK. I wanted it to be. Christ, you'll never know how much I wanted it to be.'

She didn't remember deciding to go to him, but the impulse was good. They stood for several seconds in a comforting asexual embrace and Clare felt his trembling gradually quieten, control return.

'Come on,' she said at length, 'let's go and sit down and be close and talk about this. We mustn't pretend that nothing has happened.'

It was a grim tale, and not what Clare had expected. Joe was adamant that he was not homosexual but said gay men were always attracted to him, seeing him at once as one of them, and it appalled and disgusted him. He had been brought up by a stiflingly possessive and embittered mother who had taught him that his body and its needs and functions were gross, never to be mentioned or acknowledged. So powerful had her influence been that his sexuality had been totally repressed; physical contact with either sex repelled him, yet he was an affectionate and gentle man who dreaded being alone all his life..

'But why did you choose to go into the services?' Clare asked when they had talked, haltingly and with painful pauses when she had simply held his hand and waited, for a long time.

'It was banned there, wasn't it? That's what they told you, anyway. That's what I believed as a young lad. They'd get rid of anyone who ... Christ, what a joke.'

But had he been drawn by an instinct he didn't even recognize to the company of men? Clare ached for that boy's naivety and optimism.

'When we got on so well, in the beginning, at Marbury,' Joe continued with a sudden burst of courage, 'I used to wish I could find some girl like you. I used to think about you all the time, live for those weekends. Then after the − well, this summer, when your letter came, when I was about to leave, it seemed meant, a fresh start, you know what I mean? You were living up here and I'd got a job in Scotland. It seemed to fit. I remembered how easy everything had always been when we were together and I thought if I had a chance with anyone it would be with you. It's been great, really great, these last few weeks, but then I began to feel I should − that you'd be − you know −'

'That I'd be wondering why you weren't trying to get me into bed?'

Even after all they had just talked of so frankly, Joe found this unacceptably outspoken and blushed hotly. 'I thought you were beginning to want − not *that*, I don't mean, of course, but more, you know −'

Clare felt herself blushing too. Her motives had been no less self-centred than his.

'What happened with Martin?' she asked. To her this was the vital question. They, she and Joe, didn't matter. 'They' didn't exist and never had.

It was so simple. Martin had made advances which Joe had rejected; Martin had had him removed under a cloud of suspicion, effectively destroying his chances of promotion, while at the same time appearing to deal leniently with him.

'You remember that flight sergeant from Medical Centre who

came to Capel with us a few times?' Clare really didn't. 'He was there to keep an eye on us, see when we were alone, talking late in the kitchens, walking back to your hut, that sort of stuff. If I'd cut up rough all your husband had to do was court-martial me for going after an officer's wife. He had me either way.'

And Martin could at the same time satisfy himself that his wife wasn't enjoying an affair on her own account. 'But you could have reported him,' Clare said, horrified.

Joe gave her a twisted smile. 'You've got to be kidding. I wouldn't have stood a chance. And I couldn't drag you into it, could I? It was a real can of worms, believe me.'

Clare was tempted to tell him about the irony of Martin's funeral, but instinct warned her that for Joe service conditioning would still be strong.

There was an unexpected peace in being alone that night, an absence of regret or humiliation. There was only compassion for the lonely man in the next room, whose unhappiness extended far beyond this night or this place.

CHAPTER TWENTY-SIX

The next day was cold and overcast, the sitting-room dreary beyond words, lamp quenched by the bleak morning light, sofa as Joe had slept in it, the pale flames of the newly lit fire giving out no warmth.

Joe was unable to meet Clare's eye and his briskness as he cooked breakfast for them both was so painful that presently she caught his arm and checked him, making him look at her, saying softly, 'It's just us, Joe, the same people as we were yesterday.' He clamped his hand hard over hers for a second and nodded a grateful acknowledgement.

'I'd best pack up,' he said as they finished breakfast, a substantial meal as it always was when he was there.

'There's no need.' Clare profoundly wanted the house to herself, but that could wait.

'I'd rather—' he was beginning, when they heard voices outside.

'We'll not disturb you at your breakfast if we take the door off?' Pete asked with his sly grin. Ewan was propping the disputed window against the wall.

What a moment to choose. But perhaps after all it helped. They didn't start work at once, of course, but settled down at the table and finished off what was left in Joe's teapot and Clare's share of the toast (though Pete carefully pushed to the side of his plate all the pieces of peel in the marmalade). They did their best to get Joe to agree that the whole plan of closing off the door was a mistake to begin with, but didn't find that he entered into the spirit of the thing satisfactorily.

There was not much chance for deep emotional exchanges with the door off and cold air pouring in, with Pete whanging away at the frame and Ewan whistling as he went back and forth raiding the pile of stones Clare had gathered by the kitchen door for quite other purposes.

'Look, stay today,' she did find time to say to Joe. 'You don't have to be back till tonight, do you?'

'Would you like to go out?'

Clare hesitated. She would have liked to ease this for him, but knew she couldn't face that sort of day together. 'Well, not really, Joe. I'd prefer to be here while this is going on. But if you want a day on the hill you could come back here afterwards for a bath and dinner.'

'The hill. I still call them mountains,' he observed wryly. 'No, I couldn't stand it on my own today. If you don't feel like coming out I'll push off. Probably best anyway.'

'You don't have to take everything away, you know.'

He said nothing but went on with his packing. Clare had a hard lump in her throat as she helped him. How many times in his life had he reached emotional dead ends like this? She saw him hesitate over the station plaque.

'Will you want this now?' he asked.

'Joe, I don't want you to remove every trace, of course I don't. But if you would like to have it for the flat, you take it.'

He still hesitated. She saw that this single item had held real significance for him. 'I suppose it makes up the set,' he said, too casually, and with a quick movement took it down and rammed it deep in his bag.

'You know you can come back whenever you like, don't you?' Paltry, placating words.

'Oh, I'll be back. You won't get rid of me that easily. We'll have some great weekends, you'll see.' But the words had a hollow sound and Clare looked quickly away from his smiling face.

'I hope the job goes well.' She had not meant it to sound so final.

'No worries. It'll be fine. Can't expect it to be like the Service, can you?'

She ached for him.

'I'll leave you the rest of the compo, shall I? Just so you don't forget me.'

'Joe, you must come back,' she said fiercely. 'We were friends before any of this, don't forget.'

'Yes, well, it's not quite the same now, is it?' He concentrated on pressing down the last bulge of cagoule impeding the zip of his sports bag.

As Clare watched the jeep take the slope in a long curve she knew he was right. Her own need had helped to create the Joe she had admired and relied on in the early days; the need was his now, but she would not be able to give him help. She waited in the chill misty air till he was out of sight.

Pete and Ewan had their heads down, carefully industrious. Clare was glad they were there, glad that silence would not immediately overtake the house, glad there was something positive to occupy her.

There were many thoughts of Joe, and of Martin, to deal with that day. Martin must have been very sure of what he saw in Joe to have risked such an advance, and equally he must have known Joe was no threat where Clare was concerned. His reaction had been pure revenge for a humiliation he couldn't accept. And Joe had not considered challenging him. Because he couldn't involve her, as he had said, or because deep inside him there was a terrified confusion about his own sexuality? But someone, in the end, had challenged Martin, threatened him with exposure at a time when his career was critically vulnerable. And Martin had taken the only way out which would preserve what he had already achieved.

Clare was also able, during that long day, to put her own part in this into a more honest perspective. She had wanted an affair, had clutched at the relationship with Joe because she couldn't have Donald, but in her heart she had known it was all wrong, and she could admit it at last.

Pete and Ewan had the window in by dusk, after entertaining themselves by telling Clare there would be a week to wait for the cement of the new sill to set before the frame could go in. It had seemed quite reasonable to her.

The character of the room was startlingly changed, a feeling of space and solid shelter instantly created. Clare felt one pang of loss for the door standing open to the sun on fine days, but knew keeping out the much more prevalent wind would be adequate compensation. As soon as she was on her own she cleaned the room from top to bottom and then, needing to be busy, started altering Lilias's velvet curtains.

Pete and Ewan were back the following morning (what had Donald said to them?) to put in the inner porch door at the end of the kitchen and to be paid, departing in haste to cash the cheque they'd wanted made out to the Inverbuie Hotel. Clare prowled about her snug, light cottage in great contentment, delighting in the view across the loch from the long window and making gloating comparisons with the room as she had first seen it. Catriona must come and admire it as soon as possible; and Sandy Maitland would certainly approve of the transformation. And Donald, what would he think? Donald who was always somewhere behind her thoughts.

He came that afternoon, to see that the work had been properly completed, he said. Clare guessed that he had already made sure it had. 'Just what was needed,' was his summing up, when he had examined both jobs minutely. 'This room looks twice the size.'

'It actually seemed warmer in here last night – or was I imagining it?'

'Oh, you'd notice a difference. You'd never have kept the draughts out with that hollow step no matter what you did, and these old doors weren't ever a tight fit in the first place or they jammed up with the damp in the wintertime.'

'Even my feet were warm for once.'

'So you think you'll be able to face the winter after all?' Donald asked, running a hand down the dense pile of the heavy velvet curtains.

There was an emptiness in the thought of being at the Larach without him at Rhumore which Clare honestly didn't know how she would cope with. 'Oh, take it as it comes, I suppose,' she said lightly.

Donald turned and shot her one of his searching looks, but made no further comment. Whether she stayed long-term in the glen or not could hardly interest him much now.

'You'll be putting some kind of cushion on that sill?' he asked.

Was he casting round for something to say? Were things so changed between them? 'I've got a piece of Dunlopillo in the loft I thought I might use.'

'I'll fetch it down for you while I'm here.'

'Oh no, Donald, please don't bother, I can easily get it.'

He said nothing, but went through to the bedroom and set the heavy wooden ladder in place with one easy swing. 'High time you rescued it, by the look of it,' he observed, dropping the length of rubber mattress down to her. Chewed fragments showered lightly on her face. 'Your friends have been enjoying that.'

'Little devils. I'd heard them up there again. I've been meaning to set the traps.'

'You're not too bothered about them these days?' he questioned with a small smile.

Clare laughed, remembering the panics of her first night, and not for the first time amazed at how oppressively dark and cramped the house seemed in her memory of those early days.

'They'll be coming in now with the cold weather,' Donald was saying. 'I'll set the traps for you.'

How normal it felt to have him there, how his presence seemed to fill the cottage, and fill her with happiness. He set to work as a matter of course to help her to cut the cushion, making a neater and more accurate job of it than she would have done on her own.

'You're meaning to cover it with that?' he asked, nodding at the pieces left over from the curtains. 'Let's have a look then.'

He's a farmer, Clare thought, amused and oddly touched, as he laid out the material and tried the cushion this way and that, avoiding faded patches and seams. He has no right to be so good at this sort of thing. But any job was a job to Donald, and she allowed herself the pleasure of watching his big hands deftly at work, enjoying his concentration and competence.

She found herself wanting to drink down the scene like wine: the room put together bit by bit and now so satisfying and comfortable; Trim sleeping with her nose on her paws, the glow of firelight on her coat; Lilias's dark-leaved begonia against the white wall; the little lamp Trudy had given her throwing its soft light up the book-filled dresser shelves; the occasional hiss as water leaked from the base of the spout of the old kettle and bounced and sizzled to extinction on the hob.

Gradually they talked more easily, about the stalking, about the best primer for the new window frame, about the visible effect Lucy's disappearance had had on Lilias and Gerald. Donald told her about the cottage between the Luig road and the loch which the Markies used to rent long ago for Stephen's school holidays, the excitement when Tigh Bhan unexpectedly came on the market, and how Lilias had flown from Singapore to buy it and more or less camped there with Stephen when he came home for Easter.

The cover for the cushion was cut out and pinned, they had had coffee. Then suddenly, it seemed to Clare, Donald was on his feet and picking up his cap. Trim had come out of apparently fathoms-deep slumber the moment he moved and after one instinctive cast towards the former doorway was ready at the kitchen steps. Clare experienced the familiar sensation of something inside her being pulled up by the roots, which she always felt when it was time for Donald to go, increased now by an irrational fear that this might be the last time she would see him, that he might leave the glen without ever coming to say goodbye. He had seen to it that the work on the cottage was completed, as he had promised he would. There was nothing to bring him back. She watched him mutely.

He went towards the door, then checked, turned back and asked abruptly, almost as though against his will, 'Has your friend moved out?'

Of course he had seen Joe's things here the day he had helped with the water tank and he could not have failed to notice today that they were gone. Also Pete and Ewan were sure to have spread the news. All the same this bluntness, unusual from him, took Clare by surprise.

'Yes, he's gone,' she said, floundering among the hundred things she wanted to add and knew she couldn't.

'You're all right?'

She looked up into his face, saw the understanding and concern there, and her pent-up feelings surged up uncontrollably. 'Donald, it was awful!' She turned away from him, feeling tears rising in a choking tide. She hadn't even known that she wanted to cry.

'He's gone away for good? I'm sorry, lass, if that upsets you.

I don't like leaving you here on your own if you're unhappy. Would you like to talk about it? Talking always helps.'

Clare suddenly saw how he would interpret her distress. 'Oh, no, it's not like that! It's not me. I mean, it's Joe I feel so sad for. There was nothing between us – it would never have led to anything.'

'I know that.' The calm words, interposed with such certainty, arrested her.

'You know?'

'Come on,' said Donald, tossing his cap on the table again, 'let's sit down and talk about it.' Trim slipped back to the hearthrug.

'But Donald, how on earth did you know?'

'I met him, remember.'

'But what did you say? I mean, you hardly spoke to each other. And in any case, then there was—' Nothing to know. She cast her mind back to that encounter in the shop, but could remember little about it except her own anxiety to get away.

'I knew he wasn't the man for you and never could be.'

Clare stared at him, remembering Joe's anguished words returning, shaken to find them so swiftly corroborated. 'You thought he was gay,' she said flatly.

'I did. But it will have come as a bit of a shock to you if you've just found out.'

'But he isn't,' Clare said wildly.

Donald waited.

'He told me he isn't,' she insisted.

'And did you believe him?' The quiet question forced her to be honest.

'He believes it. I think – yes, I think he probably might be. And I should know, shouldn't I?' she added bitterly.

'Because of your husband?' Donald's voice was matter-of-fact.

'Oh God,' she sighed, giving up and admitting it. 'All the signs were there. And he never responded to females, never even seemed to notice them. The girls on those expeditions to North Wales tried everything they knew, but he was totally impervious.' She remembered the flower-arranging wives discussing the same problem in the mess that afternoon. 'It's so tragic for him, Donald. He thought he ought to have a male–female relationship; *ought* to. He's never in his life understood his own feelings. They're all tied up with fear and disgust and despair at his own inadequacy.'

'And you? It will have been a – blow to you.' He clearly had trouble with which word to choose.

'It makes me sad. And guilty, for not seeing sooner, and for—' But how to explain to Donald that she had been using Joe? 'Once, in the past, I needed him and he helped me. But things – people – move on, I suppose.' Looking at Donald's big frame and brown strong face, savouring the reassurance his clear perceptiveness always brought her, Clare wondered how for one second she could have imagined herself attracted to poor Joe.

'Did he and your husband know each other?'

How had he put his finger on that? 'Oh yes,' she said grimly. 'They knew each other. Martin propositioned Joe, Joe turned him down – and paid a nasty price. I suppose the fact is that Martin manipulated us both.'

'Tell me.'

How remote the mean little story seemed from the mood of this peaceful room. Donald sat well back in Murdo's chair, listening without interrupting, his face shadowed.

'You had to see him again,' he said definitely, as Clare finished. 'You're free of that guilt now.'

'No links left with the past,' she assented with faint irony, but she had a new guilt to contend with. She had encouraged Joe for her own ends and had hurt him badly in the process.

'You mind that?'

'I'm glad, really. It had to be this way, I suppose. It's different from when Magda left. Then I felt I belonged nowhere, had no aims or motivation. Now –' She paused, her thoughts drifting.

'Now?' Donald prompted, and he had taken some care to make the question easy.

It would seem presumptuous, she felt, to talk about her feeling of having begun to put down roots here. 'Oh, I suppose it's having so much to do,' she temporized. 'The Old Mill – Trudy wants a hand with stock-taking at the end of the month – then I've great plans for Fergus, and Lilias needs more company these days, I think.'

'You're busy,' Donald agreed.

'Oh, well, for the time being,' she said, embarrassed. It did sound pretty trivial listed like that, conveying none of her sense of having found a small foothold of her own in this place.

'Indeed, for the time being.' Donald glanced at his watch. 'I'd best be off before it gets dark. No, don't come out, you'll get cold.'

He was suddenly brisk, evidently satisfied that Clare had recovered her equilibrium. She went down to the jetty with him in spite of his protests, wanting to hold on to every moment with him, wanting things to be as they had been, knowing that they never could be and that time was slipping though her fingers at a dreadful rate.

CHAPTER TWENTY-SEVEN

Joe vanished from Clare's mind with a speed she was ashamed of but could do nothing about. She did write to him to reassure him that friendship was still there but, certain that he would hate her to be too explicit about what had happened between them, it was hard to know what to say to him. His reply, which took several days, was a pink and silver card cut in the shape of a rose, with a verse that ran:

> Because you've been so very kind,
> So very thoughtful too,
> This little note just comes to bring
> A grateful 'Thanks' to you.

Under this he had written, 'I think the above verse says it all. Take care, Joe.'

Clare felt rebuffed by this impersonal message for a moment, then humour came to the rescue. She and Joe? Never. She must have been out of her mind.

Other matters rapidly absorbed her, the first of which was driving Lilias and Gerald to Inverness to meet Oliver and bring him back to Tigh Bhan. A short while ago they would have managed this for themselves without question; now they had virtually given up driving altogether – to the general relief of the glen, it had to be said. Stephen came up bringing Libby, and Clare found herself included in all plans, a useful buffer during a long edgy weekend.

After it Lilias seemed more than ever reduced and frail. Clare guessed that Stephen had kept his own counsel and that, while Lilias would respect his reticence, her meddling soul must have been tormented. She was so much less ready to take up arms these days, gratefully accepting proffered help and even prepared to sit down occasionally and do nothing. Gerald on the other hand was more compulsively garrulous than ever, needing the customary squabbles and embattled interaction to maintain a pretence that all was well. He followed Lilias about obsessively, referring every detail to her like an insecure child.

'I shall strike him,' Lilias told Clare, though looking scarcely capable of it.

'Hold off for a bit if you can,' Clare begged her. 'I've had an idea that may help.'

There was no reason why her plan for Fergus should not include Gerald too, and as a by-product give Lilias a little of the peace she yearned for. The following week Clare drove her to Inverness on a squally day of lurid sunshine flaunting across the autumn landscape under damson skies, and bought a word processor, the most idiot-proof available.

'You do have electricity, I suppose?' she asked Catriona, having taken it up to Glen Righ House in Lilias's Metro the next morning.

'You know quite well we do.' Only the sockets turned out still to be fifteen amp.

Watty Duff, keenly interested, hurried off to fetch an adaptor from the MacGillivrays and stayed to watch with an excited Catriona and a puzzled but amenable Fergus as Great-Aunt Sofia's three-page account of what she had worn to the Northern Meeting began to appear on the screen. Fergus, suddenly riveted, crouched with his head close to Clare's to watch the text spreading magically before his eyes.

'Remarkable, remarkable,' he murmured, in the gentle voice so rarely heard and, drawing up a chair without taking his eyes off the screen, he settled down to watch. When Clare had printed out the first page he walked excitedly about the room with it, going from window to window to examine it in rapture.

'It's so good of you, Clare,' Catriona said when Watty Duff had been driven away to resume his normal pretence of work and she and Clare were putting together a meagre lunch, 'and of course we must pay you. If you have an invoice I could send it off to the estate office with the rest, only I'm not absolutely sure how soon it would be paid.'

'No,' said Clare, determined to scotch this at once. 'It's my machine. I'm lending it to you.'

'But you can't use it at the Larach.'

'Exactly, which is why I'd be very grateful to keep it here. So no argument.'

'It really is the most marvellous idea for Grandfather, but mightn't he do something frightful to it?' Catriona asked worriedly.

'I've printed enough pages to keep him happy for a while. When I go I can take out the disk, and I can always have a back-up safely stored away at the Larach.'

'But the machine itself? It he sees it there and doesn't remember what it is?'

'We'll have to risk that. If there's no text visible, perhaps he won't connect it with Aunt S and think someone's been interfering again. But look, I do want to ask a favour, to help Lilias really.'

'How could I ever help Lilias?' Catriona asked, dubious and anxious at once, forgetting the bread she was holding in its wire holder under the Aga lid. Black check toast would be for ever associated in Clare's mind with spartan Glen Righ meals.

'Would you let Gerald come up sometimes and put his regimental record on disk too? If he and Fergus get on well together, then perhaps you'd feel able to leave them on their own sometimes.'

Clare could read in Catriona's eyes the excuses rushing through her mind, and watched her waver for a couple of tense seconds. Then, very unexpectedly, she gave Clare a quick strangling child's hug, and Clare found herself wondering how long it was since she had made any such gesture.

Gerald gobbled down the bait. He saw himself not only as coming to the rescue, the one person the laird would accept in the house, but also as modern man, able to deal with a technology quite beyond poor old Fergus, his senior by about five years. Clare did wonder what she had let herself in for as his stubby fingers swept the screen clear or gratuitously underlined whole pages of text, and he raged and swore with military vigour. But he was blissfully happy editing and polishing the well-worn anecdotes which, as Stephen thankfully remarked, should effectively delay an end result.

It never seemed to occur to Fergus, most luckily, that he could touch the word processor himself. When Clare was working he was happy to sit beside her for hours at a time, abandoning his paper-shuffling and endless annotating for this new and fascinating spectacle. He never questioned Gerald's presence and they were perfectly content together, scrupulously taking it in turns to talk but not going in for anything silly like listening to each other. Extra supplies of disks and paper had to be rushed in.

'A stroke of genius,' said Lilias, as Clare drove her in to Fort William to shop. 'Being shut up in the house with Gerald is quite unendurable. I can't send him out to do the digging because of his back, and I can't escape to the moor with the dogs because of these useless knees of mine which simply refuse to work properly any more. Don't ever get old, Clare, it's not to be recommended.'

'Well, let's hope neither of them loses interest in the new toy too soon. You should hear them "working" together, Fergus rambling on about some ancestor called Finlay the Fair who hunted his daughter with wolfhounds when she ran off with a tacksman, and Gerald telling him by way of reply what it cost to insure the mess silver in 1934.'

Lilias laughed. 'I pray I am never called upon to read either of the finished opera.'

On the way home she told Clare that Stephen had received a letter from Lucy, a letter which had just about destroyed him, detailing as it did with agonizing minuteness all that had been wrong with their marriage from her point of view.

'It was so senselessly cruel. If she could see that so clearly, and analyse his character so accurately, then she must also have known what it would do to Stephen to have it spelled out like that.'

Lilias saw the letter as unforgivable self-indulgence. From what Clare had seen of Lucy she could guess at her sincere intention in writing it, and also imagine what it must have cost her to do it.

'Where is she, did she say?'

'She's joined some artistic group in Norfolk. Do they still call them communes? One can hardly keep up. But as far as I can gather they go round the countryside advocating music and poetry and art as a means to draw people back into harmony with their environment. Well, all I can say is, part of Lucy's environment is two children . . .' But she could not go on and Clare patted the trembling hands clutching the well-polished worn crocodile bag and didn't look at her.

The marriage must have been foundering for some time, yet Stephen was devastated by its breakdown. What was this bond that held people together when feelings had changed or died? Clare found the question often in her mind in the days following this conversation. Why had she herself stayed with Martin? And her thoughts would turn, inevitably, to Donald. Ishbel might not have been his first choice, they might never have established the sort of communication he would have liked, but he had married her of his own free will, had lived with her for more than twenty-five years, had brought up a child with her. He would grieve at her death, and break his life apart when she had gone.

Clare did her best to keep this firmly in mind as Donald was at the Larach a good deal these days. He brought down a section of screening to fix between house and shed; spent a couple of afternoons sawing up wood already collected by Clare and dragging more fallen branches down from the promontory to add to the pile; laid some monster stones in the paved corner which Clare couldn't possibly have shifted alone; and even gave a hand with painting the new doors and window, which Clare knew was his least favourite job.

He brushed thanks aside. 'To tell you the truth I'm glad to get out of the house,' he said. 'Those sisters of Ishbel's are just about driving me mad. I know I need the help and I'm grateful to them, but a little goes a long way. We never seem to have been free of them. I could count on one hand the number of Sunday dinners we've had on our own since we were married.'

Fiona and her husband appeared one weekend and there was a major row which Donald seemed glad to be able to talk about to some neutral listener. 'That damned man of hers thinks she should get Rhumore if I don't stay on there. Wants to build time-share cabins on it.'

'Time share! On Rhumore!'

'They'd bring up their caravans too, put them down in Righ

Bay and use the remains of the old settlement for bottoming the roads. They've got everything worked out. Well, I suppose if they don't do it some other bastard will. It's all the rage these days.'

Clare looked down on the proposed site a couple of days later, wincing not only to think of this disfigurement but also of the changes ahead. But she pushed the images aside, determined not to spoil a precious day. Donald had offered to take her stalking, or, more accurately, had insisted that she went. He had not forgotten their early arguments on the subject of blood sports and said that since Clare hadn't been involved in the shooting (they both preferred not to go into the reasons for that) she had better come and see what stalking was all about.

About to leap in and air her prejudices once more, Clare had suddenly remembered Annabel. And turn down a whole day with Donald? Was she mad? Hastily she had accepted the offer, agreeing that she had everything to learn.

As they had set out along the farm track that morning she had belatedly realized that Dougie Stewart would almost certainly be coming with them, and was doing her best to pretend she wasn't disappointed when Donald had driven past The Birks without stopping. She had given up pretending, dizzy with relief.

Being on the hill with Donald was so different from being with Joe. No racing along the highest ground in sight, ticking off Munros, doing sums about altitude and distances. Now it seemed to Clare that they were part of the landscape, accepted by it, and as they moved on at Donald's leisured deceptive pace she learned from him more of the rudiments of seeing and hearing.

'Sparrowhawk,' he would say, and have to point out to her the big bird floating against the dark plantation. 'Grouse.' And when she screwed up her eyes against a silvery sky he would grin and nod to the droppings at her feet. He showed her the slots of roe deer, where they had drunk, where they had crossed a fence, where a fox had made a meal. 'You can still smell him,' he said.

'I can't.'

'Stand here. Shut your eyes.' Clare picked up the rank scent immediately, and at the same time became aware of a dozen sounds she hadn't noticed before.

They walked, looked, listened, smelled, crawled and lay pinned down, interminably it seemed to Clare, by the shifting wind on boggy ground where Donald improved the hour by showing her half a dozen different mosses growing within a few inches of her nose. She had not known there could be this deep contentment in someone's company, a warm certainty of rightness and completeness, of living without reservation in the moment.

They saw deer on every side – Clare mostly had to be shown them – and after a long stalk came up on a stag lolling at his ease in a shallow corrie, his half-dozen hinds feeding near him. They lay and watched him for a long time, saw him scratch behind his ear like a puppy, wrinkle back his dark rubbery lips and yawn, stretch his neck and roar a half-hearted challenge to a stag across the glen, letting the sound subside into grumbling petulance.

When Donald trained and cocked his rifle Clare's stomach gave an unpleasant lurch. Kill this splendid creature, whom they had seen at his ease by his own fireside with his slippers on? Then she remembered Donald's lecture about the pressing economical reasons for this whole exercise. Too many deer reduced feeding for the sheep. Stalking, shooting and the sheep themselves meant jobs for the boys – no, not the boys, but people she knew, Dougie supporting a family, the MacGillivrays, Calum and Peggy Macdonald, and Fergus and Catriona themselves come to that. I eat meat and wear leather, Clare reminded herself. I have never done anything to save an animal from suffering in my life. She also kept Annabel firmly in mind. She braced herself for the shot.

Then she felt Donald's hand on her arm, signalling her to move back. Obediently she inched herself down the slope by her boot toes, her jacket riding up under her armpits as she went. To her surprise Donald came too, the safety catch back on. She glanced at him enquiringly as they stood up out of sight of the deer.

'You didn't shout or wave,' he teased, but he was looking rather closely into her face with that penetrating gaze of his.

'Well, some of your arguments to kill the poor things seemed not altogether unreasonable,' she said mock-grudgingly.

'Is that so?'

'But why didn't you shoot him?'

'Seemed a shame to spoil the old boy's afternoon.'

'Then why did we stalk him?'

'Oh, I thought it might focus your ideas a little,' Donald said, gazing out across the glen.

'You mean you never intended to shoot him?'

'Oh, come now,' he reproached her. 'Would I do such a thing? With stag stalking over, too.'

'You mean to say we crawled all those miles and got covered with bog and soaking wet and half frozen into the bargain, and you weren't ever going to—?'

But Donald was off long-strided down the hill, grinning happily, setting such a pace that she had no breath left for having a fight about it.

CHAPTER TWENTY-EIGHT

'Can't we lump all the herbs together?'

'They're different prices.'

'Well, I'm not going to weigh them, I'm just going to guess.'

Dusted with flour and smelling pungent, Trudy and Clare were deep in stock-taking. Ben was in Glasgow collecting plaster.

'God, what about this lot under the counter? I don't even know what half of it is. Do we really sell this disgusting stuff to people?' Trudy demanded, licking her finger and pulling a hideous face.

'Throw it out.'

'Good idea.'

'So what's this place like where we're going for dinner?'

'Shut, probably. You know what it's like up here at the end of the season.'

'Pity Ardlonach isn't still open. Lilias says Una Urquhart is a brilliant cook.'

'Una! Good job you reminded me,' Trudy exclaimed, hitting her head with a hand which showered an unknown greenish substance over her hair. 'She left a message for you. She's wondering if you could help her.'

'Help her how?' Clare asked, straightening up from trying to guess how many kilos of berrymeal were left in a sack she didn't want to lift.

'Spreadsheets for accounts or something. I was telling her about your word processor and she said they've bought a computer for the hotel which so far has the upper hand. Anyway, she wants you to give her a ring some time.'

So I shall, Clare decided.

She hadn't felt so frivolous for a long time as she and Trudy set off in the fish-smelling van after leisurely baths (strictly non-herbal) and lots of padding about half naked deciding what to wear from Trudy's wardrobe. Clare was now in a wrap-around skirt that looped her twice and did most of its wrapping round her unaccustomed shins, and her almost forgotten 'smart' boots, dug out from her bedroom cupboard at the Larach covered in green mould. Trudy, in a vivid caftan, resembled some well-built tribal chief and what they were both enjoying most was that they didn't give a damn what they looked like.

The high life didn't hold out much promise as they huddled in the lit one-eighth of an empty hotel dining-room, where curtains covered only the two nearest windows and a lot of black Highland night stared in at the rest. The only sound was the crunch of melba toast.

'Using up the leftover bread at the end of the season,' Trudy hissed. But they were too full of a highly inflated sense of achievement and freedom to be subdued, dinner was mostly good and they were in excellent spirits as Trudy drove home, handling the van as though she was breaking it in at a rodeo.

After constructing barricades of cushions to stop themselves falling through the gaps in the sparse arrangement of wooden bars and leather straps which Trudy called a sofa, they opened the door of the wood-burning stove and settled down in its fiery glow to drink sloe gin and talk.

They talked about Joe and they talked about Ben, but Clare said not a word about Donald.

'Are you minding about Joe?' Trudy asked, in the neutral voice that says I'm interested, not prying.

'Not a bit. To be honest, it's rather a relief that he's gone,' Clare confessed, hitching her bottom up the sofa but sliding back at once to a semi-prone position as the leather was slippery and her thighs too short for the deep seat.

'What happened?'

Clare swivelled her head on the bulging cushion to scrutinize her, alerted by the casual tone.

'What did you think of him – honestly?' she countered.

'Um. Bit willowy.'

Apt, funny, then painful. 'You thought he was gay?'

'I think it was watching him tidy a shelf in the storeroom one day as though he was enjoying it too much. Happy fussing.'

Martin. Fussing about his hair, his tie, the set of his aiguillettes. Why had she never seen that for herself? Suddenly it was easy to talk, to range through memories, touch on buried associations of pain and find they had lost their power to hurt, be honest about failures she had justified to herself for far too long. For a moment, encouraged by the rich warmth of the sloe gin spreading through her, the soft lights and fire glow and the relaxed frankness of their mood, she even thought of confessing to kind, down-to-earth Trudy how she felt about Donald, but it was too important, too private, and in any case Donald deserved her discretion.

The moment passed as Trudy said with a long sigh, 'This is good, isn't it? There was no one to talk to till you turned up. Funny how one knows in the first moment. Do you realize what a difference it's made, having you around?'

'It's made a difference to me too, meeting you,' Clare assured her.

'No, I mean the *actual* difference,' Trudy persisted, impatiently for her, bouncing up with a vigour that nearly tipped Clare sideways and lifting her long hair out of the neck of her caftan with a large gesture that flopped it over her face.

'What are you talking about?'

'You know Ben and I almost split up in the summer, don't you?'

It was Clare's turn to flounder upright, wishing she hadn't eaten so much. 'I don't know anything of the sort,' she said.

'You must have realized something was going on.'

'Well, only that you always seemed rather – independent of each other.'

Trudy snorted. 'We were jumping down each other's throats most of the time.'

'I really hardly ever see Ben,' Clare pointed out.

'Exactly, he's never bloody here. This talk of a new enterprise together, going in search of our personal freedom. All he wanted to do was get out of teaching. Looking back on it, I don't think he'd really have minded staying in Watford. Anywhere would be fine for Ben so long as he could do his own thing from morning till night and have the necessities of life laid on for him at the same time. As a matter of fact things were going wrong before we ever came north; it was one of the reasons we agreed to try a fresh start.'

'But aren't things better now?'

'Not really. He's making noises about being out of the main-stream, cut off from his creative roots and all that garbage. He means people don't want to listen to him in the pub. But I've had enough of picking up the dirty socks, and any other job he finds menial or boring. I'd rather be on my own.'

'Do you honestly mean that?'

'Yep. I feel totally pissed off with him. Bed's a bore – well, a non-event, more like. He's made no effort to integrate up here. He'd leave tomorrow if he thought he could find as good a work set-up. But I love the place – what little I've had the chance to see of it so far anyway. I like the people and their outlook and the general pace of life and I don't want to move again.'

'Could you keep the mill if Ben did go?'

'Not a hope, but it would be far too big anyway. I won't know till the audit's done, but I *think* I could get a living out of the shop on its own. A living just for myself, of course.'

'I'm sure you could. Business has been building up steadily. You've definitely found a gap that needed filling in Luig.'

'I've been looking around, as a matter of fact. There's a place down by the harbour I've got my eye on. You know that row of terraced cottages someone's started to do up by the old pier?'

'Oh yes, I noticed something was happening to those. They're gems. I'd always wondered why no one had snapped them up long ago. That would be an ideal position for a shop too, near where the buses come in and much closer to the centre of town than you are here. But wouldn't it break your heart to leave this place? You've made it so beautiful.'

Trudy looked round the shadowy reaches of the enormous room and shrugged. 'It's so much Ben, though, isn't it? Just think of creating a new place of my own, working for myself, not being perpetually messed about by someone else – or arguing, with him and in my head, all day long. God, I'm so tired of arguing! But you'll be around, won't you, Clare? I couldn't face doing it without you on hand. I don't mean dishing out the old lentils necessarily, but being there.'

Clare really didn't know how life would be when Donald had

gone. She was afraid she would find the Larach so desolate that she would not be able in the end to endure it. But she was coming to see that many other factors might bind her to this place. Perhaps she could find a cottage in Luig, see Trudy into this new venture if that was what she decided to do, then look around for some occupation for herself. And there was Catriona; Clare wasn't ready to abandon her, or poor stricken Lilias.

They talked for hours and Clare had plenty to think about as the bus carried her over Luig Hill the next morning. She called at Tigh Bhan for lunch as promised and found Lilias tight-lipped and exhausted and Barbara Bailey even grimmer than usual, and an alarming brick colour after a morning spent making green tomato chutney. Clare got rid of Barbara, tucked Lilias up on the dogs' sofa, gave her a large gin and tonic and made macaroni cheese for lunch. Gerald had taken advantage of Clare still being at the Old Mill to treat himself to a good go at the computer, which had to be an unmixed blessing.

'So you'll go and see Una?'

'She's going to pick me up in Luig on Friday. I'm not sure that I'll be able to do much to help, but I can certainly have a look at whatever's bothering her.'

'My dear, don't be silly, take the Metro. Yes, of course you must, it's just sitting there doing nothing. Gerald always takes the Peugeot.'

'That's very kind, Lilias, thank you. But why not come with me? Una wouldn't mind, would she?'

'Of course she wouldn't. I should love to come. We'll telephone her directly after lunch.'

Una sounded perfectly happy about this plan, and said what Clare could not say at her end, that it would be good for Lilias to get out without Gerald for a change. The meshes were weaving closer, Clare reflected as she set off for the Larach over the headland.

The cottage wasn't as cold as she had expected and she soon had the fire lit and the gas heater blasting away. As she went out to fetch more wood she saw the nicest sight in the world, Donald's boat putting into the bay. He seemed to have a perfect grasp of her timetable, she reflected with amusement, going down joyfully to meet him. She wondered what he had brought as she saw him holding a box out of Trim's reach. And Trim was behaving oddly, balancing on her hind legs eagerly trying to nudge the box and, even more unusually, taking no notice of Donald's commands to get out from under.

Pheasant? Venison? Or was he bringing the hind's liver he had promised her when she said she had never tried it? But would that arouse such interest in Trim? Donald held the box aside to come up the steps from the jetty and Clare felt the familiar glow of pleasure at the smile he gave her.

'Got the beans counted?' he asked as they went up the slope.

'Don't mention beans to me, I never want to see one again as long as I live.'

'And you celebrated well afterwards?'

'Does it show? But it was talking mostly.'

'Is that so?'

'That is so. What's in the box?'

'Down, Trim, do as you're told.'

Trim walked beside him across the sitting-room on her hind legs, deaf and intent. Clare saw the box lurch as Donald put it on the table.

'It's not something I have to kill for dinner?' she asked in sudden alarm.

'Oh, here now, I didn't think you'd want to eat him,' Donald said reproachfully, lifting out a tiny blunt-faced puppy, its coat a rich fox-red, which squeaked in piercing indignation as Donald put it into Clare's hands. Canny Donald. The puppy stilled its protests as it found itself close to a warm, living body. Clare breathed in one whiff of mealy, milky puppy smell, felt the warm silkiness of the red coat and the small head nuzzling against her chest and was lost.

'Aye, that'll stop your wheeking,' Donald said sternly to the puppy, folding in the flaps of the box and putting it on the hearth. 'This will do for him till we get something better. What do you think of that then, Trim?'

Trim paid no attention beyond one flick of her ear, still stretching up to nose at the puppy.

'But it's not hers?' Clare asked.

'Her sister's. A good working dog, though judging by what's she produced there I can't speak for her private life.'

'But wait a minute, I don't want a dog.'

'Give him back to me when I go then.'

'I don't know what to feed him on. I haven't got anything here for a puppy. I couldn't leave him when I go out . . .'

Donald didn't bother to reply but began to build up the just-lit fire which was dying of neglect. 'I'd best put a kettle on the gas. This won't do much for a while.'

'Donald –'

'So what are you going to call him?'

The puppy splayed its tiny paws against Clare's sweater and hooked itself on with needle-pointed claws. Its fur was as soft as down.

'You'd have to call him something red with a coat like that,' she said generally.

Donald said nothing.

'Rufus.'

'Rufus! What kind of a name is that for a self-respecting collie?'

'What's the Gaelic version then?'

'Ruaridh.'

'Rory. That would do.'

'Well, when you can get your tongue round it.'

Clare had never imagined anything like the pleasure and amusement that little dog brought her. He seemed to give the final touch to the cottage, providing the living presence it had lacked. But more importantly for Clare, Rory was Donald's gift, associated always in her affections with him, a small but precious substitute for what she could not hope to have.

CHAPTER TWENTY-NINE

Ishbel died a few days later and Donald vanished. Had he known when he brought Rory that everything was about to change? Clare wondered often as the dark November days succeeded each other in a series of gales that savaged the coast, driving racing waves up the loch to break in high, whirling spume which obliterated the jetty and crusted the cottage windows with salt. Keeping dry and warm became a priority and a battle. Several times a day Clare found herself fervently thankful to Donald for seeing to it that Ewan and Pete had finished putting in the new window. The door in the eastern end of the house was a huge improvement; in fact in these weather conditions she decided it was all that made survival possible, especially as Rory was being house-trained and had to go out at frequent intervals. More than once, walking round the front of the cottage and meeting the full force of the wind, she was driven back and almost carried off her feet. To struggle round that corner carrying kindling, coal and logs would probably have been more than she was capable of. As it was she had some breathless tottering struggles and would slam the door behind her giggling weakly, sure she would never have been able to shut the original door at all in the face of that ferocious blast.

The damp that pervaded the house didn't worry her any more. She knew once the rain stopped it would retreat to a level she could live with. The stains reappeared on the kitchen walls, she discovered mildew on unexpected things like wooden spoons, the rolling-pin and the plate rack, the gas lighter she had bought as the final answer to wet matches rusted and refused to spark, but in general her hours of labour clearing the earth from the outer walls had paid off. The kitchen floor showed no visible puddles – she didn't risk lifting the strip of carpet Donald had put down to see what was going on underneath – and the rooms no longer had that starkness in the air that had been so miserable when she first moved in. The fire was now her friend and she had long ago mastered the art of keeping it in for nine or ten hours at a time. She had huge stores of dry sticks and wood to hand and with the front door gone the problem of smoke billowing round the room on stormy days had vanished too.

She tortured herself over the question of whether or not she should go to Ishbel's funeral. They had never met, but she knew there was a strong tradition of attending funerals in this part of the world. On the other hand she was not local and she was not Highland. In the end she decided that to go would be an intrusion – but would Donald see it that way if she wasn't there? Would Donald notice if she wasn't there? She was separate from that side of his life, a life he might soon leave behind him anyway. When would he go? She knew nothing of quarter-days, or when it would be a good time of year to sell a flock or, indeed, how long the sale of a farm could take.

There was a huge turn-out for the funeral, as Lilias told Clare. She and Gerald came home blue and shivering in spite of Ina's revivifying brandies, and Clare was glad she had thought of being at Tigh Bhan to take care of them.

'Was Ishbel very popular then?'

'Ishbel? Absolutely not,' Lilias replied with all her old forth-rightness. 'But Donald is. It was out of respect for him that everyone came.'

'And for Ishbel's family,' Gerald put in.

'Certainly,' Lilias agreed, making Clare nostalgic for battles long ago.

'But why not for Ishbel?' The sort of question one knows one should not ask.

'Because she was the laziest and most selfish person who ever walked the earth, except that she saw to it that she almost never did walk it. No, Gerald, no use muttering about *de mortuis*, I didn't say it when Ishbel was alive and it can't do her any harm now she's dead.'

'But I thought she did everything on the farm?' Not a fishing question this time but asked in real surprise. This was not the picture of Ishbel that Clare's lonely envy had created.

'On the farm? Not a thing. I think she'd had enough of that when she was a girl, though as the youngest she was let off more lightly than her sisters. But at Rhumore? Dead wood. Wouldn't even learn to drive. Can you imagine it, living out there? She left the bottle-feeding during lambing to Peggy Macdonald, and the clipping and shooting lunches as well, and she screamed for one of her sisters the moment anything went wrong. Thoroughly spoiled, was Ishbel Macrae.'

With the conventional image Clare had built up shattered, beguiling fantasies rushed in. How different if she . . . She caught herself up. What rubbish. Lazy Donald's wife may have been, but she would have known more of everything to do with his world than Clare could ever hope to learn.

She did her best to shut out pictures of Donald at Rhumore alone. Margaret had plenty to say about Fiona leaving her father on his own and Ina Morrison, though not quite as frank as Lilias, allowed herself some very unflattering reminiscences about Ishbel and her sisters when they were all at school together. But no one mentioned Donald's plans. Clare waited numbly, fearing that every time she saw Margaret or Dougie, Angus or Nicol, she would hear news of his departure.

The days of wild weather had given her an idea of what it would be like living at the Larach without his reassuring background presence. She saw them as some sort of testing time but in fact, at that very deepest level of decision which is unaffected by any anxious weighing up of pros and cons, she knew she wasn't going anywhere at present. Even perhaps realizing that without Donald as a vital part of the scene she would learn more about her true intentions and the value of other relationships she had begun to build here. And there was Rory. With him it would not be quite so simple to take off, find some arbitrary place to live and work. Here he could be fitted into whatever pattern developed.

She drove Lilias over to Ardlonach on a day so soft and damp that it was hard to believe in the wildness of the gales that had battered the coast during the past week, or to take seriously the white wintry crowns of the inland hills. Rory was on Lilias's lap safe from the attentions of Topsy and Poppy, who had officiously taken on the role of well-meaning but inept aunts.

Ardlonach was a lovely place. In complete contrast to the stark granite block of Rhumore facing the winds off the sound, it was tucked down into a wooded bay on the south shore of the Luig peninsula, a cream-painted sprawling house with cotoneaster and roses still blooming against its walls. Stone-faced terraces, their outlines blurred with neglect, descended through riots and tangles of shrubs and ornamental bushes to a strip of sandy beach and boathouse and slipway. Even at this time of year there was an impression of trapped warmth and profuse flowering.

Una, looking very attractive in rugged check shirt and dunga-rees, her soft dark hair tied back, was halfway down the terraced slope with secateurs and big green garden waste container, attack-ing a wildly straggling rambler rose which had almost buried a stone seat placed to look out over the loch. A pair of pugs flew at Clare and Lilias in bulgy-eyed rage, and Topsy and Poppy, without discussion, headed smartly back to the car. Rory hung out of Clare's arms, quivering with interest.

'Thank goodness I can stop,' Una exclaimed as they threaded a way down to her. She had a couple of long dotted lines of blood down her cheek and her wrists were liberally scratched above a pair of too-short gloves. Lilias had known Ardlonach of old and she and Una fell at once into ardent gardening talk. Clare was chiefly impressed, as she looked at Una's slight frame and air of elegance even in her heavy working clothes, by the scale of the reclamation being so airily outlined.

Una led them in by a side door, kicking off her muddy boots to lie where they fell, and padded ahead of them in her socks into a big kitchen midway between scruffy fifties' gloss paint and modern stainless-steel hotel efficiency. Tony Urquhart, in naval uniform trousers and guernsey, daubed with the paint of the off-season hotelier, was taking a couple of bottles of wine out of the fridge.

'What are the pugs called?' Clare asked, holding Rory firmly as they circled her, balancing themselves upright with cold little touches of their paws against her knees, a highly unreliable look in their glistening eyes.

'Iolanthe and Hermia,' said Una, with an innocent glance at Tony.

'Hernia, more like, when I've finished kicking them round the kitchen,' he growled, beating them away from Clare with a waiter's cloth smelling of turps.

Not a new joke, Clare surmised, but one they obviously enjoyed, seeing the exaggerated look of loving disgust Tony gave Una as she crooned idiotically, 'Aren't they swe-ee-eet?'

Lunch was delicious – celery soup with Stilton, smoked mackerel pâté, bread from the Old Mill. 'Should be pug pie,' muttered Tony as they were solicited in turn with greedy gulps and snuffles.

After lunch Una showed them over the semi-dismantled house where she was struggling to maintain a faded chintzy country-house look in spite of mandatory emergency lighting and fire doors and the alterations necessary to provide en suite bathrooms everywhere. Then business could be put off no longer. Leaving Lilias in the library professing an interest in Tony's grandfather's collection of local press cuttings, but clearly longing for a nap, Una, sighing heavily, led Clare to the office.

'I hate coming in here,' she confessed. 'That arrogant machine sits there mocking and gloating and I can't meet its eye. Tony could probably best it but he's deep in wet rot and dry rot and loos going the wrong way. I thought if you could just point me in the right direction . . .'

The office was a wide-windowed, white-panelled study, cluttered with a miscellany of objects – boxes of what looked like job lots from Rory McMunn's saleroom, a pair of spindly rosewood chairs without seats, binoculars, cartridges (Donald would certainly think those should be locked up), game bags, cased rods, an oil painting of the pugs waiting to be framed, and a sagging dress box full of yellowed lace and linen which Clare longed to examine. Squatting on a leather-covered director's desk, a hostile alien, the computer bided its time.

'They sent us a software package,' Una told Clare in a business-like manner, adding at once, 'Do I mean that?' with a giggle that was very engaging. She explained her present accounting system and Clare closed her eyes.

'You'll be there for ever,' Lilias prophesied as they took the long way home by the shore road, now empty of tourist traffic.

'Una only wants me to start her off.'

'You'll never see either of them in the office again.'

Possibilities. Doors opening. Clare thought of the secluded beauty of Ardlonach, the huge enticing amount of work to be done, the charming office, Una's shy friendliness and eager commitment. Was Tony quite so committed? He'd certainly made a lot of intolerant references to the punters. And the pugs were a definite drawback. Also the open physical pleasure Tony and Una took in each other, revealed as much in their sparring as in the contact which seemed so vital to them, might be hard to take.

Emotionally she felt rather fragile. It might be easy to add up the practical reasons for staying put, stitching together some agreeable patchwork of mini jobs and friendships, but she missed Donald desperately. Would he come to say goodbye? Surely he wouldn't go without a word, leaving her to hear from someone else that Rhumore was sold and he had left for good? She wasn't sleeping well and in those restless nights fantasies she was ashamed of by day filled her imagination – Donald announcing that he couldn't live without her and taking her off to Canada with him; Donald saying he couldn't live without her and abandoning the farm to live a simple life at the Larach (making plans for the necessary extension was one of the better ways to lure sleep); Donald unable to support life in Canada and turning up as Joe had done, walking towards her, a mysterious stranger against the sunset. Et cetera.

By day she missed him frequently for many practical reasons. The care of Rory for one thing. It was Lilias who gave advice, not all contested by Gerald, on inoculations and dew claws and feeding and training, though Clare hadn't too much faith in the last, knowing what Donald thought of Poppy and Topsy.

Turning over the idea of helping Una she wanted first and foremost to discuss it with him. She suspected that Lilias was right; a permanent job probably existed at Ardlonach. Her mind was carried forward past the winter, which had been the hurdle she had set herself to get over, to summer here without Donald. A sequence of images seared across her brain – Donald in jeans, denim shirtsleeves rolled up over tanned muscular arms, thumbs in his belt, laughing at her attempts to put the tractor exactly on the required spot for lifting bales; Donald jumping long-legged to block an escaping ewe; Donald tucking her comfortably down beside him out of the wind to watch a red sun rise or twitching her up out of the boat and on to the jetty like another bag of shopping without even noticing he was doing it. These pictures would swarm up with such stinging nostalgia that sometimes it seemed sheer madness to stay here and expose herself to such pain.

She pulled her mind back firmly to the present. Circumstances had changed and she had to adapt to them. The time had come to buy a car, but before she could take up Catriona's offer of letting Watty Duff look for one for her Lilias offered the Metro.

'I shan't ever drive again and Gerald shouldn't either, only he's not prepared to admit it yet.'

'But I can drive you wherever you want to go.'

'Well, so you can if the car is yours.'

Apart from the simplicity of the arrangement, Clare was quite happy to buy a vehicle which would have to be left at the farm. Let the little house keep its remoteness till other changes overtook her life there.

Catriona thought a good many changes had already overtaken it and was full of amazed approval when she was finally persuaded to come, no longer able to pretend that Fergus needed her when he and Gerald could barely be dragged away from their labours to eat. Today, leaving the pair of them with one of Lilias's steak and kidney pies to heat up in the Aga, which Gerald would make sure of doing even if Fergus forgot, she had at last brought the dogs on a visit of inspection.

'I remember how it looked when Murdo lived here. Brown varnish. And I'm sure the ceiling was lower and the fireplace took up all that wall and you could hardly see. And wasn't the kitchen like a sort of lean-to, damp and freezing cold?'

Clare thought, not for the first time, that Murdo had not been the owner of the Larach.

'You are so lucky,' Catriona went on enviously, 'to live in a tiny house. That's what I'm going to do one day.'

It was the first time Clare had ever heard her refer to the future. 'One of the cottages on the estate?' she hazarded.

Catriona hesitated, then with a frown of irritation at herself because she found it hard to talk about such things, she answered gauchely, 'It would have to be, wouldn't it?'

'Not necessarily,' said Clare.

'Well, how could I live anywhere else? How could I fit into any other place? Everyone knows me here. Anywhere else I'd be regarded as a lunatic.'

Revealing, thought Clare, with a stab of compassion. 'Hardly,' she said, deliberately judicious, and was rewarded by a reluctant grin. 'Was that why you put off coming here for so long, because breaking the pattern is alarming?'

Catriona gave her a sudden sharp look, her small face pinched and mutinous, then with evident resolution she explained, 'I feel as if I've been living under a glass dome and it's been cracked and all kinds of draughts are coming in and I'm not sure I can deal with them.'

'Do you wish the dome was still intact?'

'Oh, Clare, *no*. I knew it had to happen and I'm so grateful that you came along and stirred things, but I can't imagine what will happen next. I watch Grandfather and I know he's failing. Not his mind but his health. I can hardly get him to eat and sometimes recently I've seen him sway when he stands up, and I've heard him stumble on the stairs. He fumbles for things and has trouble picking them up and he gets so upset when he's clumsy. I know I should have someone to look after him properly, but Mr McInnes is always saying there's no money . . .'

She turned her head to look out of the long window, her jaw set. Clare gave her a moment, going to the oven to get out the baked potatoes and the rabbit casserole — courtesy Dougie Stewart, since Margaret wouldn't cook rabbit for the dogs let alone the family.

'Talk to me about money,' Clare said breezily, emerging victorious from a brief tussle with Braan for the oven glove.

Catriona laughed. 'Why not? There isn't any.'

'Well, that's straightforward enough.'

'The whole place is mortgaged, as you might suppose. It costs more than it makes, no matter how frugally we live. My father ran through everything there was, income and capital, and the estate has never recovered. All I can hope to do is hang on as long as Grandfather is alive. It would be unthinkable to ask him to live anywhere else. I wish we could afford care for him.'

'A nurse?'

'He'd loathe it, loathe the very word. No,' she said slowly, 'what I really think might be the answer would be some kind of valet or manservant. We couldn't possibly manage the wages, of course. And there's another thing I think he might like if only we could afford it – something that may surprise you.'

Clare couldn't begin to imagine what Fergus might be secretly yearning for.

Catriona grinned at her. 'A television,' she said, sure of Clare's reaction.

'A television! At Glen Righ House?'

'More interesting for him than the word processor – at least, one supposes so. I could do a course in social studies at the same time,' she added, mocking herself but at the same time bravely expressing an idea which she didn't want laughed at.

'Well, they don't cost that much,' Clare said, understanding perfectly. 'Surely the estate could run to that?' Could I buy them one? she wondered, but it would be difficult to find a pretext this time.

'Oh, I never hear anything from Mr McInnes but the size of the overdraft. I'm sure he'd never agree.'

Clare felt that Mr McInnes should perhaps be checked up on. 'What about the Bentley?' she suggested.

Catriona stared at her.

'Are you very much attached to it?' Clare asked.

'I hate it,' Catriona said vigorously. 'Iain and I always did. We felt so sick with the smell of the leather and rolling round on the back seat when our feet wouldn't reach the floor.'

'Why not sell it?'

'But Grandfather would – well, I suppose in actual fact he never sees it nowadays, does he?' Clare waited. 'Goodness, how I should love never to have to drive the horrible thing again. I do envy you whizzing about in Lilias's little car – your little car. Watty would probably give notice, though.'

'It must be worth a fortune.'

Catriona gazed at Clare with growing hope. 'Is there a garage in Fort William where we could sell it?'

'Fort William! You're joking. No, I know the very person.'

One of the Carlini brothers could make himself useful – the first impulse Clare had had to make contact since Magda left.

'But would it really be worth something? It's very old,' Catriona said doubtfully, and was puzzled when Clare laughed.

The Bentley fetched a price that rocked the glen and Watty Duff had to be carried to one of Ina's chilly beds after rounding off a maudlin night in the bar by throwing himself off Inverbuie pier into two feet of water, to the infinite entertainment of his cronies.

It was Gerald who had the best idea. 'Get Watty to look after Fergus. It might fill the gap the Bentley has left in his affections. He comes and goes about the house as it is and no one could say he's fully occupied.'

This simple answer seemed to suit all parties. Fergus found nothing strange in the increased presence of Watty, who having found a Fiat Uno for Catriona which he could barely bring himself to touch set about making the big house as warm and comfortable as the garage had been.

Clare took Catriona to Fort William, where she had thought it was only possible to shop at Maclennan's because the account was there. They bought a television set and Clare introduced her to the simple process of cashing a cheque. Mr McInnes would be pleased. Gently, carefully, Catriona was lured out of her tower. She joined in the coffee sessions at the Old Mill, where Ben was not visible and not mentioned, and called at the Larach whenever she felt like it by simply extending one of her daily rides. There she played for hours with Rory, dived with joy into Clare's books, and dutifully tried to extend her cooking range while remaining on the whole baffled by basic principles. She was often at Tigh Bhan and enjoyed long glen chats with Lilias, who had an excellent grasp of local relationships and events.

'It's good to hear her talking so easily,' Clare said to Lilias.

'I've never seen her so alive. You've made a big difference to her.'

'I've asked her to teach me to ride.'

'Ideal. In fact the classic therapy, allowing her to show you something for a change. And you'll find it a very different way to get to know the glen too.'

She was right. The garrons they rode, working hill ponies

with a marked tendency to follow routes of their own choosing which ended up at grouse butts, were steady and sure-footed and had a comfortable swinging gait. Clare loved the long rides on the hill in the early winter days, Rory tucked inside the front of her jacket or lolloping along trying to keep up with the other dogs, and Catriona was delighted to range further afield than she had felt she could for a long time, often talking about her brother Iain and of Fergus as he had been when he was the one adored and stable adult of their childhood world.

So many good things, but Clare knew that in spite of them all she felt herself to be once more a person alone.

CHAPTER THIRTY

Christmas arrived, cutting arbitrarily across normal life, and still Clare had not seen Donald, had barely had news of him. The glen at large seemed to want to respect his privacy, seeing it as natural that he should wish to be alone at Rhumore in the weeks after his wife's death, having grown accustomed over the years to his preference for an increasingly unsocial existence there. Lilias did talk of inviting him to Tigh Bhan for Christmas, but Gerald routed the proposal most emphatically while Clare, who was already invited, coped privately with a sudden breathlessness induced by longing and also panic at the thought of meeting Donald for the first time again in such circumstances.

'But I feel so guilty that we're doing nothing to help him,' Lilias objected. 'It seems so unfeeling to leave him alone like this.'

'When was the last time he accepted an invitation here?' Gerald demanded.

'He used to be such a sociable creature as a young man,' Lilias told Clare, neatly avoiding answering Gerald. 'He and Stephen were good friends and he was often here, and both of them used to spend a lot of time at Ardlonach with all the Urquhart cousins. I wouldn't say Donald was exactly wild in those days – I do miss the word gay – but he certainly loved ceilidhs and dancing and parties, and he was a great shinty player.'

'That delightful little blonde he came home with changed all that,' Gerald commented.

Blonde, Clare thought with irrational and fierce jealousy. I don't want her to have been blonde.

'Yes, I've often wondered what Donald's life would have been if that affair hadn't hit him so hard. Ishbel was pure rebound, of course. Then under his wild ways he was always very conscientious, and Mary, his sister, had already made her escape by then. He really did see Rhumore as his job and his ultimate responsibility.'

Would he abandon it now? Clare found she couldn't bring herself to ask.

Trudy and Ben were going south for a couple of weeks over Christmas. To sort out their business affairs, Clare knew. 'See you in the New Year,' Trudy had said, giving her a crushing hug. 'So *be* here.'

'I will,' Clare promised. That much anyway was certain.

Lilias had begged her to come to Tigh Bhan not only for Christmas itself but to stay for a few days. 'If you're here I won't badger Stephen,' was the way she put it, with calculated candour, and it was clear that Clare was not going to be allowed to refuse. 'And we might be able to persuade Catriona to bring Fergus down for Christmas lunch,' Lilias had added as an extra inducement.

'Done!' Clare exclaimed, delighted at the idea.

She had been to Ardlonach several times by now and had sorted out as much of the backlog of the season's accounts as she could, but Una's mind skated apprehensively off the most elementary explanations of how to proceed from there and Clare had promised to go back after the holiday to carry on. For the time being, however, she concentrated on Lilias, seeing her through her catering-scale Christmas shopping and cooking. She also took Margaret, Lynn and Sheena for a day's shopping in Inverness, an ordeal from which she emerged in poor shape.

Angus came down the loch with a load of coal, gas, paraffin for the lamps and various bulk supplies.

'Now, are you sure that'll see you through?' he teased her, but there was approval there too. 'Good luck to you, I say. There's been plenty folk come up to try this simple life carry-on, and had us all running round helping them out with their daft notions, but they've mostly taken off fast enough at the first sniff of winter. At least you're giving it a go.'

From him Clare learned that Donald's mother was at Rhumore, and that Fiona and her husband were expected for Christmas. The news made her feel as though Donald's real world had engulfed him and she knew she had no part of it. She admitted at last that she had been hoping all through these weeks of underlying loneliness that he would come to the Larach looking for company or merely for a listener as he had so often when Ishbel was ill. But he had not turned to her for that help and he would not need her now.

Clare's only link with him was Rory who was an endless delight to her. To be the focus of that intelligent brain and unstinting affection was a new experience and one she was grateful to have discovered. She couldn't imagine life at the cottage without him now.

Catriona agreed to bring Fergus to Tigh Bhan for Christmas lunch, then did her best to get out of it. 'He hates crowds of people. He hasn't been out of the house for years. He'll wonder where the Bentley has gone and when we have to explain he'll be so upset . . .'

'Tell me,' Clare demanded, 'is this anxiety for Fergus a smoke-screen you're putting up to hide behind yourself?'

Catriona reddened and Clare thought she'd been too outspoken, but Catriona didn't lack courage and after a moment said awkwardly, 'Yes, that's probably it.'

Treading more cautiously, Clare pointed out, 'Your grandfather has accepted me and Gerald coming to Glen Righ, and Watty looking after him. He's so gentle and amenable I wonder if he wouldn't accept anything that came along in much the same way.'

'Like television, you mean,' said Catriona dryly, and Clare was glad she could produce a small joke.

Fergus had become an instant addict, marvelling by the hour at the antics of an alien world, shaking his silver head and murmuring, 'Extraordinary people, quite extraordinary, so rude to each other, so unhappy and so unkind.'

'Then you'll come to Tigh Bhan? If it seems too much for Fergus you could take him home early. Everyone would understand.'

The day was a festive assault course. Present-giving took place after breakfast, including bones for 'the girls' tied up in ribbons and Rory galloping madly through seas of wrapping paper till the children were weak with giggles. Lilias, via Stephen, the children and even the dogs, had lavished gifts on Clare. Trudy had left a bottle of sloe gin for her with the message, 'Keep it for our next heart-to-heart – who knows?', and Una had tucked a diary between a jar of mint jelly and a jar of pickled nasturtium seeds with the instruction, 'Fill in the Ardlonach days NOW.' Touched and grateful, Clare still longed to have something from Donald, and to be able to give him something. She wrenched her mind resolutely away.

They walked through the village in the mild yellow morning, greeting people not normally at large and strangely clean, and church had the inexplicable brightness of Christmas, that atmosphere of best hats and full-voiced singing and goodwill as yet in place, the satisfaction of presents newly acquired and the prospect of gluttony.

When Catriona and Fergus arrived in the middle of pre-lunch frenzy Clare knew she wasn't the only person to feel a pang to see Fergus in a faded kilt jacket which hung loosely round him, and Catriona in what looked like a 'Sunday' dress dating from school which still fitted her childish frame. Though she was speechless with nerves it was good to see Fergus calmly at home in a scene once familiar, talking gravely to Libby and Oliver about their presents, discussing the state of the pheasants with Stephen, questioning nothing.

Lunch was a huge and perfect meal. Looking at the smiling faces round the laden table Clare wondered what festivity there would be at Rhumore and found herself passionately longing for a glimpse of Donald, the sound of his voice. Then she remembered that she was not the only person at this table who had pain to hold at bay. She recalled Lilias's words when she had come to Clare's room to say goodnight: 'I'm only thankful that I can still cope with having them here, especially now.' Clare watched Stephen carving for his father, pouring the wine, saying and doing all the required things; the children boisterous and therefore presumed happy; Fergus affable and calm; Catriona relaxing as Gerald embarked on a long tale about Christmas in Sicily in 1943 and she realized that she needn't say a word.

In fact, Catriona became slightly high on warmth and wine, relief and attention, and Clare saw that everyone found her a useful focus for affection, even the children recognizing in her someone who needed their care, an adult who did not belong to the adult world. I shall never go away from here, Clare found herself thinking fiercely, high herself, smiling across the table at a Catriona pink-cheeked and happy. I shall be here for her when Fergus dies and her world falls to pieces.

A move was made to the drawing-room to listen to the Queen. Everyone stood for the anthem and Rory sicked up a balloon. Then mass dog-walking took place in the fields beside the loch and Clare's thoughts sailed away down its silver length to where the last of the light was held. They came back for mince pies that burned their mouths and Christmas cake by the fire.

Fergus looked tired but was tranquil as Stephen helped him into the Fiat. Clare felt Catriona's tremulous gratitude in her farewell hug. She was wound up to quite a pitch and Clare hoped that the cold, gaunt, silent house waiting for them would not be too harsh a contrast. But it was her home; she would be all right.

Even Lilias conceded that no one could possibly be expected to eat dinner and agreed, as though it was some daring innovation, to let Stephen and Clare make turkey sandwiches for supper, while Oliver fried slices of Christmas pudding so that he could finish off the brandy butter. Quite soon he and Libby trailed off to bed with the portable spoils of the day, shortly followed with apologies by their weary grandparents.

Stephen and Clare, comatose in the warm softly-lit room, were not yet ready for sleep, or solitude.

'I can't tell you how grateful I am to you,' Stephen began rather formally, breaking a drowsy silence. 'I know I shall have to make proper arrangements soon, but it's been such a relief knowing you were close by and keeping an eye on the parents.'

'I love coming here, you know that, and they've been very good to me too.'

'I've an idea mother's match-making,' he said casually, after another pause.

'Us? Oh, surely not,' Clare exclaimed, waking up suddenly.

He laughed. 'Flattering.' But they both knew exactly where they stood. 'It makes me terribly defensive on Lucy's behalf, I'm afraid.'

Clare had not expected him to be ready to talk about Lucy yet, but well-dined-and-wined torpor can stimulate confidences from the least articulate people. 'Lilias will only ever see your side, you must realize that.'

'Yet she knows what a marvellous person Lucy is. I could never match up, could never hope to give her what she needed –'

The floodgates were open. Here was an honest man, capable of assessing his shortcomings, his lack of imagination and artistic sensitivity, the product of the forces that had shaped him and unable to change, yet still hopelessly in love with a woman of a very different fibre. 'I persuaded her to marry me. Bludgeoned her into it, more like. I don't know how many times she refused me. I just wore her down.' He had no illusions about her coming back and knew that all he could do was to make the best of it for the children.

'Will they see Lucy?'

'She thinks better not. She sees herself as the odd one out in the family, the disruptive element. But a part of them comes from her, is her . . .' Raw pain.

They talked on quietly with lengthy silences. There was evident solace for Stephen in this but no answers, and there was only a certain amount he could make himself put into words. Almost without Clare noticing it he had drawn the conversation round to her own marriage.

It was easy now to say straightforwardly that Martin had been gay, she had already taken that hurdle, and to go over the business of Joe with someone who understood the service environment. Stephen's calm acceptance of the sordid little story, his matter-of-fact air of having heard it all before, made her able to express her deepest fears.

'I think – I'm almost certain – Martin was being blackmailed. Oh, I don't know, it sounds so outlandish even to say that.'

'What makes you think so?'

'He'd been paying quite large amounts to someone. And he was drinking far more. It was becoming such a struggle for him to get himself together each morning to go to work. Perhaps it was beginning to affect his competence in his job. He had to be so utterly meticulous, and he always told me he had an enormous amount of information to keep abreast of.'

'What was he doing at the time?'

Stephen knew precisely, far more precisely than Clare guessed, the importance of the unassailable image in a senior staff post, and the damage not only to Martin's career but to those very much more important than his if a scandal had burst. Stephen had no doubt that Martin had taken the only way out that he could see. There could be no making a clean breast of it for him, no appeal for help, no quiet oblivion in some Service backwater, if indeed a man who sounded arrogant and egotistical to a degree could have endured such a solution.

'They gave him a military funeral, you know.' The irony of this had bitten deep and Clare had never talked of it to anyone. 'The whole rigmarole – valuable young officer, dazzling career cut short, flag draping the coffin, the volleys over the grave.' She shivered even now to think of that dank Cambridgeshire churchyard, the east wind biting to the bone, rime on the clods of turned earth, their rattle as sharp as the shots fired for a hero as they fell on the coffin holding the body of the man she had once—

Stephen's warm hand came down over hers. 'Hold up,' he said in a bracing tone. Clare understood Lucy's flight even as she was filled with gratitude to be able to free herself finally of this poison.

She even told him about something buried more deeply yet – her shameful behaviour to Martin's parents.

'It was such an agonizing farce, and I was terrified that I would somehow give something away. They were so proud of him and I should have tried to help them. They were grieving, devastated, and all I could think about was the nagging question, had Martin gone out deliberately to make it happen? And about what he must have been going through to reach that point. And I hadn't known, hadn't ever tried to understand. Do you know, I wouldn't even let his parents stay at the house? Can you imagine such utter selfishness? I drove them straight to the station after lunch in the mess. I can hardly believe I did it. I can still see their bewildered faces as I put them on the train . . .' That, she knew, was the core of her guilt. That and the fact that she had never been in touch with them since, had wiped them out of her life as something she was quite unable to deal with.

But at least she had finally admitted it, had put into words those deep-buried, festering memories, she thought as she snuggled down at last in Lilias's soft guest-room bed, with the faint scent of verbena rising from the cool smoothness of old linen. Stephen was the last person she would have imagined as the one to exorcise these devils, but his phlegmatic calm, as though he heard similar stories every day in the normal course of his duties, had put them finally into perspective for her. She could not alter or recall her failures in generosity or courage, but she could put them behind her.

CHAPTER THIRTY-ONE

On the way back from Tigh Bhan two days after Christmas Clare called in at The Birks to thank Margaret for her plant-holder with the poker-work view of the Pap of Glencoe. Finding her alone (since Dougie had gone to do a quiet bit of fencing and who could blame him?) Clare had stayed to tell her about Christmas with the Markies, an account Margaret would certainly have enjoyed more if Clare had been able to tell her that Fergus had gone for someone with his *sgian dubh*.

As she passed the farm she looked for mail in the old dairy and found a card from Joe. She opened it eagerly as she had put a long letter in her Christmas card to him. It said, 'Merry Xmas, take care, Joe.' She felt cross, amused and then sad for him.

When she reached the Larach and went out for wood she found a large box waiting in the shed, an envelope tucked into the flap with a message on the back: 'Sorry to have missed you, thought you were coming back today.'

Clare was furiously, blindly angry with poor Margaret, shaking with disappointment to think that Donald had been here, perhaps not an hour ago, and she had not been there. One chance, one single chance, and she had missed it.

His card was a painting of grey seals by a local artist and he had written, 'I hope your first Christmas in the glen has been a happy one and that the coming year will bring you peace and contentment wherever you are. With all good wishes, Donald. (I suppose that pup of yours will be beyond hope by now anyway.)'

So much; but not enough. In tears Clare knelt there and then on the rough cobbles and bits of bark of the shed floor to open the box. A beanbag for Rory was tucked round a handsome old flour crock. When she lifted its glazed lid she found the slim shape of a book neatly wrapped. Naomi Mitchison's poems. Reading them later by the fire they hurt so much that she couldn't go on. Scotland, Donald's Scotland, honed, pared, its beauty laid bare.

And she had not been able to give him the present so lovingly chosen for him – a pair of photographs she had come across with astounded pleasure in a junk shop in Inverness, one of a clipping scene on a croft on the eastern side of the glen now obliterated by plantations, the other of a garron pulling a plough in the field by the hump-backed bridge. She had had them framed and then had swung violently and absurdly from the conviction that Donald would be delighted with them to equal conviction that he would have seen them already, that everyone would know them, that he probably had copies, that she shouldn't attempt to give him bits of his own history.

She longed to thank him for his presents, so perfect, so carefully thought out. She considered with a perilous excitement going to the village and phoning him, but knew she couldn't trust herself to handle it. But she could write to him. The first letter covered twelve pages and did her a lot of good. The final note achieved the tone of his own message and the only satisfaction it gave her was knowing that absolutely nothing could be read into it.

During those first days of the new year Clare had to work hard at positive thinking. Though Trudy was still away and the Urquharts swamped by friends and family, who believed they couldn't be any trouble since Ardlonach was a hotel after all, whether open or shut, Lilias needed her support and help. Stephen had gone south but Oliver and Libby had stayed on at Tigh Bhan and Clare spent a lot of time with them, glad of their uncomplicated friendliness. She took them off to spend book tokens, squander Christmas money, ski in Glencoe and ride at Glen Righ.

Catriona welcomed them nervously, but their enthusiasm soon reassured her, while Watty Duff took to the new scene with zest. One morning as he sat at the kitchen table with his tea and yesterday's *Daily Record* while Clare, Catriona and the children were engaged in putting together a pheasant casserole over and round him, he remarked, 'I've always fancied trying my hand at a bit of cooking,' and, folding up the newspaper and stuffing it into his pocket, plunged into the fray. After that there was no stopping him and he was a far more rewarding pupil than Catriona would ever be. He got the Aga going so well it rocked at its moorings and the kitchen was nearly as hot as Margaret's.

Oliver went hind stalking with MacGillivray while Libby, deep in the pony phase, was blissfully happy dragging out the remains of old jumps and banging them together with Catriona's help. The ponies preferred to go through rather than over them, but quite without malice.

They spent a couple of rainy afternoons exploring the further reaches of the house, a great success with the children. Clare was afraid that Catriona might find it sad, but she seemed to view abandoned nurseries and mouldering rooms with the detached eye of the tourist and to enjoy the forays as much as anyone.

Clare got Great-Aunt Sofia safely completed and printed out, and began transferring the rest of Fergus's rambling account of the Finlays on to disk. He wrote very little now, content to sit for hours reading and rereading what Clare had produced.

When the children went back to school Lilias did admit that, much as she had loved having them, she was quite glad to have the house empty again. Trudy returned without Ben and the pottery was silent and unused. In the winter the shop was much quieter, though Trudy was gratified and reassured to find how much steady local trade she had won, and though Clare went as often as before it was more to enjoy Trudy's company than from any need to help.

At Ardlonach she had become very fond of Una, scatty as she could be and frighteningly vague, from a business point of view, about the relation of costs to charges or expenditure to returns. Tony Clare wasn't so sure of; he was charming, friendly, even slightly flirtatious which she decided he couldn't help, but she observed that he did very little actual work and was off whenever he could manage it to stalk hinds, ski or indulge in his latest passion of ice climbing.

Early in February the first heavy snow arrived, driven by a screaming, relentless blizzard that shut down all movement in the glen, closed the road over the moor and imprisoned Clare for several days of total isolation at the cottage. In a way she relished the experience. In practical terms she knew she could deal with it, but much more importantly she discovered how far she had adapted, feeling no anxiety or restlessness or fears about being able to occupy herself. She read avidly (I've finished *War and Peace*, Donald), scraped and painted the bathroom ceiling, a nasty job which had been abandoned in the summer when outside work became too attractive, cut down and replaced the border on a beautiful (and beautifully thick) bed cover Lilias had given her, listened to hours of music, her mind on Donald, with Rory pretending he was still small enough to get on her lap, and she slept sound and warm while the wind screamed and tore unavailingly at the solid little building.

She was enchanted by her altered world after the storm died down, its newly sculpted contours flowing in smooth white billows under a blinding sun, its calendar-blue loch. Rory went quite mad and was irresistibly funny in his ecstasy in this new element and Clare longed to share her laughter, and this sparkling beauty. But even in her delight the thought dragged at her that every day brought nearer the moment when she would hear that Donald was going, had gone. When, as swiftly as it had come, the snow vanished and the whole landscape came alive again, rippling and flowing, sunny and mild, she was terribly afraid that with life back to normal it must be the first news she would hear.

And then it happened. She met him, simply and naturally, at Tigh Bhan. Calling with some shopping for Lilias she had found Donald's Land Rover parked outside, Trim poking her nose out of the back and after one duty bark smiling toothily and giving whimpers of welcome to Rory.

Clare put him into the back of the Land Rover with his excited aunt and, her arms round a big box, her knees oddly trembly, went in to find Donald about to set off for the plantation by the ravine where the rabbits had been causing terrible destruction among Gerald's young trees. She could never afterwards remember what she said or what she did with the shopping or quite how it was decided that she would go with him. There was such a buzz of greetings and orders and questions about boots (which Clare always had in the car for going back over the headland anyway) that probably she hadn't given herself away too badly, she thought, waiting in the stillness of the wood. She could only remember Donald's smile and his calm voice saying, 'Here you are, just in time for another lesson in straight thinking,' as though there had been no weeks of absence, of wondering, of dread.

More a vibration than a sound, she caught the quick drum of panic underground and, glancing at Donald, saw that he was watching her to see if she had picked it up. He nodded, satisfied. Leaning against a leafless rowan, not moving, Clare watched the nets, waiting with mixed feelings for the explosive bulge, the frantic flailing, the heart-pounding check when escape was found to be impossible.

I eat rabbit, she reminded herself. She had been told that after a couple of mild winters (really?) they were increasing at crisis rate. Ferrets working surely followed natural laws, and she couldn't deny that she felt a primitive excitement each time they sent a victim into the waiting trap. Yet she would have been incapable of killing one herself and covered her ears and looked away from the flurry and thud of death.

Every sense alive and aware, incredulous to find herself there, Clare was enjoying not so much the drama of the job but its methodical quietness, Donald's practised hands swiftly coiling the nets, releasing them with a flick that laid them exactly where he wanted them, his intent face and steady movements and the shared silence of the waiting and listening. She had been unexpectedly charmed by the ferrets, too, though self-control had been challenged when Donald put one into her hands. Quelling instinctive recoil, she had made herself look properly at the delicately made but astonishingly powerful creature, liking the immaculate cleanness of its pale yellow coat, its redcurrant-jelly eyes, its inquisitive busy checking out of the stranger, as though willing to give her a couple of minutes of its time before real work began. And they were such engaging creatures when they abandoned business to play briefly at the mouth of a hole, writhing and leaping with boneless speed and lightness, ignoring Donald's disgusted whispers till they were ready to get on with the job again.

There had been thin silvery rain for most of the time from soft white clouds mounded against a pewter sky. There had been the rich smell of earth and ancient leaf mould, and the sharper smell of wet rhododendrons and rotting wood as Clare had crawled through the undergrowth to close off hidden back doors. There had been a feeling of conscious explicit happiness to be where she was, doing what she was doing.

Eyes on the nets, body still, vaguely aware of cold striking up from the damp ground through her boot soles, of the nip of wet, icy fingers thrust into her pockets, Clare let her thoughts drift, thankful beyond words to be with Donald again, engaged in some shared task, at peace. Before she had known him she had looked ahead along the years rather like a road, herself a dot bobbing somewhere along the first part of the route, assuming that she would come before long to some recognizable arrival point. Briefly, with Martin, she had imagined that this had come. The husband, the house, the accepted slot in the structure of society, the mapped-out future. But the feeling of waiting had soon re-emerged. Unfulfilment. Was there such a word? Then she met Donald, and when she was with him that looking ahead vanished. She had found point and purpose. It was very simple. Now she had unexpectedly been given this day, these hours, with him and, though nothing had altered, that in itself was marvellous.

'I think that'll do for today,' Donald said at last, when dusk had deepened round them and all Clare had seen of the last fugitives hunted from their homes had been the flash of white belly fur as Donald tossed them down to join their dead friends and relations. They wound the nets round thumb and finger for the last time and the ferrets were put into their carrying box. The evening air was full of a distillation of the scents of the day which Clare knew would always hold an intense nostalgia for her. As they went down the path above the burn towards the lights of the house Donald lifted a laden arm round her shoulders in a small hug.

'You'd make a good rabbit-catcher's assistant.'

Clare laughed, but felt herself stiffen involuntarily against his arm. She knew if she allowed herself to respond in any way to this gesture her body would betray her, turning to him, folding against him with a message he would not be able to mistake.

Trim was blasé as they dumped the rabbits in the back of the

Land Rover, but Rory was appalled to find himself in the company of twenty still-warm corpses and not impressed with the way Clare smelled either.

'I suppose you'll want to bring him in,' Donald said, lifting him out by the scruff in a way Clare knew she mustn't mind.

'Trim as well then. Fair's fair.'

'Dog'll be ruined,' he grumbled, jerking his head at Trim resignedly and selecting the couple of rabbits Lilias had said she could use. 'A nice young one here for you. Can you carry that home if I put it in the boot?'

Tea in the warm kitchen of Tigh Bhan, muddy moleskins steaming, chilled fingers wrapped round teacups so fine you could see through them, freshly made drop scones and raspberry jam and huge slices of coffee walnut cake. Trim lifting a warning lip as Topsy and Poppy tried clumsily to play with Rory, Gerald saying yet again that next time Donald must let him come out with a gun, only way to do it, and Donald swiftly skinning and cleaning Lilias's rabbits, ignoring her objections that she could perfectly well do it herself later. Piercing happiness. Happiness which Clare knew could not be held on to or recaptured. Without warning she felt tears sting, her throat constrict.

Donald was on his feet, Trim at the door. Hubbub of thanks and farewells, shouts at Topsy and Poppy to stay. He's going. But we haven't talked, haven't said – said what? If only she hadn't had the car, he would have driven her up to the farm and then perhaps ... But heading a few minutes later up the glen, with Rory standing up on the back seat with every muscle tense and quivering, nose questing towards that irresistible scent from the boot, she realized that no one had mentioned Donald's departure.

CHAPTER THIRTY-TWO

The next day was bright and cold, with a crisp wind swiftly drying out the landscape. It was a day for out of doors and indeed Clare could not have stayed inside, restless and stirred up by the meeting with Donald. She had severely depleted her store of kindling during these winter weeks and decided that under the pines on the rocky promontory would be the driest place to replenish it.

Yesterday had been so strange, like a slice of last year presented to her again, wonderful but finite. Donald had been so exactly the same, his manner kind and easy, gently teasing and friendly. Nothing could have made it clearer that for him the weeks without seeing each other had had no significance. Odd that the job they had engaged in at this first meeting had meant quiet hours together when talking was impossible. It had been dream-like, time drifting unmeasured. And it had changed nothing.

Rory loved the cones and was playing happily near her, batting one about, squirming on his back to juggle it in his paws, rolling over with ferocious growls when he dropped it. They were well back from the loch up three big shelves of rock and Rory was moving with Clare as she filled her basket.

It happened with unbelievable speed. A puff of wind took the cone and Rory galloped after it across the sloping rock. As Clare shouted to him he had already followed it down on to the next shelf and as she went after him, sure he would stop, he was racing in pursuit down the smooth slabs. Screaming at him now, her limbs slowed by dragging weights, Clare was yards from him as he rolled, gathering speed, and disappeared with one sharp yelp of fear over the edge of the sheer drop to the greedy currents of the loch below. There was just one glimpse of a wisp of red coat before the dark waters sucked him down and he was gone. Clare was almost over after him before she woke to her danger and clawed herself back to safety, sobbing with shock, her mind refusing to take in what had happened.

She scrambled, shaking, up the broad ledges and tore down the flank of the promontory to the shore, searching for a sign of the small body. But her brain told her that he could not possibly survive the powerful drag of that racing current, and that if his body ever surfaced it would be far from here. Still she searched and called, distracted with grief and guilt.

She stumbled back to the cottage at last. Her primary need was to tell someone, to pour out her horror. Donald. But comfort from that one essential source was no longer available to her. She had set off towards Tigh Bhan before she thought how it would distress Lilias to see her in this state and turned, nearly blind with tears, towards The Birks.

Probably it was the best choice. Dougie was home for his dinner and he and Margaret, while concerned and kind, were sympathetic only up to a point. Rory was just a dog after all; there'd be plenty other pups. Also the children were goggling with interest, which made Clare realize how wild she must look. Then again, the crude flavour of the tinned tomato soup Margaret gave her was shock enough to brace the most distraught. Grateful to them for reducing the tragedy to everyday terms, Clare set off for home. She must deal with the reminders of Rory waiting there. There was no one else to do it. And she would have to live with the stark fact that because of her stupidity and negligence that loving, exuberant little creature was dead.

Face stiff, hands unsteady, she collected up rubber bone, grubby slipper, ball, chewed stick, lead, bowls. So much property. The problem at the Larach was that you couldn't simply walk outside and drop things into the bin and never see them again. The beanbag from Donald would have to go up into the loft for the time being. Chippy might like it – no such luxuries at Glen Righ House.

How could she not have seen the danger? How could she have taken him to such a place? No, don't think about that; get on with what has to be done.

She didn't hear the door open, too deep in grief to be aware, but suddenly Donald was there at the kitchen steps and she scrambled to her feet and went to him without conscious decision and was caught into his arms, enwrapped and comforted. She could feel his strong fingers running up under her hair as he held her head against his chest.

'I couldn't stop him. It happened so quickly.' Tears flowed in a drenching tide, words coming in painful gouts. 'I should never have taken him up there. But we were miles from the water, right back among the trees. But then the wind, he was playing with the cones, I should have been watching him, I should have realized . . .'

'Oh, lass, don't grieve so,' Donald's deep voice soothed. 'Don't grieve.'

'He was so happy. He was such a good little thing.'

'I know.'

She drew back in his arms, trying to get the tears under control. 'Donald, I can't believe you've turned up, just when I needed you so much.'

'Dougie phoned me. He said you were upset.'

'Oh, how kind of him.' Tears of gratitude now. Her voice was still tremulous. And how good of Donald to have come at once. Realization of where she was returned. Donald felt her movement to pull away and his arms slackened. He said in that easy way of his, 'You'll want this lot out of sight for the time being,' and, stooping, he tossed the pathetic collection of favourite objects on to the beanbag and carried it away. Clare didn't ask what he would do with it.

'Where's Trim?' she asked as he came back.

'In the boat. She's fine where she is.'

'That was kind, Donald, not to bring her in,' Clare said, chokily in spite of her efforts.

Donald gave her a moment, then she felt his hand firm on her shoulder. 'Come on, Clare, get your coat, you're not staying here on your own.'

'Are you going to the village?'

'I'm taking you to Rhumore.'

It was bitterly cold on the loch. The wind smoothed over Clare's face like an icy hand, setting it in a stiff mask. She huddled in the circle of Donald's arm, turning her head occasionally to breathe in the comforting smell of his jacket, and to shut out the sight of the dark racing waves.

Going to Rhumore. Donald's world. Yesterday's meeting at Tigh Bhan had seemed out of context in either of their lives, as though only the immediate moment had had importance. She had offered condolences about Ishbel when they met and Donald had accepted them with the same formality. Now the reality was coming close.

'Donald, I never saw you to explain. About Ishbel's funeral. I didn't go because I wasn't sure whether—'

'Don't worry about that now.'

'I didn't want to intrude – a newcomer –'

'It's all right. I understood.'

'And it was so awful to miss you when you came at Christmas. I'd called at Margaret's on the way home. I haven't even thanked you properly for your presents, they were perfect . . .' The knife-twist of those poems, Rory's beanbag.

His arm tightened round her. 'Don't think about it. You wrote to me, remember.'

That careful, attenuated, anxious letter. And her present to him was still waiting. She could have given it to him today. It had never occurred to her.

Going to Rhumore, something she had never thought would happen. Certainly now he would talk of his plans. Clare shivered, feeling she couldn't face any more blows, but at the same time warning herself that she mustn't overreact whatever he told her. Emotions were so raw, it would be too easy to give herself away. And this is only about Rory, she reminded herself. He's being kind about Rory, nothing more.

From the Rhumore jetty a vehicle track made a long swing up the cliff but Donald led Clare up by a steep path, taking it at a steady pace with her hand in his, and they came out on to sheep-clipped turf where the sweep of the wind met them and a great view of the islands and the sound opened before them. Beyond a gap in the dyke sprawled the steading buildings, the square granite house staring out to sea above their blue-slated roofs. In spite of what had happened Clare felt excitement rise in her as Donald led her to a stone porch at the side of the house, where Trim hopped up into a raised wooden box padded with sacks and watched them go in with pricked ears.

A narrow lobby, dark with coats. 'I'd better take my boots off,' Clare said. She had put them on to go and collect kindling; it seemed like days ago.

'Don't worry about that,' said Donald, sounding almost irritated, opening a door into a kitchen which startled Clare into open-mouthed silence. Uniformly white, as clinical as an operating theatre, its strip lights blinked on in a glare that blinded her. It had built-in everything, except for a puny formica-topped table and two tubular metal chairs set in the middle of a wide expanse of floor. Dismay and disappointment chilled her.

Donald made a harsh sound which might have been a laugh. 'How about something to warm you up? Brandy? Sherry? Or I could make some soup.'

'Just coffee, thanks. Or have you missed lunch coming to see me?' It was hard to work out what time it was.

'I'll get something later.' He went to fill the kettle and Clare looked around her. No colour, no soul. Donald's dishes from breakfast were in the draining rack. On the worktop lay a newspaper, a couple of buff envelopes, a catalogue. The room was warm but she shivered.

'Donald?'

'Yes?'

'Could Trim come in?' She hadn't known her voice would sound so quavery.

Donald gave her a sharp look over his shoulder, put down the cups he had taken from a cupboard and went out without a word. Trim hesitated in the doorway, smiling ingratiatingly, then padded carefully across the shiny floor to sit at, on, Clare's feet, pressing back against her legs and nosing up in search of a reassuring hand.

They sat at the absurd table and drank their coffee, pin figures in a black and white painting. For the first time they had nothing to say to each other.

'Would you like to see the rest of the house?'

How she had longed to know what his home was like, yet now she felt unsure, disconcerted by that terrible kitchen, conscious of the presence of hostile ghosts. It was a house ill at ease, its solid structure and original furnishings silted over with the sort of stuff Martin had liked – smoked-glass coffee tables and ruched cushions, dyed pampas grass and marble table lighters. The bathroom was lilac and plumber's aubergine, complete with bidet and plastic quilting round the bath. The louvre-doored and mirrored 'master bedroom' in white melamine with gold twiddles showed no sign of the master's occupation, Clare was silently thankful to see. Donald was using a room which looked as though it belonged to no one and had a disquieting air of transience. There was no trace anywhere of his boyhood, or of Fiona's childhood, come to that. The unused rooms were cold, severe, blankly unwelcoming.

Clare felt disillusioned, hollow with loneliness, as she followed Donald down a curving stair with an elegant wrought-iron banister and a strip of carpet very like that in Ina's lounge laid over wood rich with years of polishing.

Then Donald opened a door and stood aside to let her go ahead of him into a small room that might have been a stage set for all the relation it had to the rest of the house. Clare's first grateful reaction was that it was warm, with a big fire banked up in a tiled Victorian fireplace with wooden surround. There was a tall secretaire, its flap down and covered with work in hand, a worn Turkey carpet, deep leather chairs, books along one wall, oak shutters never vandalized with paint, cluttered mantelpiece, farming magazines lying about.

The room was Donald, felt of him, breathed of him, and she turned to him on an uprush of relief. He was watching her, his face giving nothing away. She didn't know what he saw in hers but the next moment she was in his arms.

Clare could hardly stand when he released her, her brain whirling and her body pithless. With an exclamation of exasperation with himself Donald swung her off her feet and sank down with her in his arms into the big armchair beside the fire. 'I'm sorry, love, I should have been more gentle.' He was holding her close, his cheek against her hair, and she was moved and startled by the emotion that roughened his voice.

'Oh, Donald, no, I've wanted that. I've needed you so much.'

'Do you mean that?' he demanded, drawing back to look at

her and letting her see a face so altered, so naked with feeling, that her heart lurched.

'Oh, Donald.' The feel of his hair under her hand, the solid bar of the arm against which she leaned. Their eyes searched each other, read the same message.

'There's nothing to cry about!' His voice was lighter, gently teasing, with a new loving note in it that pierced her.

She remembered why tears were so near today. 'This isn't because of Rory?' she asked in sudden doubt.

'It is not. I was coming to see you today anyway.'

'You were?' A host of implications swept through her mind.

'I could hardly believe it when you walked into Tigh Bhan yesterday. I'd been wondering how soon I could let myself come and see you, then leaving a bit more time, a bit more time, making myself wait, wanting to see what you would decide to do about the Larach, about your life in general. But being with you, up there in the plantation, in the quietness, seeing how you involved yourself so easily, how you fitted into the whole scene and were part of it, I knew I couldn't wait any longer. Only it was no use getting into it then – there'd have been no rabbits caught, that's one thing certain. And in a funny way it was perfect as it was, being together again, knowing that soon we would talk. There, at Tigh Bhan, with the Markies, it wasn't exactly the place or the time . . .' He laughed, sounding very happy, and crushed her to him, folding her comfortably against his big body. 'You know damn well this isn't only about Rory.'

Time and the world outside this room forgotten, they pieced the pattern together.

'I thought every day that I'd hear you were leaving,' Clare said.

'I couldn't plan anything as long as you were at the Larach.'

'But I thought you'd decided to go to Canada?'

'It was an option. If you weren't going to stay I couldn't face carrying on here, living on my own, nothing to work for, nothing ahead of me.'

'I didn't know if I'd be able to bear the Larach without you nearby, the memories and associations. But I didn't want to move away entirely.'

'Do you really mean that?' Donald's voice was suddenly alert and Clare realized he had no idea of how tightly he was gripping her.

'I don't want to live anywhere else now,' she said. 'Where would I go? Where would be better?'

'That's what I needed to hear,' he said, letting out a held breath on a sigh of satisfaction. 'That you'd decided for yourself that this was the kind of life you wanted.'

She nodded. 'I know. I had to be certain too. Everything had always been so tied up with you, from the very beginning. When I thought you'd be going away I had to face up to the question of what I wanted, where I wanted to be. I might perhaps have moved from the Larach itself – without you it could never be the same – but I'd have stayed somewhere in the area, in the village, maybe, or near Luig.'

'I've wanted so much to convince myself of that.'

'You thought I'd be like Annabel.' It wasn't easy to say, even now.

Donald didn't deny it. 'I was afraid you'd need more in the end, just as she did. I thought you might enjoy this kind of life for a while, but then you'd be restless and want to be off.'

'But you must know how much I've loved it here.'

'You wouldn't ever commit yourself, though. I could never tell how you really felt. You were making friends, seemed to be settling in, but then you'd say, "I'll be gone by winter." It was like a knife going through me to hear that. When I asked you if making alterations to the cottage meant you were planning to stay, you said glibly it added to the selling price. I could have wrung your neck.'

'I was so terrified of giving myself away. You never gave me the slightest hint you cared about me.'

Donald rubbed his hands harshly over his face, and stared into the fire. 'I wanted to be fair to Ishbel. She had a poor deal in me, after all. I married her because she was shoved at me, and because Annabel had gone, but it was my choice. And there's a lot of guilt attached to knowing that when your wife dies it will be a release. That's not easy to live with. But for God's sake, how can you say I never showed you how I felt? Wasn't I down at that cottage of yours just about every day, grabbing at any excuse to see you? And when I was there you must have noticed it was all I could do to drag myself away. I've never actually wanted to get up for the lambing before.'

'So when did you——?'

He laughed at her. 'The first day I saw you. You can't imagine how I hated leaving you in that dismal place. You were so lost and forlorn. I wanted to come back that very night to make sure you were all right. I was afraid you'd be off the next day.'

'I nearly was. But you didn't come to check.'

'Everyone else did though, didn't they? Oh, I was keeping an eye on you all right. Then when you did stick to it, I loved to see the way you adapted and changed, losing that brittle defensiveness, getting past the drink problem, accepting things as they were. And the new clothes – you looked years younger and so bloody sexy! I wasn't too pleased when you hacked your hair to bits, though.'

'I remember your face when you saw it. But you were so good to me, you took care of me at every turn.'

'I had to take care of you. You weren't going to stay unless life was at least half comfortable.'

'Devious.'

'It was a bit of a shock when the boyfriend turned up, though I suppose I should have expected there'd be somebody. Then when I met him in the shop that morning I could have laughed aloud to realize there was nothing to worry about – except that I was afraid you might be hurt again.'

'Did Pete and Ewan tell you when he left?'

Donald grinned and didn't answer. 'I used to balance things endlessly in my head. You were helping Fergus with the Italian stuff, but that couldn't last long. You were working at the Old Mill and Ardlonach but neither job was full-time or permanent. You bought a car but not one that was much use for the Larach.'

'I wanted you to go on calling for me in the boat.'

He laughed aloud and kissed her with an exuberance she would never have suspected in him. Then the kisses changed, became intent, exploratory, as though he wanted to find out all of her, arousing feelings she had never known before but which she had an exciting conviction he was going to be able to satisfy. Had everyone else crashed through this stage; or had she herself never felt anything approaching love before?

'God, Clare,' Donald said, his voice husky, and she could feel him mustering the effort to draw them both back to control and normality. 'I always thought you were so cool, so disciplined.'

'I was so sure the feelings were all on my side. And also—' Terror suddenly filled her at what he would think of the way she had lived at Carlini's. 'Donald, I'm not as – I mean, I think you should know I'd been leading a pretty rackety sort of life before I came up here and—'

He stopped her firmly. 'I don't want to know. You had the guts to get hold of your life and change it. I let mine go on being a lie. And in any case—'

He stopped, his face grim, and she pulled herself up to look at him, surprised by his tone. 'In any case what?'

'There's something I want you to know. No one else does – and that has to be a miracle in this part of the world – but I don't want any secrets between us; I don't want to start out like that.' Whatever was coming the promise implied in that felt good to Clare. 'There was somebody else, a relationship that lasted a couple of years. I used to see her when I went down to the sales in Stirling. She was . . . I needed someone, that was all. She was married, had a family, it would never have come to anything, but she was kind, good-natured, generous. I just needed something outside this place.'

Clare felt a storm of jealousy whirl up and with a single determined effort dismissed it, put it out of her mind. There had been no note of loving nostalgia here to sear into her memory; she could accept this woman as Donald had accepted Joe. She didn't want to hear any more about her, but she could bear this.

'Don't tell me her name, that's all I ask,' she said, and Donald raised his eyebrows at the pragmatic tone.

'I don't think I'll make a habit of talking about her,' he remarked dryly, amused and relieved at her reaction. 'But I didn't want you to have any ideas that I've been the perfect husband, loyal to Ishbel through thick and thin. And more importantly for us, I wanted you to know because sometimes it seemed to me that my whole life with her was a lie. I haven't felt at peace with myself. I stopped seeing . . . X . . . when Ishbel became ill. Placating my conscience, I suppose. With you I want everything to be out in the open from the beginning. We are who we are now and we take it from there.'

Rejection, deception, guilt. The past. They had taken a huge step away from it today.

CHAPTER THIRTY-THREE

'Come on, out of this, woman, I've got work to do.'

Jolted out of their dreamy closeness Clare asked dazedly. 'Work? What work? Can I help?' Wanting only to be near him.

'You stay in the warm. Get some supper going, perhaps. I'm starving.'

'What?' Clare exclaimed indignantly. That wasn't the way things were going to be.

'I'm going to feed the dogs, love,' Donald explained, his voice gentle.

She leaned for a moment against him, memory returning. Poor Rory. 'I'd like to come. I want to be with you.'

He smoothed her hair. 'I want you with me. I just didn't want it to upset you.'

'I'll be fine.' As long as he was there she knew she would be. 'Come on, then.'

It was the first real flavour of Rhumore for Clare, to go out to the kennels with Donald in the early dark, the wind lighter but with a mean bite to it, stars appearing in a sky that promised frost, the smell of meal and the coats of dogs that lived out of doors, battered tin feeding bowls icy to her fingers. Sharp longing for Rory, tears for him, but she could deal with them with Donald there.

Back indoors they ate quantities of bacon and eggs and sausages in the kitchen, its glaring sterility unnoticed now, then moved to the firelit study and talked and talked. But Donald didn't seem to want to make love to her, and didn't suggest that she might stay. Instead around midnight he put her into the Land Rover and drove her to the Larach, and Clare told herself that this was the way it should be. Taking their time; behaving well.

Small comfort that was when she found herself restless in her solitary bed, the cottage cold after being empty all day, cold without its other life.

She jerked awake. White light at the chinks of the curtains, a sound in the next room. Rory – no, not Rory – remembering pang of loss. Donald's voice, 'Stay, Trim. Stay where you are.' Happy sensuous anticipation filled Clare as she heard him at the door of the bedroom.

'Don't move, keep cosy. I'll put the kettle on.'

Put the kettle on? Donald Macrae! But as Clare pushed herself up on one elbow about to call a protest after him she caught it back. This had to be Donald's way, not hers. The careless habits of the past would not do now. He was here, he had come up the loch more or less at first light to see her. And he was staying for the known future at Rumore; that surely was enough for now.

That day was theirs. After a leisurely and prolonged breakfast, in itself an extreme concession for Donald, they went down to the farm where Donald saw to a couple of jobs and had a word with Dougie and Calum who were trying to track down an ignition problem on one of the tractors. Then he and Clare took the Land Rover and headed for Righ Bay to look at the ewes.

'How do you feel about people seeing us together?' Clare asked as he drove along the cliff track and the farm dropped out of sight behind them. To her surprise he stamped the Land Rover to a halt and demanded with an anger rare for him, 'What kind of a question is that?'

'Because of Ishbel, I meant,' Clare said, taken aback. 'I only wondered – it's not very long.'

He reached out a hand. 'I'm sorry, biting your head off like that. It's just . . .' He paused, gazing out across the still-rimed grass falling away to the sheltered cup of the bay and the dark traces of ancient dwellings. Safe from the threat of time-share now, the thought flicked across Clare's mind.

'Tell me,' she prompted.

He gave a quick shake of his head as though not wishing to be too sombre. 'Oh, just that I seem to have spent most of my life doing what other people want. These past months, since

Ishbel died, I've gone on doing the right thing by her, by her family, by Fiona, by whatever rules I was brought up to observe. Finishing off a job,' he said, as though to himself. Then he turned to her and said savagely, 'Can you imagine what it's been like, sitting in that damned empty house alone and knowing you were there, so near, not sure if you intended to stay or go, trying to decide how soon I could *decently*' – with heavy irony – 'come and see you. I needed you, your company, talking to you, getting things into the open between us at last. Yesterday, being with you in that absolute peace again, I knew I'd done enough. That's the end. From now on I'm going to look at things only in relation to you and me and my own conscience.'

The words seemed to hold a promise which Clare, in the days that followed, had to accept she had misunderstood. Feeling that everything between them was now resolved and declared, she wanted Donald to make love to her, saw no reason on earth why he shouldn't. She had to remind herself his standards were different from hers, he would need time to adapt to the new situation, and that she wouldn't want him to behave like the casual amoral lovers of the past.

Oh, yes, you would, she admitted, finding herself once more tucked up alone in her bed at the Larach, senses aroused, alive, after an evening of closeness and caresses. Well, it's good for you, she told herself firmly. But it was hard to see how.

In fact in practical terms, except that she saw Donald every day and was often at Rhumore, life was very much what it had been the previous summer. She continued to go to Ardlonach, she went to Glen Righ House, she took Lilias to Fort William to shop and to Inverness to have her eyes tested. Trudy came to the Larach for dinner and stayed the night, a plan made weeks ago and postponed because of the weather and for a variety of minor reasons, and not even to her did Clare feel free to talk about this dazzling development, not sure that Donald was ready for anyone to know how things stood between them.

But how did things stand? She was increasingly uncertain. They saw each other at every available moment, they were confident of how they felt about each other, yet more and more restlessly Clare realized that nothing had been decided. She was angry with herself for this frustration, and ashamed. A few weeks ago she would have wanted nothing more on earth, she would have thought, than to know Donald loved her. She was concerned, too, about a growing physical restlessness, the terrible feeling of anticlimax each time she returned alone to the silent cottage, her growing short-temperedness. Sometimes it even seemed as though she was returning to the impatient person who had first arrived here. Had the need for sex, after all, been an addiction which she hadn't kicked as she had the need for alcohol? Had it merely been submerged, waking again as soon as someone roused the familiar sensations? But then she would protest angrily that surely this was natural. She had never felt for any man what she felt for Donald; he attracted her enormously, he was everything she had ever wanted. She was just finding it hard to play this his way, hard not to take the initiative. She had been so sure the need he aroused would be swiftly satisfied.

Yet another part of her wanted to take things slowly, respecting Donald's scruples. But gradually, to her dismay, she noticed a constraint growing in him as the days passed, a constraint which transferred itself to her as she became more and more doubtful and worried. They had not become publicly a couple, which on that first rapturous day of revelation she had supposed would be the case. Did Donald feel, in spite of what he had asserted, that Ishbel still deserved her due of time and respect? It was only a few months since she had died. Or was something else worrying him? Or had she assumed far, far more than he had ever meant?

Then the most frightening question of all assailed her: was Donald in fact not much interested in sex? Had he been influenced by a Calvinistic Scottish upbringing? Or was she herself promiscuous and over-sexed? She remembered Martin and she remembered Joe. Then, with an irony that did not escape her, she found herself remembering almost eagerly Donald's relationships first with Annabel and then with the nameless woman who had provided him with a brief escape from an arid marriage. She would remind herself of how good it felt to be in his arms, and compare her present situation with the lonely weeks when she had simply waited numbly to hear of his departure, and she would tell herself not to be a fool, to relax and enjoy each day, there was all the time in the world.

She was invited to dinner at Tigh Bhan when Stephen and

Libby were up for half-term. Already it felt wrong to be going alone and she could barely get through the evening civilly, then felt guilty towards these loving friends for her impatience to be away, walking home under the stars, her thoughts back on Donald. She must talk to him; she must ask him outright what was wrong. It was absurd that they had not discussed this. Lack of communication seemed to have been the fundamental problem in his marriage; it certainly wasn't going to be a problem with them. Or was it natural that Donald needed time; should she let things take their course? And so the argument swung once more.

Though it was not much further to Tigh Bhan over the hill than it was to the farm she had brought the car tonight, specifically to prevent Stephen offering to see her home. When she drove into the farmyard her lights picked up a waiting vehicle which, after one startled moment, she recognized with delight as Donald's Land Rover. He came to open her door and she leapt out happily and into his arms, hugging him tightly.

'What a marvellous surprise! How long have you been waiting here?'

'Anything to bring?' Donald had returned her hug with marked restraint and his voice was curt.

'What's wrong, Donald, has something happened? Your mother? Fiona?'

'Nothing's wrong. Come on, get in. I'll take you down.'

Subdued in spite of herself at his tone, Clare felt her elation at the sight of him fizzle out. He put in four-wheel drive and ground away up the slope; it wasn't a moment for insisting on frank and open discussion.

Once at the Larach Donald made no move to help as he usually did, but stood planted in front of the fire, rather in the way, in fact, as Clare shoved in the poker to bring the flames leaping up and pushed the just-simmering kettle further on to the heat. She made coffee in a silence novel for them. Tonight Donald accepted a dram as well.

'So what's this about?' Clare demanded finally, when Donald was settled in Murdo's chair and she in her turn was standing warming her back at the fire, too tense and too aware of his strange mood to relax.

'You enjoyed your evening?' Donald asked. He sounded more hostile than interested.

Provoked by his tone and by what seemed deliberate prevarication, Clare answered blithely, 'It was lovely, thanks.'

'Lovely. A damn fool word to use about a dinner party.'

'Well, not exactly a dinner party,' she corrected him, still lightly. 'Just the family.'

'And Libby went off to bed, and the old folk went off to bed – and it's after one in the morning, for Christ's sake!'

Clare looked at him in disbelief. 'Is this what this is about? Because I'm out late? Because I was out without you?'

Donald stared back at her, his face granite, his eyes cold.

'Because *Stephen* was there? You cannot be serious? Please tell me I'm imagining this!'

'Don't you think you should have told me how things were?' he demanded, yet with the look of a person who wishes the words could be recalled.

Clare sank down on to the sofa, her heart beginning to bump, but not wishing to make this a confrontation. 'You'll have to explain,' she said as evenly as she could. 'I don't understand.'

'You should have told me about Stephen.'

'Stephen?' In one leap of intuition she knew. 'Has Lilias been talking to you? Donald, tell me, what has Lilias said?'

'Something I'd rather have heard from you.' He stared at her grimly, but beneath the anger she saw that he had been most deeply hurt.

'Oh, Donald.' She was beside his chair, dropping on to her knees to be close to him, taking his hand. 'Did Lilias tell you Stephen and I were – well, however she put it. You cannot possibly have taken her seriously. What did she say?'

Donald closed his eyes for a moment, leaning back, his face tight. Then with an effort he put into words the idea that had been biting into him since that chance meeting with Lilias outside the shop. 'Oh, you and he, how suitable it was, you know.'

Clare's eyes were full of loving sympathy. 'Donald, she was only making up a little story for herself because she hates Stephen being unhappy. It comforts her; you must have realized that was all it was. Stephen and I haven't the faintest interest in each other. He's totally wrapped up in Lucy. You couldn't really believe—' The enormity of what he had suspected began to reach her.

Donald saw it in her eyes and, angry with himself, reached for her with a rough exclamation. 'Oh, Christ, I didn't know what to think. Lilias sounded as though – I don't know, it seemed so plausible.'

'How could you listen? How could you think for a moment that I—?' Clare was breathless as the implications sank in at last. 'Without asking me, without even talking about it – how could you?'

'Clare, listen –' He grabbed her hands as she snatched them away, and she balled them into fists, resisting him. 'Listen to me. I'm sorry, I was a fool. But when Lilias hinted like that I was completely winded. The thought had never crossed my mind. Then I thought – well, they're your kind of people, you and I come from such different backgrounds, perhaps I'd been assuming too much. And after all, we'd never talked about the future.'

'Because you wouldn't talk about it!' Clare exclaimed. 'You've never even suggested there was a future!'

He looked at her blankly. 'But you know what I want.'

'No, I don't,' she retorted.

'Jesus, Clare, I want to marry you more than I've ever wanted anything in my life. But I wasn't sure if that was what you wanted. I thought I should give us both a bit of time to get used to being together. I was terrified of rushing things. But I'm perfectly happy to live with you married or not, if that's the way you prefer it. I'll live at Rhumore, at the Larach or Timbuctoo if you like. Just so long as we're together.'

Clare couldn't speak, couldn't even control the muscles of her face. She saw the familiar loving amusement fill his eyes as he said, 'Shall I take that as some kind of yes to the general idea?'

She buried her face against him, above her clenched fists which he still held against his chest. 'Donald, I'd live anywhere in the world with you.'

'Rhumore?'

'Rhumore especially, but not if you want to be free of it.'

'With you it would be different. With you the place would come alive again, be the home it should be.'

It was evident, however, that he had no intention of returning there tonight. Well, I'm all for a spot of male jealousy, Clare thought contentedly. Stephen, I owe you one.

'Hope old Murdo's bed is up to the weight,' Donald remarked as he joined her there. He had undressed her in front of the fire and drew her warm body into his arms with a sigh of pleasure.

'I wanted you, I wanted you,' Clare whispered.

'I must have been out of my mind. Come here.'

There had been good love-making in the past, enjoyment given and received, expertise and sometimes tenderness, but never this loving with trust, never this certainty of feelings deep and matched. Clare had never known that every detail of herself except that one focused sensation could be forgotten, vanish entirely. Nor had she known the sense of another person being an extension of herself so that returning to earth, which was really how it felt, there were not two separate beings, heavy limbs, withdrawal into sleep or the longing to be alone, but a delicious sinking into shared peace.

Much later Donald said, 'Two things I would like.'

'Anything,' Clare murmured.

'Long may that continue,' he remarked. 'The first is to go and see my mother.'

Chill of the world outside. 'She'll mind, won't she?'

'To be honest, I'm not sure, but I want her to know before anyone else. Will you come?'

'Of course I will, I want to. And the second is to tell Fiona?'

'It is not,' he snorted. 'I don't give a damn what that one thinks. No, I'm looking ahead a bit. I want you to go on seeing your friends here, giving Catriona a hand with Fergus, helping Trudy and the Urquharts.'

'But I'll want to be with you.'

'Well, I can understand that,' he said reasonably, 'but I don't want you shutting yourself away at Rhumore. I've watched how you've moved on from being handless and helpless – all right, then, being looked after by everyone – to being needed and depended on, and I know how much you like people and involvement. No, hang on a minute, this is important to me. I've grown up in this place but I've let myself become totally cut off from it, and not only because of Ishbel's illness. It's been happening for years. Apart from her family we saw no one.

Stephen Markie and I saw a lot of each other as boys and I used to fish and shoot with Tony Urquhart and John Irvine, but nowadays I never see any of them. I'd like to get back in touch. More than anything I'd like to have friends round my table, make that dreary house welcoming again.'

'It would be wonderful.'

'It will be. And part of that would be you continuing to get out and about.'

'Well, I don't think poor Fergus is going to last much longer and Catriona will need company, that's certain. And Trudy will have a move on her hands, she'll need some help with that.' And with being alone. 'Ardlonach's a long way round from Rhumore, though.'

'It's no distance if I put you across the loch.' In that single sentence the picture took on reality – Rhumore her home, living there with Donald, heading out across the loch with him on summer mornings (or less idyllic mornings) a part of normal life.

Clare was exceedingly nervous as Donald parked at the head of a cul-de-sac of neat bungalows at the western end of Fort William and walked with her up the ribbed concrete path.

It was all desperately stilted. Donald's mother was carefully dressed, her hair newly set, and she must have been cleaning and polishing the whole morning since every object in the room shone. The table, with lace cloth and best china and minute napkins knobbly with embroidery, was crammed with perfect baking which Clare was far too uptight to do justice to, though Donald in his calm way disposed of enough to keep his mother happy.

He had come over to break the news to her a couple of days earlier, but admitted to Clare when he returned that he hadn't been certain how she felt. Now she was so anxious to be positive about everything she never let him finish a sentence and Clare could see his frustration mounting. After tea conversation foundered. They had dealt with life at the Larach, glen news, the storm; had avoided Fiona and Rhumore. Finally Donald said he was going to clear the leaves out of a drain, which he had been meaning to do since last back end, and took himself off. Clare badly wanted to go and give him a hand.

Mrs Macrae began to clear the table, making routine protests when Clare started to help but allowing her to carry the tray through to the kitchen. Clare was glad of a glimpse of Donald's broad shoulders through the window.

'That's something you'll not be bothered with,' said his mother. 'Leaves. At Rhumore.'

So brave. Clare seized her chance. 'Mrs Macrae, I know I'm probably not the sort of person you would want for Donald—'

Donald's mother rapped down the milk jug and whipped round. 'Now don't you go putting words in my mouth,' she said fiercely.

Clare was startled, thinking for one horrible moment this was a declaration of open war.

'I'll take my chance while Donald's out of the way and say what I have to say.' Mrs Macrae's faded eyes looked at Clare out of her small wrinkled face with precisely her son's concentrated gaze. 'He should never have married Ishbel. There, that's said. I've no wish to speak ill of the dead and she wasn't entirely to blame anyway. I let it happen and it was wrong of me. Donald's father was keen on it and so was hers – they'd been friends all their lives – but that didn't make it the right thing. And Donald should have been given the choice about the farm, I see that now. All these years he's made the best of it but he's never once been happy.' Her small bony hand darted out and grasped Clare's arm. 'I was watching you out of the window as you came up the path together and I saw the way he looked at you. I've never seen that look on his face before.' She gave Clare's arm a shake and released it. 'We none of us know what's round the next corner, but if he's found happiness then I want him to take it and hold on to it. And I've one more thing to say – I'll say it to him too when he comes in – if Rhumore is to go at the end of the day I'll not fret. Stones. There's more to life than a pile of stones, though the lord knows it's taken me long enough to see it.'

'But we want to stay at Rhumore,' Clare told her, choosing the one thing easy to say out of the responses this honesty and courage had stirred in her.

'Stay there?' The tense old face lit up. 'But not because Donald feels he should? There's no future in hill-farming nowadays, you know. There's folk selling up all over.'

'We really want to be there. I think Donald has some other ideas. He'll tell you.'

'Well, now,' Mrs Macrae exclaimed, delighted, 'that would be grand. I've surely something to put in my letter to Mary this week.'

Mary, the sister who had not allowed Rhumore to entrap her, the sister Donald had planned to go and see in Canada. The thought could still shake Clare. She wanted to say to his mother that she must come to Rhumore whenever she liked, but it had been her home for over forty years and Clare wasn't even living there yet. Later she would see to it that she came, as often as she wanted to.

Clare was glad she and Donald had decided to get married and not just live together. She knew that was how he preferred to do things and she herself wanted to belong to him, but now she understood how much it would matter to his mother.

Until the wedding they moved as they felt inclined between the two houses, though the Larach was usually their unspoken choice for love-making. They had taken pity on Murdo's old iron bedstead and migrated to the big sofa-bed, and some of the most precious memories of that winter-into-spring were of long firelit evenings spent there. Clare wondered if she would ever be able to make Rhumore a place where they felt so relaxed and contented and secure. She agonized over the question a good deal before taking it to Donald, for it was difficult to find a tactful way to say she thought his house had been ruined. 'Would you mind if I put up curtains in here?' she asked tentatively in the kitchen one day. 'Or rugs on the floor?'

Donald glanced around. 'After we gut it, do you mean?'

Clare goggled at him and he laughed. 'Come with me,' he said, reaching for her hand.

He took her into the old stone barn and up into the loft. Stacked against the wall was the frame and top of a monstrous table. 'Must have been built in situ, we had to take it to pieces to get it out. The Aga's still around, but you can decide what you want for cooking. And how about this?' A tall pine dresser, pale with age, scarred with long use.

'It's a beauty, and the table. But won't it be a bit ruthless to tear out all those units?'

'It's up to you, but that kitchen used to be the heart of the place and nothing would please me more than to see it back the way it was. That goes for the rest of the house, too.'

Clare was surprised at the interest he took, the details he was ready to discuss as well as the work he put in helped by Calum and Dougie, and occasionally by Pete, but as the modern veneer was stripped away what emerged was the home he had once loved, and recreating it gave him deep satisfaction. He was a lot more ruthless than Clare would have been, especially about the room that had been his and Ishbel's, and his parents' and grandparents' before that.

'No sense in our being driven out of it. It has the space, the light and the view. We'll get whatever you want for it, and for that damned bathroom.'

'What happened to the original furniture?'

'My mother took what she could, but you saw the size of the bungalow and pretty well everything is built-in anyway. The wardrobe's in one of the back bedrooms. Come and look.' Mahogany, wide and high, with fitted drawers that whispered in and out, brass rails, an enormous mirror.

So out came the melamine, the peaked and buttoned headboard of the bed, the patterned wallpaper and the shaggy off-white carpet trodden flat and grey in busy places. Back went the dressing table filched from one unused Rhumore bedroom, a tallboy from another, and the big wardrobe was returned to the spot for which it had been designed. Long brocade curtains of faded gold, wrested by Trudy and Clare from Rory McMunn before they ever reached the saleroom, hung against pale walls. Donald could not hide his delight.

'Are you sure your mother won't mind?'

'Wait till you see her face.'

She trembled, clinging to Donald's arm, looking tinier than ever in the high-ceilinged room. 'I never thought I'd see it like this again.' But in the kitchen she broke down and wept, and later, when they had had tea at the big table, Clare saw her run her hand over the time-smoothed corners of the big dresser with a gesture of love.

Fiona came and flounced about in a fury which she had just enough sense to keep within bounds. Donald's wooden face held a warning which Clare thought she wouldn't have ignored herself, and though Fiona made a lot of remarks she was stupid enough to believe subtle she did refrain from open attack on the house or Clare. Her resentment was understandable and Clare would have liked to have established a basis for some kind of future relationship, but Fiona's antagonism was too irrational and undisciplined to give her the chance.

Her husband Norrie kept up a maddening patter of what he considered tactful if not conciliatory remarks. Clare guessed that he would pay for every one on the way home.

'Don't let them get to you, love,' said Donald, as the beat-up Jaguar surged away.

'I minded for you.'

'Then don't. I've put that kind of minding way behind me.'

CHAPTER THIRTY-FOUR

Trudy had had an offer for the Old Mill and her bid was in for one of the cottages down by the harbour. Ben had returned to take what he wanted from the pottery and had left everything else for Trudy to get rid of. Clare was afraid when she told her her news that it might seem as though she was deserting her too, but Trudy saw it quite differently.

'Thank God, that means you'll still be around,' she said when they had calmed down a bit.

'But I don't think I'll have time to help you in the new shop very much.'

'Pff, anyone can do that. Have to pay them, of course, that's a drawback. But the main thing is you won't be getting any silly ideas about "going back", wherever back is, or doing something "worthwhile" with your life.'

'I'm glad I know what you mean. Anyway, I'll help you with the move.'

'You certainly will. And that man of yours can buy his dog food from me in future.'

Lilias took a similar view. 'Oh, my dear, to have you close at hand, settled in the glen for good, what could be nicer?' Preferable to being married to Stephen and somewhere else, Clare thought, amused. 'And it's so good to think that Donald will be happy at last.'

'Knew it the day you were here ferreting.' Gerald asserted airily. 'Knew it the moment the pair of you walked into the kitchen with the dogs.'

'Oh, poor *dear* little Rory,' Lilias put in, 'but Gerald's right,' (did I hear that? Clare wondered) 'you did look very relaxed together.'

'Now, have you set the date for the wedding?' Gerald enquired in a distinctly family manner.

'It will have to be after the lambing,' Clare began seriously, which they found very funny.

Margaret didn't let her off quite so lightly. She couldn't get over it, as she said every two minutes. 'And to think that all the while ... Dougie said Donald was always away down to the Larach, but I didn't think there could be anything in it. I mean, with Ishbel ill and that, and then Donald's not really the type, is he? And besides, he's so old, well, not *too* old, of course I don't mean, but you know. Oh, here, I'd best keep my mouth shut. I'm really pleased for you, though. Wait a minute, why don't we have a wee drink to celebrate? There's that sherry from Auntie Bella, where did I put it now ... ?'

She was so pleased with herself for thinking of it that Clare downed the sickly brown syrup without protest and went on her way up the glen with glowing cheeks.

'Neighbours!' exclaimed Catriona. 'Really and truly neighbours, that's lovely.' Hadn't she been a neighbour at the Larach? 'It's so perfect I can't believe it. Donald's the kindest person in the world and I'm so glad for you both. Perhaps you'll buy this place when Grandfather dies and make Glen Righ one again. Then you can sell *me* a cottage.'

Clare knew that Donald longed to buy at least part of the estate if it came on the market. He had shown her on the large-scale map on his study wall what the benefits would be. Rhumore was fortunate as it was in having an alternative income to sheep-farming in its shooting and stalking, and reducing the flock still further would bring in more deer, already driven to search for new feeding by the afforestation of the eastern side of the glen.

'With Carn Righ and the big corrie below it taken into Rhumore they'd have shelter in all weathers and the stalking would be vastly improved. Then if I can raise some cash those cottages above the Macdonalds' could be turned into self-catering accommodation – or how would you feel about having shooting guests in the house? God knows it's big enough.'

'I'd love it,' Clare said eagerly. 'Orgies of cooking in my wonderful kitchen. But we could do up the cottages as well. It would be fun.'

'That's what it's going to be,' he said, hugging her. 'Fun. I'm going to enjoy this place again. But how will you feel about an economy based on killing creatures?' he added slyly.

'I don't suppose the sheep die of old age.'

'You're learning.'

He didn't want to use her money, though he was startled when she told him what it amounted to.

'So you'd rather borrow at some exorbitant rate of interest? That's an intelligent decision, and really makes me feel part of things,' Clare mocked him.

'I'm not used to these wealthy career women,' he admitted. 'I see I'll have to change my ways. We can certainly put it to good use. Everything between us will be shared, I promise.'

They were married in May. Clare would have been happy with the Register Office and a few friends, but to Donald being married in Inverbuie church was not so much a matter of religion as of tradition and a feeling that a wedding wouldn't be a wedding anywhere else. He warned Clare that there would be the inevitable 'and his wife barely cold in her grave' comments in the village if they were married there, but Clare thought it unlikely they would actually hear them.

They would even have braved a wedding breakfast at Ina's, but Lilias was adamant; Tigh Bhan was the place for that. Clare was afraid that it would be too much for her but everything was worked out in the usual glen way, with Barbara Bailey and Mrs MacGillivray (who turned out to be sisters, which Clare thought she should probably have realized before) taking over the catering with jealous zeal.

Donald had asked Clare if she wanted to invite her father, but though she toyed with the idea for a day or two, dreaming up cosy reconciliation scenes, she knew there was no point in getting in touch again. She had gone to find him before because she had wanted to put right what her mother had done, believing he would welcome her when he understood. But there had been no welcome, no contact, no trace of feeling. It was absurd to pretend that he would take any interest in the fact that she was getting married.

She did write to Magda, who sent as a present a tiny vivid

modern Italian painting. It was quite beautiful, and Clare spent a lot of time wandering about Rhumore failing to find a place where it looked right.

She didn't write to Joe. There would be more hurt than pleasure for him in this news.

Donald's sister Mary had arrived from Canada with her husband the day before the wedding, back in Scotland for the first time since the fight with her father which had driven her from home. She and her husband and Clare and Donald had dinner at Rhumore and Clare heard the full story of her rebellion when her father had refused to let her accept a university scholarship on the grounds that she was needed to help at home.

That determined girl could still be traced in the direct and positive woman she was now, and she lost no time in making her approval of the marriage clear. As she and Clare stacked plates in the dishwasher, which Clare had not stripped out of the kitchen, she said, 'I can't tell you how glad I am to see Donald so happy. Only I want to take my chance and say one thing – don't let him be lumbered with this place unless it's what you both really want. He's more than done his stint. First Dad, then Ishbel, and to be honest with you she was someone I never could stand. You make your own choice and enjoy yourselves.'

Clare's first clear memory of her wedding day was of walking from church over the hump-backed bridge to Tigh Bhan with her hand in Donald's. Then there was a jumble of dislocated fragments – Poppy coming to meet them looking woeful because she had raided a rack of curry puffs and burned her mouth; Libby feminine and grown up in a dress, and the ache to think that Lucy wasn't there to see her; Gerald cockahoop because he had given the bride away so brilliantly; the wonderful flowers Lilias had arranged in the cleared sunny rooms, though Clare could never afterwards remember where the food was set out; and Stephen drawing her aside and saying, 'I know this is hardly the moment, but if you are ever thinking of selling the Larach do let me know before you put it on the market . . .'

Leaving the Larach had been an underlying sadness during these last weeks, but letting Stephen have it would hardly be like selling it at all. 'We'll talk about it some other time,' he promised, laughing at Clare's readiness to make a deal there and then. 'I was just putting down a marker.'

Fergus, less and less aware of what was going on around him, had been left at home in Watty's care, but Catriona was there looking very pretty indeed. Trudy and Clare had taken her off to Inverness, forced her to get rid of some of her hair so that she could see out, and then gone shopping. As Clare had found almost at once a silk dress the exact colour of her hair, and Trudy said she had something in a box somewhere and was broke at present anyway, they had been free to concentrate on Catriona and somewhere around five o'clock had run to earth a dress she was not only prepared to wear but which perfectly suited her slender build and dark colouring.

She was being chatted up by a young man in a kilt, looking shy but not at all unhappy. Clare hadn't been prepared for the kilts and could hardly keep her eyes off Donald. She kept catching glimpses of him and thinking, Who is that marvellous man? and realizing with disbelief that she had just married him.

Sandy Maitland was there with a girlfriend with hair as red as his own. Will Morrison, florid of face and with a very tight collar, looked like a publican on the loose, while Ina, against orders, had disappeared without delay to the kitchen.

Una was sleek in dark red, her elegance somewhat marred by blue sticking plaster on three fingers, and Trudy was draped in a Mother-Earth-for-the-Great-Occasion number which was splendid with her brown hair and healthy skin. Clare knew that for her, as for Stephen, the day would bring pain and she was thankful that Trudy had agreed to stay at Tigh Bhan for the night.

Donald's mother had been very much on edge at first, defensive and over-eager to make her support clear. When she found she had no one to fight except her granddaughter, who rather surprisingly had elected to come, she began to enjoy herself tremendously, blinking and beaming through intermittent tears and allowing herself to be made much of.

Clare asked her who the young man talking to Catriona was.

'That's Donald's nephew, Alan.'

Clare tried to work it out; Mary had no children.

'Well, Ishbel's nephew rightly,' added Mrs Macrae. (Impossible still for Clare to take in that she was Mrs Macrae too.) 'He's always thought the world of Donald. There's one or two of Ishbel's family can see past the ends of their noses, as that one will find out –' with a disparaging jerk of her head in the direction of Fiona. 'If she was thinking she'd get some sympathy here today she has a surprise coming to her.' She appeared to be right. If any of the guests shared Fiona's views they were far too busy enjoying themselves to waste time on them.

The plan had been, Clare had thought since she had made it, church, reception, buffet, send-off and a dash to catch the ferry to Mull. (She and Donald had seriously discussed the Caribbean, Corfu and the Norwegian fiords.) Now she was puzzled to see, in spite of her general floating sensation of being in some unreal world anyway, three little men in dark suits opening the piano and getting out violin and accordion. As they played a commanding chord Clare found Donald laughing down at her.

'You look totally thunderstruck. Come on.'

'But what's happening?'

'The bride and groom are about to take the floor in the traditional manner.'

'Dance? But shouldn't we be leaving?'

'None of your cold English ways here. This is a Highland wedding.'

'But the ferry, the hotel –'

'Trust me.' Smiling at her like that, so happy, so handsome, Clare didn't find it difficult.

The carpets had been rolled up and disposed of by willing hands and everyone but Clare seemed to know exactly what was going on.

'Come on now, you'll know the Gay Gordons, surely?'

If she hadn't Clare couldn't have gone wrong. The beat of the music was irresistible, Donald turned out to be an excellent dancer, bringing back to Clare Lilias's description of him as a young man, and with the lover-like words that she weighed less than a half-bag of meal, he put her exactly where he intended her to be. They were barely allowed one lap of honour before everyone surged on to the floor to join them, and faces whirled by which Clare was certain hadn't been there earlier – Angus and his wife, the Irvines, Peggy and Calum Macdonald, Kenny dancing as expertly as Donald with a girl in a black leather skirt all of ten inches long, Pete with a firm-faced female who Clare judged from his subdued manner to be his wife. And there was Nicol McNicol carefully turning Lilias under his arm in a quiet corner, Watty Duff wildly swinging Libby.

'But what about Fergus?'

'Gerald's gone up for a couple of hours. Watty would never have forgiven us if he hadn't been able to dance at your wedding.'

'But Donald,' she pleaded breathlessly, 'we mustn't be too late.' He relented, swinging her round and round as the dance ended and bending his head to confess through the applause, 'We're not going to Mull tonight. I've booked a room in Onich. We wanted this evening to be a present to you from the glen. Do you mind?'

'Mind! It's wonderful. But poor Lilias, will she have to feed everyone? Did she know about it?'

'Come and see.' Half the glen seemed to be in the kitchen unpacking bags and baskets. Margaret, now minus her cartwheel hat of straw-effect plastic, was piling éclairs, hopefully made by someone else, on to a big ashet in a very slapdash way.

'Everyone's brought something,' she exclaimed excitedly, giving Clare a rough hug which made her give an unworthy thought to the back of her dress. 'Mrs Markie isn't to set foot in here. Isn't this brilliant? Who'd ever have thought it when you first came? I never believed you'd last two minutes . . .'

Clare danced in a whirl of bliss, spun and twirled by guiding hands, and on every side friendly faces smiled on her. She could hardly bear to leave.

'Lilias, how can I ever thank you enough?'

'Darling girl, we've loved every second of it.'

'I hope you're not too exhausted.'

'Nobody's allowed me to do a thing. And Trudy's here to take care of me.'

'You're coming back, you know,' they teased Clare as she was passed from hug to hug and clung to them tearfully one after the other. 'You'll be home in no time . . .'

Home. As Donald drove up the steep twists of the road above

the village and out on to the moor she repeated the word to herself, a word that had not meant very much in her life till now.

Coming soon from ALEXANDRA RAIFE

SUN ON SNOW

'A welcome new storyteller' *Rosamunde Pilcher*

No one really wants Kate at Allt Farr, the rambling house in Scotland that sometimes seems more of an albatross than a family heirloom to the Munros. But they are used to dealing with the consequences of Jeremy's fecklessness, and Kate – a cast-off girlfriend – is one of those consequences.

A fragile 'townie', Kate is unused to the rigours of a harsh Scottish winter and unfamiliar with the way of life in a house like Allt Farr. Her ignorance of country ways exasperates Max Munro, the head of the household, who has worries enough trying to run the estate. But her gentle manner, intuitive sympathy and cheerful willingness to tackle any chore quickly endear her to Max's mother and sisters. When disaster strikes, Kate finds she has earned herself a place at the heart of the family.

HODDER AND STOUGHTON PAPERBACKS

Coming soon from ALEXANDRA RAIFE

GRIANAN

'A real find ... the genuine storyteller's flair' *Mary Stewart*

Abandoning her ordered life in England after a broken engagement, Sally flees to Grianan, the beloved Scottish home of her childhood. Running Aunt Janey's remote country house hotel is hard work, but at least it will be a complete break.

Sally's brief encounter with Mike – gentle, loving but unavailable – cures the pain of her broken engagement even before she reaches the Highlands, but leaves a deeper ache in its place.

Caught up in the rhythms and concerns of Grianan, Sally begins to heal, putting behind her not just her recent loss, but a whole lifetime of hurt and rejection. And when fate brings Mike into her life again, tragically altered, she has the strength and faith to hope that Grianan might help him too.

HODDER AND STOUGHTON PAPERBACKS

ALEXANDRA RAIFE

DRUMVEYN

Four months after Sir Charles Napier's death, his widow, Madeleine, finding it hard to free herself from his lingering domination, still maintains the oppressive lifestyle he had ordained, and which had finally driven her children from their large and remote Scottish home.

Then Madeleine becomes aware of people needing her: her betrayed daughter Lisa; her son, Archie, with his plans for the estate and the problems of his foundering marriage; a friend at a crossroads in her life; an abandoned child and an unwanted baby. In meeting these challenges Madeleine discovers self-confidence and independence, and a new beginning at the heart of a wider, happier family in a transformed Drumveyn.

'Warm, friendly, involving … lovely' *Reay Tannahill*

'*Drumveyn* had me hooked from the first page' *Barbara Erskine*

'An absorbing story with a perfectly painted background' *Financial Times*

HODDER AND STOUGHTON PAPERBACKS

ALEXANDRA RAIFE

BELONGING

An encounter she never expected to face prompts Rebecca to abandon her high-powered, successful life in Edinburgh to seek refuge at Ardlonach, the family home on the West Coast of Scotland. But Rebecca does not find the haven she expects.

The sprawling old house, now run as a hotel by the cousin who owns it, is in turmoil – and full of people with more immediate problems than Rebecca's own. Never one to resist a challenge, she puts her future on hold and sets about making the venture a success. In doing so, Rebecca finds the answer to her own dilemma – and achieves at last a sense of belonging.

'*Belonging* has all the emotions ... we have come to expect from Alexandra Raife's characters' *Woman's Weekly*

'The power of a natural-born story-teller' *The Lady*

'A love story with an unconventional twist and a very readable novel' *The Times*

HODDER AND STOUGHTON PAPERBACKS

A selection of bestselling paperbacks from Hodder & Stoughton

Belonging	Alexandra Raife	0 340 73830 8	£5.99 ☐
Drumveyn	Alexandra Raife	0 340 73892 8	£5.99 ☐
Painting out Oscar	Nina Dufort	0 340 71683 5	£6.99 ☐
Defrosting Edmund	Nina Dufort	0 340 71682 7	£6.99 ☐
In the Heart of the Garden	Helene Wiggin	0 340 69571 4	£6.99 ☐
Trouble on the Wind	Helene Wiggin	0 340 69569 2	£5.99 ☐
That was Then	Sarah Harrison	0 340 70731 3	£6.99 ☐
Flowers won't Fax	Sarah Harrison	0 340 65389 2	£6.99 ☐
The Trespassers	Pam Rhodes	0 340 71236 8	£5.99 ☐
Delphinium Blues	Stevie Morgan	0 340 71802 1	£6.99 ☐

All Hodder & Stoughton books are available from your local bookshop or newsagent, or can be ordered direct from the publisher. Just tick the titles you want and fill in the form below. Prices and availability subject to change without notice.

Hodder & Stoughton Books, Cash Sales Department, Bookpoint, 39 Milton Park, Abingdon, OXON, OX14 4TD, UK. E-mail address: order@bookpoint.co.uk. If you have a credit card you may order by telephone – (01235) 400414.

Please enclose a cheque or postal order made payable to Bookpoint Ltd to the value of the cover price and allow the following for postage and packing:

UK & BFPO – £1.00 for the first book, 50p for the second book, and 30p for each additional book ordered up to a maximum charge of £3.00.

OVERSEAS & EIRE – £2.00 for the first book, £1.00 for the second book, and 50p for each additional book

Name _____

Address _____

_____

_____

If you would prefer to pay by credit card, please complete:

Please debit my Visa/Access/Diner's Card/American Express (delete as applicable) card no:

Signature _____

Expiry Date _____

If you would NOT like to receive further information on our products please tick the box. ☐